JAYMIS

PATTERNERS PATH, BOOK 2

STEVE TURNBULL

TAU PRESS 2020 LTD

CHAPTER 1

The private garden on the roof of the castle at Corlain was filled with the new green of Spring and a few of the trees were already blossoming. The scented air was fresh but not cold and Elona paced its length with her shawl loose about her shoulders. It could have been idyllic but she saw the walls as if she were a caged beast.

And every other time she turned, there was the tower in which she had been imprisoned.

This might have been her home once upon a time, but not any longer. Almost every memory was pain of one sort or another: the tower where she had been chained, and had felt betrayal seeping from the very stone of the walls. The place under the stairs where she had strangled her dearest friend to death. The room where she had stabbed Bejeren, though he had survived.

Sometimes, even now, she wondered what had been real, and what had been a delusion caused by the conniving of Lady Metrid. In the end it did not matter, because the only thing that was not a dream was her sister, the Slissac woman Chara. Elona smiled quietly.

"Her name is Chara ko-Tek Tegina ar-Tek Guala ar-Gey Aytrueth..." It had been like music when Chara named herself.

Perhaps her name was different now, because she was a matriarch. Chara ar-Tek?

Elona had not told anyone about that part of her adventures. It was private, and it was likely they would think her mad. Most did not believe the Slissac still lived or, if they did, they were very far away.

No one wanted to know that the lizard people lived almost among them. So close that the Slissac could see the Taymalin every day if they wished, but nobody from her world ever saw them.

She had ridden in a basket carried by a giant *tekrasa* across the sky, and the thought of it still made her queasy. She had discovered her wild magic—certainly she told no one of her natural healing and that she could control animals without the use of patterns—and she had seen a Kadralin shaman take the form of beasts using the power of the Mother's Milk. Though Elona had messed that up very badly.

She had learnt to light a fire, cook, milk the beasts, care for horses and *kichesa*. All the things a high-born lady should never do.

And now she was pacing a walled garden as if she were a wolf caught in a trap. Perhaps that was why the aristocratic ladies of the world were never taught these things because if they were, they would rebel.

Just as she planned to rebel today.

She glanced around quickly in case someone might see her and guess what she was thinking but the garden was empty. She almost felt she could cry but that would have been the old Elona. The new Elona had killed a man when her blood was running hot—and a woman, when it seeped through her veins stone cold.

She ran her hand across her scalp. In the Slissac town she had to shave off all her hair, and then in Aris she had pretended to be one of the Sisters of Taymar. But now it was growing back, she was not sure which she preferred. For now, she might be mistaken for a boy, and that could be convenient.

Corlain castle stood on a rise above the main town. Beyond the houses and the defensive wall were the fields where new shoots were emerging from the ground. If she leaned out across the parapet, she could see the Apra road crossing the Timalay and winding north. To the east rose the nearest mountains, there were more to the west and they defined the width of the land of Faerholme. Another separate range in the north marked the boundary there, where the city of Apra lay. There were no Slissac in any of those mountains as far as she knew. Chara's people lived in the great ranges further east, beyond Dirdin, to the south of Taltia and Tirnia.

But the great outdoors beckoned to her, and there was nothing to hold her here.

Her father had all but disowned her. It was true she had been pardoned for her crimes by the Dragonblade himself, with the consent of the Conclave, but that did not make living here any easier. To most of the staff, she was still just a crazy woman who had committed murder with no retribution.

Her father had paid the family of the maid well, and even now brought up the orphaned son as his own, and the boy would inherit all of Corlain. While Elona would get a stipend to live on, and her quarters here at the castle for the rest of her life.

No one cares what happens to me, they would be happier if I were not here at all.

"And that has been arranged," she said into the air.

AFTER THE MIDDAY MEAL, which she took in her rooms, she sent the maid away to have her horse saddled. She could have done it herself, but it saved time. A young woman in her position was not supposed to dress without assistance but Elona seldom allowed the maid to do more than lay out her clothes. She preferred to maintain what little independence she had.

Elona was tired of pretty dresses, though once she had revelled in them and dreamt of the prince that she would marry. Proper ladies rode side-saddle whether on horse or *kichek*-back. It was long since that Elona had any pretence she was a proper lady. So she changed into the travelling clothes she had gathered, men's breeches with a white shirt and a leather jacket tailored to her shape. A big warm cloak of simple design. She wore long riding boots and made sure her little knife was hanging on its chain around her neck.

This was the tiny magical weapon Lady Metrid had given her, perhaps thinking Elona might take her own life with it. That gift was the only good thing the woman had done, all else had been lies, deception and magic. The knife itself had been recovered from the castle at Canvor when she had vanished into thin air.

The chest at the end of the bed was the same one she had all her life. It contained memories she would be happy to forget. As a child, she had been betrothed to the Crown Prince of Faerholme, but now Drahail, the current Dragonblade, was married to another and they had an heir. That was something that could never be changed, besides she no longer wished for the closeted life of a queen.

She opened the chest and dug through the dresses of her youth, to find the rest of the items she had secreted for this day. She buckled on the dagger. It was an ordinary thing, unlike Metrid's gift, but it was sharp and useful. The pouch of coin. She opened it and examined the contents. It would do for a while.

And when you run out? said a voice in her head.

"I do not lack for skills. Not anymore."

She forced on her riding gloves angrily. Though why should she be angry? If Metrid's plan had been successful, they would be at war with Tirnia now. She did not know what the history books would say, but she knew her name would not be in them. Yet, without her, no one would have stopped Lady Metrid and the invading Tirnian army.

With Jaymis's help, said the voice once more.

"Yes, I couldn't have done it without Jaymis."

Metrid's own son.

With her preparations concluded, Elona hurried down to the courtyard carrying her travelling bag, forcing all the thoughts of the past into the place they belonged. The hammering of metal on metal came from the forge. Another memory.

"Lady Elona?"

She turned towards the man heading her way from the building that housed her father's administrative offices. He was in his mid-thirties and had, for a long time, been her tutor until her madness. Perhaps they had even been friends once. But no longer.

"Bejeren?"

"You're going out?"

"If it's any business of yours."

"Do you not think you should have an escort?"

He approached but stopped as if her glare were a palpable barrier.

"I will be fine."

"Your father would prefer it."

She bit back the words she wanted to use. "If he cared that much, scribe, he would speak to me himself. When he deigns to do that, I will consider listening."

Not that he will get the chance.

At the sound of iron horseshoes on cobbles, she turned away from him. The mount she chose to use was brown all over apart from a white splash on his forehead and a white sock on his left back leg.

"You're taking Whitestar?" said Bejeren. He sounded aggrieved; this mare was his favourite.

"I am."

"She's a good horse."

"That's why I chose her." She did not add that, since all the horses were the property of her father, Bejeren had no right claiming one for his own. There were plenty more now than there used to be, he could find another.

Elona took the reins from the stable-hand, gathered them up, placed her foot in the stirrup, and was into the saddle in a smooth strong movement. The summer and winter here had softened her but not too much.

"Where are you going?" he asked.

"Out."

"When will you be back?"

"Later."

"What shall I tell your father?"

"Anything you please, Bejeren."

She whipped Whitestar around and walked her towards the gatehouse. She settled her seat better and allowed herself to move with the beast. Bejeren had annoyed her and she was tense.

THEY WALKED down the main street of the town that led from the castle gate and came out into the main square. This wasn't the day for the livestock market but it was busy nonetheless. There were all sorts of stalls, and one selling fresh fruit was particularly busy—someone had travelled a patterner's path to bring them from the far south.

People stared. Most did not recognise her—though her mount and clothes marked her as one of high station. But some did know who she was and they whispered to their friends while their faces turned ugly.

All the more reason to get away from here. This was no longer her home.

She reached the northern town gate that gave out onto the Apra road, and took it. Moments later she was crossing the stone bridge that spanned the Timalay. Along its shores were the women cleaning clothes on the wide flat stones.

Elona had done that too when she lived in the village with the old woman Usala and Chara. When she had learnt not to be scared of the Slissac girl, they had curled up together in bed for warmth during the long mountain winter.

If only her life could be that again.

But Usala must be dead, and Chara was the head of a Slissac family in a constant battle with the other houses, trying to rebuild what had been stolen. It was still the closest thing to being home Elona knew, but she could not return there. Any Slissac would kill her on sight, and even if she made it through, all it would do is make things harder for Chara.

All she had now was the road that stretched out in front of her.

"I have never been to Apra," she said aloud. Whitestar's ears twitched at her words.

But she didn't stay on the road that led there. At a fork not long past the bridge, she turned to the right, heading towards the nearest mountains but even that was not her destination. This new road was almost as wide as the one to Apra, and used considerably more.

It was not long before the encampment around the Wellspring ley-circle came into view. The buildings furthest from it were constructed from stone and made up the permanent garrison which, she thought, seemed to have more men than before. And why should it not, when Tirnia presented such a threatening force.

Distance meant nothing when an army could march a patterner's path between ley-circles. That had been the whole purpose of Metrid's betrayal in Aris. She and a force of Tirnian armsmen had planned to take the ley-circle and thence allow in a greater force. Meanwhile she would murder the King and his heir so she could control the throne through her daughter's baby son.

Metrid had managed to kill the King but Elona had saved Drahail and the attempt on the ley-circle had been foiled by Jaymis—though he went by another name at that time and she did not know his lineage.

The past still followed her. She needed to go somewhere else.

She heard hoofs pounding up behind her.

"Running away isn't going to help."

Another good mare, piebald like her old Teaser, drew up beside her and matched her walking pace.

"Stop haunting me, Bejeren."

"I cannot tell you what to do, my lady, but I would be failing in my duty to you and your father if I did not at least accompany you."

The road past the garrison was lined with more buildings. There were several hostels to provide temporary accommodation for travellers, even a few shops. She ignored the hawkers selling food.

"Go back to my father, say you couldn't find me."

Past the buildings, they entered the area of ground that was badly affected by the ley-circle's feeding. Many of the plants grew strangely. The patterners would destroy them. Here the buildings were of wood and could be disassembled. Some of them were even on wheels. There was a fence ahead and beyond it the ley-circle proper. Elona could feel it but she chose not to focus on its power.

"I can't do that, Elona."

"And I can't stay."

She took a closer look and saw he was dressed for travel with several bags. She frowned at him but refused to ask whether he had been spying on her. She would not believe his answer if he said *no*. He had been working for the arch-mage all the time anyway, not for her father and certainly not for her. She had no reason to trust him.

"Where are you going to go?"

She ignored him and dismounted then led her horse towards the gate into the ley-circle.

The last time she had walked a patterner's path was when she had returned to Corlain from Aris. And before that? She did not know how but it must have been a patterner's path that aided her escape from the tower in Canvor.

Escaped was hardly the right word. How had she had fallen from a high balcony to certain death—and woken up in one of the main ley-circles in Dirdin?

Even if someone had asked, she could not have answered since she had not the slightest idea. Her wild magic involved only two things: healing and her ability to control wolves. Metrid had that skill too, in the end it had been a battle between them to see who it was the wolves slaughtered. Elona still lived.

"My lady?" said the armsmen at the gate.

"Is the next path the one to Avakending?"

"Yes, my lady."

She nodded. "How much for me and my horse?"

The man looked at Bejeren and back at her. She pulled out her pouch of money.

"Just me and my horse, armsman."

He looked confused and waved over a patterner.

"Lady wants to go to Avakending."

"Lady Elona?" The man looked uncomfortable, as if unwilling to agree a price. Then he looked at Bejeren.

"I am the one making the deal, patterner."

"Yes, my lady, but you're on your own?"

"By what right do you bar my way?"

"I do not seek to bar it, my lady, but someone of your importance does not travel without their entourage."

She closed her eyes and fought to control her temper. "How much to go to Avakending? Myself and my horse."

He hesitated, glanced at Bejeren once more. "Seven tay, my lady."

She did not haggle, though it seriously diminished her funds. She dropped the coins into his palm.

The guard stood back and opened the gate wide. She led the horse through.

"Where do I wait and how long will it be?"

"The path should be woven before evening, my lady, we will travel together after the evening meal. There are waiting areas over there, though they are for common folk and merchants."

"That will be acceptable."

She walked away without looking back but she heard Bejeren talking to the patterner, but did not listen.

CHAPTER 2

The waiting area indicated was a wooden building, with a corral for livestock—there were about twenty *kelukisa* with their stockman watching—and a place to tether riding animals outside. She tied up Whitestar, and was removing the saddle as Bejeren arrived. He looked at what she was doing and just stood there.

Elona sighed. "You don't know how?"

"I don't, isn't there someone to do it?"

"Let me, what's her name?"

"Oceanmoon, I think."

Elona loosened the buckles, showing Bejeren what to do. "Now just lift the saddle off and put it next to mine."

She didn't wait for him. She mounted the steps and entered the waiting area. Inside were chairs and tables spread about in a haphazard manner as if the different groups who came and went, rearranged it to their own preference. At the centre was an unlit metal stove heater.

There were ten people inside in two mismatched groups. The first group were dressed in peasant clothes, while the second was composed only of two men in merchant garb of reasonable quality. All of them had the swarthy skin complexion of those who came from Mirriasmia. She and Bejeren had the palest skin in the room.

They glanced up at her as she entered carrying her bag, then again as Bejeren followed her. The eyes of one of the merchants followed her longer. She took a chair at the side of the room and did not argue when Bejeren sat next to her.

"Water?" said Bejeren pulling out his bottle and a small cup.

"No, thank you."

There was another long pause.

The oldest man in the farming group was talking loudly. She found it hard to follow his words, but as Bejeren had once said, it took a little while to become attuned to a specific variety of the Taymalin language, but they were all basically the same.

"When we arrive at Mirriasmia, it will be night," said Bejeren.

"Yes."

"Have you given any thought to where you will stay?"

"Yes."

A LITTLE LATER A MAN CAME IN selling pies from a tray, the delicious smell of them filled the space. The family turned him away but the two merchants bought one each though they complained over the price. He came over, and gave Elona a long look then spoke to Bejeren.

"Pie for your mistress, goodman scribe?"

"How much are they?" asked Elona.

The man hesitated. "Just a tay each, mistress."

"That's ridiculous," said Bejeren. "They'll milk you dry if you're not careful, Elona."

"We have expenses, scribe, we have to pay the patterners for the privilege of selling here, and the armsmen want their slice for letting us in at all."

"I'll take one," she said, though she knew Bejeren was right, when the place was busy there could be dozens of people to buy. The pie-man probably did very well here.

The man smiled through his beard and reached for a pie near the front.

"Wait," she said, "I'll choose the one I want."

She reached for one nearest to her but felt warmth coming from ones further to the back of the tray. She stretched until she found the hottest. "I'll take this one, thank you."

The fellow did not look entirely pleased but did not argue. Elona fished out a tay from her pouch and handed it over.

"A good choice, my lady. Has the scribe decided to buy?"

Perhaps Bejeren was being the spoilt child now, but he waved the man away. Since there were no further potential customers inside, the fellow left.

The thick golden crust of the round pie was slightly smaller than the width of her palm. There was a representation of a pattern on the top.

"What's that pattern for?" she asked.

Bejeren shrugged. "I don't recognize it. It's probably nothing, or perhaps it's supposed to be a preservative."

If she had been alone, she might have tested the pattern to see if it could channel magic. More likely Bejeren was right, people put patterns on everything, whether they had meaning or not.

She pulled out her knife and managed to cut it in half though the crust was thick and dense. Steam went up from the inside and juices ran out, soaking into the wooden table. She quickly laid each piece on its side to keep the rest of the liquid in.

She noticed the merchants were looking at her. Perhaps they were envious of her hot pie when theirs were not steaming at all.

"Do you want half, Bejeren?"

"It smells good."

She started on one piece and between chews she added. "I won't be able to eat it all, and we don't know how long we'll be on the path."

Her final comment seemed to persuade him. He took the rest and they ate in silence. The light was fading outside and an older boy from the farmer group went to the heater and set about lighting it.

It would get cold quickly if the sky was clear.

She stared at the stove which leaked its flickering light into the darkening room.

"The path is complete."

Her reverie was interrupted by a man who put his head round the door. Elona quickly repacked her bag and stepped outside into the cold air. The sky was filled with glinting stars, though they were made dim by the cold white of Lostimal hanging one third full above the eastern mountains. Colimar, the red companion to Lostimal, was not in sight but it usually managed to make an appearance on any given night as it shot through the heavens.

She saddled Whitestar taking extra trouble with the straps since she could not see each buckle clearly. She did not fully tighten the girth since she was not planning to ride.

"Could you?" asked Bejeren with a slight hesitation.

She said nothing but sorted out Oceanmoon—*ridiculous name.*

"The saddle is only on loosely, don't mount."

"We're walking?"

"You can just go back to the castle for all I care, Bejeren, I did not ask you to accompany me. I don't want you here."

She fell silent as the two merchants came out of the hut and down the steps beside them. It was not that she didn't trust anyone, it was just that there were only a very few she had found in her life that could be trusted. And half of them were now dead. Bejeren did not figure among those that remained alive.

She threw on her cloak and raised the hood so her face was in shadow.

Taking up Whitestar's reins, she headed across the field towards the ley-circle. She could feel it now. Its chaotic patterns filled her mind even though she tried not to look. The Wellspring was very powerful and she couldn't block it out. It was disorienting and the dark of the night made it worse.

She focused on the lights of the patterners and guides up ahead. Off to the side the farming family were herding the *kelukisa* who were not too pleased about being forced to move at night.

There were even more people waiting, several with mounts, mostly *kichesa* though there was one other horse. There wasn't enough light to see people's faces, although the merchants apparently had servants and were now on the backs of *kichesa* being led.

She wondered how skilled the patterner was because the precision of their patterning affected how long the path was. The portal was invisible to most people but not to Elona who could sense the way it manipulated the World's Pattern.

Then the guides, who carried oil lamps on poles, started forward. One of them stopped just short of the portal while the other stepped through and simply vanished. The party of travellers, thrown together for this single journey, followed. It was disconcerting the way they simply slid into nothingness.

The merchants were directly in front of them and they disappeared, the tails of their *kichesa* being the last things visible. Elona strode forwards steadily. She felt the pattern flow through her, almost as if it were twisting her. It did not cause pain, but it was uncomfortable nonetheless.

With the transition completed, all of those who had disappeared were now visible again, all walking ahead just as they had been before.

On her journey back from Aris, she had been self-absorbed and had paid little attention to the path. Now she stared. The ground beneath her feet was as firm as stone, and completely smooth, though her boots did not slip on it. The horses' hooves made no sound, though the clinking of the harness did not change. Yet the whole sound of the place was different, they were cut off from the real world, the only sounds here were what they made themselves.

They were surrounded by the World's Pattern; it was as if a tunnel had been made through it. The sides were not stone, or wood, but more like water. Lights moved, patterns formed and separated. She did not know what others saw but, to her eyes, she could see the deep complexity of it all.

Yet this was not like the reservoir of power from which the ley-circles were composed. Nor the raw chaos of the Mother's milk when it ripped from the conjoined moons to the earth in a feeding, with a power that warped all patterns nearby.

There was order here.

There were those who said the World's Pattern was set forever and that all things were part of it, their destiny fixed from the past into the future.

Elona refused to believe it because if that were true then she was nothing more than a cog in a mill turning in its allotted spot. Her life had no meaning. It may not be chaos but it was not predestination.

But the Revered Malea spoke prophecies, she had given one when Elona was young. She had said Elona would go into battle and defeat an army. And that had happened, although the prophecy had involved a huge battlefield and Elona had been at the head of the army.

Instead, there had been a skirmish where she had prevented Lady Metrid from carrying out her plans. Elona sighed. This was exactly the sort of question Bejeren had taught her to ask when she was being educated—far beyond what any young lady might be expected to learn.

"So, Bejeren, do you think prophecies can be changed?"

The pause before his response was so long, she wondered whether he had heard her, or perhaps did not wish to answer.

"If they can, then you are free."

And, if not, then I am still in its thrall. "If we have free will, we can avoid them."

"Is that what you're running away from?" he said.

"I'm not running away."

And that was why she didn't want to talk to him.

IT WAS hard to know how long they had been walking. The path itself seemed to go on forever both ahead and behind. The air though completely still always seemed fresh—though the animals complained increasingly as time wore on.

There were horror stories of patterners who died in the middle of the path they had made, causing it to collapse and all those within to be absorbed into the World's Pattern. But they were just tales to tell round a dying fire. How could the story have been told if everyone died? Sometimes it was different and the patterner had constructed the path so poorly that the travellers were inside for days and turned on one another, and it was only the patterner threatening to kill himself that prevented more bloodshed.

She believed that was possible.

But this patterner was not incompetent and it was not long before she saw the shape of the exit. Then they stepped out into air that was thick with heat, filled with strange smells and wet with rain.

CHAPTER 3

Despite the warmth, Elona kept her cloak on with the hood up as she tightened the saddle. When she was done, she looked at Bejeren standing there, dripping with the rain.

"I could just leave you."

"You could."

The livestock came streaming from the portal, indifferent to the sudden change in weather.

"I did not ask you to accompany me."

"You did not."

She sighed again handed the reins of Whitestar to him and dealt with Oceanmoon's saddle.

Then she mounted and headed away from the ley-circle across the sodden surface. There were armsmen at the gate but they did not stop anyone leaving. Faerholme and Mirriasmia were on good terms.

They passed the point where the buildings were demountable and reached the shops and hostels. Each of them was constructed from stone and lit by flickering oil lamps outside and friendly-seeming lights inside.

Elona checked the names on each of the buildings as she passed them.

She found the one she wanted, rode through into the stable yard and dismounted. A boy came out and took Whitestar. Bejeren arrived moments later and seemed very happy to relinquish his mount to someone else. Elona ignored him and went to the door of the main building. She pushed into the main room, full of chairs and tables, most of which were empty. She threw back her hood and dripped rain water as she looked around.

A serving maid approached. The girl curtsied as if she recognised and acknowledged Elona's rank, despite her attempt to disguise it.

"I require a room for the night, how much?"

"For you alone, sister?"

Her accent was strange though understandable. But *sister*? Then Elona smiled and ran her hand across her bristly scalp. It was an easy mistake to make, besides she had been promised to the Sisters of Taymalin before Revered Malea's prophecy had changed her future.

"Yes, me alone."

"That will be two tays, sister, and your servant can sleep here on a bench for nothing or the common room with a bed for half a tay."

"He's—" she sighed, "he'll sleep in the common room."

"Thank you, *sister*," said Bejeren. Elona recognised the sharp sarcasm in his response.

"Elona!"

She looked up and smiled. "Jaymis."

He was halfway up the staircase coming down. Taking the remaining steps fast, he hurried over, brushing past Bejeren.

"You made it."

He looked as if he was going to hug her but hesitated. She lifted her arms slightly, he moved in close and wrapped her in his. She could smell wood smoke on his clothes. She closed her eyes and clung to him. The last person she had held had been Chara, before that—no, that memory hurt.

She did not want to let him go and he did not object. Finally, they separated and she felt embarrassed. Glancing at Bejeren who was frowning as if he had a right to comment on her behaviour.

"When did you arrive, Jaymis?"

"This afternoon from Dirdin."

"They let you go?"

"They weren't happy about it but I used a false name when I enlisted so it was complicated. And since I had just helped save Aris, they decided it was simpler to just discharge me from their Lord's service."

"You didn't even need to go back, what could they have done?"

He smiled. "Let's sit down, are you hungry?"

"Ravenous, only had half a pie since midday."

Elona started to remove her cloak and Jaymis took it, then she shrugged herself out of the leather jacket. They sat down.

"What happened to the other half of the pie?"

"He had it." She nodded in the direction of Bejeren.

Jaymis looked at him for the first time.

"Bejeren of Canvor, Lord Jaymis. I was once tutor to Lady Elona."

"But not anymore," she said quickly.

Jaymis turned and looked at her, clearly too polite to ask the question but desperate to know.

"I didn't bring him, Jaymis, he followed me."

"It was my duty."

The serving girl reappeared and took their order for food and drink. To keep up the pretence of Bejeren being her servant, she ordered for him too.

"You owe me a tay," she said.

"Yes, my lady."

Then the conversation faltered. There were things Elona wanted to say but Bejeren's presence made it impossible. The food arrived, she downed the first beer immediately to quench her thirst, then ate rapidly and washing it down with a second mug. Everything was warm here, unless it was hot. The stew had curious flavours she did not recognise—once upon a time it would have worried her, but now she simply enjoyed it.

"How long have you been planning this?" said Bejeren conversationally.

"A few months," said Elona. "As soon as it was clear there was nothing for me in Corlain."

"What are you planning to do?"

"Travel."

"But where?"

Elona looked at him square in the face. "I spent my life doing as I was told, Bejeren. Then two years chained to a wall or running for my life. I am not that person any more. I am choosing my own future." She finished off the second beer. "And you are not any part of it." She pointed at him. "So, you can go back to Corlain, or Canvor, or wherever the Arch Mage is, and you can tell him I am no longer playing his game. I have taken myself off the board."

She realised she was slurring her words, and stood up feeling a little woozy from the beer. It was stronger than she was used to, Jaymis was on his feet and took her arm to steady her.

"And now I am taking myself off to bed." She was amused by her play on words.

Jaymis gathered up her things with his free hand.

"It's been a long day," he said. "Walking a path can take it out of you."

"So, can drinking that much strong beer too quickly when you're not used to it," said Bejeren.

"You don't know what I'm used to," said Elona. "But now I am going to bed."

Jaymis smiled. Bejeren attracted the attention of the serving girl. "My lady is going to retire; can you show her to her room?"

The girl led the way upstairs which Elona managed well enough, as long as she concentrated but she kept seeing them as patterns in her mind, and then it got confusing.

The maid held the door open and Jaymis helped Elona inside and sat her on the bed. The sheets were simple but clean and there was a thin coverlet over the top. It had the sheen of satin and she stroked her hand across its sensual surface.

The maid hovered at the doorway as Jaymis hung up her jacket and cloak.

"Are you all right?" he asked gently leaning over her.

"I'm fine," she said in the most sensible voice she could muster. She turned to the maid and moved her hand as if shooing a fly. "You can go."

The girl hesitated and looked as if she wanted to say something. Then decided against it and left, closing the door behind her.

Jaymis turned and headed for the door too. Elona surged to her feet and regretted it immediately as the room swayed. She went to follow him, tripped on the edge of a rug and crashed into him as she stumbled forwards.

"Elona!" He turned awkwardly and managed to prevent her from hitting the ground.

"Kiss me."

"You don't know what you're saying."

He was holding her at arms-length but she wriggled her shoulders and stepped forward pressing herself against him.

"I know what I'm saying," she said. "I want you to kiss me, and I want you to take me ... to bed."

"Hush, Elona, someone will hear you."

"You don't want to? Why not, you're all the same. Styvan, the outlaw, Krazak..."

She sank to her knees and couldn't stop herself from bursting into tears as the men who had attacked her loomed in her mind. None of them had got what they wanted but they were all dead, all ghosts and demons who never left her alone.

She felt a hand on her shoulder and lashed out. Jaymis stumbled backwards and fell on his behind. Elona sobbed. There was a pattern in this. She saw it.

Three men. Three attacks. In the first she was a victim but rescued. In the second, she fought back but it was futile. In the third, she killed him.

And Jaymis, was she supposed to be the victim, fail to defend herself or kill him?

She shook her head but it didn't clear.

"Am I going mad again?"

"Mad people never doubt their sanity, Elona."

"What do you know? You've never been one." But he was right, in all the time she had descended into mental chaos she had never once doubted that she was the one who was right. The rest of the world was wrong. She was not the one polluted, everything else was corrupt.

Except, of course, there had been truth in her madness too.

She took a deep breath.

"I can get some fruit juice," he said. "It's good for inebriation."

"No," she said quickly. "I mean, it's all right. I don't want you to go."

"I won't sleep with you, Elona." There was a hesitation. "Not when you're like this."

She gave a little laugh. "But you might."

"We don't know each other well enough, relationships formed under duress are unreliable. We should give ourselves time."

"We should find a feeding and debauch ourselves with the peasants and the Kadralin."

"I don't think that is a good plan."

She remembered the Kadralin shaman, Yolandra, it hadn't been a feeding and that had gone very badly indeed.

"You're right."

Through tear-blurred eyes she saw him stand up. "Time to get into bed."

She let him help her to her feet and he guided her to the bed. He pulled her boots off and plumped up the pillow as she carefully lay down.

He kissed her on the forehead and she slept with the touch of his lips lingering in her mind.

SHE WOKE next morning with sunlight slanting in through the window and beating against her closed eyelids. The heat was already stifling as she threw off the bedclothes and sat up.

Her head did not ache but she felt as if her mind was numb.

She had no trouble remembering where she was, nor the fact that she had made a fool of herself the previous evening. Nobody would mention it, of course, it would not be polite. That wouldn't stop her from cringing over it.

What had possessed her to drink so much when she normally only consumed a glass of wine with a meal? She had been trying to prove herself to Bejeren, and what she had achieved was the direct opposite.

She took off her clothes and wiped herself down with water from a bowl on the dresser. It was cooling. She caught a glimpse of herself in a small mirror and stared at the short hairs on her head. In the end she decided to leave it. If people mistook her for one of the sisters that was fine.

In the end she was forced to dress in the same clothes, but it felt better.

"Elona?"

"I'll be out shortly."

CHAPTER 4

It was just Elona and Jaymis who broke their fast. Bejeren was nowhere to be found. Elona didn't care.

"Are we going into Avakending today?" she said between bites into a fruit she did not recognise but recalled the taste of.

"If you like."

His answer was controlled and he had not volunteered much the whole meal.

"If you want me to say I'm sorry, then I'm sorry," she said. "I was drunk."

"You remember?"

"I wasn't *that* far gone," she said. "Sufficient to forget myself but not enough to forget my actions."

"I see."

"I'm apologising."

"I know."

"What's wrong?"

He took a long time answering and filled it with drinking from his glass filled with green *tasa*.

"I didn't want you to think I didn't find you attractive."

"You think I'm attractive?"

"Of course, I do. You are."

She smiled. "It's nice of you to say so. At least I've filled out a bit now." She noticed the horrified look on his face. "I mean I was barely more than a skeleton when they took me to Drahail's wedding."

"I remember."

Of course, he did. He'd been at Dirdin.

"And," he continued, "you look much better now. Healthy."

"And you have a beard."

He rubbed his hands across the stubble. "I don't know whether I want a beard. Lower ranks weren't allowed them in Dirdin's forces."

"I expect it will make you look more distinguished."

"You mean older."

Her smile broadened. "Yes, older."

The cold green *tasa* was pleasant enough, the bitterness was disguised by mint and honey.

"How far to Avakending then?" she said.

"Less than half a day if I haven't been lied to."

"The sooner we set off the better."

"What about your shadow?"

"I'm packed."

"Me too. And I asked for the horses to be saddled."

"Even Oceanmoon?"

Jaymis's brow crinkled with pity. "Your horse is called Oceanmoon?"

She laughed. "No, that's Bejeren's. Mine's Whitestar." She leaned forward. "If he's not with us, I would be a lot happier."

Elona got up and hurried back to her room to collect her bags as Jaymis did the same.

The serving girl, the same one as the day before was at the door as she was leaving.

"Is there more to pay?" asked Elona as the girl seemed intent on getting in her way.

"No, mistress, but your servant—"

"What about him? Let him sleep in, he can catch us up."

"Oh no, mistress, he's gone, went early."

Elona settled back on her heels. "Oh." Then, "Did he leave a message?"

"He said he must run errands and would speak with you soon."

Not if I can help it. Elona smiled. "Thank you. When did he go?"

"Shortly after dawn."

"You wouldn't happen to know if there was a patterner's path open?"

"One going out to Dakastown on Esternes, mistress."

"And did he go that way?"

"Don't know, mistress, I was at my duties."

"Yes, thank you for letting me know."

Elona went out, less happy and more thoughtful. A quick glance at the horses showed that Bejeren had not taken Whitestar.

"What's wrong?"

"He's gone."

"Bejeren?"

She nodded. The stable-hand was holding both horses by their bridles.

"Did you see which way my servant went this morning?"

He smiled at her but looked confused.

"I thought…" she said.

"What?" said Jaymis.

"The girl in the hostel must have known we came from the north, and was speaking so we could understand. I thought perhaps the problem with the languages being different had been exaggerated."

It took a while, with much gesturing and using simple words that seemed to be in common, to ask the question of which way Bejeren had gone. The boy pointed back towards the ley-circle.

"Then he's really gone," she said, still not quite believing it. And there was still the ominous comment about speaking soon.

They mounted and headed south along the main road at a trot so the horses could stretch their legs, but returned to walking as the heat increased.

The road was a lot muddier than the one to the Wellspring in Faer-holme. It very rapidly came alongside what looked like a large river but as they travelled, they could see that what they took for the far bank, was just an island—though covered in trees. And there were very many islands, occasionally they got a view between them and the river stretched away.

"The Avaki," said Elona. "Some say it is the widest river anywhere."

"When we have been everywhere," said Jaymis, "we will know."

There were boats filling the river. Mostly small fishing boats with just one or two people aboard, but there were larger ones with crews of perhaps ten or more. Then they passed by a very large vessel under sail, travelling slowly upstream.

The shores were lined with huts. Children played around them. Women washed clothes in the river—though Elona thought it would be too dirty. If it had been in the north, she would have been sure the buildings would be clumped together in villages and towns, but here people just lived along the banks and on the bigger islands. The clothes they wore were loose and baggy but with bright colours. The crews of the boats seemed to be wearing very little.

Their skin was dark—so dark she had trouble distinguishing the Taymalin from the Kadralin. Anyone living here would never care which was which, and they probably intermarried all the time. There were part-Kadralin people in Faerholme, she had seen them.

Perhaps Yolandra had been wrong when she said: *We will pay the price of defeat until the day the sins of the Taymalin cast them down and we are free once more.* Perhaps the day would come instead, when there was no longer any difference between the two races. But then the knowledge of the Kadralin would be lost forever.

The huts and the people went on. She looked with interest at the occasional frame across which was stretched the skin of a scaly creature with four legs, webbed feet, and a long wide tail. Their colourings ranged from green to brown. The skins were reminiscent of *kichesa* hide but the shape suggested these lived in the water. Not as monstrous as a *nachak*, but probably dangerous.

They passed through a town where there were buildings built of stone. When they entered a market square they were surrounded by traders, trying to sell them all sorts of things from fruit to fabrics. But they pressed against the horses and made them uneasy.

"You stay mounted," said Jaymis as he slipped off his horse and led them.

The crowd thinned out as they left the market and they were only pursued for a short distance by a couple of persistent traders.

THEY NEGOTIATED a second town a short while later though there seemed little to distinguish it from the first. They ran a similar gauntlet through the market though Jaymis dismounted earlier and managed to keep them moving.

The sun was rising towards midday and there were fewer people visible outside their huts. The sky was not cloudless but the sun was very strong. Elona had long since taken a scarf from her bag and draped it over her head. Jaymis had thick brown hair which seemed a satisfactory protection.

The road finally turned away from the banks and led up a slope with hills on their left. *Kelukisa* grazed on brown grassland. They topped the ridge and stopped. The ground fell away from them, fields of glistening damp green were lay ahead stretching out for a league or more until it faded into the blue of the sea. From this height, they could see many more of the channels as the Avaki split and divided into the distance.

Elona imagined that even the river's mouth could be several leagues across, she had seen the maps but they did not reflect the truth. No one could have mapped the islands and the hundreds of mouths—perhaps it changed. It was beyond comprehension.

She focused on the city. Avakending rose in mounting terraces to a great height—she sighed with dismay, why could they not build these cities in flat places? The walls were enormous even from this distance, she guessed they might be the height of ten men, and the buildings behind were big enough to overlook it. They were shaded with bleached browns and whites, with black holes for windows.

It reminded her of the Slissac town where she had stayed with Chara, though she doubted this one had the strange double- and triple-level walkways going between the buildings.

"Do you want to rest, or keep going?" It was the first thing Jaymis had said for a long time but the silence had not been awkward.

She reached down and patted the side of Whitestar's neck. Then she looked ahead, there were buildings on both sides of the road.

"They need water and a rest," she said. "Let's see if we can get something there."

Nobody was in sight as they came up to the buildings. One of them seemed to be an inn and there was a horse trough with good water with an awning to create shade. Their mounts were grateful. Once they had drunk their fill, Elona and Jaymis tied them up and went inside.

The main room had perhaps fifteen people sitting around, some were sleeping. Elona wasn't sure whether the place had gone quiet when she and Jaymis had entered. They all had drinks, there were plates of food as well.

Flies buzzed lazily through the place while a gentle breeze flowed through the open slats covering the wide windows.

They purchased a jug of sweet mint *tasa* and sat down with it. The man at the bar brought them rolls of fresh bread and wafer-thin cooked meat.

Elona was surprised at how hungry she was and ate her fair share while washing it down with the *tasa*.

"We should probably get a guide," said Jaymis.

"Why?"

"Because we don't know where anything is, and communication can be a problem."

Elona shrugged. She had been halfway across the world, certainly further than Jaymis, without a guide or interpreter. But then she hadn't been visiting only to see what was there.

"All right."

"When we get into Avakending, we'll find somewhere respectable to stay and see who they can recommend."

"How much money have you got?"

"Enough," he said, "for a while."

"I brought some trinkets we can sell if we run out of coin."

"What sort of trinkets?"

She shrugged. "Nothing my father would miss. Let's call it my dowry—or part of it."

"Dowry?"

She shrugged. "I am not much a catch any more, the crazy murderess. I think he would have to put a lot more into it to get someone to take me off his hands."

Jaymis hesitated. "I think there might be some who would be very happy to be with you, dowry or no."

She reached out and touched his wrist. "You?"

He seemed to jump and though he did not pull away, his face took on a strange expression. She withdrew her hand.

"Sorry," she said simply. "I didn't mean it." The happy mood of the moment before crushed in the knowledge she was indeed damaged goods.

"No," he said. "I mean… it's not a problem."

She glanced around and felt the other patrons were all staring at her.

"Let's move on."

CHAPTER 5

It was mid-afternoon when they finally approached the towering walls of Avakending. It was built on an island formed from the tail-end of a ridge running down from the hills inland.

They crossed a wide stone bridge which brought the road across to the first island covered in a haphazard collection of wooden houses—some barely more than single rooms. But the place seemed to teem with people, most of them seemingly undernourished, something she knew about.

Then there was a second bridge which led up to the city gate itself. As they approached, the number of people seemed to increase. Almost everyone was on foot, some pushed barrows, others carried large packs on their backs and heads. There were a few carts. And the noise of talking, shouts, animals braying, growling or shrieking slowly built. Elona and Jaymis dismounted and led their mounts as the crowds packed around them.

The city walls were pitted with ancient scars and wounds. In places there were patches where the stonework must have been completely replaced. The arch of the gateway was large enough to take three carts side-by-side and was as high as two men. Pulled back were the two gates themselves. They were formed of timbers bound by iron. They were split and scarred with moss growing in the cracks.

"If Bejeren was here," said Elona, "he could probably have told us all about the history of the battles that made these marks." Even as she said it, she noticed that the nearer gate, on her left, had deep scratch marks running down it, from a point well above head height down to near its base. They looked recent but surrounded by so many people she felt too self-conscious to point.

There were guards all the way along the enclosed passage. They did not stop anyone but every time she looked, each one seemed to be staring at her, or Jaymis. Their pale faces would have stood out even if they weren't also the only ones with horses.

They passed through the gatehouse and out into an open area where people dispersed in various directions. But even here she recognised the defensive construction. None of the buildings had windows or doors facing on to the square except from the third storey upwards, and those were barely larger than arrow-slits.

"Faerholme, yes?"

The speaker had approached them from the city and was dressed in the loose shapeless clothes of most of the lower classes, but the clothes were clean. He had a scarf of the same material draped over his head. His skin was smooth and very dark while his features seemed mostly Taymalin. It was an odd contrast to her eyes.

"Looking for hostel, yes?"

Jaymis glanced at her and she gave a nod—surprised he was looking for her opinion in the matter.

"You know one?"

"I know many, lord. But for you and your lady—" he tilted his head towards Elona, "—only the best."

THEY FOLLOWED the man through the streets. Once past the entrance square, the buildings took on a more normal look with doors and windows at ground level. Wide awnings with colourful stripes spread across the narrow streets, shading it in the intense sunlight. There were raised wooden walkways at the sides, which their guide used; he introduced himself as Athlem of Liralain.

Elona doubted the city had any indoor conveniences—though they were rare anywhere—and all effluent was simply deposited in the streets. Leading the horses single file, she and Jaymis had to take care where they trod. She knew there was a concerted effort in Canvor to create under-street channels to carry away both rain and unpleasantness. She supposed Drahail would continue the plan.

But thinking of him presented an open door to the painful memories and she tried to focus on what Athlem was saying, but he talked only to Jaymis who was in front. She was not surprised since she was merely a woman.

All the buildings seemed to be joined together, though the differences in stone used, style and ageing showed it had been a haphazard process. They were heading up hill for the most part, and went under great archways that had been built on. Then they passed over a bridge where workmen were doing something to the parapet on one side.

The ground dropped away precipitously. Elona clung tighter to the reins and guided Whitestar to the middle of the bridge. Her head spun with vertigo and she reminded herself the bridge was solid stone but it did not help. So instead she tried to face her fear and looked out over the edge of the bridge. In the brief moment she dared to look, she saw water a long way below, squeezed between near vertical cliffs. Somehow there were dwellings built into the walls with precarious-looking walkways and ladders joining them. It seemed the city was built on more than one island after all. And they had already climbed further than she would have expected in the time. It did not please her.

Looking up from the bridge in an effort to take her mind off the drop, she could see the towers of the Liralain castle. They alone were similar in look to those at Corlain, Canvor and Aris. It was the mark of the Taymalin. That too failed to ease her mind but a dozen more paces finally got them to the other side and they were once more surrounded by the comforting closeness of the buildings.

It occurred to her she hadn't seen the Ziri Tower, she was aware they had one here. The racing of the *zirichasa* had been covered briefly by Bejeren, he did not seem to be interested in the great feathered beasts—much like her father. But without their own Ziri Tower, Corlain could not be expected to breed the animals, besides there was no one to ride, women couldn't. Horses were easier, they stayed on the ground and had far more practical use.

They turned off the main thoroughfare, went under another arch and into a courtyard. The four sides were walled by a building displaying four ranks of windows, and it was all on the flat. In here there was no hint they were high up on a hill. Another arch led out on the opposite side to the one they entered and in the middle of the cobbled area was a fountain with a constant spray of cooling water.

"The water is come from rain," said Athlem with a wide encompassing gesture, "and the magic of the patterns. It does not stop."

Sure enough, there were pattern inscriptions cut into the stones from which the fountain was made: round the outside and up the central column that was shaped like some sea creature. Even so Elona was sceptical, they were a good distance from the ley-circle and while patterns could work everywhere, it would need to be constantly replenished to run forever.

Besides, she opened her senses, and saw nothing special here.

"Elona?"

"Sorry, I was away with the Tahulin."

"Please, mistress," said Athlem abruptly.

They both turned to stare at him.

"It is bad luck to speak the name of ghosts."

"But—"

"No, lady," He was clearly trying to suppress his upset and speak calmly. "No, it is bad luck. Please. Athlem—" He touched his hand to his chest as if to remind them who he was. "—he is wise in the ways of the world. He knows things are different in other places. In this land, lady, do not speak their name. You will fetch bad luck."

Elona frowned at him but took a deep breath. "I am sorry if I have offended you."

He gave a little bow in acknowledgement.

A couple of young lads emerged from the other arch and offered to take the horses. Athlem spoke to them so quickly Elona could only catch the occasional word although she felt she was getting a feel for their word rhythms. Bejeren was right, of course, all the Taymalin originally had the same tongue. It was only when they settled and spread through these lands that there were local variations—at least among the lower ranks.

Elona and Jaymis unloaded their limited number of bags and the horses were guided away. In these hotter lands, *kichesa* were still the preferred mount. They liked the heat a great deal more than horses did.

Athlem guided them out of the sunlight, through a wide and open door, into a dark and cool reception area. It took a moment for her eyes to adjust. The interior was as different to the outside as could be imagined. Here all the stone was dark and polished.

"This is the House of Jalima of Kotulain. The home for the great visitors to Avakending, where all needs are met."

A man emerged through a door. He wore something similar to the baggy shirt and trousers that were popular here, but these were a little more close-fitting and made of far finer cloth. They were still woven in bright colours which seemed quite at odds with the dark solemnity of the room.

"Travellers from Faerholme, honoured brother," said Athlem.

"I am Jalka of Betlain, and this is my sister Parthia."

Elona bristled for a moment but realised it was the best choice. Though she did not like the name he had given her. They should have discussed it. She turned toward the man and smiled but kept her mouth shut, that was the way women were supposed to behave, it didn't matter what part of the lands of the Taymalin you were in. Unlike the Slissac, where the men were subservient.

"My name is Yolan, noble sir and lady. I am the concierge of the House of Jalima, and that is how I should be addressed. If there is anything you need that cannot be supplied by the staff then I will find it for you."

"That is good to know, concierge. If you have modest rooms for my sister and I, that will be acceptable."

Elona was grateful he had managed to get in the idea they did not have a lot of money, this place might be beautiful but it would also be very expensive.

"Modest rooms? Of course, noble sir. We have a delightful and cool suite that looks out on the city below—"

"No," said Elona abruptly, then controlled herself. "No, I'm sorry, concierge, I prefer a room that looks only onto the courtyard and the fountain."

Jaymis looked at her with a question in his eyes. She glared at him until he turned back to the man called Yolan.

"As my sister says, good sir. Overlooking the courtyard, if you please."

"It shall be as you wish, noble sir," he said smoothly, "and your staff?"

"We travel alone."

If the concierge was even slightly surprised, he did not show any reaction but clapped his hands and two boys appeared. They took their orders from the concierge, which Elona could not follow, and gathered up the bags.

"You will require a maid for the noble lady." That was a statement and not a question, there was no way out of it. A matter of protocol.

Elona responded. "Thank you, concierge, that will be helpful."

Athlem cleared his throat. Jaymis pulled out his money purse and hesitated.

"A tay, noble lord," said Athlem quietly then bowed as Jaymis handed one over. "When do you require me again, kind sir?"

"Tomorrow morning, Athlem. We would like to see the most interesting places in the city."

As long as they don't involve heights, thought Elona.

～

IT WAS NOT clear to Elona how much the concierge had understood from her outburst but the rooms they were given were inward-facing and only one storey above ground level. She could look at without an overwhelming fear of falling—as long as she was holding on.

"That should keep the price down," she said as she looked around the central common area. The two bedrooms led off on opposite sides, though her one had an additional antechamber where there was another simple bed. For the maid they were being given, it seemed. Protection for a young woman.

Their suite was directly across from the reception wing of the building, which meant the entrance arch was on the left as they looked out. The fountain in the centre of the courtyard continued to spray its water into the air. None of the windows had any glass but they all possessed adjustable shutters, a novelty which she played with for a few moments.

There was also an ornately carved screen that stood in front of the window to provide additional privacy. It reminded Elona of the painted glass one in the tower at Canvor. The one that had shattered, its shards becoming a weapon in her hands. She rubbed her palm where the glass had cut into it. There were no scars, she had healed. She shook herself, that was then, this is now.

Like the rest of the building, the interiors here were polished stone, with rugs over them. Although she imagined the stone would be very cool against her bare feet. The furniture was simple in design and did not have a lot of padding. Her bed, however, was comfortable.

"Good idea about the sister," she said as she wandered back into the main room, the only room that possessed a fireplace.

"It seemed the best choice," said Jaymis from where he lay on a divan, propped up with cushions and eating fruit.

"Comfortable?"

"I am. You should settle down too, this is supposed to be a relaxing and educational trip."

"No one is supposed to know where we are," she said. "And that part of the plan is already ruined. They'll be coming after us. You and me alone together? It will confirm everything they ever believed about me and your reputation will be ruined."

"The son who killed his father?"

"But you didn't."

"And you weren't mad."

She sat on a hard chair beside a table where she could see into the courtyard but had the wall behind her for security.

"Your mother turned out to be a traitor," she said. "So, you have that evidence on your side. I was mad, and I am a murderess. Being pardoned by the King doesn't mean it didn't happen. I will never escape it."

"But my mother did that too."

"Indirectly, and nobody cares—"

She was interrupted by a knock at the door.

"Come," said Jaymis.

The door opened slowly and a young girl entered, she wore a light flowing robe in the multitude of colours they preferred here, with a band of cloth around her waist.

"Lady Parthia." She said it so hesitantly it was as if she had simply memorised the sounds without knowing what they really meant.

Elona sighed and stood. "I am Parthia."

The girl glanced at her once, and then cast her gaze to the floor. "Lady, I am Keeli. Maid to you."

Elona nodded and pointed to her rooms. The girl went.

"I expect I'll be hungry soon."

Jaymis laughed. "You're not very good at being a lady."

"I was once," she said. "The world taught me how little value it had."

CHAPTER 6

The girl, Keeli, tried not to express her horror at Elona's meagre selection of clothes. However, since they could barely communicate, it was the least of Elona's concerns.

The sky was growing dark when the evening meal appeared. She and Jaymis ate at the table in the main room close to the window. The maid stayed out of the way, though Elona got the impression the girl was watching them.

She found the meat course to be pleasant enough if heavily spiced, and the dessert was some sort of milk dish that had been chilled—which impressed Jaymis more than her. The final dish was just fruit. She stuck to what she knew, which meant oranges.

"Look at that," said Jaymis, pointing with his knife. The courtyard was suddenly full of people, mostly servants but there were two groups of eight men carrying two large sedan chairs. They came to a halt at the reception entrance and gently put it down. Some of the staff laid out rugs to go from the chairs to the entrance and moments later the heavily embroidered curtains were pulled back.

Three women and one man came into sight, with their backs to Elona and Jaymis. One of the women took the man's arm as they disappeared into the building, the others followed.

"More guests," said Elona.

"Very rich ones. I don't recognise the designs on the sedans."

Outside the servants seemed to be milling around aimlessly but a short time later, half a dozen entered the building while those who carried the sedan lifted them again and headed around the fountain.

"Keeli!"

She was there in a moment—which added to the idea that she had been listening or watching at the door.

"Who is the man with the woman?"

"Man? Woman?"

"Which family? All those servants?"

Elona wondered if the girl understood as she hesitated so long.

"Roshalain." She kept her eyes downcast.

Elona looked askance. "Never heard of them."

"You wouldn't necessarily know every family," said Jaymis.

"Have you heard of them?"

"I haven't."

"I know there might be many families in all the kingdoms we don't know," said Elona. "How many of them would be as rich as that one looks, but neither of us have heard of it?"

She noticed Keeli still standing there. "Go away, Keeli."

"Lady."

She went.

"I don't trust that girl."

"Why not?"

"Because we're in a foreign land where we stick out like an uncooked loaf in a baker's shop."

"Like a what?" he laughed, then stopped under her stern gaze.

"We're obviously aristocracy, travelling without a retinue." She sighed. "This was the stupidest idea I have ever thought of."

"I suggested it," said Jaymis.

"You did. So, it's the stupidest idea I've ever agreed with."

"Aren't you being paranoid?"

Elona froze. She even stopped breathing. She stared at the candle on the table as it moved and flickered from the gentle breeze coming in from the window.

"Don't say that," she said through gritted teeth.

"I—"

"Never. Ever. Say that."

"I didn't mean anything by it."

She closed her eyes and forced herself to breathe.

"You don't understand."

"No, Elona, I don't. Not if you don't tell me."

She stood up and went to the window. The cooler air brushed against her cheeks. Jaymis's chair scraped on the floor and she could feel him behind her.

"Don't touch me. She's watching. Stand away."

She heard him move and she sensed the space behind her becoming empty.

"When your mother—" Elona knew she was trying to hurt him by pointing out who had done this, she couldn't help herself. "—invoked the patterns that corrupted my perception of the world. I did not understand it was me who was wrong. The one thing I was absolutely certain about was that I was right."

"I see."

"No, you don't," she hissed. "You can't know, but that's not the point. How can I trust my perceptions now, Jaymis? How can I know that my suspicions are not being caused by an external corruption of my mind?"

She turned away from the window and faced him.

"What if I have been permanently damaged, and nothing I perceive is true?"

He opened his mouth but no sound came out. He looked as if he wanted to encircle her in his arms and a part of her was desperate for him to do it. But what if that was false too?

"I don't know what to say," he said eventually.

"There is nothing you can say."

"Perhaps we should just go to bed, we're tired, we'll think better in the morning."

For a moment there was a light in the sky, in Elona's mind she saw it as a streak of golden light but when she stared up, it was gone.

❧

ELONA ALLOWED Keeli to undress her, though the girl seemed unimpressed at the clothes she was peeling away. Elona had no embarrassment—it had been burned away in the furnace of her life. Keeli used a small soft cloth, dampened with cool water, to wipe Elona's skin. It was refreshing in its own way. But now she was reminded of Goodwife Akatha, her nursemaid, who had cleaned her on that day when they had fallen from the tower.

So many from her old life were dead, and so many of them by her own hand.

She let herself be put into the bed and covered with the light sheet. Keeli moved about the room and then shut the door. Elona imagined her preparing for her own rest in the next room. Ready to defend Elona's honour if a man should come.

Elona was perfectly capable of protecting her own honour.

The sounds of Avakending seemed very distant. Another reason to have a room facing into the courtyard. At one point, she heard shouting and singing, then raucous laughter echoing through the streets. But no sound of animals. They were in the heart of the city, the only thing they would find would be *kikisa* being chased by *chakisa*.

A latch closed. Her hearing, so sensitive in the quiet of the night, made it sound like a hammer falling. It had been close by.

Elona slipped naked from the bed, extended her senses and grabbed her knife necklace from the table. She placed it around her neck. Its magical blade, bright to her perception, hung between her breasts.

With a silence she had learnt in service to her paranoid delusion, she crossed to the door. She could hear nothing beyond it. She did not need to close her eyes, the night was black enough and sight did not interfere with her seeing, it just made it easier for her to adjust.

She focused on the patterns. A *kikik* was close to her feet, frozen in terror at her presence. There were other small creatures in crevices and corners, the tiny sparks of their patterns barely made any impression. The wall too had a simple pattern but she could see past it without effort. What was important was that there was no one in the next room. Keeli was gone.

The hostel—if it could be called that—had supplied a thin silk dressing gown. She pulled it on and tied the belt around her waist.

She went through into the main room. All was still but she could hear Jaymis snoring in his room. For a moment she considered waking him but decided against it—he would ridicule her suspicions.

But there was something she could do. She locked the main door to the suite, it even had bolts, so she threw those as well.

Now she felt safer, she returned to her bed and managed to sleep.

SHE WOKE EARLY, a habit she had never lost since she living on the small farm with Chara and Usala. She checked to make sure Keeli was still missing from the bed, which she was. Elona sighed. At least she hadn't dreamed that.

She dressed, went out and unlocked the main door. She found Keeli asleep on the floor outside. The girl woke immediately and prostrated herself at Elona's feet in the corridor.

"Get in here."

Keeli scrambled on all fours into the middle of the room and once again lay down. Elona shut the door.

"Where did you go?"

"Punish self, lady."

"What? Oh, no, I don't think so. Just answer my question."

"Punish self, lady."

"Stop that. Tell me where you went last night. Did you think I wouldn't notice?"

The door to Jaymis's room opened. He was wearing a loose robe that brushed the floor and hid everything except his feet.

"I'm not crazy."

He came all the way into the room and stared at the girl cowering on the floor then back at Elona. She dared him to challenge her.

"I never said you were, sister," he said in a voice that barely seemed to stir the air.

Elona pointed at Keeli. "She went off in the middle of the night. I locked the door, and found her outside this morning."

"She was waiting?"

"Yes."

"Too scared to go back to whoever sent her to spy on us, perhaps?"

"Not spy, master."

"You know that word?" he said. "Perhaps your understanding of the northern dialects is not so bad as you pretend?"

"Not so bad, master." She lifted her head and sat back on her heels. Much less subservient even in that pose than she had seemed yesterday.

"If you weren't spying on us," said Elona harshly, "what do you call it?"

"My mistress desired to know if you were lovers."

"Ha," said Jaymis. "How could a brother and sister be lovers?"

Both Elona and the girl stared at him.

"Yes, all right."

Elona turned her attention back to Keeli. "What did you report to your mistress?"

"You are not lovers, and you are as close as kin."

Jaymis smiled but Elona kept her face expressionless.

"But you are not kin."

"What else?"

"My mistress wanted to know who you are. I could tell her nothing more."

"Who is your mistress?"

Keeli's face became fearful. "I cannot say."

Jaymis took a step towards her.

"I am forbidden, master. Do all you wish to me but I cannot say."

Elona glanced at Jaymis and he withdrew. Elona did not think he had it in him to beat someone so helpless.

This was difficult, she knew what she should do but it was not entirely up to her. The only other time she had travelled with someone it had been Chara and they had spent the entire winter together. They were already as close as sisters.

But this was not the same. The few things she and Jaymis had in common all revolved around his mother and the defence against the expanding Tirnian empire. It had been foolish to agree to this journey.

But here she was.

"Keeli, go and arrange for food so we may break our fast."

"Yes, lady."

The girl moved quickly and the door closed gently behind her.

"You let her go?"

"She'll be back."

"She might be listening at the door."

"She isn't." Elona headed for her room. "We need to talk."

Which is how Elona found herself sitting at one end of Keeli's bed wearing nothing but flowing silk, while Jaymis sat at the other, possibly only wearing his robe. It didn't matter, she had no interest in him, not at present, and she trusted him not to make a fool of himself —at least not in that way.

"Why not one of the other rooms?"

"No windows."

"I see."

She hesitated. "The way ahead is not clear."

"What? Are you a seer now?"

"No, of course not. I just mean there are a lot of choices we could make."

"There is no danger we know of, Elona. Yes, we may not have been as secretive as we might like and perhaps people will know we're here, but we can still do as we intended. We can tour the places of interest here and then move on."

She sighed and looked down at her hands clasped in her lap. "Do you think that will work?"

"This is our own time, Elona, we can do what we like."

"Until the money runs out."

"Then we sell your trinkets."

She smiled.

~

WITH BREAKFAST DONE, they dressed. Keeli had returned with a basket containing clothes for both Elona and Jaymis. She instructed him on how to wear his, and then dressed Elona.

The costume she ended up in, Elona thought, was a ridiculous riot of colour but it was comfortable and they would fit in perfectly—apart from the colour of their skin. The loose material was gathered at her throat, wrists and ankles with a wide belt around her waist. There was a scarf to go over her head that hung in folds over her shoulders. The lack of constriction was quite pleasant.

"How much for the clothes?" she asked as Keeli adjusted Jaymis's attire. His clothes were a similar confusion of stripes. The material was heavier and instead of a scarf he had a jacket. Then she realised the stripes constituted a regular pattern and it was the same on both their clothes.

"Whose colours are we wearing?" she asked abruptly. There had been omissions in Bejeren's lessons, but he had mentioned how the colours had meaning.

Keeli turned and bowed. "My mistress sends this gift, lady and master. The colours belong to a family that is no more, but one with great honour."

Elona gave a short barking laugh. "Again?"

Both Keeli and Jaymis looked at her quizzically, but Elona had no intention of explaining.

"Is there any duty attached to the wearer?"

"Lady?"

"They're just clothes, E-Parthia."

"Symbols stand for something, Jalka, you should understand that. Will we have to fight another noble house? Will anyone be insulted by us wearing it?"

Keeli bowed again. Elona had the idea she did it to gain time to think about her answer as well as the best way to frame it.

"My mistress offers this gift in apology for spying."

"And that is not an answer."

"I do not know any deeper answer, lady, but she understands you have been offended and wishes to make that up to you. She does not wish you ill will."

"So, no one is going to send assassins to end our lives."

"I cannot know all the workings of the world, lady."

"Enough of the games," said Elona. She went to the window and looked out across the courtyard. Athlem was sitting on the stone surround of the fountain, as if he had caught her movement, he looked up, stood and bowed.

"Let us get on."

CHAPTER 7

Keeli guided them down to the courtyard.

"Lady! Master! How much better you appear on this new day."

Elona did not miss the appraising look Athlem gave both of them and their clothes, nor the glance that went between him and Keeli.

"You will blend into the crowd as if you were born and bred one of the Avaki."

"Unlikely," said Elona. "Do we ride?"

"They who ride know not the pattern of soil nor stone."

"And did Taymar say that?" said Elona.

"Athlem's words, my lady," he said with a bow, sweeping the ground with the tips of his fingers.

Elona wasn't unhappy at the prospect of walking. She was not keen on crowds but the prospect of crossing one of those bridges with the additional height of a horse did not enthuse her. At least, on foot, she wouldn't feel like she could just fall over the parapet.

"Where are you going to take us?" said Jaymis.

"The Mother's Kitchen," said Elona, the words had simply popped into her mouth and then she remembered it had been in one of her lessons.

Athlem looked confused.

"Would you not like to see the Courts of Justice? They are very grand, raised by the first of the Liralain dynasty in Avakending."

"The Kitchen," said Elona perversely, the mere fact that Athlem did not want to, made it a desirable location as far as she was concerned. She turned to Jaymis and glared at him.

He held up his hands. "What is this Mother's Kitchen? Why not go there, we can see the Courts later."

"It is a long way," said Athlem, "and it is not interesting."

"Then we should stop arguing and start now," said Elona.

Athlem smiled. "Of course, master, lady. We shall go to the Mother's Kitchen. Do you have a sword, master?"

Jaymis frowned. "Do I need one?"

"The Mother's Kitchen is in an unruly place."

Elona turned to Jaymis. "I am sorry, brother, but we shall find another guide who will take us. Athlem probably does not even know the way."

"I can fetch my sword."

"You won't need it," she said.

"It is possible—," said Athlem.

"We go now. Or we find someone else."

Athlem raised his hands as if in surrender.

"Master, lady. Follow Athlem to the Mother's Kitchen."

As far as Elona could tell, Athlem led them in a great circle around the hill that was topped with the citadel. They did not descend as far as the huge gash in the ground between this island and the one next to the mainland. Instead they wandered through streets and alleyways, heading downhill at a gentle pace. There was no room for wheeled traffic in most of these tight places, people carried goods in baskets on their heads, both men and women.

Thankfully there were no precipitous drop-offs either. Elona could pretend that they were at ground level except for the rare moments when the arrangement of streets was such that she could see away into the distance. Sometimes the vista revealed the mainland with the huge Avaki river leading north. At other times it was the sea, blue and cold. In both cases the view was so distant she felt no fear. It was not height that scared her, it was the prospect of falling.

Most of the areas they passed through seemed prosperous while the people they encountered were clean with clothes in good repair, and they moved with purpose going about their business.

But that changed without warning as they passed along a particularly narrow passage, almost a tunnel through a building, and they emerged into a square where all was still.

Yet there were people here. Their faces were gaunt and deepest black. Elona recognised at once they were the purest blooded Kadralin she had seen since they arrived. But they were not like the traders she had travelled with. Those people may have had justifiably bitter thoughts towards the Taymalin, but they had purpose and they worked hard.

These seemed barely alive.

She wandered into the square—her companions forgotten—a thin child sucked at the breast of a mother that had no milk.

"This is wrong," she said to no one in particular and her words fell flat in the hot air.

"This is not a good place," said Athlem.

"You don't understand."

"Is this the Mother's Kitchen?" said Jaymis.

"This way."

Athlem picked his way across the square and into another passageway.

Elona followed but she kept staring around. Her eye caught that of another, older, woman and she hesitated. There was something familiar about her. But Elona's feet carried her forward, she was swallowed up by the passage, and the square was gone.

There were nearly a hundred steps down and without light it was hard to keep one's footing. Elona slowed and took each step carefully, pressing her hands against the opposite walls. The light of the exit far below made her head swim, there was nothing she could see to tell her she might not fall.

Closing her eyes improved matters but only for a moment because now that she was completely in the dark her other senses came into play. Out of the inky blackness shapes formed. The dull solid pattern of the stones around her, and the spaces beyond where living things dwelt.

Her little knife glowed hard at her breast. The complex shapes of Jaymis and Athlem ahead. The figure behind who watched them descend. She knew it was the woman who had attracted her attention, and Elona recognised the fire within: a shaman of the Kadralin, like Yolandra.

They emerged once more into sunshine. Blinking against the brightness, Elona opened her eyes.

The first thing she noticed was the grass that covered the ground, thick and short as if it was tended. Then there were the rounded rocks, set in a circle, that looked as if they had grown from the ground. That was what she could see with her eyes, but her other sense told a different story. Between the stones was a darkness like a great well or the void between patterns. She felt the vertigo as it seemed to pull her in.

"The Mother's Kitchen."

Jaymis stared around. "There's nothing here."

It took an effort for Elona to force her attention away from the ley-circle, because that was what it was—and yet completely unlike any she had encountered before. Even the one high in the mountains that she had used to heal her many wounds—and to draw the wolves that had almost caught and killed her.

This curious shelf in the side of the Avakending hill faced towards the sea. The sun shone down from almost directly above them. To the left and right, the city's buildings descended towards the water. There did not seem to be many windows facing this way. The structures behind towered upwards, aloof and disinterested in this strange place.

Elona returned her attention to the ground before her. She stepped forwards and ran her hand across the rough surface of the rounded boulder. It felt like a ley-circle but where was the power? And there was never one in the heart of a city. They were dangerous. The real ley-circle for Avakending was the one that lay leagues to the north.

But she could feel it. She fell to her knees and spread her fingers between the blades of grass and dug them into the soil. Her eyes closed, she tried to see. A wave of vertigo went through her as a chasm of patternless void opened.

She screamed and fell forward. To be brought up short against the ground.

"Elona!" Jaymis was at her side in a moment and lifting her up. "What's wrong?"

"It's empty, Jaymis," she said breathlessly opening her eyes in an effort to block the void from her senses. "There's nothing here."

He managed to get her to her feet and she tried to help as he walked her back the way they had come. Once free of the circle she recovered—no longer feeling as if she stood on the edge of a precipice above an endless abyss. There were enough high places in Avakending.

"What happened?"

She shook her head, then turned to face the Kadralin woman who had appeared as if from nowhere.

"What is this place?" Elona demanded of her. "Where is the Mother's Milk?"

The woman glanced at Jaymis and Athlem then shook her head.

Pushing Jaymis away, Elona forced herself to stand on unsteady feet then pointed back at the passage. "Wait for me up there."

"I'm not leaving you alone."

Elona said nothing and watched his inward battle, the desire to protect her against her simple request.

"Very well, don't be long."

He turned and went, beckoning for Athlem to follow.

Elona sat on one of the boulders, though the hole in the world behind her made her skin creep. The Kadralin woman perhaps only in her thirties or forties, though she looked older, waited patiently.

"*Old mother-mistress, I am Elona-stranger. Where is the Mother's Milk, hey?*" said Elona, knowing she was pronouncing the Kadralin very badly. She didn't even know if the people here spoke the same dialect she learnt with the traders.

"Elona-servant speaks the People's words, hey?"

"I am sorry, mother, I am not skilled. I travelled with the People for a time. I served the shaman Yolandra in the northern mountains."

"That is strange."

Elona smiled. "Very strange."

The woman sat and they faced one another.

"This was a ley-circle, mother."

The woman nodded. "And now it is not."

"But how? Do the moons not feed it, hey?"

"The world changes, child. The Mother's Kitchen is ancient. It was here before Taymalin came. It was here before the Kadralin wandered the lands. But never in the memory of the People has the Mother's Kitchen been fed from above."

Elona frowned and looked around. It was clear the city builders had intentionally left this place free of construction. Perhaps they felt its strangeness.

"Who named it then?" Perhaps the name is corruption of something else, she recalled Bejeren talking about how words changed over time.

"What do you see, child?"

"There is a hole in the World's Pattern, mother. It scares me."

The woman looked at Elona more intently as if trying to divine her thoughts and intentions.

"What brought you here, child?"

Elona shrugged. "My home is unwelcoming. Bad things happened there and it was better for everyone if I left."

"But what brought you *here?*"

"It was the furthest place I could come."

"But today? What brought you to this place?"

"When I was young my tutor told me of Avakending in the land of

Mirriasmia, and that there were many things of interest here, including the Mother's Kitchen."

The woman stood and spread her arms as if to encompass the green space. "And this is interesting to your tutor?"

Elona did not answer. Perhaps it was strange Bejeren had mentioned it, after all there really was nothing to see apart from the grass and a few rounded rocks, and who else could perceive the emptiness below them.

"I don't know."

Bejeren had been working for the Arch-mage the whole time, and everything he had done was at the behest of that manipulative old man.

"One of you has the sight, Elona-stranger, as if you were of the People, hey?"

Elona leaned forward and knelt, putting her head down. She thought she must have misunderstood the shaman's words because they did not seem to quite make sense.

"*Receive the blessing of the Great Mother who feeds the world.*" The woman's hand came down on Elona's head and she felt a tingle run through her. "*Do not betray her.*"

The hand released her and Elona stood, she embraced the shaman —who returned it—then headed away and up the hill to the passage.

In this direction, she did not feel the vertigo she had going the other way, but she made a point of not looking behind. She seemed to traverse the distance more quickly even though she was going up.

Jaymis and Athlem were surrounded by children chattering and laughing. It was in the Kadralin tongue but too fast for Elona to follow. The two men looked uncomfortable and were very relieved when she appeared.

They headed up and out of the buildings that surrounded the Mother's Kitchen. It was clear Jaymis was desperate to ask her what had passed between her and the woman. Elona was not entirely sure she was going to tell him.

"What place would you like to see?" said Athlem. "The sewer

system for the palace has great majesty. The entrance is not far from here."

Jaymis laughed at the joke. Elona merely felt horrified, she had dug holes to use for the less pleasant bodily functions, and had no desire to see any that others had built no matter how majestic.

Athlem frowned. "No, master, lady. The Great Sewers of Avakending." He said the words clearly as if they had not fully understood him the first time.

They looked blank.

"You must see them."

"No, thank you," said Elona.

"The Courts," said Jaymis.

"But—"

"The Courts, Athlem, if you please," said Jaymis. "After that we would like to see the Avaki Gardens."

Athlem stomped away and they followed at an appropriate distance, so they did not lose him among the busy streets. But far enough that they could speak without him hearing.

"Sewers?" said Elona.

"Believe me, I have seen the sewers beneath the palace at Canvor and they are not anything you want to experience by choice."

"You've been in the Canvor sewers?"

"It wasn't Jaymis, it was Captain Jalka."

"Yes, but you were in Dirdin."

"The year before there had been a state visit. We were being shown around."

"The sewers?"

"If you were one of the Farahalek, it would be a fine way to gain entry and assassinate someone important."

"I see. Though I suspect their victim might smell their approach."

Jaymis shrugged and smiled. "They worry about it, but I don't think anyone could possibly succeed."

"Why?"

"It's a labyrinth down there. Canvor has been built and rebuilt a hundred times. There are crushed buildings that form the foundations of more buildings on top. Anyone going in there is more likely to get completely lost and die of hunger."

"Or thirst."

"They wouldn't die of thirst, the walls run with water."

"Would you drink it?"

Jaymis paused. "Perhaps not."

"Speaking of labyrinths," said Elona staring around at the buildings towering above them, feeling as if they might at any moment collapse in. "Can you tell any part of this place from any other?"

They were passing through another narrow passage although this one, for some reason, had not been built across and they could see the blue sky above, even if the sun was completely unable to penetrate.

Moments later they came out into a small square, filled with people. Some were seated at tables, all of them either eating or drinking.

"Perhaps a midday meal, master, lady?"

Elona realised that one of buildings was an inn, at least at street level. Before either of them could reply Athlem had gone to a table, said a few words, and the men eating there immediately got up—although one of them clearly had some choice words to say before they left.

"Here, master, lady."

Elona was almost reluctant to sit since the table had been cleared so rudely in their favour. Jaymis seemed to have no such qualms and held one of the chairs for her. She sighed and sat. Jaymis next to her.

She could not deny she was hungry and there followed a conversation with Athlem about what it would be appropriate to eat. Fruit juices and fruits were obvious, and they were going to try a local dish which involved seafood and vegetables in a type of soup—with bread to add more solidity to the meal.

Athlem was pleased. Elona really didn't mind one way or the other. She had starved at various times in the previous few years—especially when she was certain, in her distorted version of reality, that all the food being offered to her was corrupted and poisoned.

Since then she found she was happy to eat whatever she was given. She never wanted to be hungry again.

The drink made from the fruit juices was delicious and reminded her of the first orange she had ever eaten, when she was at the Conclave. That Bejeren had been the one to give it to her put a dampener on the memory.

They were halfway through the soup—though stew might have been a better description—when she realised the crowd had gone quiet and seemed to be thinning. The reason became obvious as a man approached them, dressed in the most colourful clothes she had seen yet—which included a ridiculously tall hat with a dozen feathers poking out at different angles.

As he reached their table, he removed his cap and executed a low bow, sweeping the hat across the ground in front of him.

"Lord Jaymis of Betlain. Lady Elona of Corlain. I am Jussian of Lira, First Keeper of the Royal Wardrobe. The Great and Wise High Lord Liralain of Avakending offers you greetings and the hospitality of his house."

Elona closed her eyes. *Taymar's stinking teeth.*

She opened them again and exchanged a glance with Jaymis. She shrugged. There was nothing they could do. They were caught in the trap of protocol and diplomacy. Anything they did now would reflect on Faerholme.

Jaymis stood and Elona followed suit.

"Lord Jussian," said Jaymis, "thank you for your lord's kind greeting and offer. Lady Elona and I would be delighted to accept."

Because we have no choice, thought Elona. She noticed Athlem was staring at her with an odd look on his face. She was no longer Parthia but was now someone he might just have heard a rumour of; after all what part of the kingdoms and lands had not heard of the crazy daughter of Lord Corlain? So they were gathered up into the bosom of the aristocracy that she desired to escape.

It seemed they were not expected to walk up to the castle, instead a pair of sedan chairs were provided—Lord Jussian had one as well. Elona found that hers came with two female servants who made sure she stayed in the middle of the chair and away from the curtained windows.

It was stuffy and hot, while its swaying brought on a form of her vertigo and made her sick—but not quite enough to throw up, which was probably just as well.

CHAPTER 8

The journey did not last very long but she knew they were climbing the whole time since she spent most of the time with her back pressed against the cushions, while the maids gripped the cords attached to the chair's frame.

The sounds of the city diminished around them as they climbed higher and soon all she could hear were the echoes of feet: the men carrying the chair and their escort. They stopped while a gate was unbarred and opened. And she heard it clanging shut behind them again.

Now she really was trapped. The most likely outcome here was that they would be given generous hospitality while being prevented from leaving the palace, until such time as they were sent back to Faerholme.

After that, she would be watched to prevent her from running away again and perhaps causing some diplomatic incident. It didn't matter. She realised the mistakes she had made, being open about leaving and then travelling with Jaymis. She had treated the whole thing far too lightly. Next time, she would simply disappear.

Finally, the chair was set down and, after another long pause, she was invited out. The curtains were held open letting in a flood of sunlight that temporarily blinded her. She stepped down onto the smooth flag stones.

They were in a small courtyard, the main gate of which was shut. Elegant columns held up a higher storey creating a covered walkway around the edge. And hers was the only sedan chair here. Nor were there any men. Several female forms were prostrating themselves in her direction but one woman, in the same sort of clothing as Elona, though not the same pattern, smiled and held out her hand.

This woman looked as if she had seen at least forty years though her skin was very pale as if she seldom permitted the sun to touch her.

"Lady Elona, welcome to the palace of Liralain. We are so glad you were able to accept our invitation."

Elona bit down on a caustic comment. It was not this woman's fault, and there was no need to make anything harder for her.

Instead: "Lord Liralain is very generous."

"I am Princess Miriatali, and it is my duty to assist you in all ways during your visit. Please to come this way."

Elona racked her memory. Miriatali? Yes, Bejeren had given her all the royal houses to study, such as they were known. Miriatali was Liralain's first born—and not the son all kings wanted. In fact, there was no male heir at all, even after very many years of trying. Which meant that Miriatali was the only heir to the throne of Mirriasmia and, when she married, the Liralain dynasty would end.

That Miriatali was not married yet, when she must be nearly forty, seemed very strange. Elona shook her head. It didn't matter. The political machinations of Mirriasmia had nothing to do with her.

Following Miriatali, she walked through a wide doorway into an airy hall. Passages led away in two directions, both lined with windows, one set of which let in bright sunshine.

The air was cool in here after the stuffiness of the sedan chair, and the beating heat of the courtyard. Polished stone was everywhere, just as it had been in the House of Jalima. Between the two passageways, a spiral staircase wound upward. But it was not like the tight constructions of the northern houses, on this one five people could climb side-by-side.

However, in this case, Miriatali led the way and Elona stayed on the outside edge and clung to the smooth wooden rail. The tight turns of Corlain castle felt safer than this.

The stairs continued up but Miriatali moved off into a passage, Elona at a polite distance. There were no doors on the inside wall, while the windows looked out on to the city. Elona took cautious glances as they passed them. It seemed she was to be imprisoned in a tower once more. She could see the tops of the nearest buildings, which might have been part of the palace, and then nothing but the ground in the far distance. Hills to the left, then the shoreline and the sea. Almost at the furthest distance was a smudge of grey where rain fell.

The passage ended in a pair of double doors. Female servants, who had been following behind, moved forward smoothly and opened them into rooms of marble, onyx and alabaster. A translucent domed ceiling let in light without showing the sky.

"Quarters fit for a queen," said Miriatali.

Elona turned sharply, had that been a deliberate dig? Only the madness had prevented Elona from becoming queen in Faerholme.

Something moved in the room, Elona saw it with her mind and whirled round. Then relaxed, it was a *zatak* and an old one at that. She reached out with her pattern-sense and laid her mind on to it. It stood and shook itself, padded across to her with its talons clicking on the stone. In a young *zatek* the scaly skin glowed with iridescent blues and greens. Though well-tended, the colours of this old beast had faded, leaving nothing but browns and whites.

Elona crouched as it approached. She had never had a *zatek* as a child, but Usala had one, as old as this though not as large. They made good guards when tamed—and here, where it was warm, it would be so much more active.

The beast responded more easily than wolves ever had, but then it was already domesticated and it placed its snout in her lap as she scratched it behind the ears.

"He has taken to you, Lady Elona."

"What's his name?"

"Doda."

"Isn't that a Kadralin word, Lady Miriatali?"

There was a moment's hesitation. "It means loyal in their tongue."

"A good name then."

Elona stood up. Windows covered one wall but they were shuttered allowing air through but hiding the view. Another set of doors led away on the other side of the room.

"Through there are your private chambers; you will have a staff of four," said Miriatali. "This room is intended for entertaining."

"Am I expected to entertain?"

"Not unless it is your wish," she said. "My father invites you to stay as long as you wish, his home is yours."

"Thank you."

"There will be a banquet in honour of your visit this evening. I will leave you now so you may prepare."

"All afternoon?"

Miriatali smiled. "We can make the preparations fill all the time, Lady Elona, however I understand you have travelled with very few changes of clothes. We must have the royal dressmakers prepare something more suitable."

So I no longer look like something fished out of the gutter.

"Of course, I understand."

ELONA OBJECTED TO, and was embarrassed by, the attentions of so many staff—the most she had ever had before was a single maid, and that person had been her friend. Before Elona murdered her.

But she tolerated it. She even tried to get information out of the maids but they had either been told to keep their mouths shut, genuinely did not understand what Elona was saying, or perhaps were conditioned not to speak to someone so exalted.

The most she could gather was that they were in the guest wing of the palace.

Elona lay in the bath while her toe-nails were trimmed and

polished. Apparently, the shoes she would be wearing would reveal her toes. There was considerable amount of rubbing with a stone in order to remove the hard skin from her feet. Elona did not miss the occasional judgmental glance between the servants.

She was clearly just an uncouth northerner with callouses on her feet due to too much walking. She could not deny there had been a lot of walking. They had wanted her to remove everything, but she refused to take off the knife—despite the giver being a traitor she felt safer with it than not.

To amuse herself she called the *zatek* and tossed a rag for him to fetch. He did it slowly but he always licked her hand.

In the end, she lay back and let the water soak into her scalp. Staring at the ceiling while all sound was silenced. She closed her eyes and thought of her mother, still lying in the cold room in Corlain. Not dead but barely living.

She felt a pang of sadness even though she had never known her mother alive. There was something between them even now. There were those who expressed the idea that the Sisters of Taymar kept the body breathing and healthy simply to receive the money from her father.

Elona sat up suddenly, pulling her feet away from the maids and sending a sloshing wave up and down the tub.

Why did I never use my pattern-sense on my mother?

It seemed such an obvious thing to do but then she did not even know she could do it when she was growing up and, since her return, it had not occurred to her.

Now she was hundreds of leagues away.

It could at least confirm to her whether there was anything of her mother left. She would know if the Sisters were simply bleeding her father's money, or whether they were indeed keeping alive a person who was there.

The maids were looking concerned. Elona let herself slide back into the water and gave them access to her feet once more. Another maid arrived at her side and wanted her hand. Elona lifted it from the water and submitted to the treatment.

What about the Mother's Kitchen? Even thinking about it made Elona feel uneasy. It felt like a precipice into an abyss that would never give her up if she fell into it. How could there be a place where there was no pattern? Everything had a pattern. It scared her.

The *zatek* gave a quiet whimper.

Elona forced her mind to other thoughts and the animal settled again.

Once she had been thoroughly cleaned, they dried her and the seamstresses arrived. They measured and re-measured. Elona was not sure why, since their clothes all seemed so baggy. It was more like throwing on a sack.

Then all the fuss died away and she was left to her own devices as the sun slowly descended. Its slanting light was caught by the shutters but she could see its brightness as it made its way towards the horizon.

Clouds were building up in the distance and the blur of rain she had seen had expanded as it grew closer. The sun would not make it to the horizon, the clouds would obscure it first. She could feel the beginnings of a fretful breeze that buffeted the shutters and swept through the open spaces.

THE SUN HAD BEEN SWALLOWED by the clouds when the seamstresses reappeared. The shutters were opened to let in more light but the wind was stronger too. No one seemed to take any notice, not even the *zatek*. Perhaps this was normal for Mirriasmia.

She had imagined they might take someone else's clothes and simply adjust them for her. But, when they laid out the colourful materials, she realised they had chosen the same pattern as the clothes Keeli had given them.

The identity of Keeli's mistress became apparent.

There was a set of pantaloons of a semi-transparent material through which her legs could easily be seen. This was followed by an inner dress which came down only to her calves and revealed a great deal of her chest. Over that another dress, except it was more like a long close-fitting jacket that fastened at the front. Then there was the headdress. She was aware they were uncertain about her short-haired head, she heard someone mention the Sisters of Taymar but they simply covered it.

The shoes were not shoes at all but simply a sole with straps to hold it to the foot. Little wonder they wanted to clean her feet so thoroughly.

The final addition was a cloak, and everything seemed to include the original pattern of colours that Keeli had given them to wear. She continued to be concerned as what that might mean, to be given the colours of a house that no longer existed reminded her too much of the way Chara had been given control of a family in the Slissac town. The suicide of the previous family matriarch still gave her shivers.

The wind rattled the shutters and gusted through the room as the maids set about closing the windows completely. It seemed they were in for quite a storm, the world outside was almost completely black and rain lashed the dome above.

The room flashed white for a moment. The *zatek* growled as thunder boomed across the palace, so deep and powerful it shook the floor.

"Is this normal?" said Elona to the one she took to be the chief among her servants.

"Big storm!" the woman shouted though her words were consumed by a massive thunderclap.

Then the dome above Elona's head shattered.

CHAPTER 9

The storm blew in and ripped around them, extinguishing lamps and candles. Wind-driven fragments of the dome tore through the air. A woman screamed. The *zatek* whined. Elona's skin stung as the glass-like material sliced through the gossamer material of the pantaloons and cut open her flesh.

Elona ran for the further wall, away from the broken dome. There was another scream that cut short too quickly. She heard heavy boots crunching broken fragments on the polished stone.

Men.

Lightning flashed and she saw three shadowy shapes. One of them with an uplifted dagger.

The light destroyed any night-vision she might have gained, but if she could not see, neither could they. And she did not need to. She dropped behind a divan and took a deep breath in an effort to slow her heartbeat, and to focus.

Focusing her other sense, she perceived the figures in the room. Two of the women lay on the ground with their lives seeping away into the World's Pattern. Three others cowering. Three men, spreading out, one of them coming towards her.

With an effort she let herself feel the *zatek*. She became him. He knew the invaders were enemies and could smell blood. And, praise the Mother, he could see in the dark; it was not detailed through his old eyes but it was enough.

She suppressed his desire to simply attack the nearest one—he was not like the wolves, there was no cunning—instead she made him circle the room to come at the furthest from behind.

As he did so, Elona gently unclipped her knife and withdrew the blade. It seemed ridiculously small, barely the length of her longest finger.

Her plan was vague. These were almost certainly Farahalek, the assassins for hire that were forbidden, yet every great house used when it suited them. She had no training, but she had experience, and it was unlikely they would be expecting much resistance.

The *zatek* was in position and she did not think any of the men had noticed him. The one in front was still heading in her direction while the second was making for the main door where the other women were huddled. She could not understand why they had not simply run out.

Elona waited for the right moment—

Another flash of lightning illuminated the room. And was gone.

—Elona-as-*zatek* launched her attack, his old legs invigorated with excitement. He bounded onto a chair and launched himself at the rear-most attacker. Elona slipped from her hiding place, just as Doda's honking attack sounded, and the shocked cry of his prey distracted the other two.

She aimed for the nearest one's groin but he half-turned at the sounds behind, and the blade plunged into his thigh. His reaction to jerk away from the pain should have ripped the blade from her hands, but not this weapon. Instead a piece of his muscles was carved out. He screamed in agony and she perceived his arms lifting to strike a blow. She threw herself forward, beneath his attack, and sliced upward. Gushing blood coated her hands. Something heavy landed on her back as he staggered away clutching at his wounds.

Even the greatest healer would be hard-pressed to save him.

Something cut her cheek and clattered to the floor behind her, followed by two solid thumps.

Elona threw herself to the ground again. The third man was by the far wall. He couldn't have known exactly where she was, yet his attack —whatever it was—had been dangerously accurate.

Doda let out a screech of pain. His opponent was fighting back. Elona felt a momentary twinge of guilt. She found the dagger that had fallen on her back when her attacker had dropped it. She focused again and saw the third man was running away from the fight. She did not think he was a coward, but clearly the attack was supposed to go easily, after all, what could a bunch of women do?

She saw him pause at the second man and perceived a movement that might have been a weapon strike. She stood up and hefted the dagger. She had no idea how to do this but it would be better if he didn't get away.

Lightning in the distance illuminated the room through the shutters and she saw him clearly—though shrouded in black. He was at the window and looking back at her. She threw the weapon with all her strength. Another lightning flash illuminated the blade as it curved between them.

He caught it.

And moments later it was embedded in her own shoulder.

It knocked her off balance and she fell back as the pain ripped through her.

Never give your opponent a weapon.

She lay on her back breathing hard. Trying to gather her senses. The black figure appeared above her. She couldn't see his face but he was probably grinning behind the black scarf. He had every right; she had been stupid.

She closed her eyes and focused. She needed time, she needed him closer. Everything was about patterns and what she needed to do worked more slowly but she had done it before. She was a helpless woman and he was a man with lusts. Here was an opportunity. He could have her; no one would stop him, and then he could finish her off.

It was like the wolves. You couldn't force them to do something against their nature but you could guide, you could indicate a way forward.

A hand landed on her calf. It stung as the embedded pieces of the dome scratched. The hand ran upwards. He forced her legs apart and leaned across her.

She still held the little dagger in her hand, and just as she had killed Styvan with a rock to the temple, she slammed it with all her strength into his neck.

His forearm moved like lightning and blocked the blow. She heard his muffled laugh as he knelt back and peeled her fingers open forcing the knife to drop. His hands gripped her wrists and forced them back to the ground. Pain seared her shoulder and she almost passed out.

He jerked once and his weight collapsed on her. Something heavy crashed to floor beside them. Her head was filled with the unwelcome memory of Krazak lying dead across her in her mother's chamber. But where the archer's arrow had saved her and killed him, this one was not yet dead.

Elona choked back a scream as the remaining women pulled him off her bumping the dagger still embedded in Elona's shoulder. She took a deep breath and focused. They were no longer being attacked.

Elona ordered them to relight the lamps but the wind still whipped through the room and snuffed out every attempt. Rain poured through the gaping hole in the ceiling. Elona managed to get into a sitting position. She was covered in blood and this time a great deal of it was her own. The dagger was a burning poker in her shoulder.

"Where's my knife?" She looked at the floor and saw it glinting. "There, give it to me. Don't touch the blade!"

A combination of gestures and words made them understand and she got the blade back. The man on the floor next to her groaned and moved. Forcing the pain to the back of her mind, Elona leaned forward and sliced the blade through his neck.

There were squeals from one of the remaining maids. The chief maid simply put her hand to her mouth and stared at Elona in wide-eyed horror.

"He's Farahalek," Elona said. "If he can move, he can kill."

She pointed at the bedroom. "Help me."

The head maid shook her head and pointed at the dagger. "Get help."

"No. Not yet. All stay here."

"No help?"

"No. Later."

Elona again pointed at the bedroom and they helped her stagger across into it. They shut the door, blocking out the wind and rain. With the lights lit, the only thing that marred the perfect room was the trail of her blood across the floor. They assisted her in lying down.

"Water."

She drank and lay back.

"Mistress, you lose too much blood. You will die without healing."

Tell me something I don't know.

"I am a healer."

That was easy to say but, to heal herself, she needed a source of power and the Avaki ley-circle was too far away. She could barely sense it, and there was no other source of the Mother's Milk nearby.

But the void drew her.

The Mother's Kitchen was a well of darkness among the teeming patterns that surrounded it. Across the citadel it lay, easy for her to perceive by what was not there. But if it had no power, how could it help?

There was no choice, she had to try. The Farahalek had known exactly where she was, and somehow got in from above. The Liralain could not be trusted, nor could any healer they might supply, and she did not intend to stay for the banquet. She needed to get out before they tried again, with Jaymis if she could find him, but without him if she could not.

Fighting her vertigo, she focused on the void of the Mother's Kitchen. If this was a real source of power, it would flow to her like a river and she could use it to heal herself. Taymalin healers, even those of the Kadralin, used patterns to focus the power like all patterners. Elona had no need of tradition.

Her heart pounded as she opened herself up to whatever lay within the void.

Patterns winked out as something—or was it nothing—expanded and came towards her. She held her nerve though she knew she was sweating with fear, her attention focused on the blackness.

It came to her as if she was commanding the Mother's Milk. But it was a nothingness that moved like congealing blood. Even so, there *was* something she could use, though it filled her up until she felt she was drowning.

The tiny scratches inflicted by the wind-driven fragments of the shattered dome closed up. She could feel it happening, and she knew there was something wrong. The wound across her cheek succumbed in the same way. It was healed but not the way she expected.

In the distance she could feel the women's fear growing and their words were filled with terror. One of them went for the door but she twisted its pattern to make sure it couldn't open. The wound in her shoulder was resisting. She realised she had to remove the dagger— just as she had the lethal arrow that almost killed Drahail. She reached across her chest with her other hand, took the handle and yanked it free. There was no pain and the wound closed almost immediately.

She let the void go and felt it tearing away from her flesh as it reluctantly withdrew.

Her head swam as she sat up but she pushed the sensation away and took another drink of water. It refreshed her and she opened her eyes.

The maids were huddled by the door, terror on their faces.

"I need to get clean," said Elona. "Quickly. And I want my other clothes back."

THEY DID NOT RESPOND IMMEDIATELY but when she insisted, they set about their work. The chief maid was the one who stripped and cleaned her, using a bowl which had to be emptied twice to replace the reddened water. They dried her and helped her dress in the clothes Keeli had provided.

Then she noticed her hands. The healing had not worked properly at all. Each cut was mended but instead of the skin being woven together magically, almost as if there had been no injury at all, here it was as if no healing had been performed and the skin was simply sealed.

She raised her hand to her face and felt the gash on her cheek. The ridge remained, scarring her.

"Mirror!"

One of the maids nervously handed her a small one with a handle. Elona held it to her face. The gash remained, though the blood had been wiped away. She used the glass to look at the dagger wound and there, again, it was still there. Just sealed with a layer of skin. She touched the wound. The edges were rough and jagged while the inner skin seemed hard as leather.

Elona sighed and placed the mirror face down on the bed. That explained why they looked on her with such horror. It was almost as if the wounds had simply frozen. But she there was no pain and she knew she was fit to travel.

She stood up, taking a moment to ensure that she still had the little knife hung about her neck.

"Listen to me," she said slowly and clearly to the chief maid. "You have seen my power, so do not disobey me. You will do what I say."

She managed to get them to understand and had their reluctant agreement.

"I am leaving the palace."

That got them very upset again.

Beyond the door, she heard a banging above the noise of the wind, then a crash. Footsteps thudded across the floor. Voices were raised in alarm and she could hear orders being shouted.

Someone tried the door but failed to open it. There were shouts from outside, the three maids looked at her and she put her finger to her mouth. That did nothing for their courage but they obeyed. Something slammed against the door but it did not even shake. She had no idea what she had done to prevent it from opening, but it was completely stuck.

Elona grabbed the chief maid by the arm. "Is there another way out?" She had already looked around and seen nothing. There was something about the way the woman looked.

"Where is it?"

The woman kept her mouth shut until Elona fingered the little knife in its sheath. It was not that she liked to threaten people, but if they weren't forthcoming, what choice did she have?

"There is a way."

"Show me."

CHAPTER 10

A panel behind one of the bedside cabinets clicked when pressed just so, and the whole section of wall, including the cabinet, slid out smoothly when pulled. Elona had the chief maid take a candlestick.

She did not want three maids in tow but she could not leave them behind, so hustled them into the hidden passage ahead of her. The solid thump of an axe against the door echoed through the room as Elona stepped through and pulled the wall closed. There was only slightest line of light at the bottom from the bedroom, there would be no clue as to where they had gone.

The passage was just wide enough for one person so it was a squeeze for Elona to get to the front and take the candlestick. She led the way as the passage ran along the inside of the back wall of the bedroom and then, at the point Elona judged to be the outer wall, it turned abruptly left and steps led down.

The light from the candle did not shine any great distance and, apart from ten steps or so, it was a dark and empty void below them. Their feet scuffing on the steep stone steps was the only sound as they headed down. That and their breathing.

It was stone on both sides and there were no other entrances to rooms. The banging from the bedroom behind them soon faded to nothing.

"How many know of these escapes?" said Elona as she focused on each step, trying not to imagine the kind of fall there might be if she slipped.

"Senior staff," said the woman behind her.

It wasn't long before they were all panting from the exertion, and it was getting warm in the passage. It did not run completely straight but turned from time to time.

After a while the quality of the walls and ceiling changed. Where they had been made from shaped stones like the rest of the castle, now it changed to seamless rock. It had still been cut and smoothed, and the steps were as crisp as the day they had been chiselled.

They must now be beneath the level of the palace itself, and there had not been a single other exit. It did mean these passages could not easily be used for spying. But did it go to the heart of the earth where the rocks melted and the undying patterns of evil-doers burned? Or would it just end in the majestic palace sewers?

Elona was almost surprised when they reached the bottom. It had felt as if the steps would continue forever. But they stood in a short passage with a candle that had only burnt halfway through its length. The passage went forward another twenty paces, turned to the right abruptly and ended in a blank surface. A lever was mounted on the wall.

"You go back now," said Elona to the maids.

"Lady Elona?"

"I don't want you with me. If I get attacked again, you might get hurt or killed. Just go back up." She waved her hand in the direction of the stairs.

"These will go, but I stay."

"Don't be stupid."

"You may give me any name, my lady, but I have been charged by the High Lord Liralain himself to care for you. I must stay with you."

Elona sighed. It was obvious arguing would achieve nothing, and she suspected that threatening the woman would have the same effect.

"In that case, I will tie you up here."

"And one of these girls will take my place."

"I will tie them too."

"Then we will die here, who will find us?"

"Someone will come down."

"Or they may not."

"But for me that will be safer, you will give me away the first opportunity you get."

"My promise to my lord is to serve you, Lady Elona."

"That is a twisting thing—what's your name?"

"Kerlyn of Lira, Lady Elona. I am Third Under-Chatelaine to High Lord Liralain in the Palace of Avakending."

"You have keys to the Palace?"

"I will not betray my lord."

"But you'll help me?"

"I will serve you as commanded but I will not betray my lord."

"But I've just run away."

"To protect your own life, which is as my lord would intend."

Elona chose not to argue that point, since she was certain the precious High Lord was responsible for the attack. Though the reason for it eluded her. She could not deny having someone who could speak the language fluently and knew their way around, would be very useful.

Before she could say anything, Kerlyn had told the other two to head back up the stairs. They complained of being tired and having no light. Elona considered the light to be a fair point, though there was no chance they could get lost, and handed over the candlestick. There was probably sufficient wax to last them.

Elona pressed her ear to the exit but could hear nothing through the stone. Nor was there any breeze coming round the edges. She hoped it was an exit and that she hadn't given away the only source of illumination.

She waited until the candle light had completely faded, put both hands on the lever and pushed it hard into the wall. It resisted for a moment, then moved with a clunk that reverberated through the stone at her feet. The exit moved enough to allow grey light and wind to seep in. Her ears were assailed by the constant roar of waves crashing on stones.

It required Kerlyn's help to pull the stone door round on its hinge. Soil along with moss and grasses, had become embedded in the cracks. It dropped away as the door ground open.

Elona looked out and groaned. It was not the sewers, though they might have been preferable. There was a great chasm between this opening and the opposite cliff that rose up to the buildings of the city, and down to the wild water of the sea. Huge wind-driven waves pummelled the rocks filling the air with sea-water spray. Elona could taste salt.

The wind was cold, despite the usual heat of this place. And rain came down in sheets.

There was a path but it was as thin as the passages they had come through, with no barrier on the seaward side. The stones were slick with water.

"Why?" she moaned.

"That does not look safe," said Kerlyn peering round her.

"No," said Elona. "It does not."

She seriously considered simply staying here but eventually soldiers would come down looking for her.

"Do you know where this path leads?"

"We only know of the escape door."

"You never explored?"

"That would not be acceptable—I might be caught and tortured for the information."

"You might even yet," muttered Elona.

There was no choice. She had to simply hope the path did not go far before it became safe. She got down on her hands and knees.

"I recommend you do the same," she said. "One nasty gust of wind could knock you straight off and into the water."

"The rocks, lady," said Kerlyn. "I think you would hit them first."

"All the more reason to stay safe."

"Yes, mistress."

Elona crawled from the safety of the passageway. She wanted to close it but it did not seem practical to try. There really was no room for any mistakes out here.

The wind buffeted her as she moved across the damp, hard stones. Edges cut into her knees but she simply had to put up with it. She leaned in against the solid rock of the cliff to provide more stability, and kept her eyes on the surface in front of her—trying not to see the drop-off on her left. She moved slowly, just one knee or hand at a time, while the spray came up from below and the rain soaked her through from above.

She did not try to see how Kerlyn was doing.

The path reached a corner and turned towards the right. They were still descending though slowly. Past the corner she saw a stony shoreline below instead of the sea itself. If she fell, she might still be dashed against the rocks but she wouldn't drown.

Something shrieked in her ear and pecked at her from the cliffside. As she panicked and jerked away, the edge of the stone she was resting on crumbled under her. She dropped forward as her hand slid away and landed with face in a gooey white mess. The thing shrieked again and attacked the hood over her head. She managed to regain her balance while her thumping heart threatened to pound its way from her chest.

"Shoo!" came from behind, then something seemed to whip over her head and there was another annoyed shriek as a something stepped on her head and then disappeared.

"*Sikechak*, mistress. It's gone."

Pity it couldn't take its shit with it.

Elona pulled herself up again. She spat and wiped her arm across her face. The sound of the creature, however, did not go away and Elona could hear it continuing to squawk angrily as it wheeled around them.

She pushed herself forward and kept moving. The descending slope finally intersected with the rising shore of the small bay. The wind was less here, with the cliffs all round, and the rain fell in a constant deluge.

"I thought it was always sunny here in the south."

"Sea storms are rare, mistress."

"I was just lucky then."

She was grateful to be standing on solid ground once more, and with nowhere to fall from. Still the views up were vertiginous in themselves. On both sides, the cliffs ran up almost vertically and in the dark all that could really be seen was the lights of the buildings at the top.

"How do we get out of here?"

"Boat, mistress."

She was right, in the dim light Elona saw several small vessels drawn up on the pebbly beach. "Come tomorrow, the storm will be gone and the fishermen will return to the sea."

They found shelter in one of the boats where an oiled cloth could protect them from the worst of the rain and provide some warmth. Elona had no embarrassment sleeping close to another, but Kerlyn was less keen.

"We are wet and cold," said Elona, "together we will be warmer."

The woman's voice became stiff. "I do not sleep with another."

"I—very well, if that's what you prefer. Is it against your custom?"

There was a pause as if Kerlyn was trying to interpret what Elona had said. "Not my custom. Yes."

Elona shrugged, even though it would be invisible in the dark, wrapped herself in the cloth, managed to find a reasonably comfortable position and was asleep almost immediately.

CHAPTER 11

The sound of men's voices woke her. She was stiff and her clothes still damp. There had been no Chara to strip her of her wet clothes or build a fire to warm her. Elona smiled at the memory and her original notion that Chara had only wanted to enslave her.

A note of surprise in one voice brought her back to the present. There was a stream of angry words and the men laughed. Elona recognised some words that implied a Tahulin had fallen from the sky and become human. Clearly these people were not as precious about naming the spirit creatures as Athlem had been.

Forcing her protesting joints and muscles to obey her, Elona pushed herself to her feet and allowed the cloth she had used to drop away. The boat moved slightly and the pebbles crunched beneath it.

A grey pre-dawn light filled the small beach and left the shadows very black but she saw half a dozen men surrounding a boat that was drawn up nearer the cliff. In the dim light, she could see a precipitous stairway cut into the rock. In some places, it was less stairs and more ladder. She would not be using it.

The men had turned at the sound of her movement and stood staring. Elona could see Kerlyn looking angry with her cloth still wrapped around her. She had not been dressed for travel—Elona's clothes were better.

"Tahulin," muttered one, and two of the older men went down on their knees. The younger ones simply stared first at her and then the old ones prostrating themselves.

Elona closed her eyes. They thought she was a spirit? She stepped out of the boat as neatly as she could, stumbling might have dispelled their ideas.

"I am Parthia," she said. "And I require passage on your boat."

An argument broke out and Elona took the opportunity to summon Kerlyn who got away from the men and stumbled across the pebbles to her.

"What are they saying?"

"Their common accent is very thick."

"Just tell me."

"They are very common. They argue whether you truly are a Tahulin fallen from the clouds, or—begging your pardon, mistress— that perhaps a courtesan thrown out by the High Lord for failing to satisfy him. They wonder whether helping you will bring good luck or bad."

"Good luck if I'm Tahulin?"

"They cannot say. Perhaps dealing with a Tahulin will curse them. There are many stories."

"I'm sure there are," muttered Elona. Bejeren had told her enough of them, but he had never bothered mentioning where they had come from. None of them were any part of Taymar's lore but the poorer folk lived a strange mix of Taymalin and Kadralin beliefs. Though some believed Taymar was on a par with the Mother, while others disregarded the Kadralin stories completely. Though how they explained the feedings, Elona did not know.

"What are your intentions, mistress?"

Elona noticed how the maid's eyes flicked to Elona's cheek every other moment. The wound must look bad in the daylight. There were those who believed the Tahulin were patterns of the dead and, at this moment, her face probably made that a good argument.

"I can't tell you that, you would tell your lord when you next see him."

"Oh no," said Kerlyn, concerned at the accusation. "How could I serve if I could not be trusted?"

"You mean you wouldn't tell them?"

"I am your loyal servant, until you leave these lands or dismiss me. I will not tell during or after that time."

"I need to get on a boat and let them take me to a place outside of the city. I must find out what has happened to Jaymis, and see if I can rescue him."

"I understand."

"Tell them I need passage now. I'm sure it won't be long before they come from the tunnel after me."

Kerlyn spoke quickly and one of the older men—who had bowed low—volunteered. It seemed that he was not concerned about any curse, even if he did think she might be some sort of spirit.

Elona lent a hand as the man pushed the small vessel towards the sea. He seemed surprised but did not protest, although his eyes did linger on her damaged cheek. Perhaps it would help to hide her identity.

The moment they were all on board and the little boat moved out into the waves Elona regretted her choice. The constant rising and dipping made her empty stomach want to heave and she clung to the side as if the movement might flip her into the sea.

She could not swim and her only experience of deep water had been the glass-like lake in the mountains when she and Chara had been fleeing the soldiers. They had almost drowned.

But the fisherman moved confidently back and forth, the small sail was raised and, as he sat in the back, the vessel whipped round and headed along the channel between the cliffs at a good pace. Elona focused on the coastline. There were dozens of little inlets and bays. Each one seemed to have a stairway leading down into it and boats just like this one, drawn up on the beach. Men were working in them, some drawing them down to the sea. The channel was filling up with small vessels.

The water became much rougher as they passed out from between the cliffs and into the open sea. They would rise up one crystal green slope, tilt over the top and plunge down the next one. All around the other vessels were doing the same. It was all very well seeing it happen and not a single vessel sank, but every time Elona felt as if the boat would spill them all into the water.

They did not seem to be heading inland, or even along the coast. The great city of Avakending moved away until, at the top of a wave, she could see the whole of it brilliant white in the sunshine.

"Kerlyn, ask him where we're going?"

There was some rapid discussion between the other two that she could barely follow.

"He wants to fish first."

"But why? Would it not be easier without us?"

"He is testing you, mistress."

Elona closed her eyes but realised that just made the feeling worse. "Why would he do that?"

"He wants to know if befriending a Tahulin would be a blessing or a curse."

"But I'm not one."

"He knows you might not be."

"But it makes no sense."

Kerlyn made a noise like a shrug.

Time went on. The other boats had spread out. The man—Garoon was his name, according to Kerlyn—finally brought down the sail and they bobbed on the huge waves.

From a small cabinet under his seat in the rear he pulled out a long line with hooks at regular intervals. There was a bucket containing wormlike creatures and he went along the line impaling a worm on each of the hooks. As he did, he let it trail out into the water.

He said something.

"He wants to know if you will do a pattern and bless his hooks."

"I'm not a patterner."

"I think it would be good if you did something, mistress."

Elona pulled herself into a sitting position in the bottom of the boat. It was wet but it felt safer with her back pressed against the side.

She closed her eyes and spread out her senses. Her vertigo hit her like a stone. *"Mother's Milk,"* she hissed between her teeth.

"Mistress?"

Elona shook her head. How could she explain that the depth of the water terrified her? She could make out the bottom but it was a long way below it was as if she was standing on a cliff-edge, or flying. While the sea itself was teeming with brilliant flashes of patterned life. So much more than land.

How could it not be terrifying?

But she tried to pull herself together, this man wanted a sign and it would be a decent thing to do to return his gift of taking her from the city by filling his boat with fish.

"I might be able to do something but I need to see one of the fish he catches." There was no telling what she might drag out of the deep if she did not have a clear picture of what she wanted. She was not even sure she would succeed anyway.

Kerlyn passed on the message and Garoon nodded as if this was the sensible and obvious thing to be done.

They waited and the sun bore down. Elona arranged her hood to cover her face. She was warm and tired, the movement of the vessel changed to something soothing; she knew she was drifting off to sleep.

"Hey," sounded the deep voice of Garoon.

Elona pulled back her hood and saw he held the glistening form of a fish about the length of one of his arms. It was sleek and wriggled. The hook still embedded in its mouth. Carefully Garoon pulled it out.

"Tell him to hold it still."

Elona made sure she kept her weight low as she moved to the rear of the boat. Garoon was staring at the wound on her cheek again.

"I've never tried this before," she said to no one in particular, and Kerlyn didn't translate it. Perhaps Garoon understood anyway.

The fish was wriggling but Elona closed her eyes and focused her attention on it, trying to understand its patterns. Slowly she reached out and lay her hand on its slick skin. She became the fish, and found it to be more aware than she had imagined. It was scared.

"Let it go," she said to Garoon. His eyebrows knotted—she knew he had understood her and she pointed over the side. "Put it back in the sea."

He obeyed with a great deal of reluctance, this was his livelihood and a lost fish was lost money.

Elona went back to her place and closed her eyes. Trying to ignore the depth below her, she stretched out to touch the fish's pattern. The brightness of the life was blinding and she could not imagine how she could find a single fish among it all.

A mass of light caught her attention. It reminded her of the wolves and she realised it was not a single creature but a mass of them, hundreds and thousands, and her target was among them.

She could barely make it out, they were all so similar. She was not even sure how she managed to see *her* one among the teeming mass.

Her experience with the wolves had taught her to find the leader and influence that one, then the others would follow. But these were not wolves and, though she searched, she could find no single creature among them that led the rest. Yet they were in constant motion and stayed together. She could feel their hunger, they searched for patches where smaller fish, also in groups, fed on their own prey.

Then she understood. One of them would find a source of food and would turn. The ones around it would feel that movement and follow. Within moments the entire shoal would be following in that direction. There was no leader, they simply followed whichever one seemed to know where to go.

Familiarity made it easy for her to connect with the one Garoon had caught. Once more she matched its pattern, feeling its constant contact with its shoal. It did not know where the boat and its lines were, but she did. Elona brought her fish around and felt the others follow. She pushed him forwards and up. She could not see what it saw only encourage and guide.

"*By the Mother's tits!*" shouted Garoon as the boat was inundated with water. Elona was ripped from her reverie as a wave of water crashed down on her. The boat shuddered in the water. The sea was alive with fish, their silver bodies turning across the surface. Kerlyn screamed as one of them threw itself over the side and lay flapping in the boat.

Shrieking birds and *sikechasa* filled the air. Diving into the water, or grabbing at the fish with their talons.

Garoon shouted something Elona couldn't translate but Kerlyn lay down as a bird went low over the boat looking for anything to grab. Elona followed suit. Garoon batted away a small *sikechak* as he pulled on the rope to raise the sail. Another seabird slammed into the mast with enough force to make the boat rock and Elona thought she heard something crack.

There was no way to tell if the boat was moving but she could see the sail filling with wind. Air and sea were alive with creatures. The noise of the birds was deafening. Elona remembered the Slissac boat with its curious living hull, she had almost drowned Chara when she used her magic to drive them—the way the Slissac must have done. But she did not know the patterns and her raw power was too much. She had killed the mosses and the boat-creatures when her fear had caused her to lash out.

At first it almost felt as if Garron's vessel was sailing over bumpy ground but soon it smoothed away and they were riding up and down the big waves again.

"Tahulin!" Garoon shouted above the noise of the birds and he laughed out loud.

Elona sighed. It seemed he was convinced. Now perhaps he would take her where she wanted to go. Although she had no idea what she would do next.

IT WAS a small village along the coast where Garoon finally tied up. The bottom of the boat was filled with fish he had removed from his lines. They twitched unnervingly and Elona tried not to think about how she had lured them to their death.

They had to wait while he sold the fish. Kerlyn explained that the price out here was a lot lower than in the city but Garoon was happy enough to do it. He was thoroughly convinced of Elona's divine nature.

If only he knew what I really am.

He had arranged for them to stay in someone's house, after explaining the miracle she had wrought on the open sea. She hoped their new hosts did not expect their own magic—it was never safe.

They had been brought food and a change of clothes.

Elona tried to hide the damage to her cheek with a scarf but it tended to slip. She examined the dagger wound in her shoulder; it did not seem to be healing any further. As if even the natural process had stopped. It was the same with the scratches on her hands and legs. If she had ever hoped for a husband, there was little chance she would find one now with her body permanently and grotesquely scarred.

The strange magic of the Mother's Kitchen was powerful but it did not seem to care for patterns.

After some discussion, Kerlyn had agreed to go back into the city and find out what had happened to Jaymis—if she could—and to speak to Athlem, if he could be found. In exchange, Elona agreed she would stay in the village and keep out of the way.

She could only imagine the stories that Garoon would be telling his friends. They would have seen the way the seabirds and *sikechasa* had arrived when the shoal surfaced. Would they think she was a Tahulin fallen to earth too? She hoped not, it was a complication she did not need.

Once more she thought about how she would rather be in the Slissac town with Chara.

She was exhausted and slept the moment her eyes closed, dreaming of her sister.

CHAPTER 12

The previous evening...

Rain poured through the blackness at a sharp angle driven by the wind. From a window of the suite of rooms he had been given, Jaymis stared out across the haphazard roofs of the palace and across the town. Down from his window was a great dome which glowed from its inner lights.

Jaymis stepped back as lightning flashed directly overhead and the deafening thunder rattled the shutters. He had asked them not to close this one because he liked thunderstorms. But he had never seen anything this fierce, the Kadralin would probably say the Mother was angry.

It was only early evening but outside it was like night as the rain tumbled from the thick clouds, except when the lightning showed everything in a monochrome of white and black. He was still waiting to be called down for the banquet, and he was nervous.

He had attended plenty of banquets, and with lords, princes and kings he did not know. But this one would be with Elona. He knew she was no longer under the influence of his mother's magic but simply knowing that could not dispel the thought that something might go wrong.

She spent so much time looking inward.

She was right, of course, his mother might have accused him of murdering his father but he had not done it. The accusation was a wound on his heart—he had loved his father and his mother had ripped him away—but Elona had suffered so much more.

He felt responsible. That it was his duty to somehow make it up to her, and make amends for the harm his family had caused. But she was so self-sufficient, she did not need him. He doubted she would admit it even if she did.

He had been in disguise as Captain Jalka, an armsman of Dirdin, when he had been called to the ley-circle because she had appeared there. Almost as if she had walked a patterner's path. Yet no path had been made.

It had not been hard to arrange for her escape, money in the hands of the Kadralin traders and a promise they would not be pursued. He had not known of her extreme fear of heights at the time and the route arranged did her no favours. He had watched from a distance as she crawled across the roof top, and finally made it into the traders' cart.

He had managed to put himself in charge of the pursuit and had managed to guide his men in completely the wrong direction, until it became too obvious.

When he finally caught up with the Kadralin traders, the master and the shaman told him how she had given herself to the raiders as payment. He was horrified and could not understand what had possessed her to do such a thing.

They gave chase but, after the battle at the Slissac bridge, he lost her. He found the cave with the raiders' leader dead, his skull crushed by a rock, but Elona was gone. He had his men search for another day but the weather closed in and they had to leave before they were trapped by the snow and died.

He guessed she must still have been alive to elude him—she did not know he was on her side—but did not see how she could possibly survive the winter in the mountains.

Except she had.

He had been among the forces sent to aid Aris in Taltia against the Tirnian offensive. In its protected valley with a ley-circle, the city could hold out against any siege—which is why it had such military importance. The ley-circle meant that food and troops could be brought in all the time.

The betrayal of his mother had been intended to allow Tirnian forces through the ley-circle, while she murdered the Faerholme king and his son, so she could control the throne through her daughter and grandchild.

It was Elona who had stopped her.

He sighed. How could he *not* try to make up for all the harm his mother had caused? That woman had destroyed Elona's life.

He was brought abruptly back to the present by a brilliant flash, and another tremendous thunderclap followed by the shattering of something very large.

"What's that?" He turned to the servant he'd been given who gave a shrug that in Faerholme would have been inappropriate.

From somewhere outside, through the window, a woman's scream started and cut off. The servant opened his mouth and then closed it again. His eyebrows knotted in worry.

Jaymis spun back to the window. There was nothing to see in the black, he stared out, certain that something was different. Lightning flashed again and he glimpsed what had been the glowing dome, now shattered, its edges like a broken egg.

There was another cry—this time it sounded like a man.

The wind changed direction and rain pummelled him.

"What's that place?" he shouted at the servant, who would not come any closer and said nothing.

Jaymis was across the room in a moment, grabbed him by the arm and dragged him to the window.

"The broken dome, what is it?"

"Women's place."

Another female scream pierced the blackness.

"Take me there!"

"You will not be safe, I cannot."

Jaymis stared across the dark roofs. Then directly down. There was a ridge that ran in the right direction.

Slowing himself down, trying to act naturally. "No, you're right. You go and alert the palace guards."

"Yes, master. I will go, you will wait." He turned and hurried towards the exit.

Jaymis was out of the window before the door closed, and soaked through in moments.

This is not a good idea.

A gushing drainage pipe made a ladder down to the main roof below him. He wiped the rain from his eyes then, on all fours, made his way up the opposite slope to the ridge. Looking back, he could see his own window with the lights flickering from inside.

He gripped the slick ridge tiles in both hands with his feet on the roof slope, then clambered sideways along its length moving just one hand or foot at a time.

He looked down under his arm and saw the roof below him now ended in a drop into darkness.

This really isn't a good idea.

He reached the end of the ridge. The dome was not too far away but there was nothing below him except a chasm of blackness which probably ended in flagstones. His fingers ached but he managed to pull himself up until he was sitting on the end of the ridge.

Looking down, he noticed this end of the building was angled compared to the next one and further down the gap narrowed. Lightning flashed above him and he saw the drop to the ground in perfect clarity. He would not survive if he fell—perhaps Elona could magic him back to Dirdin if he did.

Except she wasn't here and she might be in trouble.

He knew she wasn't a woman who screamed, though a niggling thought suggested she might be the sort to make someone else scream. But he pushed it aside, even if she had been the cause that didn't mean she wasn't in trouble.

He swung both legs over to the other roof slope, rolled on to his stomach and tried to control the slide down. His clothing caught and tore as he descended. He jammed his toes into the tiles as hard as he could. His feet struck a ridge and he came to a jolting stop.

Then something gave way beneath him and one foot lost all support. Flailing his arms to try to regain his balance he went over—

His arm caught on a cord hanging in space and he came to an abrupt dangling halt with one foot on a solid surface.

The line was taut and solid, about the same diameter as his smallest finger. He clung to it and managed to get himself upright. The rope was tightly woven and of the very highest quality. Not the sort of thing you found on a castle rooftop.

Farahalek.

They had sent assassins for her. His heart sank. Someone wanted Elona dead, and how could she possibly survive against those trained killers? The fear for her safety gave him new strength. He hooked his arms over the cord and lifted his legs until they too held him on it.

He knew he was too slow as he made his way across the dark gulf between the buildings. Above him, the only place he could see, lightning flickered through the clouds and low rumbles tumbled across the city. The cord cut through his thin clothes and into his soft damp skin.

One arm, other arm, both feet. Repeat.

He had thought about Elona's escape from the wedding a dozen times. He had compared the time when she had disappeared from Canvor to when she had appeared in Dirdin.

One arm, other arm, both feet. Repeat.

Taking into account the difference in sunset, because Dirdin was further east, it did not add up. If she had taken a patterner's path, it could have worked.

One arm, other arm, both feet. Repeat.

But Canvor's ley-circle was beneath the lake. It was impossible. And her wounds were almost healed.

One arm, other arm, both feet. Repeat.

There were only two possibilities: Elona had sent herself to Dirdin using some form of pattern that wasn't a patterner's path—and healed herself at the same time—or someone else had done it to her. But they would have had to have been there at exactly the right moment when she fell and be able to make the patterning to transport her instantly—and that was a piece of magic, as far as Jaymis knew, no one possessed.

One arm, other arm, both feet. Repeat.

The ability to transport from anywhere to a ley-circle? Perhaps anywhere to anywhere? That would be very dangerous. Elona had always claimed she knew nothing about it but then, she was insane when it happened.

One arm, other arm, both feet. Rep—

His head collided with the wall on the other side. He lifted himself and managed to wriggle the rest of the way and came down sitting on the edge of the wall. The only sounds were the wind, the rain, and the rumbling thunder.

His muscles ached but he forced himself to his feet and made his way carefully across the solid flat roof that led to the shattered dome. He peered cautiously over the edge as the wind whipped round him. The room below was in complete darkness, he couldn't even see the floor. Why was there no lightning when you needed it?

There was no sound either—wait, no. Someone breathing, whimpering slightly almost like an animal.

If the assassins broke the dome to gain entry, there would be a rope.

He moved quickly round the dome until he found three ropes. He realised that he had not bothered to pick up his sword, or even a dagger. But he was sure he was in no danger now, the Farahalek had had time to get in, do what they intended, and get out. Yet they had left their ropes behind? Surely they would have gone back the way they came and removed all trace? It added to their mystique.

He took a rope and went over the edge. He controlled the drop as best he could without gloves and landed near the centre of the room. The wind blew through but the rain had stopped, at least for now. The floor beneath him had puddles that reflected light from beyond the dome.

Lightning finally gave him a momentary view. He saw five bodies and a great deal of dark liquid. Two women who might have been maids, two men wrapped up in night disguise, and a *zatek* who lay half on top of one of them. It was the animal that was still breathing though, from the laboured sound, it would not be for long.

"Good boy," said Jaymis.

He had also seen a sword not far from his feet which he picked up. Holding it did a great deal for his confidence.

There was a battering coming from the main door. Trying to avoid stepping in the blood he headed that way but it was hard to see. Beneath the door were moving lights and the shadows of many people. They were battering on it.

"Stop," called Jaymis. "I'm going to try to unlock it."

There was a great deal of talk outside and finally someone shouted. "Who is it?"

"Lord Jaymis Betlain, give me a moment."

He had to explore the back of the door by hand but eventually found the bolts which shifted with a great deal of effort. There was also a lock but the key was missing. He relayed that information and stood back.

The battering started again and moment later the door burst open. Armsmen poured through and someone slammed him up against a wall. The sword was ripped from his hand.

Lights were brought in though the wind kept snuffing them out. Jaymis was forcefully walked out into the corridor where the lights were steady. They sat him on an ornate wooden chest.

"Lord Jaymis, why are you here?"

Jaymis looked up at a man he did not recognise though his skin was quite pale, he had an aristocratic bearing.

"Who are you to ask me? As the head of a recognised family, I have the right to be questioned only by my peers."

"Lord Nemon of Tiralain."

"You're a long way from Tirnia, Lord Nemon."

"Why I am here is my business, Lord Jaymis. But why you were in that room with the doors barred and people dead is, at this moment, mine."

"My room overlooks this wing. I heard the dome shatter and screams. I came across the roof, and found dead Farahalek."

They were interrupted by repeated crashes against the inner door. Glancing back inside Jaymis saw six armsmen holding a divan and swinging it against the door which seemed surprisingly resistant.

"You had a sword."

Lord Nemon's words brought Jaymis's attention back.

"The sword? I picked it up from one of the dead Farahalek. Look at me, I am dressed for the banquet just as you are. Ask the servant in my room, he was there at the time. We both heard it. I sent him to raise the alarm."

"And I am to believe you made it across the roof when there is a wide gap?"

Jaymis frowned. "You are surprisingly familiar with the castle, Lord Nemon."

The man pursed his lips and changed the subject. "Did you kill the Farahalek?"

"They were already dead when I arrived. I was looking for Lady Elona, have you found her?"

"Wait here."

Nemon stalked away back into the women's suite. They were still trying to open the other door. Someone had an axe yet seemed to be making very little impression. It was clear to Jaymis that magic was involved, should he add this ability to Elona's list of talents?

They finally gained entry when someone had the bright idea of attacking the frame instead of the door itself.

And the bedroom was empty.

Jaymis was summoned to Lord Nemon's side, he took the opportunity to look at the bodies—two maids as well as three Farahalek. One had bled heavily from his groin, another on his back with his neck sliced open, while the third had been killed by the old *zatek*.

By Nemon's orders, the bedroom was cleared and the two of them looked at the bed. It was stained with a great deal of blood but there was no way of knowing who it had belonged to. A blood trail led from the door to the bed but no trail away from it. Yet the room was empty.

No sign of any writing implements that would have been needed for a healing pattern. There was a bowl stained with blood and blood-soaked clothes piled in a corner. The colours of the clothes matched what Jaymis was wearing. It still did not mean the blood was hers—he had made that mistake before.

"Can you explain this, Lord Jaymis?"

"I'm not sure what you mean."

"Don't act the fool, Betlain!"

"What can I say? I expect you've heard the story of Lady Elona's disappearance from Canvor."

The man was silent. "You're suggesting she made a patterner's path away from here without a ley-circle?"

"The room is empty."

"I'm told she had five maids in total."

Five? All I got was one. "They aren't here either."

"You don't seem concerned, Lord Jaymis, your friend might have been kidnapped."

Jaymis sighed. "In that case, Lord Nemon, I pity the person who has done it."

CHAPTER 13

He had been escorted back to his suite and locked in. He changed into the clothes Athlem had supplied, since they were more practical than the others. There was a guard in the suite with him who had orders to remain in the same room.

Rather than use the bed, which did not seem the best idea under the circumstances, Jaymis made up a place to sleep on the floor of the bedroom close to the wall near the door. He invited the armsmen to use the bed, even to lock the door and keep the key. But the man said nothing, and simply remained standing.

He must take his job seriously.

Jaymis, as Jalka, had spent many nights on his feet performing guard duty, until he was promoted. It was possible to sleep on your feet as long as you had somewhere to lean.

Nothing happened in the night except that Jaymis woke feeling stiff and aching. He had spent too much time in comfortable beds over the last few months.

The guard was changed when the morning meal was brought to the room, and Lord Nemon accompanied it. He did not look as if he had had as much sleep as Jaymis. They sat on opposite sides of a table.

Jaymis poured out his fresh *tasa* and pushed the cup across to the older man who took it without a word. He drank while Jaymis ate the fragrant cooked fish and fresh bread.

"You did not find her, Lord Nemon?"

"No," he said, "but there was no impossible patterning."

"What do you mean?"

"The room she was in had a secret escape passage that led down to the bottom of the cliff. The maids were heard crying when they were trying to get out this morning."

"Did you find Lady Elona?"

"We did not. The passage led to an empty beach used by fishing vessels, though there was a ladder going back up."

"But no sign?"

"None."

Jaymis set down his knife. "I am curious, Lord Nemon, how is it that you of such a distinguished family of Tirnia, are involved in what must surely be just a minor matter for the Liralain?"

"We have a close relationship."

"You must have."

"If you must know, Betlain, I am betrothed to Lady Miriatali."

"I thought you already had a wife."

"I did."

For one astonishing moment, Jaymis was certain he heard real pain in the man's voice. But when he looked into his face, he could see nothing but the bland arrogance he seemed to wear as his armour.

"I am sorry, Lord Nemon, I did not know."

"It was a recent loss. I prefer not to discuss it."

"Of course."

The older man took one a piece of Jaymis's bread.

"I have been in conference with Lord Liralain and, I'm afraid," he said after swallowing it and washing it down with the last of the *tasa*, "the High Lord wishes you out of Mirriasmia."

"I see."

"He will return you to Faerholme at his own expense, of course."

"But what about Elona?"

"We will find her and send her back as well."

"I would like to wait."

"The path will not be opened until this evening. If we find her before that, she will be sent back with you."

"But until then I have to stay here."

"I'm glad you understand."

"I have horses and my belongings at the House of Jalima."

"I will arrange for them to be fetched."

He stood and left.

THERE WAS nothing to do and Jaymis did not relish spending the entire day in enforced idleness. Yet it seemed there was no choice, in addition to the guard in his room there were now two on the door.

They knew he had not attacked the dome—or done anything useful as it turned out—but they still didn't trust him.

How had this happened? All he wanted was to help Elona find some peace. Travelling to see some interesting places had seemed harmless enough. Yet within a day they were embroiled in *something*. Someone wanted to kill Elona and were willing to employ Farahalek to do it.

He shook his head. He wouldn't even know where to start if he wanted to have someone killed. He'd just do it himself.

But why Elona?

She had managed to stop the Tirnian advance by exposing his mother's betrayal and killing her. Jaymis had roused the defences at the ley-circle to fight off the invaders who had carried Dirdin insignia.

Who had a desire to kill Elona? The Emperor would have been angry at his plan going wrong, but would he be so petty as to attempt this?

It did not seem likely because what's done was done.

The armsmen looked at him askance when he went round the room collecting rugs, pots and small decorations. He cleared a space in the middle of the floor and spent a little while creating a map of the kingdoms.

There had been that trouble in Esternes last year. He didn't know much about it except some major families had been plotting to break the Great Concordance and when they were discovered by, who was it? Jakalain? Had attempted to take their castle by force but had been beaten back.

But nobody was really sure which families were involved. Except it had to be based in Tirnia. The Emperor was always trying to extend his boundaries. He flouted the Concordance but Tirnia was too powerful to be punished.

That was the problem with the Concordance, it only worked as long as everybody agreed to it.

Jaymis put a big pot plant in Tirnia. Then distributed other items to the power centres of the world.

He wasn't sure how far south Mirriasmia was from Tirnia, but it was at least three hundred leagues and the central range of mountains was between them. The island of Esternes was over in the west just off the coast from Umran or Tenya.

Elona had disappeared from Canvor and appeared in Dirdin. Escaped northeast into the mountains and reappeared in Taltia.

While she was away the attack on the Jakalain family had occurred. He had heard from one of his friends—a princeling of Umran—that they had ridden their racing *zirichasa* into battle. Led by a Kadralin girl apparently, he had seemed quite taken with her. Like Elona's family, the Betlains did not have *ziri*, too busy playing politics for such frivolous pursuits.

The existence of the ley-circles and patterner's path meant that distance did not really matter. Mirriasmia was as close to Tirnia as Esternes, or anywhere else.

Jaymis looked at the guard. "Let's say that the attack in Esternes last year was also arranged by the Emperor. Why would he do that and show his hand?"

The guard was looking at the map and then glanced at Jaymis.

"You're right, my friend," said Jaymis, "he did it because he had been found out, his hand was forced and he was trying to squash the opposition." He went and stood on the central mountains then took long strides across to Esternes. He knew anything he said would be relayed back to the High Lord—or perhaps just Lord Nemon, who undoubtedly had the ear of the Emperor.

What if Elona had gone from the mountains to Esternes?

"No, that doesn't make sense anyway," he said out loud, "she's not Kadralin and she's never mentioned it."

He picked up a delicate vase and placed it in Faerholme, then moved it to Dirdin and from there into the mountains. He walked it all the way to Esternes and then to Taltia. "Just in time to stop my mother."

Even if Elona had nothing to do with what happened in Esternes, the Emperor might think she did—and that would be a reason to kill her. She had blocked him once as a certainty, and perhaps twice.

So, she and Jaymis are spotted here in Avakending, Lord Nemon hears about it and sends a message to his master. The orders come back to get them into the palace and kill her. Jaymis gave a little laugh, it seemed that he was not important enough to warrant being killed.

Perhaps she was being watched in Faerholme and the Emperor was alerted as soon as she left. There was no way to know the answer to that and it probably didn't matter.

Lunch came and he found himself surprisingly hungry. There was wine which he drank watered down to quench his thirst in the heat that was slowly building through the day.

The storm had completely blown itself out.

A servant arrived shortly after lunch with his clothes from the House of Jalima, they had been cleaned. The man who brought the clothes insisted on bringing them through to the bedroom and began to lay them out.

"That's not necessary," said Jaymis.

"Lady Parthia sends her greetings, master."

Jaymis blinked once. "That's generous of her, you must convey my good wishes."

"She had hoped to meet you again."

"That would have been my wish too, but I am travelling back to Faerholme this evening."

"She will be sad to hear it, I am sure."

"Perhaps she could come and wave goodbye."

"All things are possible under the Mother's eye, master."

The man finished unpacking and left. Jaymis had to force the smile from his face when he turned away from the clothes. He had been considering the possibility of leaving by the window again, cutting the Farahalek cord, which had yet to be removed, and using it to get down to the ground.

It was not a good plan since it would involve jumping while clinging to the wrong end of the rope, and he would still be in the palace if he survived.

But it seemed Elona was out, and had found friends.

CHAPTER 14

Elona waited in the backroom of the house, she had tried to catch up on some sleep but found she couldn't. Her hand kept finding the badly healed wound on her cheek then she would trace the rough edges with her fingertips.

Outside she could hear constant noise of people going about their lives, and the persistent smell of fish filled her nose. The heat was barely tolerable. She enjoyed summers in Faerholme but the warm days were varied and changeable. Here there was only the constant oppression of the sun.

She admonished herself, she had barely even been here two days and that was not sufficient to judge—but that was the impression Bejeren had given her of this place in his lessons and, so far, he had been right.

A sudden outburst from the next room brought her to a sitting position, two people were arguing but she couldn't quite understand what they were saying. Then it went quiet and someone knocked.

"Yes?"

The dark-skinned and wrinkled face of the woman who lived in the house poked round the side of the door.

"Come please."

"Is it safe?"

"Safe."

"Where's Kerlyn?"

"She is here."

Elona stood and headed for the door. Her hand went to the little dagger about her neck for the security it gave her.

Kerlyn was not alone, and she came to stand beside Elona like a protector. Though perhaps she saw Elona as protecting her.

"Athlem?"

It was him, grinning. "Mistress. I am pleased that you are well, I bring your clothes and your horse." But his eyes stopped on the gash in her face.

Apart from the people who owned the house, the other two were rough-looking men who disturbingly reminded her of Krazak though they were darker in complexion and their skin even more heavily wrinkled.

"Sit, mistress," said Kerlyn.

"What's going on?"

The men she didn't know were staring at her which was unnerving.

"She is not Akralain," said one.

"The people will not follow her," said the other.

"No one pretends she is true Akralain," said Athlem. "It will be said they are not all dead."

"What's going on?" said Elona.

"Mistress," said Kerlyn, "the patterns are changing."

"What's that supposed to mean?"

Athlem hesitated. "Mistress, we know you have been attacked by Farahalek in the heart of the palace. It is the influence of Tirnia."

"I know about the emperor," she said, surprising herself with the amount of venom that leaked into her voice.

"Perdu of Akralain was a wise man and had the ear of the High Lord. Always he advised our great leader to deny the approaches of Tirnia—because evil always comes from that place."

"Akralain was a citadel that stood on the shore, many leagues from here. It had a strong ley-circle." This time it was one of the rough men speaking. "My brother and I worked stone for Akralain, there came a night when we were away and, on our return, all within the citadel were dead. They said the water was poisoned but we two had drunk from the well before we left and we did not die."

"The hand of Tirnia had touched Akralain and laid it waste," said the other of the two.

"There are many across Mirriasmia who mourn the loss of Akralain and the wisdom of its lord," said Athlem. "We do not welcome Tirnia and we resist it where we can but there is little we can do because no family will stand against them."

"And you want me to do what?"

"Nothing, mistress," said Kerlyn. "You are Corlain from Faerholme, this is understood. But if you wear the colours of Akralain, there are those who will see. You defied Tirnia and survived their assassins. I saw you kill two with your own hands, and the old *zatek* killed the other in your defence, though he was the gentlest of beasts. I saw you heal yourself from mortal wounds, and then bring the fish from the sea."

"As if you are Taymar reborn," said Athlem.

"Or the Mother's Daughter," said Kerlyn.

"Stop that!" Elona jumped to her feet and pointed her finger at him. "I am neither of those things. I'm just me. Heal myself? You can see what happened to me, I don't call that healing. And the fish? I almost sank the boat."

"*Fahain*," said Kerlyn.

"What?"

"Perhaps you are *fahain*, mistress"

"I do not know the word."

Kerlyn nodded. "It is from Kadralin, though old like the other ancient words. I have not heard it used by Taymalin, they like their patterns too much."

"You're Kadralin?"

"My mother was but my colour favours my father," said Kerlyn. "*Fahain* is someone who does not need patterns to change the world."

Elona fell silent. She couldn't even pretend that it wasn't true. Kerlyn had seen it with her own eyes, twice. The evidence was pasted across Elona's cheek.

"I am not Taymar reborn or the Mother's Daughter—" which was not something she had heard of but she did not know a great deal of the Kadralin beliefs, "—so please do not call me that but if there have been *fahain* before and, if there is a name for it there must have been, so yes, I suppose I am."

"And you have no Kadralin blood?" said Kerlyn.

Elona shook her head. "I don't think so."

The idea that a Taymalin could be *fahain* did not seem to please her.

"I don't believe her," said one of the brothers.

"You say I'm lying?" said Kerlyn.

"Stop it!" said Elona, the tension in the room did not lessen but no one said anything. "It doesn't even matter. I just want to get out of here with Jaymis, if I can. If you want me to dress up as member of the Akralain family as a symbol, then so be it. But I sent you, Kerlyn, to find out what was happening to Jaymis."

"And I have found out, mistress. He is under guard but they are sending him back to Faerholme tonight. My brother spoke with him and told him you are safe. He asked that you be at the ley-circle, you will be able to meet him."

"You seem to have it all worked out."

"Thank you, mistress."

Elona shifted in her seat. "Except I am not going back to Faerholme."

The room went quiet. The constant sound of waves on the shore leaked through to them.

"You wish to stay here?"

"Someone is trying to kill me." She leaned forwards. "Someone is employing the Farahalek which means they have both money and power. I could not return to Faerholme even if I wanted to. Yesterday, two women who had done nothing wrong, died because they were in the same room as me.

"You may think you want me as a symbol of your struggle against Tirnia's influence, but I am a liability. If it is known where I am, they will send more assassins, they may send armsmen, but one thing is certain, people close to me will die. So, you can tell your mistress, the Lady Miriatali, I am not willing to let that happen."

Kerlyn did not look as surprised as Elona had hoped. She probably thought it was something a *fahain* would know anyway.

But looking from face to face, she was satisfied to see that any enthusiasm she had seen before was gone. The two brothers were the only ones who looked content. The consequences of the attempted assassination had not occurred to them.

"I do not plan to stay here. I need to disappear again."

Athlem cleared his throat. "Yes, Lady Elona. We were wrong, we did not understand. We will help you in whatever way we can."

"I will need a boat."

ELONA CHANGED BACK into her original clothes but wore a cloak over them. The hottest part of the day had passed but she was still sweating. Athlem had not complained at any of her requests.

Reluctantly she had him sell Whitestar, which added considerably to her money. The owners of the house provided food which would last on the road, at least for a couple of days. And when she no longer had anything to do, she went out on to the raised open area that went around the house and sat among the fishing nets, staring at the sea.

To the right, the city of Avakending rose precipitously from the water on both sides of the channel. From this distance, she did not find it upsetting to look at. Athlem and Kerlyn sat with her but none of them spoke.

The sun was now behind the city which cast its shadow across them, but light reflected along the channel between the mainland and island silhouetting the fishing vessels returning to their moorings for the night.

The light changed quickly as the sun sank—so much faster than it did in Faerholme. The sky faded from blue to black and the sky filled with stars. A breeze blew across her scalp from behind and the air grew cooler. She pulled the hood of the cloak over her head.

"There," said Athlem suddenly.

Lostimal had not risen and it was quite dark. Elona could only see his outline against the restrained light of a hooded lantern burning at his side. She looked up at the dark looming bulk of the city. The windows showed many lights but one of them was winking, regularly.

Athlem lifted the lantern, and pointed its window towards the city. Three times he opened and closed the little door on the front. He waited the space of three breaths and did it again.

The flashing light on the city walls vanished.

Elona stood and stretched. It felt cold now, though it probably wasn't, at least not yet. To Elona's surprise and embarrassment, Kerlyn embraced her. It was a generous thing and reminded her of Chara.

Awkwardly Elona returned the embrace for a moment.

"Thank you for your help, but surely you must hide from the Liralain now?"

"I did not lie, Lady Elona, my service was to you only, once I was given the order. They will not blame me and I will say nothing of your plans. I have acted correctly."

"Even wanting to get rid of the Tirnians?"

"I do that for my people. I am no traitor."

They stepped apart and Elona followed Athlem to the mounts.

Her plan was simple. Intercept the party, get Jaymis away and run.

As the *kichek* made a steady pace through the dark she smiled to herself. Barely two years ago, there was an Elona who cared about little except her future wedding. If Metrid had not been her enemy, she would be the one in Canvor nursing a child. And, if things were truly different, her mother might have been alive.

She pushed the thoughts away. That world had never happened, and it never would, it was foolish to even think about it. The road they were on went over a ridge and descended towards a line of lights strung south to the city and north as far as the eye could see.

"That's the Avaki," said Athlem. "And the main road to the ley-circle."

"I need to be close to both the river and the ley-circle. And get there before Jaymis and his escort."

"I understand. Once we are on the road, we can make better time."

The track they were on finally met the road and Athlem was right. The surface was flatter and better defined. A white glow on the eastern horizon heralded the rise of Lostimal though, under the circumstances, she would have preferred complete darkness.

As long as they were close to the river and the ley-circle, she would be able to act.

THE BOAT that had been arranged was in a good position and did not seem out of place. They wouldn't notice it coming up the road. Elona looked back. The primary moon was high now and, though not full, its pure white light put the bleak landscape in sharp relief. She could feel the ley-circle now and, after her experience with the Mother's Kitchen, it felt warm and welcoming.

She had no idea how long she would have to wait. The road had other traffic and she felt exposed. People stared at her waiting at the junction. Athlem had offered to remain with her but she sent him away, still worried about other people getting hurt.

The warmth of the day was now gone and she shivered as she leaned against an old building. Timing was another concern but perhaps if she could feel Jaymis and his escort approaching it would help.

She spread out her senses and let the energy of the ley-circle flow her way. Before now she had only used smaller ley-circles for power— or used her own in a limited way. But now she contacted one of the great sources, she could feel that it had been recently fed by the moons, though she did not understand how she could tell.

The energy bubbled and flowed. It wanted to rage along her senses and fill her up. She pulled away and found herself panting with all her muscles tense. She took a deep breath and reached out more carefully. She allowed the tiniest thread of the Mother's Milk to slide towards her. Even so it seemed to fill her as she expended it to reach out to the south.

There. A dozen *kichesa* with riders, and a horse. Not far away. It would be a shame to leave the animal behind but they had no choice.

Elona reached out again, this time into the world around her searching for a creature she might use as her tool and weapon. There were no animals on the land suitable for her plan, but the river teemed with life and some of those were of considerable size.

CHAPTER 15

Jaymis and his escort made their way steadily towards the junction in the road where it split and led off to the ley-circle inland. They had been following the road. The lights from the huts marked the boundary of land and river. He was certain the water was higher than it had been when he and Elona had entered the city.

He wondered where she was. The fact that she had managed to get him a message showed she was with some organised group. There were always rebels, wanting some sort of change they claimed would be better but it always involved them becoming the ones in charge.

His horse shied at nothing and bumped one of the flanking *kichesa*.

"Keep it under control," growled one of the guards.

"She doesn't like the dark."

Then one of the *kichesa* at the front did the same but more violently. Bashing hard into the one next to him as it veered right. They didn't like the night either, it was too cold.

"Something's out there," said another guard.

"Dismount, hold your beasts. Light all the lanterns."

It took a few moments for the orders to be obeyed. Jaymis was tempted to make a run for it but they forced him from the horse too.

Where is she?

The nervousness among the animals was contagious. They were all bobbing their heads, and shuffling their feet trying to get somewhere safer—anywhere except here. The guards had more attention on controlling them than on Jaymis.

"Who's that?"

Jaymis looked round until his eyes came to rest on a figure walking out of the dark along the road towards them.

"Archers!"

The figure kept on coming, something in the walk told Jaymis first that it was a woman, and second it was Elona herself. On her own, what was she doing?

Her voice pierced the darkness. "I'm having enough trouble holding him back as it is. I strongly recommend you don't break my concentration."

On cue, something large, off in the direction of the river, bellowed very loudly. The horse ripped her reins from Jaymis's hand and, along with the *kichesa*, bolted. One man screamed as he disappeared with them, dragging along the ground.

"Formation!"

The men moved fast. Swords slithered from scabbards and Jaymis found himself pressed to the back of the group—with no one behind him. He took a step away and prepared to run when something hard and pointed pressed into his back.

"No, young lord, the empress is very keen to meet you."

"Let him go," called Elona, her voice sounded strained. The beast bellowed again, it almost seemed frustrated.

"He'll be going on a journey, or he'll be dead. Your choice, witch."

Elona's choking laugh was disturbing. "I'm *fahain*, it seems."

A sudden drumming of heavy feet grew rapidly in volume from the direction of the river. The metal blade left his neck and Jaymis threw himself to the side away from his captor. Jaymis rolled again and jumped to his feet. He didn't look back as someone screamed.

The air was abruptly filled with the hum of arrows and Jaymis expected to feel them burn into him. But there was nothing.

He reached Elona.

She almost whispered. "Come on." And, at a run, she set off towards the river but she was not moving fast.

"Are you all right?"

"Keep moving. I'm releasing him now."

Suddenly she changed as if energy had flowed through her. The stumbling run transformed into a light-footed dash and she flew ahead of him.

There was a boat drawn up on the shore between two groups of huts. Elona jumped lightly aboard. She turned back as Jaymis reached it.

"Push us off," said a voice he did not recognise, but he did as he was asked and heaved on the side of the vessel. It ground across the stones and Jaymis climbed aboard as it moved out across the water.

Looking back, all he saw was a huge creature on four low, bent legs, with a massive tail and a huge pair of jaws. The white light of Lostimal glistening off its reptilian skin.

"I think I need to sit down," said Elona. He couldn't reach her in time to save her as she crumpled into the bottom of the boat. He ducked beneath the sail that was filling and managed to get her stretched out before he pulled the scarf away from her face.

And stared at the strange wound across her cheek.

"Is the woman all right?" said the boatman.

"I think so. She's breathing. Just exhausted."

Something in Elona's past now made sense. He knew his mother had brought down a huge pack of wolves on the Dragonblade and his party. But when she was facing off against Elona the pack had turned on her instead. People had said she lost control of them but the truth was clear to him now. Elona had wrested control of them and turned them on his mother. She really had killed her.

It was hard to believe but now he had seen her hold back that monster—which she must have summoned from the river. Wolves certainly, *zatek* perhaps, and now this.

But her face?

The blood in the bed back at the palace must have been hers. The healing did not go right and left her with this terrible scar. How could a healing pattern fail in that way? He had never seen or heard of anything like it.

She opened her eyes and looked at him.

"We made it."

"Yes."

"Sorry but I didn't want them sending you back to Faerholme."

"I'm not sure they were," he said, "when you were launching your ambush, someone said I was being sent to the Empress."

"Empress?"

Jaymis shrugged. "That's what he said."

"Whoever it was, they would have used you as a hostage."

"What do you mean?"

She yawned and the mark on her face twisted. "They think I care about you."

He hesitated. "Don't you?"

But she was asleep.

There was a pile of netting which he managed to get under her head in an effort to make her comfortable.

With the rigging moving above, he decided to stay down in the bottom of the boat as well. The city rose in the distance, the contours of its shape highlighted by the glow of Lostimal.

The boat was moving swiftly downstream in the main channel between the bank on the left and the islands. He felt it turn and they squeezed through a gap between two of them. The city was lost behind thick trees.

"Where are we going?"

"Other side."

"Other side of where?"

"Avaki."

Jaymis stared at the passing trees, many had massive arched roots that went right over the water before plunging into it. Groups of dancing lights floated above the water—the boatman seemed to take trouble to avoid them.

Why had Elona chosen to go further into a wilderness they didn't understand, containing dangers they might not recognise, rather than escape back to civilisation—or at least somewhere they wouldn't stand out.

This whole journey had been a bad idea.

But what difference would it have made? Surely they would have come after her anyway? And perhaps she would have been less on her guard if the Farahalek had come to Corlain castle.

She had dispatched three assassins. An astonishing feat—they had underestimated her, after all how hard could it be to kill a woman? She might have been very well educated but she had never been taught to fight—as far as he knew. But then she had disappeared for the entire winter and spring. Who knows what she might have learnt?

BRIGHT SUNSHINE on the other side of his eye-lids woke him. His stomach told him he needed to eat. Shading his eyes, he opened them. He was still in the bottom of the boat and Elona at his side, half-lying on him. The sails were furled and the boat was not moving.

Working his protesting muscles carefully he extracted himself from under Elona and got on to his knees leaning against the side of the small vessel. They were pulled up on to a stony beach, its slope led up to a climbable wall of rocks, rounded and smoothed by time.

They were in a small bay, enclosed by high rocks while water lapped around a too-narrow entrance. All he could see beyond it, were waves and empty sea. The boat man was nowhere about but a small fire was burning further up the shore, so he probably wasn't far away.

Drying plants were scattered on the stones and he could see a distinct line of dampness in the rocks around him. As if the sea had been higher just a little while earlier.

"Are we there?" said Elona's voice behind him, it cracked as if she hadn't used it for a long time.

He turned to see her sitting up. The scarf had fallen away completely and she caught him staring at her face. He looked away.

"I don't know where *there* is supposed to be."

"Athlem said he'd get us to the other side of the river."

"Then I think we may be."

She stumbled to the edge of the boat and he held her arm as she stepped out on to solid ground. She stretched in an unconcerned way that he never saw in the women of the various courts he had visited. It was as if she did not care what he thought of her, or what he saw—perhaps the scar on her face was the exception, but that was new.

She turned round and delved into the boat, pulling out a bag he recognised from their journey here. It seemed an age in the past that they had met at the Avakending ley-circle, though it was barely a four-day.

They walked up the beach, their feet crunching on pebbles and shells.

"What happened to you?" he asked.

She didn't answer but instead pulled out cooked meats and hard bread from her bag. She handed him a portion. Then, as they ate, she related the attack, and her escape but said nothing of injuries and healing.

"I saw the blood on the bed, Elona. I saw the trail leading to it and none going to any panel in the wall."

She touched the ridged flesh on her cheek and sighed. "I can't hide it, can I?"

But she still didn't say anything for a long time but her attention was inside herself and he did not interrupt.

"There is only one person in the world I have told about this. It's a secret, Jaymis, I don't even want to tell you. I've known about it, of course, but there's a name for it which I only learnt last night."

He waited in silence as she summoned the courage.

"I'm *fahain*, or I am a *fahain*, I'm not even sure how it's supposed to go."

The name meant nothing to him and he said so.

She sighed again. "You know I'm different."

"I know you're a patterner."

"But that's just it, Jaymis, I'm *not*."

"You do magic."

"Yes, but there are no patterns involved. I just *do* it. Healing, controlling animals, I mean, I can see the patterns but I don't do any patterning."

"And cast yourself from Canvor to Dirdin."

She shook her head. "I was falling to my death, Jaymis, you don't think about anything!"

"Instinct?"

The shrug of her shoulders told him it was not a subject she really wanted to discuss.

"So you're a *fahain*, and can do magic without patterning. What went wrong?"

She looked up at his seemingly incomplete question. He hadn't wanted to mention it directly so he just touched his hand to his own cheek.

"Have you ever heard of a power other than the Mother's Milk?"

He shook his head. Everyone knew that all the power in the world came from the moons which filled the earth with magic during feedings. That's the way it was, that's the way it had always been.

"There's another power," she said slowly. "I found it in the Mother's Kitchen. I needed to heal myself, I was already exhausted and did not have much left within me. The Avaki ley-circle was too far away and I found something in the void beneath Avakending."

"Void?"

She looked into his eyes, and he saw an overwhelming sadness there. "Another thing I did not mention. It's a place so empty there are no patterns at all."

He frowned, how was that even possible? Everything had a pattern.

It was almost as if she could see his thoughts. "Yes, I know, we're told nothing can exist without a pattern. It seems that is not the truth —perhaps I am the first person to discover it."

She looked inward again. "It may not have a pattern but it is still power. I used it to heal myself. It worked but left this."

"But surely you didn't need to do that for a cut on your cheek?" The words came out of his mouth but, even as he said it, he knew whatever the cut on her cheek it would not have accounted for the quantity of blood on the bed.

She stared back at him for a moment then undid the ties at the top of her shirt, exposed the pale skin of her shoulder and pulled the cloth down.

He stared at the raw deep hole in her shoulder. There was no blood but the same curious ragged look as her cheek. "I was dying."

She covered herself back up.

"Does it hurt?"

"I feel nothing."

CHAPTER 16

There was a sound above them, Elona looked up to see the boatman at the top of the rocks. He made his way down to the beach.

"You are good?" he said.

"Thank you for the fire," said Jaymis.

"And bringing us across the river," said Elona. "Are you going?"

The man looked down at the boat. "Soon." The water, that had been at the narrow entrance was now much higher up the beach and she could see the water pouring through the gap in a torrent.

"Why's it doing that?"

"Tides," said the boatman, then he saw the blank expressions on their faces. "The sea loves Lostimal."

Jaymis looked confused but Elona remembered there had been something in her lessons about tides. The sea level going up and down. "How high does it get?"

The boatman simply pointed at the line of discolouration on the rocks.

"How soon?"

"Soon."

Jaymis busied himself collecting their things together, not that there was much.

"How far is it to the next big town along the coast?"

"Big town? Two-day by boat."

"How long on foot?"

He shrugged. "Maybe ten-day."

Jaymis shook the man by the hand. The water really was pouring in and rising fast. It would lift the bottom of the boat in a short time.

"Thank you again," said Elona.

With Jaymis's help, she climbed the rocks until they stood at the top. Looking down she could see the boatman already preparing to leave. Though she was not sure how he could get through the gap until the water stopped flowing.

To the south and east they could see the huge mouth of the Avaki and the hundreds of islands that split it into a thousand different channels. In the far distance was the city, poking above everything else, and clearly delineated in the bright sun.

The wide sea glistened. Elona stared at it for a long time. The dream of the Shocalin came to her. She knew there was no such creature, just as the ghostly Tahulin were a myth too. But the dream had been so real, even if it had been caused by the curse Metrid had put on her. Yet she remembered the words with complete clarity:

'The time has come for you to wake up. But remember this always: *Aeshtas ulchris tahlya.*'

"The journey won't walk itself," said Jaymis.

"No," she said coming out of her musings. She turned to look along the coast to the north-west. Inland there were a few hills, bare and ochre like those on the other side of the river. "I hope we can find enough food."

"Perhaps you can lure something out of the sea, or hills."

The shoreline continued on two levels. The beach at sea level in repeating small bays of different shapes and sizes, with the low rock wall above it.

Elona frowned. "I don't think so."

"I'm sorry, I shouldn't ask you to use the magic. You were exhausted."

Elona set off and Jaymis fell in beside her. It was slow going as there was no path and the boulders uneven.

"It's not that," she said, "when I try to control a creature it's as if I become them, even if it's only a little. I can't intentionally kill something I've come to know like that."

"But the *zatek* died fighting the Farahalek."

"That was different, it wanted to fight, it wanted to defend the women, it understood that was its task, even if it was old. I guided it so it could do that effectively."

"And that sea monster?"

"River monster. The same, although that wasn't its duty."

"The wolves?" he said quietly.

"Our lives versus your mother's. I'm sorry, Jaymis."

"She had to be stopped."

"But she was your mother." *And I never even had one that I knew about, just a body lying silently in a room that is a crypt in all but name.*

"Given the choice, Elona, you alive is preferable to you dead, and the same for her but the other way around."

They stopped, standing above a gap in the stones through which a stream flowed. Something moved out of sight below them before she could get a glimpse of it.

Jaymis took a step back then jumped. He landed easily and turned, holding his hand out to her.

Then she was standing in a mist that was darkening towards night, and the wolves were all around waiting to turn her into their next meal. And the gap she had to leap was wider and deeper than anything she ever imagined. Failure to jump was certain death, against the possibility of uncertain death.

"Elona?"

She smiled at him. "Just thinking." She took two steps back and ran forwards. He caught her arm but there was no need, she made it without difficulty.

"I think this might take longer than a ten-day," said Jaymis as they made their way across the jumble of rocks.

"Perhaps we could go further inland," said Elona.

"I don't want to get lost."

"Oh, I've been lost before. You always end up somewhere."

THEY STAYED in sight of the sea for the rest of the day. Elona wasn't sure but thought they might have managed a couple of leagues. But she didn't mind, she was used to it. Jaymis seemed less happy.

The sea had come in and risen to a surprising height in the little bays and inlets they passed. Then it went away again. Neither of them had ever seen anything like it, but nor had they ever been on the coast before.

"The boatman said it came and went with Lostimal," said Elona as they sat on a ledge just above an inlet. They had checked carefully as the sun went down and were sure it didn't get covered in water.

Elona had collected dry wood though she had no idea where it came from, they had not seen any trees since leaving the Avaki. It burned well as the night got colder. They wrapped themselves in blankets and ate what was left of the food Elona had.

"We'll have to hunt tomorrow," she said.

"That will slow us down even more."

She shrugged. "Are you in a hurry to be somewhere?"

She could not see his face clearly in the light of the flickering fire but she heard him laugh.

"No, Elona, I suppose not. It's difficult for me to adjust to this pace."

She stared into the fire. "I lived on a small farm all through the winter before. There was snow on the ground the whole time—and it was deep. There were chores to be done, and the cooking, and caring for the animals. But never much. The whole pace slows. You learn to appreciate the sun when it breaks through the clouds and makes the world brilliant white. The smell of the animals in their sheds—"

"You liked it?"

"You learn to. It's warm and wraps you like a blanket." She gave a little laugh. "It also stinks."

"But you can cook?"

"Yes, of course. I can wring the neck of a bird, pluck its feathers, gut and cook it. Or fish. I can grind wheat to make flour and bake bread."

"I didn't know."

"There's a lot you don't know, Jaymis."

She poked the fire and a cloud sparks went up and joined the crystal stars. The constant roar of the waves crashing on the rocks was almost a lullaby.

Something roared in the night.

Elona closed her eyes. She let herself look into the patterns about them. The rocks were solidity and firmness. The sea ebbed and flowed, impossible to grasp but full of the bright lights that she knew were living things. There were some sparks of life around them, small ones and probably no threat unless they had bites or stings that could kill.

The slow pulses of plants further inland. Larger creatures she did not recognise, some hunting, some feeding … until she found it. A monstrous form.

"*Nachak*, I think," she said out loud. And beside it were smaller ones. It moved and they followed. "With two young ones."

"I've never seen a *nachak*," said Jaymis.

She opened her eyes. "Do you want to?"

"Another day, or perhaps never. Is it coming this way?"

"No, it's teaching the young how to hunt. It doesn't seem very interested in the shore."

"You can know that much?"

"I can know more. I choose not to."

"What about people?"

"Animals are simple things, but people? They are not simple."

Except when you encourage the lusts of the small-minded.

~

SHE SLEPT EASILY ENOUGH despite the rocky floor, and dreamt of a frozen river valley under snow where she had been happy. Until the armsmen came to kill the only person who had seemed like a real mother. But neither she nor Chara had been there, they were already running.

Dawn was turning the horizon to white. Jaymis was still asleep—although he had been born into luxury, he had been driven from it, just as she had. Their lives were uncomfortably similar.

She climbed to her feet and stretched, getting the kinks out of her back. Sleeping on rocks was never comfortable. She folded the blanket and put it back inside her bag. Checking the fire, she found a few embers at its heart and managed to get it going again. But they would need more wood.

She climbed up the rocks and looked out. Black dots on the horizon, back toward the city, marked fishing vessels heading out to make their catches. Seabirds and *sikechasa* wheeled overhead, perhaps they thought they might scavenge something.

Perhaps she could see about getting something to eat. Meat of the *sikechak* was good, the birds probably were too but bringing one of them down might be tricky. She knew that being precious about luring things to be eaten was foolish, it was what fishermen and hunters did all day. Never mind the farmers who bred animals for slaughter. It was just that, for her, it felt more personal.

She wondered about what the boatman had said about these tides being linked to Lostimal. The moon was in the sky early in the evening at the moment so why would the water be rising now?

Sometimes there were questions that could not be answered.

Perhaps she could bring fish up into the bay and they could simply hook them out of the water. She preferred that idea so climbed down past the ledge and on to the stony beach of the little bay. The waves never stopped but tumbled endlessly on to the pebbles and surrounding rocks.

After finding a suitable boulder to sit on she focused on the water —and the pattern of the fish she had encountered before.

She found them almost immediately. It was as if the seas were made of them, but she was wary of the chaos she had brought down on them the first time she did it. She made an effort to identify a single fish and bring it towards her but the nature of these creatures meant that any positive move by one was immediately reflected by the rest.

The shoal split suddenly and she felt herself being carried along; a great dark form shot between the two parts which then re-formed as soon as it was past. The shoal didn't know what it was except it would eat them.

"Elona?"

The voice penetrated her concentration from above. She tilted her head back and found Jaymis looking at her, upside-down.

"How's the fire?"

"It's fine."

"You want fish or bird?" She pointed upwards.

"You don't have to pluck a fish."

"No, but you still have to gut it."

He grunted and she smiled in amusement.

"You better get down here and get ready to grab some—and watch out for the birds."

He said something in reply but she had stopped listening and reached out once more. She wasn't sure if it was the same one as before, but there seemed to be no difference between them. She steered it towards the shore and it moved like lightning through the water.

Moments later the sea was alive with motion as the fish she had brought struggled to keep their formation so close to the surface with the waves crashing all around.

Before Jaymis had managed to get halfway down to the waterline, the flying thieves were already thundering from the sky. The sound of their wings beating the air and each other, was mixed with the cacophony of waves and splashing.

Something dark, as thick as her arm, snaked from the water. A pair of jaws opened showing ranks of sharp teeth and snapped around the neck of one of the birds. It dragged it down and Elona watched as the bird frantically beat its wings trying to escape. But now its head was underwater, and its struggles weakened rapidly. Then the sinuous body appeared and wrapped itself around the bundle of wet feathers and sank out of sight.

Other shadows cut through the water now, sliding among the confused shoal. The birds, oblivious to what had happened to their companion, continued to dive and spear their prey.

The ones that succeeded beat their heavy wings to escape the rocks around the bay but there were always more circling above to take advantage of the space made. Jaymis had reached the water's edge and, after a couple of failed attempts, managed to spear a fish on his sword.

His triumph was short-lived as a *sikechak* cruised in at speed and snatched it away. As it soared through the melee, deftly twisting to avoid the ones who wanted to plunder what it had stolen, a huge green-grey fish-shape launched itself twisting from below. Its huge wide-open jaws snapped shut on the *sikechak* so that only the tip of its beak, wings and tail were visible. It hung for a moment then dropped back into the water taking its victim with it.

Jaymis tried again and this time managed to get the fish inside his shirt before the birds—bigger up close than they seemed when in flight—mobbed him.

"Can't you get these damnable things off me!"

Elona tried to focus on the birds wheeling and turning above the waves. But it was hopeless, they were not like the fish. Even when she managed to suggest there was something dangerous in the bay, the single avian flew off only to be replaced by another.

Instead she went back to the fish. She managed to engage one that was deep enough not to be confused by the waves. With a mental nudge on its pattern, she sent it away from the shore and into the safety of the depths. All those around it responded and followed as the message went out in a great ripple through the shoal.

Within moments most of them were heading away. Only those at the surface remained and the birds quickly finished them off.

Jaymis staggered back up the beach with a final haul of three fish. He kept them hidden until the seabirds dispersed.

"Let's not do that again," he said, touching his hand to the back of his head. It came back bloody.

"I should check that," said Elona.

She saw his eyes flick to the ragged scar on her cheek but he said. "Thank you" and turned round so she could examine his scalp. She found the injury hidden beneath his dark hair. The scratch wasn't deep, just enough to break the surface. She pressed it with the tips of her fingers.

"Ow."

She let go. "You'll live."

The sea was still coming in and the waves reached their boots. They climbed to the ledge and, after checking the sky, Jaymis slapped one of the fish down by the fire and hid the other two under his pack.

"We'll cook everything," said Elona. "These will last us at least until tomorrow evening."

She set to work with her knife, tossing the parts she didn't want over the edge and into the sea.

They still managed to attract a few smaller birds who collected what she was discarding but other than that they were not molested again.

CHAPTER 17

The next three days continued in a similar manner. The weather remained clear although, on the second day, high level clouds obscured the sun from time to time.

The great white moon was waxing now as it tracked slowly across the stars. Colimar always moved much faster but did not cross Lostimal's face at any time. When that happened there was always a feeding, though it was strongest when Lostimal was full, and that only happened over a major ley-circle like the Wellspring at Corlain.

Jaymis estimated they had managed to travel a total of twelve leagues.

"That's not too bad," he said on their fourth evening from Avakending, "considering the terrain."

"We could go inland."

"And then miss any major towns which will almost certainly be on the coast."

"And when we hit a really big river?"

They had had trouble today when they had to cross a river that was too wide to be jumped. It was deep and fast-flowing because it was between rocky banks. The sea was in and there was no way to get round that way. They spent time moving inland until they found a place, climb down and make the risky jump to the other side. If either had fallen, they would have been swept into the sea.

"If it's that big there will be a town, and if it's not directly on the coast we just follow the river upstream until we find a town or a crossing point. The boatman said a ten-day, we've only been travelling for four."

Elona regretted her decision not to ask for them to be carried all the way to the next town. She had thought she was doing the right thing. The less others were involved, the less they could tell.

~

THE FOLLOWING DAY THINGS CHANGED. The rocky coastline they had been following sank away within perhaps a few hundred paces, to be replaced by sand. At first there was still rock beneath it, exposed in places. In the end, it was just sand down to the edge of the water.

"I think I can say that I dislike the sea and everything to do with it," said Jaymis. "Give me Faerholme or Dirdin, or any kingdom enclosed entirely by land and I will be happy."

Elona agreed.

The heat was intense here and seemed to reflect from the sand itself. They had filled their water bottles at the last stream they had crossed and they were still full but what if there was no more freshwater? At least the sea remained full of fish.

There was little choice, they had to keep moving and set off across the compacted sand, and found their rate of travel increased. No more climbing over uneven boulders, no more jumping across gaps where the streams tumbled down to the waves.

Here they found they could stride ahead while the sea pounded in on one side, and the rising desert sands filled the other.

The lack of shade was a concern, but a cool wind blew constantly from the sea during the day.

"Your skin is getting darker," she said to Jaymis that evening as the sun went down. They had moved inland a little and found a place where a rock outcrop created a place sheltered from the wind. They lit a fire—driftwood as common here as it had been for the first part of the journey.

Jaymis dropped another branch into the embers. "I think they come from the Avaki."

"What do?"

"All this wood. It falls in the river and gets swept out into the sea, then the waves and wind bring it back in."

Their conversation lapsed again. It was doing that more often as they dredged through what they were willing to say to one another.

Elona might have mentioned Usala's farm, but she did not say anything about Chara. She did not think even Jaymis would be happy to know that Slissac lived so close. He might tell others and the humans would mount an offensive to try to wipe the mountains clean of their ancient foe.

And many would die. Perhaps even Chara herself, not that there was any guarantee the humans would win. Elona was well aware of the powerful magic the Slissac still managed to wield, though the ones she met were a shadow of the monsters she had been taught about.

That secret meant that there were other things she could not say.

So they did not talk much now.

IN THE NIGHT, a storm hit. It did not seem as powerful as the one they experienced in Avakending, but here they had no shelter. They huddled together with their cloaks over them and rainwater soaking them from the bottom up.

But at least they could fill their water bottles.

They slept no more that night and set off before the sun had risen, just as the pre-dawn light filled the air. The ground was wet, just as they were, and when the day broke the landscape steamed.

The rain also caused dried up beds to become filled and they took advantage of them whenever they could. But, by the end of the day, the smaller ones were dry again and even the larger ones were trickles in their wide beds.

The walking became automatic. As long as they kept the sea on their left, the placement of each foot required no thought.

Elona daydreamed about everything and nothing. She could not tell from one moment to the next what she was thinking about, and when Jaymis's stomach rumbled she giggled—then stopped herself abruptly.

"What?"

"You made a noise."

"No."

"You did—your stomach."

"It didn't."

Elona hesitated. "Perhaps it was mine."

The sound came again and, with their attention now in the present, they both turned to where it was coming from.

"Taymar's teeth," said Jaymis, turning his whole body slowly and moving in front of Elona as if to protect her, though all he succeeded in doing was blocking her view of the beast that stood looking at them in return.

It resembled a *kichek* in general shape and size, with the powerful back limbs, thick tail, and smaller arms. From there upwards the resemblance faded. Where the *kichek* had jaws made for cropping plants, this beast had two massive jaws full of sharp teeth and its skin glowed in multiple iridescent colours.

"That's a *nachak*," said Jaymis quietly.

"Baby."

"Baby?"

"Well, half-grown. Might have been the ones I saw before."

"How many were there?"

"One adult, two young."

"I would prefer not to die here," said Jaymis.

Elona put her hand on his shoulder and closed her eyes, spreading her senses through the surrounding area. She blanked out the sea which was always teeming with scintillating patterns. The young *nachak* was a bright spot but the others did not seem to be around.

"I can't find the parent or the other one, I think it's lost."

"If it's hungry it can still eat us."

The monster took a step towards them. Jaymis jumped at the motion and the creature stopped uncertainly.

"Perhaps it doesn't know how to hunt yet."

"I really don't want it practising on me."

Elona sighed. "We can't kill it."

"I expect we can, if you can confuse it while I cut its throat."

"No."

"What? Why?"

The beast made a strange guttural noise that didn't sound threatening, though not friendly either.

"It's already confused. It just wants its mother."

"I really don't care about that, Elona. I don't want to get used as a plaything and then eaten."

Elona stepped to the side of Jaymis, which grabbed the *nachak's* attention, it stared at her. "I need to try something."

The Slissac used creatures with patterns that had been modified to make them more useful. The moss that glowed with a magical light might have been theirs, it was common enough, but the strange creatures on the hull of a boat that propelled it definitely were. There were the giant *tekrasa* used as transport—they must have been intentionally created.

What if the *nachasa* had been created too? Perhaps for defence, or fighting, even just food.

She kept moving away from Jaymis, sideways and the eyes of the *nachak* followed her. It could be on her and biting off her head in less time than it took her to draw a breath but it was not showing any sign of aggression.

When it came to the moss and boat creatures, all she had to do was focus her attention on them and the Mother's Milk would flow. If she was right about the *nachak* it should be much the same, and then she would know.

She carefully lifted her arm and focused on the pattern that was the *nachak.*

In less time than it took to blink, the creature relaxed and sat back on its tail, just like a *kichek*. Its breathing slowed and it made a gentle rumbling sound.

"What did you do?"

"Hush."

She tried to think, this was right. The *nachak* had been changed by the Slissac for a purpose, but what? This was the most dangerous creature in the world, and yet it had been made to become as tame as a *zatek* when power was applied.

"If you could make a *nachak* as tame as this, what would you use it for?"

"I'd have a hundred of them to fight a war."

Elona remembered how all the families in the Slissac town had effectively been at war with one another. If you lived in a nation of Slissac? Yes, they probably were fighting most of the time, and developing the most effective war creatures would be a priority.

"You're right," she said, "that's exactly what they would do."

And then if control was lost and the *nachasa* escaped, they would become the most formidable fighting creatures the world had seen.

She nodded to herself and focused once more on the beast. It tensed and climbed to its feet. Jaymis drew his sword, Elona didn't object, it made no difference to the creature because it had no idea what the action meant.

On the assumption that this was one of the young ones she had seen before, the parent had to be back the way they came and inland, perhaps this one had got separated in the storm. She pictured the direction and—she was not sure how to describe it—but she gave it to the young *nachak*, along with the mental image she had had before of the parent.

Without another sound it turned deftly, almost swiping them with its tail, and ran off the way she had specified.

"Come on," said Jaymis, "let's get away from here in case it comes back."

Elona didn't argue though she knew as a certainty it wouldn't be returning for a long time. She only hoped it found its family, otherwise she had sent it into the desert, the ancient creatures might like the sun and warmth but they could still die from a lack of water.

$$\sim$$

THEY HAD NOT BEEN GOING for very long, but Elona could feel the questions boiling up inside Jaymis, until they could no longer be contained.

"What did you do?"

"I told him where to find his family."

"And it just went off."

"You saw it."

"Look, Elona, I know you have some kind of affinity with animals —the way you can draw the fish, that river monster, you made the old *zatek* fight for you, and the wolves." He stopped, seemingly not wanting to go further with that thought. "But you just saved us from a *nachak*."

"It didn't want to hurt us."

"Why not?"

She shrugged. "It wasn't hungry."

"Will it come back?"

"No."

"You seem very sure."

"Yes, Jaymis, I am very sure it will not come back."

"I'm not stupid."

"I never thought you were."

"You're not telling me something."

She stopped dead on the sand. It took Jaymis a moment to realise she was no longer alongside him. He turned back and faced her.

She looked up into his eyes. "There are a lot of things I haven't told you, my friend—" She placed her hand on his wrist. "—and there are some I may never tell you."

She set off along the shore again and he fell in step beside her.

"Last year, when I disappeared into the mountains, I discovered some things about me. When you were chasing me, I heard you come into the cave and find Styvan's body."

"Where were you? There was nowhere to hide."

"The tunnel where the river spilt out into the pool. I had climbed in there then, when you'd gone, I kept going." She remembered the biting cold of the water and the intense blackness. "I found an abandoned underground dwelling place, and eventually made it to the surface."

"Who lives underground?"

She stared at the rolling waves that thundered into the shore in a constant barrage. The power of man was nothing compared to that.

"Slissac."

"The bridge."

"Yes, once upon a time the Slissac lived there. It was there I discovered a moss that would shine like a fire if you put magic into it. And I found I could heal myself using the power of a ley-circle—there was one there although it was very small. Just as well, since I killed all the glowing moss with too much power and attracted the attention of wolves."

"We saw their traces."

"Another time, later, I was underground again in another old Slissac place."

"More than one?"

She gave a short laugh. "I expect the central mountains are riddled with them."

"But the Kadralin lived here too? Before the Taymalin arrived."

"Perhaps it was a different time—or these Slissac did not enslave humans." She took a deep breath. There was a haze in the distance ahead of them but she couldn't make it out. "You interrupted me. There was a boat on a canal made by the Slissac and it had strange creatures attached on the bottom of it. Tiny ones, thousands of them, and when commanded with magic, they moved together driving the boat forwards, without oars or sails."

He said nothing this time. She wondered if he doubted her sanity. She didn't care, she had decided to tell him this much, but she would not reveal the existence of the living Slissac. Did that make her a traitor to her kind?

"This is what I believe," she said. "The Slissac were so skilled in their patternings, they could change the nature of living things and bend them to become tools. And I think perhaps the *nachasa* were also their tools which is why I could command it so easily."

They walked on in silence.

"Giant *tekrasa*," he said suddenly.

The shock of it rocked her—she had not said anything about that, *how could he know?*

She tried hard to make her voice sound normal. "What about them?"

"There was word of such things in Esternes."

Elona's mind whirled—could there be Slissac in Esternes too?

"What happened?"

"My friend, the one who rode the *ziri*, he said the enemy had many of these giant beasts carrying armsmen. What if they have been discovered and bent to the will of man…"

His voice tailed off as he tried to imagine what it meant.

Jaymis stopped dead in his tracks and stared at her. "You weren't surprised."

"What?" she said coming to a halt, her heart went cold.

"When I mentioned the *tekrasa*. You weren't surprised. You already knew."

She nodded but said nothing.

"This is something you don't want to talk about, isn't it?"

It seemed safer, so she nodded again. He looked annoyed but set off walking. Elona appreciated him not pressing the point, though she still felt uncomfortable having been caught out so easily.

She might know about them but one thing she knew as a certainty: she was never going up in one of those again. They were utterly terrifying.

"So, you could control one of them."

It had not even occurred to when she was being carried, she was far too scared to concentrate.

"I don't know."

She glanced up as if she might see a swarm of the normal-sized *tekrasa* migrating across the sky. There were none and she didn't even know if they appeared this far to the south.

"Is that a town ahead?" said Jaymis.

"The blur? It might be."

"Perhaps we can make it by sundown."

CHAPTER 18

It turned out their destination, if it was a town, was more elusive than they hoped and they spent another night in the open, barely sheltered on a rocky outcrop poking above the sand.

Elona had become adept at clearing an area of small creatures, including a vicious-looking stinger that seemed to live everywhere here. Most of the animals and larger insects were persuaded they wanted to leave.

She could feel a ley-circle now. It gave her comfort like a child who had been alone and wants their mother's arms around them. The thought saddened her.

"Can you keep watch, Jaymis?"

"Of course, do you sense something bad?"

"No, I just want to try to perform proper healing on myself." *I cannot stand these wounds—they feel so wrong.*

"Is there anything else you need me to do?"

"Don't disturb me, regardless of what happens."

He hesitated before accepting that condition.

Elona tried to get comfortable with her head on her pack, leaning up against a low rock. She closed her eyes and reached out towards the ley-circle that glowed within her mind.

She wished she was closer but she was able to draw power from this distance. And even as she thought it, a thin stream of blinding white flowed to her. She formed a pool around herself and let it feed her. The other part of herself, the part that could heal, extended itself across her every limb such that every subtle pattern that made her was restored. Except—

Even Elona could see the empty holes in her body. The glass cuts on her hands where the strange magic from the Mother's Kitchen had done its work, stood out like tiny black lines. On her cheek, it was as if black paint had been daubed across it and no amount of healing light would change it.

And the patternless hole in her shoulder, that pierced deep, could not be filled.

Elona felt the frustration of her healing self almost as if it were separate from her. There was nothing that could be done. The patterns in those places had ceased to exist and could not be rebuilt nor fed.

And in that moment, she learnt how powerless the Taymalin truly were. They thought they commanded the world with their patterns, and with enough study they could make themselves as great as the Slissac had been.

But she knew now. Their obsession with patterns blinded them to the truth, just as it had blinded their reptilian masters. Even the Kadralin had become subservient to the tyranny of patterns. Old Yolandra used patternings for most of the magic she performed, it was only at the feast that she allowed herself to be consumed by the true power of the Mother's Milk.

And Elona was sure that she was the only one who knew of the void. Though now it was etched into her body—and could not be healed.

She opened her eyes.

The sky was filled with stars and she wondered what they really were.

Jaymis was snoring and there was no light on any horizon. Only the red glow of Colimar illuminated the world. She was refreshed but hungry, even though the power she had been using was not her own.

Although she had cut off the flow of Mother's Milk from the ley-circle she was still very aware of it.

She climbed up on to the rock outcrop and looked across at the sea. The waves rolled in, their highlights red and the rest black as pitch. The sand reflected a lighter red.

Walking carefully across the compacted sand to avoid stumbling, she made her way to where the sand fell away abruptly to the sea. The wind blew from inland as she stood with folded arms looking out at nothing.

She sighed. It was time for decisions and there was only one she could make.

THE FOLLOWING MORNING, she and Jaymis sat on either side of the fire and chewed the meat Jaymis had cooked badly the day before. She had been instructing him but he seemed to have trouble judging how long things should be cooked. He kept getting distracted.

"I'm going to Aris," she said finally.

"Is that wise with the Tirnians trying to kill you?"

"What would you suggest as an alternative?"

He shrugged. "We seem to have eluded your pursuers for now. Let's go somewhere else, anywhere, as far south as we can, get a couple of mounts and find a place where no one knows who we are."

She had been expecting that, and doubted even Jaymis thought it was a good plan.

"And be forever looking over my shoulder, or into the air, in case someone should come to kill me?" She shook her head. "No. I think it would be better to go to the source and deal with it, one way or another."

"You mean kill the emperor."

"How else can I make this stop?" she said. "The chances are, he was behind the trouble in Esternes and from what you say there was almost open war. He is not afraid of bending the Concordance until it breaks—he calls himself *emperor!*"

"Or you die in the attempt."

"In which case, it will be over. You see? I cannot fail."

His smile occupied only half his mouth and carried no humour. "Then I best come with you to make sure we avoid that particular turn of events."

She had expected him to say that as well. Of course he would, he was an honourable man. On the one hand she was grateful for his loyalty, on the other she did not want the responsibility of getting him killed.

"Nobody will care if I die," he said almost as if he had been reading her thoughts.

"I would care." Now she was annoyed with herself, she had not intended to say that. Any sort of intimacy between them would be a liability. Unfortunately she could see, from the way a genuine smile now occupied his face, the damage had already been done.

"That's settled then," he said. "We'll go to Aris and then travel into Tirnia to confront the emperor in his lair."

When he put it that way, Elona wondered whether perhaps she had once again lost her mind. They were unlikely to get a fraction of the way.

THE TOWN SAT on both banks of the river with a ferry that linked the two sides. Neither aspect was very big but the place was, as a whole, sufficiently populated for anonymity.

There were a few curious glances from fishermen as the two of them walked out of the desert but no one questioned them. They found the ferry and took it across the river. There were the beginnings of a bridge on both sides but no workers, and the stones looked worn enough to suggest it had been abandoned a long time before.

The ferry was sufficient and they still plenty of money. Being only two people on foot, the price was not high.

They headed out to the ley-circle—only stopping long enough to buy some fresh fruit in a small market. There was little organisation here and no hostels for travellers. Just a small stone hut a short distance from the circle itself where an enquiry revealed the next patterners path had been paid for privately and was going to Leket in Umran, which was a hundred or more leagues along the coast.

Leket was a real city and that suited their plans.

The patterner was happy to direct them to the house of the livestock merchant who had paid for the path. This town, Katending, was too small to have any scheduled paths because the needs were so irregular. Joining a journey someone else had paid for was how it worked here.

The house of the merchant was not large, but it was bigger than most and, from the clean-cut surface of the walls, had been constructed from kiln-fired brick rather than the sun-dried ones. It was an obvious attempt to show the owner's wealth.

Pitra of Kotu was a very big man in all directions and welcomed them into his home. He went through the house extolling its virtues, its size, and the expense he had gone to having it constructed.

Elona said nothing while Jaymis introduced them as Jalka and Parthia, still brother and sister, of Betlain—there was no point in pretending they were from the south despite the darkening of their skin in the days they had been travelling. She found this Pitra irritating, and his name sparked unpleasant memories.

After the short tour, they were seated in a shaded part of the building's garden where they drank refreshing fruit juice—though Elona was not sure which fruit they were from.

"You have walked from Avaki?" he said with a great laugh. "Who would do such a thing?"

"We wanted to see the land."

Pitra scoffed at the idea. "Desert and scrub. Only good for the hardiest *lukisa*, and they are safe only because they are so big. They have a nickname for me, can you guess?"

Elona cast her eyes down in the appropriate fashion. She could think of a few names.

"Lukikalma!" he said without waiting for any reply. "The big father *lukik*. Ha-ha!"

Jaymis laughed with him, but not for very long.

"And what do you do in Faerholme, in the dukedom of Bet?"

"My sister follows the paths of the Sisters of Taymalin, and I am an armsman."

"I could always use a good armsman, are you for sale?"

"I am beholden to my duke, good sir."

"What about your sister, eh?"

There was a long silence. Then Pitra burst out laughing and slapped his hand on the table which made Elona jump. "Good joke!"

Jaymis didn't laugh.

"We are touring the lands of the Concordance, good sir, and we understand you are opening a path to Leket?"

"Taking livestock to sell, yes. You wish to come along?"

"If that is acceptable, I believe it would be a very long walk otherwise."

"Ha-ha! Yes, very long indeed. Five or six moon-turns, at least. And dangerous."

"The wild is always dangerous, good sir."

Pitra's eyes narrowed. "It is." This time his voice carried not the slightest hint of humour. "What will you pay?"

"We have very little coin, good sir, what would you charge?"

"Five tay. Each."

Elona stiffened at the outrageous cost, this was not a major path and it was already paid for, but Jaymis laughed. "Pitra of Kotu, good sir, it is easy to see why you live in such a palace as this. It is such a sad thing but we have barely two tay between us."

"It cannot be done for such a low price. Four tay each."

"I can show you my purse, good sir, we have but three tay in total."

The merchant hesitated as if he believed Jaymis's story but was reluctant to accept such a low price, though it made no difference to him. Anything he made from additional travellers went straight into his pocket, there were no extra costs with this sort of journey.

"Two tay and a blessing from the Sisters of Taymalin," said Elona, looking him in the eye.

"A blessing is always welcome, sister, but it does not feed the stomach."

"Very well."

She took up her bag and delved into an inside pocket. She found and extracted the pair of plain silver hoop earrings Bejeren had gifted her on her sixteenth birthday. Nursey had never let her wear them because her ears would need to be pierced, and when she became mad, she assumed they were cursed. They were not expensive, but worth more than four tay.

"Here," she said and placed them on the table. "These silver earrings and nothing else."

Pitra picked one up, it got lost between his huge fingers.

"They are very small."

"They are silver and easily worth sharing a path, goodman." Her tone suggested that this would definitely be the last offer, and her use of "goodman" was slightly less polite than Jaymis's term—it was a forceful reminder that Pitra was just a merchant.

He sat back. "You have a deal, sister."

The pleasantries that followed were short and they found themselves out on the street with directions to the better of the two inns in the town. And instructions to be at the ley-circle after the midday meal.

They found a corner in the inn where they should not be overheard, they ordered food and drink, and still got change out of a tay.

CHAPTER 19

"What do you think?" said Elona.

"That's a man who cares only for himself, I wouldn't trust him as far as I could throw him."

"No, but he's opening the path today which means he won't have time to send back to Avakending even if he is suspicious of us. We should be able to get into Leket, and disappear."

Jaymis was the one who seemed unsure now.

"Leket will have armsmen, and there will definitely be a fence around the circle. Everyone is nervous about the emperor"

"We can't walk to Umran."

"Fly?"

She shuddered. "Don't even joke about it. Besides what would you use? A *tekrak* we haven't got, or a *ziri*—" she searched for a clever way to say it but came up with nothing. "—we haven't got either."

"Maybe you could control a big *sikechak*."

She knew he was joking but the mere idea made her feel uncomfortable.

"We just need to stay firm on our path."

~

AFTER THEY HAD DIGESTED their meal, they wandered back through the town and out to the ley-circle. The patterner they had spoken to earlier was busy marking out his patterns. The place was quiet and the two of them sat on a bench with their backs to the shed. Elona could have happily stayed here, feeling the power beneath them.

But was the Mother's Milk really beneath them? There were probably arguments among the patterners as to how things truly were. She knew there were ley-circles that hung in the air—where was their power? The ley-circle at Canvor was beneath the lake which meant no patterner's path could be created there. Had they tried? Did it work or did the path become filled with water?

The patterners probably knew, but they did not like to speak of their craft to others outside their guilds. Always they protected themselves, and their sources of money.

The peace was broken by the sounds of men shouting, *zatesa* hooting, and the thunder of *lukisa* hooves. The massive creatures flowed round a bend in the road like a sea of pale hair. She wondered how these long-haired beasts managed in such a hot place but they did not seem to mind it. Herdsmen walked off to the sides calling and whistling to the lithe *zatesa* who moved back and forth, keeping the *lukisa* grouped together and moving towards the ley-circle.

"Jalka and Parthia," said Jaymis.

"I haven't forgotten."

Their benefactor, Pitra of Kotu, arrived driving a trap pulled by a young *kichek*.

"Greetings, friends," he said as he climbed down awkwardly. He let go of the reins and the *kichek* waited obediently. "What do you think of my herd?"

"Impressive," said Jaymis. "They're all yours?"

"Yes and no. Most are, some belong to other farmers, but they trust me to get them the best deal in the city." He moved closer as if he were about to reveal a secret of the universe. "Just farmers, you see, the city scares them, it's too big for them."

"But not for you," said Elona.

Pitra laughed. "No, sister, because I am friends with everybody it's important to know in Leket. I know how to get the best prices and for that I get my cut."

He glanced over at the patterner who was still working.

"Not long now." He sounded impatient as if he had been expecting the path to already be open. "You should go ahead of the animals."

"Why?" said Jaymis innocently, and Elona cringed.

"Ha-ha! Unless you want to come out the other side covered in *lukisa* crap!"

Even under his tanned skin, she saw Jaymis redden, which she thought was quite endearing but then he had never been arrogant. Neither had Drahail.

Once upon a time, in the days when she had dreamed of marrying her prince, she absorbed all the stories where the prince was always arrogant but then learnt his lesson and became the perfect husband.

She realised she was smiling at Jaymis, and he was looking back at her with a confused expression on his face. She turned away and watched the *lukisa* crowding into the space in front of the ley-circle. Some of the men were bringing up fencing and constructing a funnel from the place the patterner was working. They were careful not to interrupt him.

Elona tutted.

"What's wrong?" said Jaymis.

"He's taking so long."

"And you could do it better?"

She felt the pressure of the patterning in the ley-circle as if it was going to overwhelm her. She wanted to use the power to hold herself up but worried she might damage the path being created.

"The path is nearly ready."

"How can you tell?"

She looked at where the arch was taking shape above the circle— bending and twisting the shapes on the other side of it.

"I just can."

Elona stood. She was going to insist that Jaymis did not need take her arm to steady her, but it did help so she said nothing.

Pitra was back on his trap and waved to them. "Let us go! Trade does not wait!"

"All that good humour could get very wearing," said Jaymis as they walked across the dirt floor.

There was no physical sensation when they walked into the path. It was just like stepping across the threshold of a building, except it went dark.

They walked briskly to keep ahead of the increasingly noisy herd of *lukisa* as they were forced inside. They continued in silence for a while—silence for them, but the noise of the herders and the animals filled the air. As did the smell.

THE JOURNEY CONTINUED. Beyond the walls of the path, and beneath their feet, they could see the intricate and moving lights of the World's Pattern but between the threads there was just empty nothing. A void. It made her skin crawl to contemplate it and without conscious thought she touched her hand to the ragged injury on her face.

The patterns filled the void, but if there were no patterns all that remained was void.

She wondered whether even the patterners really understood what they were doing when they made a path. One thing was known for certain though. If the patterner died, the path collapsed and everything within simply disappeared. The same if the one who created it exits the other end, which is why they always followed at the back, to ensure all the travellers are out before the path ceased to exist.

There were stories about patterners leaving people behind too— sometimes intentionally.

"So, what can you see?" she asked.

"Moving lights in what I suppose are the walls."

"How deep does it go?"

"Deep?"

"For me it's like looking into water and I can see the lights but they go far and deep. And I know there are the gaps between, though there's nothing to see."

"I just see some lights moving in a wall—well, they show me where the wall is, and the floor, of course."

The surface they walked on was very slightly yielding.

Time stretched out but their days on the sand had toughened them. And they did not tire.

She saw the end of the path, eventually, as another great arch of darkness though she could not see what was on the other side of it.

She was still leaning against Jaymis so she just turned her head and whispered.

"Nearly there."

"Can you see it?"

"Not really. It's just an impression. What about you?"

"The walls seem to continue—but then I don't know where they're supposed to stop."

She said nothing, absorbing the fact she perceived more of the truth in this place than he did—than most people, it seemed.

"How do you want to do this?" he said.

"If we act suspiciously that will put attention on us. I think we should just act normally."

"Let's walk a little faster and get away from Pitra and his men."

"Are you concerned?" she said.

"Better safe than sorry."

That was a sentiment she could agree with. They quickened their pace and drew further ahead of the animals and herdsmen.

As they covered the final, Elona counted down the last five steps.

The world returned but where they had left in brilliant sunshine, they arrived in a deluge of rain being whipped almost horizontal by a vicious wind. In no time at all, half of their bodies were wet through.

"Katending?" shouted a patterner above the racket of the pelting rain, as they hunched over against the onslaught of the weather.

"Yes," shouted Jaymis in return, "there's a herd of *lukisa* coming."

"That's right."

Elona could see that fences had already been set up to corral the incoming animals. Someone waved through the grey of the rain, gesturing to them and opening a gap between the movable barriers.

They hurried over and slipped through.

"That's the way out," he said and pointed at a small gate in a solid fence that surrounded the whole ley-circle. Dark shapes loomed behind the fence and Elona squinted to try to make them out but they just didn't seem to make sense.

The two of them hurried although it made no difference to the rain which had now penetrated everything Elona wore, and probably Jaymis too.

Jaymis suddenly said. "Ballista?"

Elona slowed and stared. Why would anyone set up these massive bows and arrows around the ley-circle? It made sense to have armsmen but you wouldn't use these against infantry—

"Mother's Milk," she said and stood still. She turned back to look at the ley-circle as first Pitra on his trap emerged, followed by a few of his men and the first of the *lukisa*. Pitra stopped and spoke to the man that had accosted them on their exit.

"What?"

"*Tekrasa*," she said but he still looked confused. "You said the emperor was using them in Esternes."

She saw the burst of comprehension on his face. "Can they travel a patterner's path?"

"Why not?"

"I don't know, I've never seen one."

"I have," she said and, before he could comment, she turned back to the gate. "Come on, we need to get away from here."

"What about the next path out?"

"Yes, but let's lose ourselves first. It might be worth selling something else to make sure we have enough. We'll have to go into the city."

They arrived at the gate. Three armsmen, one with a bow though it would be next to useless in this rain, and an officious-looking fellow, who was the one to speak.

"Names?"

"Jalka and Parthia of Bet."

He looked at them and then at the *lukisa* streaming, seemingly from nowhere, onto the ley-circle.

"You were in Mirriasmia."

"That's right."

"Why?"

"My sister is becoming a Sister of Taymalin and we were doing a tour of the lands of the Concordance before she takes her final vows."

For the first time, the man looked at Elona, and his eyes were drawn to the wound on her cheek.

"Probably the best thing for her," he said.

Elona could see Jaymis holding himself back—if he had any power, she suspected the man would be burning.

"This path comes from Katending, does it not?"

"Yes," said Jaymis through gritted teeth.

"That's a pathetic little coastal town with nothing but—" he glanced up then back, "—*lukisa*. Why were you there?"

"We are not near the sea in Bet, not even close, neither of us had seen it. We wanted to experience it. So we travelled from Avakending to this town, which has a circle and it brought us here."

The man shook his head but did not actually contradict Jaymis.

"Can we go?"

Just then another man, legs splattered with mud, rushed up and drew the official away. They spoke briefly, the official turned and smiled. Then pointed at the two of them.

"Arrest them, they're spies!"

It took the armsmen, a few moments longer to react than Jaymis, his sword was out as he stepped in front of Elona to protect her. She looked round in desperation as she grabbed at her neck for her dagger.

The only armsmen were the ones at the gate but it wouldn't take them long to find more. The ballista were also manned but on the other side of a wooden fence they couldn't get through.

The first of the armsmen reached Jaymis and engaged him. The clang of swords was bound to attract more attention. They needed to get away somehow—or surrender, but if they did that, they would be easy targets for assassins.

The fact that this would now get back to the emperor and their attempt at disappearing would be foiled again was just a passing thought.

The second armsmen also arrived and the two of them were forcing Jaymis back. They were fighting carefully, his attacks always missed and when he tried for one, they backed off and the other would move in. That he was keeping them at bay at all was a miracle. They were trying to flank him but he kept moving back.

"This way, Jalka," she called, she didn't know if it was worth keeping up the pretence but it did no harm.

In the distance she saw the bulk of Pitra standing up on his trap watching what was happening. Bastard probably thought he'd get a reward.

Revenge was petty but she didn't care.

She had reached the fence and pressed her back against it as the rain water rolled off her scalp. The *lukisa* bleated and hooted as the farm hands kept them under control. She had no time to make contact with them, she had no idea how they thought, but the half-dozen *zatesa* she understood.

Keeping her eyes open she spread out her senses and tuned them in. This was different to the wolves, with those you only had to merge with the leader and the others would simply follow because they were a single living entity.

The *zatesa* were individuals but they still worked as a pack. She found each of them and let her own patterns merge.

JAYMIS WAS TIRING FAST, and that was their whole purpose, to wear him down until they could capture him. A few cuts didn't matter, they were easily healed. Elona had told him to retreat to the fence which he didn't think was a good idea.

He jumped to one side, almost slipping on the muddy ground, he slashed at the one on that side forcing him to retreat. The other came in as expected but this time Jaymis was ready. He let his feet slide from under him. The armsman's swipe went over his head and Jaymis bludgeoned his sword into the man's knee. The armsmen screamed in pain and Jaymis rolled away.

The splash as the man hit the ground was satisfying, but the other one was running in, each stride raising a fountain of muddy water, and with Jaymis lying on his back this would be over—

An animal streaked in from the side and slammed into the oncoming armsman knocking him sideways and into the ground. Hooting *zatesa* surrounded Jaymis and Elona. The stockmen were now shouting, desperately trying to keep the *lukisa* under control but without their animals, the huge beasts did as they pleased and moved away in a great tide towards the main gate, taking down the fences as they went. While Pitra looked on in horror.

Elona helped Jaymis up.

"Come on," she went straight for the fence.

"The gate!"

She said nothing but when she reached the wooden barrier, she raised her arm and slashed downwards from a point as high as she could reach to the ground. Nothing seemed to happen but she took a step to the side and did the same again. A door-sized hole appeared as the wooden boards simply fell away.

She slipped through, and he followed as did three of the big *zatesa*.

The ballista stood on mounds which meant they could fire over the fence. Elona hurried between them and into the open land beyond. To their left, the rain glowed with the lights of a city.

"Stop!"

A crossbow twanged.

He saw Elona turn, as pain exploded in his side.

She screamed a word but there was something wrong with his hearing, as if the pain obscured it. He was still standing...he *thought* he was still standing...when the world went very black.

CHAPTER 20

"The World's Pattern hates us."

He knew it was Elona speaking but it seemed to be coming from a great distance. He was lying on his back with his head slightly raised. There was light on the other side of his eyelids and he could smell a fire.

Rain. The image of the ballista and the armsman burst on him. He tried to push himself up, he needed to protect Elona. Pain seared through his stomach and he could not help but cry out, though his voice rasped in his dry throat.

A hand pressed against his shoulder pushing him back. He had not the slightest scrap of strength to resist it. He groaned again.

"Serves you right. Lay still."

He forced his eyes open. The light was dim but he still blinked against it. He was in a cave, the entrance was not far away and, beyond it, nothing but a slate-grey daylight sky.

The fire he had smelled was between him and the entrance.

"I managed to borrow a blanket but there's no healer here."

"Where?" His voice was barely audible.

Instead of an answer he found a cup being pressed to his lips. He sipped and swallowed.

"Where?"

"I'm not sure." A dark figure rose up and stood beside him. "Anyway, I don't think you should be talking yet. You're probably not going to die but that was a nasty wound."

He knew something wasn't right but he couldn't think what it was as he drifted back to sleep.

~

THE NEXT THING was the smell of something delicious. She held the spoon and slowly fed him the soup.

"I foraged for herbs and one of the villagers brought the meat. Not too bad, though I say so myself."

"Good," he said when it was gone. He was still hungry but had trouble focusing.

The light at the cave entrance changed from day to night in the blink of an eye. He had slept again. An afternoon? A day? He had no idea.

"How long?"

"Since Leket? A five-day, more or less." She wasn't close but it seemed she could hear him.

"What happened?"

He heard her moving around in the cave shadows.

"I don't know."

He knew she was lying and it wasn't hard to understand why. "It was the same as happened at Canvor, wasn't it?"

She sighed. "I suppose."

"But me as well."

"You as well. Yes."

"I'm glad."

He heard a short laugh. "I'm sure you are. I expect Kienan would have been grateful too."

Kienan? He couldn't remember who that was, but the pain in his side was distracting. But he did remember one thing.

"You said there's no healers."

"None around here, no. Not even any Kadralin travellers who might have one."

"What about you?"

"No." Her answer was terse and filled with pain but he persisted anyway.

"But you saved Drahail and his wound was mortal. You healed yourself in Dirdin."

"You saw what I did the last time I tried it," she said. "You've seen my face."

"But—"

"Shut up, you don't know anything."

He fell silent. His memory finally delivered the information as to who Kienan was. The one who had tried to murder Elona in Canvor. The one who had toppled over the balcony, taking her with him to certain death for the both of them.

His body had been smashed in the courtyard below. And Elona had ended up at the Woodcircle in Dirdin. She already blamed herself for the man's death, even though he had been trying to kill her. Now, because she had managed to save both of them this time, it made that crime worse.

He doubted there was anything he could say that would make her feel any better.

"I think I have an idea of where we are now," she said.

"Where?"

"Somewhere in the north of Taltia."

"How can you tell?"

"The stars. Bejeren made me study them and we had a clear night last night. The Lost Lovers is a constellation that's easy to recognise and it's much higher in the sky than in Faerholme for the time of year. When we were in Mirriasmia, it was on the horizon."

"That's clever."

"It's just the sky."

"You're sure it's north Taltia?"

"Or Tenya."

"Or perhaps Tirnia?"

"Probably not, I don't think this is the Great Waste. There's too much life here."

His side was aching but it was less than it had been and he managed to push himself up into a sitting position. The light from the fire flickered on the walls of what had been a natural cave, he thought, but human hands had smoothed sections of the surface, and built a half-wall across the entrance. Enough to keep some of the weather out.

Further in, past where he was lying, the cave narrowed and then opened out again. There was a light inside, he could see a table and Elona moving about. Then he realised he wasn't wearing any clothes.

"Ready for some more food?" said Elona from the other part of the cave.

"Please." Simply being asked the question triggered a level of hunger he had never experienced.

She came out with two cups. She filled them both from a pot sitting at the side of the fire then sat down beside him and handed one over.

"You're looking better," she said.

For some reason her comment embarrassed him. He was very aware most of his upper torso was bare.

"Bit thin though," she added. "Scrawny."

"I haven't eaten properly for a five-day."

"Six. That last conversation was yesterday."

"I'm...surprised."

"Don't be. Usala taught me a lot. I found a jinder bush and added some of its root to your drinks and then yesterday's food. It's effective in making people sleep."

"This Usala was a good teacher."

Elona got up abruptly and went into the other area. Jaymis realised he had said something wrong again—but how could he know what was right if she wouldn't talk to him?

"This is not fair, Elona."

"No, it isn't. None of it is. Nothing in the world is fair."

He had a sudden thought. When Elona had arrived in Dirdin she

hadn't been wearing anything. "Why am I naked? Did we arrive…
without clothes?"

"No, this time I managed to bring everything we were wearing too.
I stripped you." There was a hint of a smile in her voice.

"Why?"

"You were wet and you needed to get dry. And I wanted to see how
bad your injury was."

He stared at the soup and wondered if she had dosed it again,
although he hadn't seen her do anything different with it than she had
with her own. He wasn't feeling sleepy though his whole body still felt
as if it had been trampled by a herd of *lukisa*. There was a cut log
standing on end next to the pallet. He put his cup on it.

"How did you get me into this cave?"

"This is where we arrived."

He was about to ask about a ley-circle when she continued.

"There is a very small ley-circle here in the cave. You can't see it but
there's a hole in the rock in the other room."

"But we're not safe, what if there's a feeding here?"

She came back out and stared at him. Once again, he was
embarrassed.

"It's the smallest ley-circle you could imagine. The feeding has
made a hole in the ceiling, through the rock, but I can barely get a
finger into it. Look around you, can you see anything that's been
corrupted? Any abominations? Even the stones in here still seem
natural."

"There's no danger?"

"We're safe. The animals keep clear, there were no droppings in
here, so that's a good thing. And no *sikechasa* of any size."

"What about the village?"

She pointed vaguely in the direction of the cave entrance. "We're
halfway up a hill. It's in the valley. Not far."

Elona came over, picked up his mug and sat on the log. She was
only wearing a sort of shift which came down to her mid-thighs. He
didn't think that had been among her things because he'd never seen it

before, and he was distracted by the way the material followed the shape of her body as well as all the naked skin she had on show.

"They must have been surprised to see you."

She nodded. "It worked out well. They think I'm special because we appeared in the magic cave from nowhere, so they're feeding us and supplying a few things we need."

A sensation suddenly developed in his lower torso. "Is there a place where I can go—you know."

"If you need to piss, you can just go out and to the left, far enough we won't smell it. The slope is not too bad, just be sure not to slip. The other will have to wait until daylight."

He continued to look at her and then glanced at the back of the cave.

She tutted and put her head on one side. "No, I'm not leaving, you're going to need help. You can barely even sit up. I would be impressed if you can walk all that way on your own. Besides, there's nothing you've got that I haven't already seen."

That did not help but it seemed he had no choice since the more he thought about it, the more he needed to go.

"How are we going to do this?" he said.

By the time he got to his feet, he was already exhausted—whether it was the lack of food or the injury he didn't know—Elona wrapped the blanket around his shoulders and it fell to his thighs.

He leaned on her with his arm over her shoulders. He could feel her hot skin above the neckline. This was not good at all as his wayward mind afflicted him with other images and thoughts.

She didn't complain but he knew most of his weight was on her as he staggered across the uneven surface, feeling every cold stone with his bare feet.

It was dark outside, which was a partial blessing. The lights of the village were below and, in Colimar's dim red light, he could make out a dozen or so small buildings. They went left, away from the direction of the village, and a few paces along. His side was aching badly now and he had lost the desire to relieve himself—or, thankfully, anything else.

Elona faced away and he managed to do what he needed but was embarrassed by the noise.

He was grateful when the torture was ended and he could lie back down. The pallet barely provided any padding between him and the hard stone floor, but he was grateful for it.

He was asleep before he had a chance to think about how tired the short walk had made him.

CHAPTER 21

It was another three-day before he could walk on his own enough to deal with his own physical requirements. Elona continued to be friendly and then aloof when he strayed into areas she didn't want to talk about.

It was frustrating but he was feeling better and able to eat solid foods.

She had disappeared earlier in the day saying she was going down to the village to see what additional information—and food—she might gather.

He lay dozing for a while but the boredom was becoming intense. Elona had found him a stick that was a good size for leaning on. He used it to get himself into a standing position. The wound in his side just ached now and his movements did not cause additional pain.

He had touched it with his fingers and found two places where his skin seemed to have been sewn together. The crossbow bolt had gone into his back and all the way through. He knew he was lucky because, without a healer, combat wounds especially in the stomach area could kill a man with a lingering and agonising death.

For the first time, he went into the second part of the cave at the back. He found the hole in the ceiling. Perfectly circular and straight up. Keeping his head back as he stared upwards made him dizzy. There was a similar hole in the ground. This ley-circle might be small but it must also be deep.

He was so used to the big circles and the feedings he's seen full of the flashing white light of the Mother's Milk, it was difficult to believe this was the same thing. At least, it was a ley-circle and not anything like the Mother's Kitchen, his skin crawled as he recalled Elona's description of a patternless void.

Elona had been using this area for storage and food preparation. This was also where she kept her pallet. He hadn't even given a thought to where she slept until yesterday. Although he hadn't seen her do it, he was sure she was still dosing his food to make him sleep. And of the collections of plants she had, he did not know which she used.

He trusted her, even if she was difficult but who could blame her? Her life had been terrible—except the part with this Usala she talked about. She had been happy during that winter in the mountains, though he got the impression it hadn't been easy. But that time had changed her, when he helped her escape, she had been like a *chakik*, hiding between the floorboards and scared of everything. When she appeared in Aris she was afraid of nothing—or had the courage to overcome her fears, more like a *nachak*.

A *fahain*.

She had returned with these strange abilities, some of which she could control, and one she definitely could not. He was not upset she could transport them across the kingdoms of the Concordance, but if she could do it by design instead, it would help.

He hobbled out of the back room and past the fire to the cave entrance. He stood there wrapped only with the blanket looking out. The day was cold and windy, but the clouds were high and not threatening rain. He went back and found his clothes.

Dressed against the wind, he went first to the steep-sided gully in the hill Elona had shown him, where their waste disappeared into the dark. The edges of it were well worn by time and plants grew inside it but Jaymis could not help but wonder whether the crack had been forced by a feeding.

His needs satisfied, he set off in the other direction, past the cave entrance and along the path that wound back and forth down towards the village.

He had managed only half the distance when he had to rest. He was already panting, and the ache in his side had intensified.

"I can't go all the way down." *If I do, I won't be able to get back.* As it was, he realised he might have overstretched himself. If coming down this far had exhausted him this much, returning was going to be even harder.

In the end, he managed to make his way back in stages. He counted a hundred paces then stopped until his heart slowed and the blood stopped pounding in his head.

He barely remembered making it back to the cave.

~

"You're an idiot," was Elona's first comment when he finally woke up as the sun went down. "I watched you come all that way down. You were like an old man going back."

"We have to move as soon as we can."

"Nonsense. We have all the time in the world."

He said nothing. She was right, how could anybody find them in this remote place? Especially when they had no idea where they were either.

"How did the Tirnian armsmen find you?"

Elona closed her eyes and sighed. "Your mother had learnt some unusual patterns. She created some sort of empathy with me, I don't know how or what exactly, she always knew where I was when I did something with the Mother's Milk."

His mind jumped on to a flaw in her story. He hesitated, this was usually the time when she would stop talking and turn away, but he couldn't not ask. "You were away a long time after spring, when the armsmen came for you."

"I discovered the link and broke it," she said abruptly and her look challenged him to question it.

And he would not have questioned it, if she had not challenged him. Her defiance told him there was more she wasn't saying.

"It is not that I have any right to know—"

"No, you don't."

"I just want to understand."

"I'm not ready to tell you."

"Of course."

BY THE TIME another five-day came and went, he was almost back to his old self. He exercised by walking over and around the hill, only to find that there were more hills in all directions. Low and rounded, most of them covered in trees. The shapes they made were curiously peaceful, compared to the south, where the mountains were jagged.

Even the small river in the valley meandered gently.

The weather had turned milder too, it rained but not heavily and the air was warm.

There was a place a short distance from the cave where a rocky outcrop jutted out into the path and a short climb took you to its flat top.

Elona and he sat up there watching the sun bury itself in the hills to their left. She had acquired an alcoholic drink from the village, she had been told it was made from the flowers of a tree.

"My father thought the best way to deal with me was to put my bedroom in a tower."

"Like a princess in a story."

"If he couldn't see me, he could pretend I didn't exist."

"But you don't like heights."

"He didn't know that."

"You didn't tell him?"

"My father is not someone you talk to—is not someone *I* could talk to. And I don't suppose it would have made any difference even if I had."

Jaymis looked at her and then at the drop beneath them. It's true that it wasn't very steep once you got past the height of the rock they were on.

"Is it okay up here? We could go back to the cave."

"I'm all right. As long as I don't look directly down."

"You drove the outlaw's wagon across a Slissac bridge."

She gave a short laugh. "The bridge wasn't the problem. It was snowing and I couldn't see very far—I had to concentrate on controlling those beasts. There was a turn before that, we nearly went over."

"I *saw* that. My heart was in my mouth—and I didn't understand why you were running from us. Didn't you hear us?"

Elona hesitated. "I heard you but I thought you'd send me back to Faerholme. I'd rather have died."

"But why did you think the traders had helped you escape at the Woodcircle?"

"Honestly, Jaymis," she said with a sigh, "I didn't even think about it. I was just so scared and I needed to get away."

"When you were driving those *kichesa,* were you using your—" he stopped for a moment. "—I don't even know what you call it."

"I don't have a name for it. I didn't even know the word *fahain.* But no, I mean I don't think I was. I learnt how to drive the caravans and wagons of the Kadralin traders."

The valley was dark. The sky above the horizon, where the sun had disappeared, was filled with reds and orange fading into blue. Stars stood out sharp in the still air above and to the right where the sky was black.

"The Lost Lovers," said Elona and pointed towards the horizon directly ahead. "If I didn't know what season it was already, I could have determined that too."

"I'm not sure what I'm looking at," said Jaymis.

She pointed again. "You see there's four stars, two pairs but in a straight line?"

He leaned his head over to sight along her arm. "I see them."

"That's their eyes. Yaily is the one on the right and there's a whole crowd of stars that are supposed to be her hair. Others are her body, though the exact ones depend on who drew the constellation. The other pair of eyes is Komas, he's not very well formed apart from his sword at his waist."

"I heard it wasn't his sword," said Jaymis.

"Oh, really? You don't know anything about the stars but you know that? Well, Bejeren never told me that version."

Jaymis hadn't remove his head from her arm, he turned slightly and kissed the bare flesh.

She didn't say anything. She didn't move, so he did it again.

He wasn't sure what to do next. He knew she was nervous—or she would be if she was feeling the way he was. Terrified.

"I'd like to kiss you," he said.

"You did. Twice."

"You didn't tell me to stop."

"Would it make any difference?" There was a strange hard tone in her voice, he did not understand—it was almost resignation.

CHAPTER 22

I *will not cry.*

And she managed not to. She knew he did not mean any harm but he caused it anyway.

Neither of them said another word as they, by mutual and unspoken agreement, climbed down from the rock and went back to the cave. Elona unrolled her bed and lay down. She kept telling herself she trusted him and that he would never do anything she didn't desire, but she still made sure her dagger was to hand.

She lay awake in the dark until his breathing had settled into sleep, and a slight snore. Relaxation came on her slowly and she spread out her senses. The rock of the walls did not create any barrier as she perceived the patterns of life around her. The day insects lying dormant, those who lived in the night crawling or flying. *Sikechasa* flitting through the air. Small hunters and prey among the rocks and grass.

Something attracted her attention, like a beacon in the sky. A golden line moving fast, very high in the air. She had never seen anything like it. It couldn't be any kind of bird because it was so swift and trailed a magical light, but what else was there? It was a long distance away and heading across the hills at an angle.

She tried to see what it was. But either it was very small or even further than she thought. Abruptly it changed direction. For a moment, she held her breath then she realised it wasn't coming directly towards her, although it was moving along the valley now. Then it simply stopped—at least the golden line became no longer and even the gold seemed to evaporate as she watched, like smoke.

She brought her attention closer to home and turned it towards the village where the livestock outnumbered the humans, and almost all of them were now asleep. Except those two, their patterns intermingled, flaring and pulsing.

She knew what it was, what they were doing, and it affected her too. The energy exploding between them. The passion. The types of pattern she had intentionally encouraged in those who kept her guarded on two occasions. The patterns that had controlled the men who had attacked her—Krazak, the outlaw, Styvan. All of them bent on only one thing.

The one she had sensed in Jaymis.

She knew he did not mean her harm but how could she separate what she saw in him with what she had felt, and encouraged, in them? At the time she had not been aware of her ability, but that did not mean she had not felt it.

She did not withdraw from the lovers though she was eavesdropping where she did not belong. She envied them and bathed in the lustful energies they generated. She fell into them and let their emotions run through her.

Then it was over. The patterns changed, the intensity was lost, the lovers' patterns remained entwined as they became quiet. No betrayal. No hate. No pain.

Then she wept.

DAWN WAS CREEPING through the cave entrance when she woke. She had slept soundly for a change despite the previous evening's upset and eavesdropping. There was something different. Once on her feet, she rolled up her bed roll.

"Are you decent?"

There was no answer and she looked into the cave. Jaymis wasn't there. She froze in fear—not only that she had failed to notice him leave but worrying she might have driven him away.

"It doesn't matter," she thought. "If he's gone, it's one less thing to worry about." *A lot less to worry about in truth.*

But once she stepped into the space, she knew he hadn't gone forever. There was a dead *sikechak* lying next to the fire. How could he have got it? She pulled it up by its neck and examined its body. There were no obvious wounds but its neck had been wrung and was broken.

She laughed out loud. *Stone-struck.* They were always a little slow first thing in the morning which, according to the saying, made them easy prey to a solidly thrown stone—although she didn't know anyone who had ever put it to the test.

She took it outside, to the gully they used for a toilet, and gutted it. Up from the gully, and feeding into it, was a small stream which she used to clean it after slicing off the head, feet and wings—which had barely any meat in them. It had no feathers and was usually cooked in its skin, though she was sure that was because it just made the job easier. She caked the whole thing in clay because she had no cooking pots.

Back at the cave she built up the fire and laid the cocoon of meat into the side of it. They were going to need more fire wood, and it was getting harder to find since they had taken everything available in the vicinity already.

Almost as she had the thought, she heard boots on the path, and the distorted silhouette of Jaymis appeared at the door. She realised he was carrying logs and jumped up to take them from him.

"Thank you," he said in a strained voice as he leaned against the man-made half-wall that partially blocked the entrance.

"Where did you get them?"

"Village," he said between strained breaths.

"Lie down."

"I think I will."

As he slowly got himself into a lying position, she stacked the logs near the fire to dry and placed one of them on to it.

His breathing slowly returned to normal as he lay there with his eyes closed.

"You're an idiot."

"You said that before."

"Must be true then."

"Probably."

She made sure the *sikechak* was close to the hottest part of the fire while the new log steamed and hissed. Then she laughed.

"You actually brought down a *sikechak* with a stone."

"I don't know why but it wasn't on a proper roost, just on the ground hiding beside a rock but still asleep. I thought it looked a lot like dinner. It was a lucky shot. I managed to stun it enough to get my hands round its neck."

She smiled and shook her head. "When did you get up?"

"Bit before dawn," he said. "I couldn't sleep. I wanted to apologise but I didn't want to wake you."

She didn't mention she had been awake as well, even if her thoughts had been elsewhere. She hoped the flush of embarrassment did not show.

"So instead of waiting until I woke up, you almost killed yourself trying to make it up to me by finding food and getting wood?"

"It doesn't sound very sensible when you say it like that."

"How are you feeling?"

"I feel like I've run a league and back carrying a dozen rocks on my back, and my arms feel as if they're going to drop off."

"The wound?"

"Aches a bit but not much."

She nodded though he wasn't looking and prodded the fire with a stick sending up a shower of sparks.

"We'll head off tomorrow, shall we? We can cook this and I'll get some more supplies from the village," she said. "If you can carry those logs up from the valley you're fit enough."

"And bring down a *sikechak*."

"Yes, we mustn't forget that."

"I'm sorry," he said abruptly, "about what happened last night."

She hesitated. "So am I."

"You've got nothing to apologise about. I was the one forcing the issue."

She dropped the stick she'd been using on the fire, stood up and turned towards him.

"Don't take away my right to apologise."

He looked as if he were about to say one thing—probably protest again—then he sighed. "Of course." It looked as if he was feeling his way in the dark, looking for the right words to say. "I just don't understand, and I want to."

"What's the weather like?"

The sudden change of subject threw him for a moment. "Cloudy, not much wind."

"Come." She stretched out her hand and helped him get to his feet. She forced herself to keep hold of his hand as she led him out of the cave and back to the rock they had been sitting on the previous evening.

Her feet were bare and the stones were slightly damp. It meant nothing. She had survived a Faerholme winter wearing only a shift, and chained to the wall in a tower. But she still shook slightly at the prospect of what she was considering.

He climbed up first and pulled her up almost without effort. He was certainly much stronger, all that remained was for him to regain his stamina which was best done by travel.

They stood there. She looked out on the valley and hills as she struggled with how to say what needed to be said.

"Should we sit down?" he said eventually.

"Sorry. I have to tell you some things and I don't know where to start."

"The beginning?"

"No." That was too painful to come at head on. She started in the middle. "Usala had a daughter, her name is Chara and she was a sister to me."

"One of the things you didn't mention."

"No, there are reasons and now is not the time for that either. But you have to understand we were close. Since Savi died—well, a long time before that—I hadn't had any one I could talk to. We talked about everything but I didn't even tell Chara about these things."

"I see."

She turned to face him. "Please sit down. This is very strange for me. I think it would be easier for me if you were sitting."

"Are you going to sit down too?"

"I—no, I'll pace."

He went to where rock ledge went into the hill and half lay down with his head propped up enough to watch her.

"The day your mother arrived at Corlain, I was attacked."

"Attacked? I hadn't heard."

She turned to him and gave a gentle smile. "You have to keep quiet, Jaymis. No comments, no outrage—because you will get angry—you have to just listen."

"Sorry," he said and then gave back her gentle smile. "Again."

"You didn't hear about it because it was kept secret. I was raped."

She simultaneously saw and felt his whole body go rigid. "Well, he tried to rape me. Nursey's son, Krazak, was his name. A thief and ne'er-do-well. He—he had been raping my mother's body. Lots of times. I stumbled on him and he tried to take me as well. But Nursey raised the alarm, she was bad but she had some regard for me. Krazak was shot by an armsman before he could...do anything." *He nearly did.*

She had stopped looking at Jaymis. Her eyes were directed at the ground but she wasn't seeing it. Only Krazak. His knife at her throat. She could see in his eyes that he would kill her afterwards.

"The life went out of him. I couldn't move. I could barely breathe. But I was still *intact.* That was all they cared about." *Except Bejeren, he cared. The traitor.*

"Your mother pretended to be concerned about what happened to me, but for her it was the opportunity she needed to cast her patterns, to bind me to her, to put a twisted mirror in my mind to make me see the world as corruption. She turned my pain to her advantage." Elona closed her eyes and took a deep breath. "Then I went mad."

She stopped talking as she tried to rip herself away from the memories of that time, only to be caught up in the next horror. "You sent me away with the Kadralin traders, I surrendered myself to the outlaws as a thank-you and an apology. Their leader, Styvan, told his men they must not touch me, because he thought I had value in Faerholme.

"But there was one, one night he tried. I was already a different person. I fought him but he would have succeeded and forced himself on me. It was Styvan who saved me, but that was when you were catching up. We ran, and you were right, I had the opportunity to escape and I didn't. Styvan may have been a thug but he was not a fool, he realised I must be a liar and did not want to be rescued."

Even she noticed the difference in the emotions of each event changed the way she held herself. She stood taller now though she was no happier about what happened next. "Styvan took me with him when he abandoned his men and we went into that cave. He sent me in first, in case it was dangerous. The only value I possessed now was my body. He made that clear enough." She hesitated. "At least he was almost gentle. He wanted something soft in his bed, not just a receptacle for his lust."

There was a sudden intake of breath from Jaymis.

"You're shocked by my words?" she said but held up her hand so he did not reply. "You shouldn't be. All refinement had been stripped from me. I had been wrapped in the softest *lukisa* cloth all my life. I had been taught facts, but knew nothing of the world. I had been prepared to become the queen of Faerholme—but I became an outlaw's slattern. The only difference is the bed they lay you in. Sometimes not even that."

She looked up from the stones and saw the grey of rain in the far distance, falling on some hill that had no name.

"I allowed Styvan to think I enjoyed his attentions. He kissed my neck and it was all I could do not to vomit. The moment I could, I smashed his head with a rock. My third kill. Savi, Kienan, and Styvan.

"But my descent does not end there. By the time I was captured by the Tirnian armsmen in Aris, I had learnt to work with the patterns. They had left a single armsman to guard me, and I was tied up. I intentionally stirred up his lust and made him want me." *I made him want me.* "And pretended that I wanted it too. When he untied me, I killed him." *I kissed him as I cut his throat.* "I kissed him as I cut his throat."

She knew Jaymis was thinking about when they met just after that and he had asked about the blood 'It's not mine' she had replied, as if it was a joke.

"I don't know the name of the fourth person I killed. The fifth was your mother."

She took a deep breath. "Even then it was not over. When the assassins came for me in Avakending, I used the same trick. Stirred a man's lust so that I could stab him through the neck." *That I failed is not the point.*

She fell silent. Drained and empty. She dropped into a crouching position with her arms over her head. She was numb. *There it is. I use passion as a weapon.*

The scrape of leather on stone told her he was moving. Now he knew the worst of it. She was a cold-blooded murderess who could never love because it would always be tainted. He would stay with her, but he would never—

She jumped as his arms went round her. Half of her wanted to pull away but the rest leaned in to him.

Without warning her entire body was wracked with sobs. She shook as he held her, tight enough that she could feel him, not so tight that she was trapped.

She lost track of time, she could barely understand what she wept for—whether it was for herself or for the people she had killed. Or those she had saved.

Eventually there were no tears left, and her throat was raw. They stood together, he helped her back to the edge of the rock and they sat looking at the world laid out before them.

CHAPTER 23

 $\mathcal{I}$ t was early afternoon when they went back to the cave. Elona turned the *sikechak* to ensure it cooked properly. Jaymis went through his minimal equipment and clothes to make sure it was all in order.

"Tomorrow morning?" he said.

"We can't stay here forever."

"No matter how much we would like to?"

She sighed. "They're trying to kill me."

"But they have no way of knowing we're here."

"We have no way of knowing if that's true, or whether they will suddenly turn up here in force."

He had no answer for that. She watched as he examined and re-sheathed his sword three times.

"You could fill the water bottles."

He went.

Elona sat with her back against the cave wall poking the fire, she had as little to do as he did but she was the one who had poured her heart on to the stones for him to see. He hadn't said anything about it afterwards, for which she was very grateful. He was not a complete fool. She just didn't know if what she said changed anything.

He was not the prince she had longed for when she was young but then she wasn't that person anymore. She liked Jaymis but she was not even sure she wanted a … *what?* A beau? Companion? Sweetheart? Lover?

Her past was only part of the problem. She feared the future.

~

HE RETURNED a short time later with their bottles. She was in the further room sorting through her own belongings. Her hands were shaking.

"Cooking smells good," he said. "We probably need to talk about the direction we're going to take."

She said nothing in response, afraid of how her voice would sound. Instead she turned and walked to where he was standing close to the fire. The water was on the floor near the opposite wall. He was always thoughtful, making sure they weren't close to the fire.

He had a bemused expression on his face as she came up and stood directly in front of him.

"What?"

His eyes flicked towards her right hand as she raised it—was he checking she didn't have a dagger?

She had never considered the fact he was a little taller than she was. Her hand went round to the back of his head, bringing her so close she brushed his chest. He opened his mouth to say something.

She prevented him with a "*Shhh.*"

He resisted when she pulled his head toward her but, after a moment, he yielded. She shivered as his unshaven cheek touched hers. *Too many memories.*

Their lips met. The tension in her drained away. Her left hand snaked around his body and pulled him tighter to her. Then his arms went around her. She slid away from the kiss and pressed her forehead against his shoulder. She felt every part of her that touched him.

"I love you, Elona."

"I don't know what that means."

"It doesn't matter."

"I don't know what happens next."

"We could lie down."

The fear rose inside her again. She knew what that meant.

"You're shaking, my love."

She had promised herself she would try to be honest. If this was to happen at all, she needed to be truthful about it.

"I'm scared."

"Nothing has to happen, Elona. We just lie down because it's more comfortable than standing."

"Are you suggesting your bedroll is comfortable?"

"I'll admit it's not the House of Jalima," he said, "but you did your best to make me comfortable here so, if you lay your bedroll on top, we may achieve some level of comfort."

"That means you have to let me go."

"That is a disadvantage."

Letting go now scared her as much as kissing him had done. "What if I am not brave enough to come back?"

"Then I will be satisfied with what you have given me."

"Pretty words, lordling."

He loosened his embrace. She pulled herself back a step and missed the comfort he had provided. Saying nothing, in case she said the wrong thing, she fetched her bedroll. He had removed the blanket and helped her place her roll over the top of his.

Then he sat—she did not fail to notice the hesitation in the motion as if something hurt when he did it.

He smiled up at her and held out his hand. "So comfortable I could imagine myself sleeping in a palace."

There was not a great deal of room and she could not sit without her hip pressing against his, but then that was why they were there. He threw the blanket across their legs then settled back as she sat beside him.

He had one arm stretched across the bed awkwardly she turned and lay against him. Her breasts pressing against the side of his chest and her head on his shoulder. His arm wrapped over her. She was grateful her damaged cheek was hidden.

Her mind filled with the tumbling memories of Savi and her lurid tales of what she and Kienan had done together. Elona had always pretended she did not want to hear, but she hung on her maid's every word. The couples kissed, touching, love making. Savi had no shame when it came to relating her experiences.

And I killed them both.

"This is nice," said Jaymis.

Elona forced herself to be brave and pushed Savi from her head. "Only nice?"

"I don't want to over-egg the pudding."

"Now you're calling me a pudding?"

He turned his head to look at her. "You're being very obtuse."

She sighed. "Sorry. This is difficult."

"I know," he said. "I have no expectations beyond enjoying having you close to me." He raised his head and kissed her on the forehead. "Try to like it, if not enjoy it."

"I am enjoying it," she said and lifted her free arm to let it rest across his chest.

"And like it?"

She hit him with the flat of her hand.

"Ow."

They lay like that for a while, and she relaxed once more. Though she thought her right arm might be going to sleep.

"Can I touch you?" he said.

She tensed. "What did you have in mind?"

"You don't want to know," he said.

She knew he was trying to be funny, but it didn't help her state of mind. "You can't say things like that," she said quickly. "I mean, it's too much. I know about men and women, I know what happens, but…" Her train of thought ran out.

He shifted slightly and gave her a squeeze. "I'm sorry, I didn't think."

"No, you shouldn't have to second-guess everything you say. I was just explaining," she said. "I'll try to do better."

"If you want me to stop, just say."

She was trying to trust him but before she could say anything, his right hand came down on hers as it lay against his chest. The tips of his fingers stroked the back of her hand, it felt weird and tickled but she kept quiet. His hand was so much bigger than hers, it was engulfed as he gently rubbed and squeezed. Then he pushed up her forearm and into new territory. There was a rhythmic nature to the way he moved.

"I can't do this," she said as his hand reached her elbow. She tried to get up and realised she had been right—her arm had gone to sleep. "And I'm stuck."

"When you say stuck?"

"I mean I can't move. You need to do something."

She felt the muscles of his arm moving under her head. "Mine's gone too."

"What do we do?"

"Two options," he said. "I roll in your direction, or you roll in mine. Either way we have to get closer before we can separate."

The prospect of him being on top of her did not appeal. The memories were unpleasant but there was the simple fact he was probably heavy.

"I'll move," she said. She took hold of his shirt then put her leg over his and bent it, bringing the knee higher.

"Careful!"

She stared for a moment trying to understand his concern. Then it came to her. "Oh."

"It's all right there, just no higher."

Elona managed to roll herself on to him and push herself up with her good arm until she was sitting on his thigh.

"This was a bad idea," she said. "Let's forget it."

"Did you like the kissing?"

She pursed her lips. *Be honest.* "I quite liked it."

"We could do more of that. Perhaps hold hands—" he must have spotted she was about to object, "—but only when safe and convenient."

She smiled and for the first time in a long time she really felt the pleasure of the smile. "Yes, we can kiss, and we can hold hands like young moon-blessed lovers."

"Let's have a little practice now," he said and held out his hand. She took it as pins and needles announced her own arm was waking up. It was a very odd sensation as her skin touched his and felt as if he was pricking her.

She brought her other hand up and held his in both of hers. She stroked his calloused and dirty skin.

"Next time you want to stroke my skin," she said, "perhaps you could clean these first."

"As you command." He was smug as if he had won a victory, and perhaps he had but she needed to keep in mind that his victories were also hers. They should not be at war with one another.

As long as he doesn't overstep the mark. If only I knew where the mark was.

She let go of his hand and knelt up. She leaned forwards until she was across his body with her hands on each side of his head.

"If I had long hair," she said, "it would drape around your face. Would you prefer me to have long hair?"

And it would hide my disfigured face. But he wasn't looking at her cheek, his eyes were looking into hers—which was disorientating.

"It is not your hair, or lack of it, that makes me care for you, Elona."

"You don't dream of taking the forbidden pleasure of a Sister?"

"Do you?"

"No!" She huffed. "You're impossible. Perhaps I won't kiss you after all."

"Was that going to be an option?"

She let her head drop to his and placed a quick kiss on his lips. And moved away again.

"There are other possibilities with kisses," he said.

"I know," she said. "I was told you can use tongues too."

"Just opening the mouth makes it a great deal more intimate. You could try that first if you don't like the idea of tongues."

She said nothing further but let herself down again until their lips touched. She closed her eyes and enjoyed the simple sensation. She half-expected him to open his mouth first but he was waiting for her. She took a deep breath through her nose and pulled her lips apart. His followed—they felt so soft, though his unshaven skin was bristly.

Something was happening to her. It was like the sea rushing inside her, building in pressure and threatening to spill over.

Hesitantly she let her tongue extend past her own lips, and she touched his. Further in, his teeth, also parted. She ran her tongue along them and then penetrated further, pushing her face harder against his. Her eyes screwed up as the energy built inside her.

His tongue touched hers.

It was as if she had been struck by the power of the Mother's Milk.

She felt a sound grow in her throat, like an animal she groaned. She withdrew her tongue and his followed into her mouth. Pressing, touching, probing.

The strength in her arms gave out. And she rolled off to the side. Her chest pressed against his, and her head buried in his neck. She kissed his cheek.

"I need to get up," she said after a long time breathing the scent of his body, as the energy that had woken within her dissipated.

"We don't want to progress too fast," he said.

"It's not that—well, it is that in part, but my knees are hurting, and I need to check the cooking."

She pushed herself back into a kneeling position and then crawled off him awkwardly. Her knees had been bent for so long it hurt to stand. Her face felt flushed, she hoped it wasn't visible. She sat on the big log by the fire and turned the encased *sikechak* again.

Jaymis got up too. He left the cave for a little, when he came back, he offered her some water which she took. He drank as well.

"Was that all right, Elona?"

"Yes."

"Good."

His question put her mind into a whirl. It had been more than 'all right', if they hadn't been in such an awkward and uncomfortable position, she would probably have done a great deal more.

She had never felt it before, but now she knew what Savi had been talking about, the way passion robbed you of your reason. And that was fine if you happened to be a servant in a castle who was dallying with their betrothed.

But they were in the wilderness where danger could come from anywhere, whether man, beast, or abomination. Or simply slipping on the side of a hill and tumbling to one's death.

This behaviour was not helpful.

But it had felt so good.

CHAPTER 24

Jaymis had suggested they might both sleep by the fire and
she acquiesced. She would be warmer and, if there was
trouble, they were together. She still kept her little dagger
under the bag she used for a pillow.

They were awake before dawn the next day. She was amused that
he had more concern for her seeing his body than she did of him
seeing hers. Her time as a prisoner had erased most of her modesty.

Once dressed, they ate some pieces of the *sikechak*, which had
cooked well, and they drank a good deal of water before refilling their
bottles again.

The weather remained settled with clouds moving above but little
in the way of rain.

They still had not properly discussed what they intended to do but,
once they had got down into the valley, Elona pointed their feet in the
direction of Tirnia as best she could, and they set off.

"This river goes east," she said. "If it keeps on going that way then it
should come out in the Sea of Taltia."

"And if you're wrong?"

"We'll be somewhere else. It's a river, it goes somewhere and there
will be other people, somebody will eventually know where they are."

"And perhaps there will be another ley-circle," he said.

"I was hoping more for a boat."

Some of the villagers gathered at the edge of their clump of houses and watched the two of them leave.

"They're probably wondering why we didn't simply vanish the way we came," said Jaymis.

"They were just good people."

BY MIDDAY, the twists and turns of the river had brought them to a place where they were forced to walk slightly up the side of the hills because the flat valley floor was just marshland. They had both got wet feet before they decided to move away from the river itself.

It slowed their progress as the valley bottom spread wider and the river disappeared into the mire of its own creation. In places the ground must have been a little higher and trees formed copses on those islands with their leaves hanging out over the water.

Elona saw a movement in the marsh out of the corner of her eye, but when she looked all she could see was a falling mist.

"Did you see that?"

"What?"

"I'm not sure."

The hills became steeper and they were forced to walk closer to the edge of the marsh. It made her uncomfortable. Every now and then a set of ripples would appear, but no sign of what might have caused them.

She could feel life in the water, it was not as concentrated or mobile as the sea, but there was plenty here that seemed to be sitting and waiting.

They trudged on through the day, the sickly smell of the dank water expanding as they did so. Midday passed and the terrain became more hilly. Here and there they came across the tops of dead trees poking up through the water—covered in green moss that gave them a livid hue—looking almost alive but their bare white branches revealed the truth. It was less marsh now, and more lake, but one of stagnant and fetid water.

"I think this is new," said Elona. "This valley has been flooded."

And it just went on.

The sun descended and they started looking for a place to rest, moving inland a little more. They came over a hill and in a flat space carved from the rock by a spring they found a small stone building with a low door and no windows. The hearth in the corner was open to the sky. They were hidden from the marsh, which pleased both of them.

"Herdsman's shack?" said Jaymis.

"I think so," said Elona. "Even if the herds are long gone."

They unpacked and Elona prepared the food while Jaymis found wood for the fire.

The sun was gone and only Colimar was in the sky when Elona needed to deal with her body's needs.

"Do you want me to stand guard?" said Jaymis.

"I'll be fine."

Elona moved quickly out into the cool night air and stepped round to a point where she couldn't be observed by Jaymis. Although any creature across the expanse of hills would no doubt be watching.

The red moon gave everything a strange hue and the shadows it cast always seemed deeper than those created by its sister.

Something flashed yellow in the sky from the direction of the marsh, Elona glanced up and her heart froze. It was hard to make out but the vast curved shape floating in the sky blotted out the stars and one end spurted yellow flame. It told her everything she needed to know.

It was heading up the valley, the way they had come and was soon lost to sight.

Was it Slissac or human? The villagers had said nothing of the reptile people—and she had asked—so she must assume it was from Tirnia.

She finished up what she needed to do and went back to the hut, wondering what she should do. In the end she chose not to tell Jaymis.

There was nothing either of them could do and he didn't need the extra worry.

She knew he would have liked to have practised kissing but the sight of the giant *tekrak* had thoroughly spoilt her mood. He was confused, of course, but she couldn't help that.

~

NEXT MORNING there was no sign of the *tekrak*, and she decided they must have just been passing by, much as she had done when she was taken to Aris. She gave him a kiss before they set out, just to be sure he understood it wasn't about him.

They headed down the narrow valley and came out at the marsh once more. They set off along its shoreline, this day turning into a trudging duplicate of the previous one.

As the morning fell away, the marsh seemed to curve round to the south, so they could not see far along its length. They climbed over a spur of one of the hills, that plunged into the water beside them, and saw the dark waters of the marsh expanding in all directions. And a black tower pointing up from its heart.

They stopped and stared. It was a good way away. It wasn't on a hill, or even a hummock. Its smooth rounded stones plunged into the water. If there was a visible door at ground level it was either submerged or on the other side—but, in the top third of the structure, there were openings into the dark interior.

"I think that's a Ziri Tower," said Jaymis. "Why would there be one out here?"

Elona scanned the sky. A *zirichak* was big enough to grab a fully grown person and, just because some had been tamed for racing, did not mean the wild ones were safe. Far from it. Besides she had a natural antipathy for things that flew.

"We'd better be careful."

"That tower's been here a long time," he said.

"We still need to be careful."

"I wasn't disagreeing, but won't you be able to deal with them?"

Perhaps. "I don't know."

"If you could control them, we could fly."

"That will *never* happen." It was bad enough being in the gondola of a giant *tekrak*, riding unsupported on the back of one of those *zirichak* was her worse nightmare.

But they didn't see any *ziri* and left the tower behind as they continued around the edge of the marsh. There were trees further up the hillside but an open space between them and the water below.

There were a lot of streams to cross that ran from the high lands into the marsh but even the widest was a simple leap to cross. They drank from those rather than getting any water from the marsh.

Unlike the southern lands where twilight barely existed and the change from day to night was abrupt, here the light lingered and they kept moving for as long as they could before they retreated up into the edge of the trees.

They laid out their bedrolls so their heads would be uphill, but with their feet against a tree so they wouldn't slip down. They ate some of the *sikechak* meat and washed it down with water.

The light faded and, as it did, lights within the marsh itself came alive. Most were green but some were a more golden colour.

"*Dakasa,*" murmured Elona and her hand found Jaymis's. "This is dangerous."

He squeezed hers in return. "Little wonder that village is so isolated," said Jaymis. "They're cut-off by this."

It explained the missing *zirichasa* as well. A *dakak* could even bring one of those down with a well-aimed arrow of water.

"As long as they don't know we're here," she said eyeing the light that was closest to the shore. What she had almost seen earlier in the day, it must have been a *dakak* trying to shoot something down. Perhaps it had succeeded.

"We should move higher," said Jaymis. He was as nervous as she was.

It didn't take long to pick up their gear and climb further into the woods. They stopped when they reached a point where they could no longer see the marsh at all. It was also slightly flatter than the first place they had chosen.

Elona lay back on her bedroll.

"We could practice kissing," said Jaymis.

"Not just now," she said. "I'm … distracted."

"One kiss then? A quick one."

She sighed. It wasn't that she was opposed to the idea, she hadn't been lying when she said she liked it, but it was dangerous being in the outdoors.

They had laid out their bedrolls next to one another. He got on his hands and knees and crawled the short distance between them. She lay on her back and watched his head obscure the dark-grey sky. His body wasn't over her so she didn't feel too bad about the position. She closed her eyes as his lips came into contact with hers.

She took a deep breath through her nose and let her mouth open. The tension flowed from her as she relaxed and focused only on him.

He jerked back.

She could see him clearly in a thin white light from somewhere.

"Something under you!" he hissed as he scrambled for his sword.

She rolled away bumping into a tree.

Jaymis yanked her bedroll away and jammed the sword into the light beneath it. She pushed herself up, stared at the ground for a moment then laughed. "I don't think you can kill moss that way."

"What?"

"Look," she said then made a fist and concentrated. Then she drew a rough circle on the ground and where her fist had been, it left a trail of light.

"Slissac?"

"Looks like it grows naturally too." She closed her eyes, wrapped her arms around herself and reached out to the pattern of the moss, the first Slissac tool she had ever encountered. Light blossomed behind her eyelids.

"Taymar's blessed bollocks," breathed Jaymis in wonder.

She opened her eyes. All round them the world was bright as day as the moss in the ground, on the trees and in the branches above them shone with their pure blue-white light.

She laughed. "What did you say?"

He had the decency to be embarrassed. "Armsmen talk. Sorry." He stared around. "This is incredible."

"Didn't you believe me?"

"I didn't understand."

"The only problem is that I can't stop it. It just wears out." *Or I kill it with too much power.*

"Didn't you say you attracted wolves as well?"

"I can deal with wolves," she said, "but I know what I'm doing now. This was just the moss."

He looked across the lit area. "You must be the only person I know who isn't afraid of wolves."

Your mother wasn't.

She stood up and ripped swathes of moss from the trees around her and gave a handful to him. "We better find somewhere dark to sleep." She found a fallen branch, wrapped the glowing moss around it and tied it on with a strip of leather. "Light without fire."

Once more they packed up their belongings, and Jaymis made his own moss torch.

Rather than head further up the hill they made slow progress along the same height. The glowing forest was left behind and vanished into the trees.

Jaymis came to a sudden halt. "Stop!"

She came up beside him and found they were on the brink of an abyss. It made her feel queasy and she backed up to the nearest tree. The walls of the gap had been perfectly smooth and there was the sound of running water echoing up from below.

"Slissac," she said. Now she really was worried but there was nothing she could say. If they were careful, nobody would be alerted— though now she was concerned about the light.

"How do you know?"

"Are there patterns marked into the walls?"

There was a pause. "Yes. Everywhere but in straight lines."

"It's them." *I hope this is another abandoned place, I don't think I could keep us alive without Chara.* Perhaps she should tell Jaymis the truth—but he would be hurt she hadn't told him immediately.

"We can't search in the dark," she said as a distraction.

"No, I know. Let's find somewhere away from this hole."

They headed uphill further into the woods and found another flatter area.

"So why did the moss light up?" he asked as they, once again, set up a camp.

"Because I concentrated on its patterns."

"I meant the first time."

She thought she knew where this conversation was going. "Because I was lying on it. It just responds to the power."

"It didn't do that until I kissed you."

"I think," she said, "that you are fishing for a compliment."

"You were excited by my kiss."

"I was *not*, I was just…"

"What?"

"Focused. It had nothing to do with you."

"Just my kiss."

"Only indirectly." She knew she was blushing but was confident he couldn't see it.

"I find that acceptable."

"Do you?"

"That I have a magical kiss? Yes."

She harrumphed, turned over and closed her eyes. As lightly as she could she opened her senses to the world around her and felt the patterns. The trees glowed with life and the creatures that lived in, on and around them. She did not sense anything large in the vicinity and there had been no further sign of the *tekrak*.

SHE WOKE with the dawn and found herself staring into the face of Jaymis. They both needed a shave: his face and her head. She rolled over the other way and sat up. The air was damp but fresh with the fragrance of flowers. Mist rolled between the tree trunks, flowing down towards the marsh. The air was filled with the cries of flying creatures and animals. She had no idea what any of them were.

In the daylight she could not tell if the moss-lights they had made were still glowing. They did not need them now, but they might later.

She stood and headed for the Slissac-made gap. The cut stone could have been either human or Slissac, but the patterns were clear and recognisable. She held tight to a tree and peeped round it but she was too far away and couldn't see the bottom. Sighing, she lay down, wriggled slowly to the edge to peer over.

It was a deep drop to a river, flowing fast. It ran in a straight line to the marsh—the sides descending and then plunging into the water, as the river rushed out to join it. This confirmed her idea that the marsh was relatively recent.

In the other direction, the channel ran a short distance and then disappeared into the hill. That's where the Slissac town, or port, or whatever it was, would be. And there should be a way in from the surface if her experience was anything to go by. What was concerning was whether this place was still occupied.

She pushed herself back from the edge until she felt safe enough to stand and headed back to the camp. Jaymis was still asleep, she remembered the story of Eftena and how the prince woke her—well, she wasn't going to do that, but she could kiss him.

He was still on his side, so it was a bit more awkward than she hoped, but their lips made contact. He tried to brush her away. She jerked back as he slapped her on the cheek. His eyes opened and looked into hers.

"Did I just hit you?"

"Yes."

"Sorry."

After they had eaten, they packed up and headed cautiously for the top of the hill above the Slissac waterway. When Elona saw the collapsed walls covered with moss, grass and even trees growing through them she breathed a sigh of relief. The place was long abandoned. They stood among the ruins of an ancient building. It was older, and in considerably worse state, than the ones she had seen before. She could barely even make out its outlines.

What she couldn't see was the entrance to the interior. There was almost nothing left to get any bearings, they needed faster transport and a Slissac boat was the best choice for her.

"There will be a way down somewhere here," said Elona. "We just have to find it."

"We can't shift all of this," he said.

She knew he was trying to be gentle and sensible, but he was the only person available and took the brunt of her annoyance.

"We have to get in!"

"Well, you find the entrance then!"

"It's right there," she said in exasperation, pointing to a place where a corner between walls had not completely collapsed. The roots of a tree had broken the stones but now they held them together

"Is it?" he asked.

She blinked and looked at her finger as if it wasn't a part of her, and then at the stones. There was a hint of patterning about them. "I think it might be."

Jaymis found a flat piece of rock and scraped away the surface grass and soil. The thin layer hid a slab of stone which he managed to clear completely. There were geometric patterns across it. He struck it several times with his rock.

"Sounds like it might be hollow underneath, but I have no idea how we can get it up. This soil round the edges is as hard as mortar."

"It is the way in," she said. "Those patterns still have some power in them."

"What are they patterns for?" said Jaymis. "Any kind of trap?"

"Out of the way," said Elona and pulled her dagger from its sheath as Jaymis scrabbled to the side. "I think it might be for concealment, but it doesn't matter."

She placed the dagger at the centre of the stone and pressed. It slid through like a hot knife through butter.

"Taymar's teeth," muttered Jaymis.

Holding the small hilt carefully Elona pulled it sideways through the stone. The energy of the patterning that she had been able to see faded to nothing as the blade cut through the symbols. Once she reached the side, she went through the process again slicing in the other direction.

The line she made was not straight but there was a clear cut running from one side to the other now. She did the same again between the other two sides.

She had expected the pieces to fall away, but they remained where they were.

"Perhaps the blade isn't long enough," said Jaymis.

"I can gouge out a channel to get deeper."

"Well, let's see if some stupid armsman strength will do the trick, stand back."

Elona examined the blade, which looked the way it always had, and then re-sheathed it before getting up and moving away.

Jaymis selected a large stone, hefted it above his head and slammed it into the cut flagstone. With a crack, the centre gave way, and the four triangular pieces fell inward a short distance but came to a stop with Jaymis's stone sitting in the middle of them.

He leaned forward and placed both hands on the wall at the side then hit one of the pieces with his heel. Nothing moved, and the pieces were now firmly wedged.

"Good work with the stupid armsman strength," she said and gave him a little shove to get him to move away. She examined the edge of the flagstone where it was still being supported and sliced a piece of stone from the corner. It fell way into the dark below and she heard it as it struck something a short distance below.

At least it wasn't too far down.

She could see now that the blade was a finger-width shorter than the stone was deep, which is why she hadn't been able to cut all the way through. Jaymis's stone had snapped the rest—it hadn't been useless.

Using the hole, she had made as the starting point, at intervals a hands-breadth apart, she made vertical incisions in the stone, top to bottom. Then she cut diagonally along the length of the stone the pieces broke away as she reached each of her vertical cuts.

Nothing happened until the final section became detached. The big triangular piece she'd been working on no longer had any support along its outer edge and it fell away into the dark. As it went, the other three parts went down one after the other, crashing and tumbling into the darkness.

"Moss," said Elona as she sheathed the dagger and held out her hand.

It took Jaymis a few moments, but he deposited some of the moss they'd kept into her hand. She focused for a moment and it glowed dimly in the daylight, she leaned forward looking into the blackness and dropped it.

CHAPTER 25

From what they could see, there had once been a wooden stairway down. The remains of it were visible among the broken stones. But the drop was not too far.

"I'll go first," said Jaymis.

"Pride?"

"I'm taller."

He let himself down into the hole until he was holding onto the edge with his hands and then dropped. She heard him grunt as he landed. Moments later he picked up the glowing moss, looked around and then tossed it further in, beyond where Elona could see.

His voice echoed up from below. "I'm just going to clear the floor then you can come down."

She watched as he did so then sat on the edge herself and wriggled in until she was supporting herself on her elbows. She managed to swing down the same way as Jaymis and let go.

His arms went round her as she dropped and caught under her arms. He grunted again as if something hurt. She thought she'd have made a more comfortable landing if he hadn't helped, but she didn't say anything. Instead she let him kiss her and let her go.

Her eyes adjusted and she found herself in a strangely familiar place. The tunnels of the Slissac were always covered with patternings though with her new experience, she knew most of them were not for magic. They were simply stories, or perhaps information. Not that she could decipher them.

But the small piece of glowing moss told her what she needed to know. Along every wall, close to the ceiling, were ledges with moss spilling over them. She tuned in to the pattern needed, spread her arms in an unnecessary flourish, focused her power, and the place lit up in all directions.

Jaymis just made a noise of surprise. And she felt very pleased with herself. It was such a different experience than the first time, and she had an easily impressed audience.

"You did that?" he said finally.

"You saw me," she said as she picked up her bag. "Let's go."

This was where she could lead. She knew more about Slissac than any scholar of history. Not only had she explored their ruins, she had lived among them and understood at least some of their ways.

It was all about hierarchy and rank. Where human peasants might get out of the way of a lord on the road, the Slissac would build two roads so the two never met. And the more populous the area, the more levels of road they built. She had almost been killed simply for using the wrong gate.

They were a good way above the river, but the passage led in the right direction, so she headed off. Jaymis drew his sword and followed.

They passed through several smaller chambers until they came out into a large one with a raised dais at the far end. It reminded Elona of the matriarchs' audience chamber in the Slissac town. There were even partitions at this end so that those of lower caste could be in the room without seeing those higher up.

She stopped in the middle and almost felt as if she shouldn't be there, as if a matriarch would call for her execution. *But I am the sister of a matriarch, I am of their rank.*

"What's wrong?" Jaymis's voice sounded strained. As it echoed between the walls, there was almost a palpable sense that he was an interloper. He was only male. She wanted to tell him to keep quiet, but then she would have to explain.

"Nothing, just getting my bearings."

Only half the moss was glowing in this room and, with barely a thought, she lit the rest.

There was a crash of metal against stone and she turned to see Jaymis crumpling to the ground. She dashed over trying to sense if there was some special magic here, some pattern affecting him that did not touch her. She felt nothing.

"Jaymis?" she pleaded with him as she tried to turn him over. The light wasn't good, but he looked pale—strained. She realised her hand was wet.

"Mother's curse, you're bleeding!" The wound must have reopened —the jump down and catching her. "Oh, you idiot. Why didn't you say?"

She pulled his clothing away to see what had happened.

It was bad. She didn't understand it but he was bleeding far worse than he had originally. How could that be? But her fingers were slippery from his blood as it dripped on to the floor.

"Elona." His voice was weak.

"I'm here."

"Heal, please."

"Hush." She stared at the wound. "You'll be fine. I'll just sew and bandage it."

But she didn't move.

"Heal, please."

"I *can't*."

"Trust you."

She touched the hard ridges of skin on her cheek.

"There's no ley-circle."

"Do best."

It had to be this place. He was male. He did not belong. It must be a patterning.

And I gave it the power it needed.

She stood up and looked about. They were almost in the centre of the room, she could not easily drag him to the exit, not without making the injury worse.

"Please."

She knelt beside him again. No choice.

She closed her eyes and placed her hands over the wound. It wasn't necessary but it helped her to concentrate her mind. She looked at the wound with her other sense. The shapes and patterns formed in her mind; she could see the normal skin around the wound as the pattern that should be. And the broken pattern of his injury—not a single one but so very many of them.

Just as it had been for Drahail, she focused on rebuilding the pattern the way it should be. She was terrified that there might be a void close by and its chaos would infect him the way it had her. But she promised herself she would simply stop if that happened.

She concentrated on one edge of the wound and mended it. The patterns joined and extended into the damaged area reducing its size. She pressed forwards closing the wound from the inside towards the skin.

What is that?

She saw instantly that there was a pattern here that did not belong. It was not complex, but it had edges like a saw and as fast as she could mend the patterns, it tore them to pieces again.

This was it. This was the curse that had somehow implanted into him. The magic she had triggered that latched on to his injury and re-opened it, destroying the patterns that held his body together.

She had to stop it, but if she did that, she would have to stop the healing. And if she failed either way, he would die. Just at that moment they were in balance, but she would tire, and all her inmost power would be used up.

She thought of her mother, the healer.

A strange duality came through. The healing continued though she was no longer focused on it. Barely trusting herself Elona turned her attention to the malevolent pattern. She did not know the symbols that would have brought it into existence—she did not think the patterners of the human world even had this knowledge.

How do I stop it?

I put the power into it, can I take it out?

She approached it, as if she were truly moving. The cutting thing sliced at her and she felt the pain. She pulled back but it did not follow her.

You are mine. I created you.

She moved in again, staying clear of its pattern-blades.

If you are mine, I can change you.

She moved in quickly and received the strange patterning into herself.

Immediately she could see that it was no longer damaging Jaymis. And in the next moment, the pain of its attack seared through her. She was power and it was eating her. Jaymis's healing stopped as she collapsed to the ground screaming in pain.

She tried to focus, to change the nature of thing that consumed her.

I cannot die. He needs me!

But she was in pain and confused, it fed on her power as it destroyed her from within.

"No!" she screamed, and her voice echoed.

The blackness of the void welled up within her, she saw it like a wave, she moulded it, guided it, wrapped it around the pattern that ate her and smothered it.

It became nothing inside of her. Just another black scar.

The healing that now seemed unconnected to her continued once more, this time unopposed and rapidly sealed up Jaymis's wound.

She took a deep breath and knelt upright. Her back ached and her hands were thick with Jaymis's blood. But when she wiped him clean, his skin was whole once more.

She felt very tired, but they needed to get out of this hall, if she unthinkingly lit the moss again it might trigger another one of these patterns, perhaps something even worse.

It took a while to drag Jaymis to the exit she thought was the best one—he remained unconscious the whole time. He had lost a worrying quantity of blood. They made it to another corridor and the top of a flight of stairs. She wouldn't be able to get him down it, so she made a camp.

He came round enough to drink some water and, when she was sure he was sleeping again, she slept too.

～

SHE WOKE in complete darkness again. The thought she might trigger another violent protective pattern if she attempted to light the moss scared her. Instead she spent time with the flints making a real fire, not that they had much that would burn here.

Using one of the burning brands as a torch she went back to the room where they had entered and collect the remains of the stairs—it was night and a drizzle was falling through the hole they'd made.

With those pieces she was able to build a decent fire next to Jaymis. When he woke, she gave him water and most of their remaining food.

He was insistent on knowing what had happened so she explained it as best she could.

"It was my fault," she said.

"You had no idea that was going to happen."

"I should have thought."

He sighed weakly. "How could you possibly know how *Slissac* might think, or what they might do?"

His comment multiplied her guilt a thousand-fold. She wondered if she could tell him the truth, but what would he do with the knowledge that the *Slissac* lived so close to them?

He would tell the Conclave and they would lead an army into the mountains to kill the ancient enemy. And one of those would be Chara.

It was a secret that could never be revealed.

When he was resting again, she went down the stairs. The air became cold and damp as she came out into a huge cave—its further limits were hidden in shadow, but water lapped against stones of the dock. Her heart froze as she saw how much it resembled the place she and Chara had entered when escaping the Tirnian armsmen. The underground *Slissac* port where Chara's parents had been murdered when another family wiped them out.

The difference here was that, as far as she could see, there was no boat. And the torch she was using was not going to last.

She could not see any way out, though there was bound to be a canal further along. She set off along the dock. Just as before there were storage areas set behind doors—but they were rotted with the years of damp revealing emptiness behind them. If there had been a boat, it would have gone the same way.

The place she and Chara had found had only been abandoned for perhaps ten years or so. It had been in use when Chara had escaped the assassins, but this place was much older.

She reached the end of the dock and her flickering light revealed the dark tunnel of the canal leading away under the hills. As she stared at the water, a piece of wood floated from the tunnel, moving sluggishly along a slow-moving current.

This wasn't the river they had seen. That was a torrent.

As she headed back her light went out.

She stopped moving immediately and sighed. That made things a little more difficult, the place was completely dark, not the slightest hint of light, and it was night outside anyway.

She needed light. This place was unlikely to have any traps, and she was a long way from Jaymis. She could probably light some moss here safely. She pulled a handful from her bag; it was already glowing gently simply from being close to her. That made it easier to focus only on this piece and feed it some of her energy.

It brightened immediately.

As did clumps of the moss which lay all around her but only out to a short distance. At the same time, there was a splashing from the water which faded almost immediately.

She worried there might be *dakasa* here, but she hadn't seen any lights in the water. She took out her dagger and held it ready as she moved closer to the edge of the dock.

The water was black but reflected the light she held.

As gently as she could, as if it made any difference, she fed her power to the moss. Instantly ripples appeared in the water moving out from the side of the dock, and she thought she saw something move beneath the surface.

She searched for a stone and managed to locate one of reasonable size. She wrapped it with glowing moss and dropped it in. The water was clear as crystal. She watched the light sink to the bottom and come to rest. It stirred up silt as it hit, which clouded the water for a few moments but then it cleared as the gentle current carried it away.

There was something growing on the dock wall. Thin, finger-length strands poked out in a dense, gently waving mass.

She tried to remember how she had driven the boat, with the tiny creatures that clung to its bottom. At the time it had seemed to be the same as when she lit the moss, she may have learnt a lot since then but there was still nothing to distinguish it in her mind.

She focused on the strands she could see and fed them the way she did the moss. In a convulsive move, a wave appeared in the strands themselves rippling outward and stirring up the surface of the water.

She sat back on the dock. These were considerably larger than the ones that had propelled the boat she and Chara had been on, but it behaved the same way. Either they were related or they were the same, but just grown bigger.

Her interest flagged. She was getting hungry and this did nothing to help them. She had been hoping for a faster form of travel but there was nothing here. If only she were able to make her patterner path on command, but she did not have the slightest idea of how it worked, nor did she want to try since she could end up anywhere.

CHAPTER 26

She hurried to the other end of the dock and found it ended in a blank wall. She sacrificed another piece of glowing moss and found the water outlet at the base of the wall. She had no desire to get wet.

The corridor she had taken was not the right one—assuming there was any exit to the outside. But this was the Slissac and, from her experience, they lived in fear of attack and had escape routes, just like the one in the Liralain Tower.

She hurried back to Jaymis.

He was awake and had added some more wood to the fire.

"I thought you'd left me."

She expected him to say such a thing with a smile, but he seemed deadly serious.

"I found a dock but there are no boats."

"You should be careful there might have been *dakasa*."

She shook her head. "Not here, unfortunately there's no exit to the lake. Only a canal that runs into the hills."

"Underground?"

"Yes. I've seen it before."

"How could they make such a thing?"

"I don't know." That, at least, was the truth.

There was a pause. "What happened to me?"

"I think I triggered a pattern that attacked you," she said. "I'm sorry."

"Why not you?"

"What do you mean?"

"Why did it attack me and not you, if you were the one who triggered it."

"I don't know. Perhaps it perceived you as the real threat. I wasn't important."

She cringed at her own lie. It was hard enough not telling him about the Slissac, but when he asked questions like that. How could she tell him the truth?

He opened his mouth to speak but she placed her hand over it.

There was a sound—she was sure of it. He had said nothing but in the light of the fire and the moss she saw him frowning at her.

She placed her finger against her own lips. Hardly making a sound she whispered "Listen."

There was nothing for a long time. Then…something. On the very edge of her hearing. Was it a scrape of something hard against stone?

She got up as silently as she could. Jaymis's hand went to his sword lying in its sheath on the floor next to him. She shook her head vigorously; he would make far too much noise. She jabbed her finger first at him and then at the floor.

There was a pause and then he nodded reluctantly. He wasn't strong enough.

Leaving all the lights behind but running her hand along the grooves in the patterned wall, Elona crept back towards the audience chamber.

She knew there was trouble before she reached it—there were lights bobbing and flickering in the far passageway, the one that they had come in by.

Elona froze against the left wall which gave her the most cover, watching the yellow light dance across the opposite wall.

"What is this place?"

"Slissac."

When she heard the Taymalin words a huge weight was lifted from her. For some reason the thought that it might be Slissac was far more terrifying then mere humans. If it had been the lizard people returned, her secrets would be revealed and, if they got out alive, Chara would be in danger. Taymalin were far less important. But this meant they must be the same group, Jaymis's friend had talked about in Esternes.

"*Kisharuk*'s curse, what they doing down here?"

The men were whispering but, in this silence, they might as well have been talking to her directly.

Elona felt about her with her senses. There were no wolves, no *zatesa*, just the smallest of creatures, *kikisa*, but although she had seen no sign of them, she could now see there were hundreds of them. They fed on insects and were encouraged in large buildings to help keep the pests down.

She called them.

"What's that?" said one of the men.

His voice was significantly louder now, and the light was more solid, he must be in the main chamber.

Elona heard the strange susurration of an uncountable number of tiny claws on stone. She took a deep breath and stepped out into the audience chamber. And pushed her power into the moss.

Everything exploded in light.

Three warriors stood there, one in the room, the other two at the entrance. They were armed with swords and bows, though not strung, and each carried their own lantern.

They blinked in the sudden brightness.

Then their eyes were on her.

"Go back while you're alive to do so," she said. It wasn't a very clever thing to say and she knew they would take no notice, but she needed to have the upper hand.

The one in the lead laughed. "I'm scared. You'll be the one we're after, I'm guessing. Your bloke hiding in the back is he, or going to ambush us from the side?"

"I don't need him to protect me."

Elona was wondering why the curse pattern in the room hadn't triggered. Perhaps it only worked once. The sound of tiny creatures had been drowned out by the talking but now it was there, all around.

"Is that so, little girl?" He was looking into the shadows trying to make out what was making the noise.

At that moment, a *kikik* hopped into the light from behind Elona. It looked uncertain, then started to clean itself.

This time all the men laughed.

Another one came into the light, and another. Their scaly skin rubbed against each other as more and more moved out of the shadows.

The men stopped laughing. Glancing around Elona could see hundreds of them but while they were visible, they hugged the edges of the room. They were not the flood she hoped for.

The men relaxed again. The one at the front grinned once more. "Do you do any other tricks?"

The *kikisa* went silent as Elona made an image in her mind. She focused and tried to impress the image on the myriad minds about her. These men were dangerous, they were threatening, and wanted to take the *kikisa*'s food.

The tiny creatures turned as one to stare at the huge men. Elona could feel their conflict, they did not want to fight. It was not in their nature. If something bigger wanted to take their food, then that's what happened. That was the way if you wanted to survive.

"Now then, girlie!"

"No!" she screamed. Blackness flowed up within her and poured out carrying her will to the tiny creatures. "*Now,*" she hissed.

Like a wave, the *kikisa* exploded into motion, the ones on the floor skittered at their targets and hundreds more flowed from the passages like a grey tide.

But the leader of the men was not looking at the *kikisa* he was staring at Elona, and there was terror in his eyes. As he felt his clothes being clawed by tiny talons he stared down. Reacting fast, he dashed his lantern to the ground where it smashed open and the oil spilt out, it caught immediately, and flames spread across the floor and into the oncoming flood of creatures.

Kikisa burned, perhaps hundreds of them, but hundreds more did not. They flowed round the flames. The man stamped his feet and killed many as he did so but the ones that remained swarmed up him biting and tearing. He cursed vociferously as he grabbed at them and ripped them from his body by the handful, but it was never enough.

The other two did not think as quickly. The tiny creatures were coming at them from all sides, but they were in a passage and if they had thought they might have thrown down their own lanterns too. Perhaps if they had started to run back along the passage, they might have reached the way out, possibly even escaped.

They did not do either of those things. Perhaps they simply could not believe what was happening. One of the dropped lanterns had fallen on its base and, by its light, Elona watched the horror unfold.

One after the other, the men collapsed to the floor. They continued to flail against the tiny creatures that bit and scratched. But eventually their screams turned to groans and, after a while, the groaning stopped. But the *kikisa* kept attacking, ripping into the flesh of their victims—not even eating them.

Elona's eyes were red and raw with tears. She tried to shrug away the void, but it would not stop, it was not part of her and it drove the little monsters on. The blackness did not respond to her will. She became desperate.

"*Stop!*" The final effort blasted away the liquid night that had engulfed her, that had driven the *kikisa* and the room was instantly silent.

Elona staggered and fell against the wall. In the dimming light of the burning oil, she stared at the death-filled room. The *kikisa* were not gone but like their victims, they too were dead. Every single one of them.

One of the men groaned. The fact one might still be alive shocked her from her stupor. Taking her dagger from its sheath, Elona went to each man in turn, trying not to step on the little corpses just in case there was still life in them. She made sure each man was dead and told herself it was a mercy.

"Sorry," she whispered to the last corpse, and to the hundreds of dead *kikisa*.

"Taymar's teeth," breathed Jaymis from the other passage.

"You can't be here, it's dangerous. You need to be resting."

He staggered into the room and glanced down as something crunched under his foot. He lifted his foot and stared at the crushed body of the *kikik*—not squashed, it had been brittle like glass and simply shattered under his weight.

"What have you done?"

"I saved us."

He looked at the dark forms of human bodies. "Who are they?"

"I don't know."

"You don't know who they are, but you killed them anyway?"

Anger flared in her. "I know they weren't friends—they knew who we are, who we really are, and they'd been sent to fetch us. Somehow they knew we were here."

"How could they possibly know that?"

Jaymis wavered where he stood. Elona managed to get to him before he collapsed and took his weight across her shoulders. She staggered but held him and guided him across the room towards the outside exit.

Once past the bodies, she let him sit down. It did not take her long to fetch their limited equipment, though she spent a little while searching the pockets and bags of the men. They had some food, swords and daggers, two bows with a good number of arrows—she would have taken their jackets too but they were covered in blood.

The remaining lanterns still worked.

She fed Jaymis and gave him more to drink. Then she ate too. They had pies and biscuits as well as some bottled ale in addition to water. She hadn't felt so full in a while.

"I saw all the *kikisa*, they ran past me."

"I summoned them."

"*Kikisa* killed them?"

She did not reply. The answer was self-evident.

"And what happened to the *kikisa?*"

She wanted to lie, anything except admit the truth. "I forced them too hard, they died." *I summoned the void and it did my bidding, but I could not control it.*

He said nothing to that.

"They came flying a giant *tekrak,*" she said finally.

"How do you know?"

"I saw it."

"When?"

"Yesterday."

"Why didn't you tell me?"

"Because they were passing us by, they weren't coming towards us at all." She could not tell whether he was looking at her suspiciously, or he was just tired with his eyelids drooping. "I made a mistake."

He didn't say anything for a long time. "We must get control of it."

"No."

"You said yourself we need to move faster."

She shook her head. "*I can't.* To be up high, floating. You don't know what it's like..." Her voice trailed away.

He raised his chin and looked directly at her.

"But you do."

She stared at him and then acknowledged with a nod of her head.

"You've been in one."

She nodded again.

"Why didn't you tell me?"

She closed her eyes and felt tears welling up again. She wiped them away with the back of her hand and saw blood streaked there. Not her own. "I can't tell you."

"This is how you got to Aris, isn't it?"

She stared at him.

"Why won't you tell me?"

"Because if I do, someone I love will die!"

"Someone you love?"

The anger bubbled up inside her again. "Is that all you can think?

That if I love someone, they must be a rival to you? Well, perhaps she is, but I won't betray her just because you're jealous."

"She? I don't understand."

"Of course, you don't."

"I don't because you won't explain!"

"I can't!" Her voice was hoarse.

His head drooped in exhaustion. "Why not?"

"Because I can't trust you."

He stopped and she could see him forcing himself to calm down. "When have I done anything to make you think you can't trust me, Elona? I saved you the very first time we met. I only chased you to rescue you. I came with you on this journey. I have stayed with you all this time. I have agreed to everything, including this crazy idea of taking down the emperor." He shook his head in non-comprehension. "I told you I love you. I have been honourable, and I have respected your suffering. And speaking of suffering, I have done that for you too. There is nothing in my actions that would suggest I cannot be trusted." He took a breath. "Whatever the reason for your lack of faith, Lady Elona of Corlain, it does not lie within me."

She stared at him and then looked down at the lantern glowing between them. She was numb. Numb from the fight and numb with the fear. As if her entire body was filled with the void. *Perhaps it is.*

Her throat was dry, and swallowing did not help.

"If I tell you, you have to promise you will never tell anyone."

"Of course."

"No, Jaymis! This is not a child's secret. This is not Elona being mistreated at the hands of bad men. This secret is bigger than the Conclave. On this secret hangs the lives of armies. If you speak of this, tens of thousands might die, and the *Kisharuk*'s curse will be on the world. You do not understand what it's like to hide this secret. It's the weight of the World's Pattern on my shoulders alone—do you think you can bear that?"

It seemed she had made him think, at least, as he did not respond for a while.

"Perhaps I can share the weight of your burden, Elona. If you choose to tell me, I promise it will stay our secret. I will not press you to tell anyone else. And I promise this on my Father's pattern."

"I do not believe in Tahulin, Jaymis," she said, "but I thank you for your promise. I won't tell you everything just the important parts now. Try not to overreact."

His eyebrows creased then he gave a slight, though tired, smile. "You met Taymar?"

"No, not him. He's been dead a very long time. But I have met Slissac, and one of them is my adopted sister."

He looked at her as if he was expecting her to laugh. "You're not serious?"

"My sister is Chara ko-Tek Tegina ar-Tek Guala ar-Gey Aytrueth Aka Hanna ar-Ku Jyrna ko-Ku Jyrna Aka Kalenaye. She is the matriarch of a Slissac family living in a town in the central mountains. I won't explain how that happened. The Slissac wanted to kill me but she saved my life. With her help, I managed to get away flying in a giant *tekrak* which brought me to Aris."

"Slissac live in the central mountains?"

"Yes, but they're keeping themselves to themselves. They want nothing to do with us and they don't want a war. And neither do we. You see? If this was known, the Conclave would lead an army into the mountains. It would unify everyone. But they would have to battle the Slissac on their home ground. So many would be killed and to what end? They would never succeed in killing them all."

"But Slissac?"

"Jaymis, you're not listening to me."

"I am, Elona. It's just hard to imagine."

"The Slissac used to have the ability to make creatures that would work the way we make machines. I'm not sure if they can still do it— but the glowing moss, the creatures that drive their boats, and the giant *tekrasa*. I didn't tell you what I saw because I thought it might be Slissac."

"And you have a sister who is a Slissac."

"I didn't want to get into this. Yes, but she was brought up by Usala who found her wandering, and they lived in this village in the mountains until I turned up. Chara rescued me, though I thought she was going to kill me, or enslave me at first. She took me back to Usala."

Her heart felt heavy as she remembered. "Then the soldiers came and Usala stayed behind as Chara and I escaped. We ended up in a Slissac town and it turned out that Chara was supposed to be dead because she was the heir to a major family who had been wiped out." She sighed. "Things happened. Eventually I left, riding in one of those things, and flew to Aris."

"How do they work? The *tekrasa*."

"They need a patterner to control them and it's complicated. At night they land and feed, but they must be controlled, tied down, otherwise they'll just fly off."

"So there's one of these things nearby with a patterner to control it."

She glared at him. She knew what he was thinking, and the problem was that she knew it was their best choice. There was no boat here and if they took the canal, there was no telling where it might end up. Flying was quicker than walking.

There was no further discussion.

She helped him to his feet and between them they carried as much equipment as they could. When they reached the hole, there was a knotted rope hanging down.

Jaymis looked at it unhappily but at least it was something.

"You go first," she said. "I can help you. I'll tie the equipment to the rope, and you pull it up. Then I'll climb up."

He nodded and removed everything he was carrying. Even the walk from the end of the passage had been exhausting for him. But there was no time to rest.

She piled up the stones, it only gave four hands-breadth of height, but it was a little less to climb. She stood on the bottom of the rope and stabilised it as he went up.

"Put your feet on my shoulders," she said as his head came level with the outside air. She guided him into place, and he stood there for a long time. Probably trying to gather his strength. Then the weight went from her as he heaved himself up.

There was nothing she could do as she watched his feet dangling while his top half disappeared into the light. His legs moved out, so they were more horizontal, and he rolled over into a sitting position above her.

"Is everything all right?"

His feet disappeared rapidly, and she knew he could not have done it on his own. There were men out there.

A brawny figure appeared silhouetted against the light above her.

"You come up nice now, miss, and we won't hurt your friend. Not any more than he's already hurt anyways."

CHAPTER 27

There were three of them. They were dressed the same as those who had gone below but, since their friends had not emerged, they were even more careful. Jaymis had been stripped of anything that could be a weapon and they did the same to her. The dagger, with its sheath and chain, was taken and put into a box along with Jaymis's family ring.

All three stared at her face, a couple of them had scars but they were nothing compared to her. She ran her hand across her cheek and knew it was different. It had spread.

"What's she doing with that?" said one of the men looking at the dagger.

"Never you mind," said the one who seemed to be in charge. "Not your business, nor mine. We just deliver everything."

Jaymis and Elona had their hands tied and their feet hobbled so running was not an option. Then they were left sitting together as one of their captors headed down through the opening.

Shortly afterwards he came back, looking white and shaken. Elona couldn't hear what he was saying but it was probably a description of the dead.

"Can you bring something to kill these ones too?" said Jaymis quietly, and seemingly trying to make it look as if he wasn't talking at all.

She was not going to summon anything if it meant she ended up killing them—and Jaymis had not noticed the wound on her face had spread.

"No."

"But we need to get away."

"They're from Tirnia. That's where they'll take us, and that's where we want to go."

"But we're prisoners."

"We can't fly the *tekrak* and it needs people to tie it down at night. This is easier."

"And if they want to kill us?"

"They would have already done it. Besides, you're still weak, this will give you the opportunity to recover some strength."

"It doesn't seem a very safe strategy, Elona, what if we can't escape when we get to the other end?"

She didn't have an answer for that but she knew that she needed to save herself for the confrontation with Emperor Myrlask, even if it meant the void would consume her, the way it had killed the *kikisa*.

Movement among their captors meant Jaymis went quiet, which prevented any further awkward questions.

The men looked grim as they came over. One of them hung back, holding his bow with an arrow strung.

"One fancy word or pattern from either of you, and there'll be an arrow through your neck sooner than you can breathe," said the leader.

They had to be helped to their feet then, in procession, they set off through the woods. Two of the men in the lead, and the one with the bow behind—still with the arrow at the ready.

It seemed Jaymis had resigned himself to her plan, such as it was, since he was too weak to get away on his own. She had to help him as they moved through the trees. Their hobbles had not been untied so they made only slow progress with Jaymis leaning on her heavily. The men did not push them to go faster.

The group descended slowly through the trees towards the mere. Elona wondered whether they knew about the *dakasa*, she would not feel so bad about using those monstrous creatures even if they did die afterwards—but the effect on her own body was enough to prevent her.

I must wait until it truly counts.

The void from the Mother's Kitchen. It wasn't a nothing, calling it a void was not right. It was something. Patternless but powerful. Perhaps it was chaos. There were stories that went back long before Taymar, and Bejeren had touched on them when she was being taught.

Before the beginning of all things was chaos. Patterns were made which brought the world from the chaos.

The smell of cooking meat dragged her from her thoughts and made her mouth water. They were descending through the last stand of trees and the huge green *tekrasa*, rooted in the moist soil, came into view. A huge net went over the top of it with ropes attached to big metal spikes in the ground. It was bigger than most of the townhouses of Corlain. In front of it, closer to them, lay the gondola in which they would ride.

The Slissac gondolas were bigger but this one seemed to be of more solid construction. It differed in style and was clearly built by the hand of man. She could not imagine how the emperor had managed to get these *tekrasa* and perhaps there was no connection with the Slissac after all.

In front of the gondola was a good-sized fire with a metal tripod over it. A fourth man was tending the fire and the food which was the source of the delicious smell. Inside the gondola sat a man in patterner robes, he would be controlling the creature even now since it was their nature to fly in daytime. The *tekrak* looked just like a bulbous plant with overlapping leaves but it was on a tremendous scale.

"Mother's Milk," breathed Jaymis as he took in the size of it.

Elona realised it would be better if she acted the same way to keep her knowledge hidden from their captors. "What is it?" She tried to add a slightly panicked tone to her voice and stopped moving.

The man behind them laughed. "Keep walking."

Their sudden appearance from the woods startled a small flock of long-necked wading birds that took off in a panic, making a strange honking noise. Moments later, a geyser of water shot up from the mere with tremendous force. It soaked half a dozen of the birds, they all staggered in the air, but one was either stunned or waterlogged and fell back.

As it hit the water, yellow-ish translucent tentacles emerged from the calm surface, folded over the bird, and dragged it down. Its fearful cry cut short. The others climbed fast and disappeared.

"Ha! You see that?" said one of the men ahead of them. In her head, Elona was calling him Baldy—he had enough healed wounds across his scalp he might have been called Scar, but she thought that made him seem too brave.

"I knew we stopped too close to the water." That was the one she thought of as Bushy because of his black beard. He was the cautious one that had insisted they were both properly tied up.

"Nothing to worry about," said Baldy, he seemed to be the leader although she guessed the patterner wouldn't see him that way.

"We should get out."

"Food's not ready." They were approaching the fire now and that last comment was from the very dark-skinned Kadralin tending the fire.

The smell was delightful, and at odds with their situation.

"What if those milk-sour *dakasa* decide we're their next dinner?"

The patterner looked out from the gondola. "I've set wards, they don't even know we're here."

Elona and Jaymis were forced over to the gondola itself, made to sit with their backs to it. Their hands were fastened to struts above their heads. It was not comfortable.

"You seen her face," said Baldy talking at the patterner.

"What about it?"

"Looks funny, you should see."

"Don't waste my time."

"Looks like a healing gone wrong."

He would have been surprised at how accurate his guess was.

"Healings don't go wrong," said the patterner.

There was silence but Baldy's face gained an unpleasant grin and she heard the patterner moving along the length of the gondola behind her until he appeared through the main opening.

He was young, probably a journeyman barely out of his apprenticeship. His hair was as dark as Bushy's, and from the similar shape of their noses, they might have been related. He peered at Elona's cheek then moved to her side, squatted down and stared.

He reached out to touch her and she jerked her head away.

"Leave her alone." She admired his spirit, but Jaymis's voice was weak and he was helpless. Baldy laughed and kicked him in the thigh. Jaymis bit back a cry.

But Jaymis's comment seemed to have reminded the young patterner that Elona was a person, he focused on her eyes. "Does it hurt?"

She stared back at him. "We're hungry."

"Tell me and you can have some food."

"Give us food and I'll tell you."

"None of that," said Baldy. "You stop asking her questions that are none of your business. You just look after the beast. And you, girl, you'll get food when I decide."

The patterner frowned at the older man but only after he had turned away—though he did not try to hide his expression from Elona. He took another long look at the damage to her cheek then got up and went back into the gondola.

Elona had lost all feeling in her arms when she was finally untied and given a bowl of meat. They let her eat first but tied her up again before giving Jaymis his food.

Their captors ate, drank something alcoholic, then engaged in bawdy talk for a while. It was nothing Elona had not heard before. Men were all the same. Bragging about the women they claimed they'd had or would have liked to. The patterner only emerged to collect his food and did not join in.

He paused to stare at Elona once more before re-entering the gondola.

She watched everything. In the distance, across the mere, water-spouts shot up every now and again, sometimes two at once. There must be hundreds of *dakasa* in the lake.

Perhaps it was a good thing they had not found a boat; they would not have survived half a day in that water.

"If I give you extra food, will you tell me?"

The voice of the patterner came from behind. She did not turn her head or give any obvious sign she had heard anything.

"Him. Not me."

"All right, let's go," shouted Baldy.

The men sprang into action, packing up the camp with efficiency. The remaining cooked meat was packed in bags and the fire extinguished with a bucket of water from the lake. The Kadralin did not seem concerned about the *dakasa* but apparently trusted the patterner's wards.

To Elona's relief her arms were released. She and Jaymis were led into the gondola and tied to struts on opposite sides near the middle—unfortunately she was going to have a clear view of the ground. From where she sat, she could see the patterner easily and watched him extract a small book. He located a page and quickly copied a pattern on to a slate.

With her hidden sense, she saw the power flowing like a gold-white stream from him as he activated it. Moments later, the *tekrak* rippled, its long roots flexed and withdrew from the ground. It strained against the net and ropes holding it down as it tried to take flight.

Tekrasa could not think, as far as she knew, so it would not even understand that it was not soaring into the sky. The control provided by these special patterns must be very precise, since its fire tube should have ignited immediately. She had never noticed that before but had been the same with the Slissac patterners.

She looked over at Jaymis, he was staring in astonishment, and perhaps a little fear, as the men unhooked the ropes and dragged the great floating monster across to the gondola.

The shadow went over them and the patterner activated a new set of symbols. The energy flowed and the roots unfolded once more and ran down the outside of the gondola, feeling their way as if each was a living tentacle. Some wrapped themselves around the struts—one barely missed gripping Elona's wrists and forearms—others simply folded into the roof. The grip tightened and the structure groaned.

The men tied off the ropes onto the gondola and climbed aboard as the next pattern took effect and the whole vessel lifted into the air. Elona made the mistake of glancing out and her stomach turned over as the ground slipped away.

She focused on the patterner. In the space at the front there were patterns etched into the gondola's structure and now he used those. He activated one and the great beast turned ponderously until it was pointing in the direction that she and Jaymis had been travelling.

One final pattern and the creature's fire tube roared into life. She was pushed back in her seat as the creature accelerated through the air. A constant wind blew through as they headed along the valley. If she looked in Jaymis's direction, she could see the hills in the distance and not the ground, which helped.

He had been staring out as well, though he was looking down, then, as if he felt her gaze on her, he turned and looked back.

The expression on his face was a combination of fear and excitement but suppressed to avoid notice from their captors. She kept her own face calm. Now Jaymis would understand why the idea of taking the vessel themselves was impossible.

There was not a lot of the day left and while a *tekrasa* could be forced to fly at night, it was simpler not to try. She was sure they would set down before it went dark.

Clouds were building up and there was the occasional gust that came in from a different angle than their direction of travel. The patterner was making regular adjustments to keep them on course.

That must be tiring, there's no ley circle so he must be drawing on his own power.

She turned to look behind, the four other men were gazing idly out into the distance apart from the one playing some card game. She turned to face forward when Baldy glared at her.

"Hey!" The patterner called back and Baldy made his way forward.

There was a heated discussion and while the patterner might have been deferent on the ground, he was a different person now. Elona couldn't make out the words but the patterner kept pointing down.

Finally, the argument ceased.

The *tekrak* was forced to turn until they were heading directly into the gusting wind and they descended. The roar from the fire tube became intermittent. She was sure the strength of the patterner must be failing as he fought to bring the vessel down to the ground in the strong winds.

Taking a breath, she made herself take a quick look at the area below her.

The big lake was nowhere in sight. They must have been blown off course—she knew the Slissac preferred to follow rivers and roads, so they knew where they were and where they were going. This *tekrak* was now surrounded by wooded hills.

She and Jaymis exchanged glances again. Did he understand there was a problem? The argument was probably sufficient to reveal it but unless he had better hearing than she did, he wouldn't understand why.

When she had been in the Slissac gondola, she had been hidden and was not aware enough to perceive how badly the mountain winds had affected the flight. But, if it had been blown about, the reptilian patterner had been very experienced and confident. He had dealt with it.

This journeyman patterner had no such skill.

But still, she did not want them to fail. At least not yet.

However, there was nothing she could do except close her eyes and pray to the Mother they landed safely.

Moments after shutting them there was a tremendous crack and the vessel lurched to one side. Convulsively she grabbed the strut tighter and felt the rough hairy surface of a root.

The strange power of the *tekrak* glowed in her hands as the vessel lurched again. She desperately wanted to feed her own energy into the patterns being made—but she dare not reveal herself and clamped down hard on her impulses.

Another crack and she was thrown forwards. It felt as if something were trying to yank her arms from their sockets—someone behind her cried out in pain. The nauseating scent of the *tekrak*'s gases filled the air making her choke.

Then they fell abruptly and came to a shuddering halt with no motion at all. She felt the root slithering beneath her hands.

No!

Without thinking she sent her wild magic through the beast freezing its motion. Instantly she realised her mistake and let go. She opened her eyes and forced herself to check Jaymis. He was still on the other side to her, trying to get back on his feet as he hung from the strut by his ties.

The patterner was still in his seat and she saw flashes of power.

The *tekrak* recovered from its momentary stasis and the roots writhed as if they wanted to let go. She hoped the patterner would not notice what had happened.

Whether he had or not he turned and shouted to his compatriots. "I'll keep it on the ground—you have to make a space for it to root!"

The way they moved quickly to follow his instructions confirmed Elona's suspicion they were not simple mercenaries, or criminals. They acted like experienced armsmen familiar with obeying orders.

CHAPTER 28

It had been a difficult period and full of action as the men leapt from the gondola. She had been horrified when Baldy had told Bushy to make holes in the *tekrak*'s body. Then she realised why—the gas helped it to lift and by letting some out they were able to keep it under better control.

The gondola slumped to the ground at a steep angle leaving her and Jaymis hanging painfully while the armsmen worked hard to clear a space for the beast between several trees. The patterner improvised as he tried to prevent the creature from flying away and managed to get some of the roots to grip tree branches.

Between them they eventually got the plant away from the gondola and staked to the ground. Then they returned to right the gondola.

"When can we get up again?"

"The *tekrak* needs to heal and recharge."

"How long?"

"A day."

"But it can fly as long as it's not leaking, right?"

"We can't travel in this weather." The patterner pointed at the sky where the clouds raced. "Unless you want us all to die."

"If we stay low—"

"Look at the treetops, it's too strong anyway but just one bad gust and we'll be dragged through the trees. And where will your precious cargo be then?"

"I'm in charge!"

"Not the *tekrak*." The patterner took a deep breath. "You can't go anywhere without me."

Baldy closed on the young man and grabbed him by the throat. "Don't threaten me. I don't have to kill you to make you piss your breeches and scream for your mama."

Then he thrust his arm out and struck the patterner with the palm of his hand. The poor fellow was caught off balance and stumbled back, falling on his behind.

"You say we can't fly, all right, we can't. But we need to be on the move as soon as we can. Understand?"

The patterner nodded.

Baldy turned away then looked back. "Set up your wards, we don't know what's out there.

The patterner looked at Elona and she returned his gaze.

ELONA DID KNOW what was lurking in the woods. There were wolves in the area—there did not seem to be anywhere they could not be found. She could feel them but the patterner's wards were also visible to her inner eye and they looked strong.

There would be no running away from here, what she had said to Jaymis was the truth. The two of them could not manage the *tekrak*, especially with Jaymis being so weak, and it was their safest means of transport even if they were prisoners.

And she feared the void.

All she could do was guess what had happened, using it to heal herself had somehow linked her to the Mother's Kitchen, and now she could summon it. She could wield it in some fashion, but she could not control it and that made it dangerous. She shivered as she recalled what had happened to the little *kikisa* once they had fulfilled the task, she had set for them.

The two of them had no alternative at this stage. Their path required they continue this journey but perhaps she could improve the quality of it.

The night passed uncomfortably but without further incident, except for the occasional wafting of nausea-inducing gas from the leaking *tekrak*. She wondered why the patterner did not simply heal it, it was what she would have done.

She had managed to get some sleep, she thought Jaymis had been unconscious for most of the time. With the light the camp became active, the Kadralin who acted as cook—though he looked as dangerous as the others—was preparing hot food.

"Baldy!" she called out to the one in charge. The other three laughed at him.

"Don't call me that. Or you'll feel my hand."

"Then what's your name?"

"Orifice," said Bushy with a laugh and dodged a punch.

"You can call me captain."

"All right, *Captain*. I would really like not to be tied to this boat all day."

"But I don't trust you, girl. You killed my men."

"It wasn't us; it was a Slissac trap, it caught Jaymis as well. He nearly died. That's why he's so weak."

"You're not hurt though, are you? Maybe he put his hand where it wasn't wanted." That drew laughs.

"I'm just a girl."

"A girl that Myrlask wants."

"Only as ransom against my father who has the ear of the Drag-onblade." The ease with which the lies dripped from her tongue scared her.

He gave her a long look.

"What do you want?"

"I know you don't trust me. I don't mind because I don't trust you either. But my friend couldn't escape even if we could get free of these ropes, then beat all five of you in a fight. He couldn't even crawl past the second tree."

She stopped to give him time to absorb that.

"Go on."

"Put him in the gondola. Bind his legs if you must but let him lie down. Let him rest and recover, even if he's not getting any healing—" she carefully planted that idea for the patterner. "—I'm not going to run without him. Keep my wrists tied and my legs hobbled but at least let me move around. I don't know where we are. I have nowhere to go."

He grunted and turned away. She watched him take his time checking the ropes around the *tekrak*, the fire, then he walked the perimeter where the patterner had laid his wards.

Finally, he returned. "All right, girl. We'll let him lie down in the gondola, but his hands stay tied. And we'll give you some rope. Maybe enough to hang yourself."

He was as good as his word. And the opportunity to have her arms below shoulder height was more of a relief than she had expected. She was able to feed herself and drink in relative comfort.

But these men were not amateurs. One of them was always watching.

Mid-morning the rain started, and they all took shelter in the gondola. Though Elona's rope only allowed her to get just inside the entrance, and she had to sit on the floor. They made no effort to make her comfortable.

The patterner busied himself studying a book. He never spoke to the others unless he had to. And they ignored him. Sometime in the afternoon the patterner went out and checked the wards. It must be a drain for him to maintain them. She couldn't feel any source of power nearby.

The grey day edged toward evening and another meal. This time cold. The Kadralin spent time making sure the fire didn't go out, but the rain was constant and heavy. Occasionally it was carried by strong winds and gusts that blew it through the empty windows of the gondola. Unable to get fully inside she took the brunt of it. The captain looked at her on one of the times the rain came in, then looked away.

Jaymis slept almost the entire time, the men laughed when he dreamt and mumbled in his sleep but Elona was happy that he was recovering. His frailty and lack of blood had shown as a thinness in his pattern, but it was thickening now. He was also out of the wind and the rain barely touched him.

As evening drew in, she realised there had been no further smells from the *tekrak* so it too must be on the mend.

Night came and the only way Elona could lie down was to go outside once more. She found a waxed cloth lying where she had slept before. The patterner must have put it there. She laid it out tucked as far under the body of the gondola as she could get. At least it would keep her off the wet ground.

~

THE MORNING CHORUS of birds and animals woke her. The sky was blue with only streaks of white cloud across it. No one else seemed to be up. She folded the cloth and, after peering into the gondola and seeing no one else was awake, she slipped it inside through a window so that the patterner would not get any blame.

Jaymis was resting peacefully, looking much stronger in the bright light that heralded a sunny day. The Kadralin was not with his fellows and she heard him moving around the fire humming a tune that she recognised as being one that Savi used to sing—a working song.

The patterner wasn't around. She walked the length of her tether to the front of the gondola and peered in. The pattern symbols meant nothing to her. Except she knew they were composed of the same ones the Slissac used for their writing and patterns. The language from which they kept all the ancient words for the animals, flying creatures and, she glanced at the huge green bulk behind her, floating plants.

There must be a fundamental truth in those symbols that they were able to focus the mind so that patterns could be modified. The patterners' mystery. Did they even understand it? Or did they just follow them by rote like a child learning to count?

"Are you a patterner?" said a quiet voice nearby.

He was standing on the other side of the front of the gondola, facing away as if he was not speaking to her at all. She leaned her back against the wood.

"No."

"I think you're lying," he said. "Although I don't blame you."

"You don't have much of an accent for a Tirnian."

"I have travelled."

"But you work for the Emperor."

"I am Tirnian, I serve my lord and master. Just as you do."

She let that go, though she wanted to point out she served no one. That would not help her case if it came to the ears of the captain.

"Tell me how you got those scars."

"I don't think so."

"They are strange. You were hurt, that is easy to see, and something sealed up your wounds. It was not a proper healing."

"If you already know the answers, why are you asking me?

He went silent. She could almost feel the battle going on inside him. He was desperate to know the truth of what caused her to look the way she did. And the price he might have to pay to gain that knowledge.

"I can get you more food."

"We have enough." *Despite the threats of the captain, he feeds us well.*

"What do you want?"

"To be free."

"No. I cannot do that."

"Then I will not tell you."

Then Bushy stepped out of the gondola yawning and stretching. He glanced in her direction and then headed off to the fire. When she looked back the patterner had slipped away.

"I can't count on him," she said quietly to herself.

"Elona?" She jumped at Jaymis's voice and turned immediately to look in through the gondola.

"I'm here."

Jaymis lay on his side. The beginnings of a beard darkened his cheeks and chin in patches. His eyes had black rings but for all that he looked better than he had for some time and the movements of his body were positive as if they were properly under control.

"I'm tied up."

"We're prisoners still."

He groaned and rolled back to stare at the ceiling. Elona glanced at where the captain and the third man were still lying at the end of the gondola. She could not risk saying anything.

"Just lie still, they'll bring food and water for you presently."

She could have climbed in through the window and reached him easily. It seemed their captors had not considered the possibility that she might simply go directly into the gondola, not round through the entrance. But she didn't plan on showing them their mistake. If they made this one, they might make another at a more opportune time.

To avoid further suspicion, she turned away and went to the end of her leash. She could still feel the wards, and she frowned. It was impossible that a single patterner could maintain such a big pattern for so long when there was no source of power nearby. Not only that, he had slept.

That was something she needed to know about. Perhaps there was something he could give her after all. But would he be willing to part with such knowledge? It must depend on how much he wanted to know what had afflicted her.

After a while the captain and the other man were called out to break their fast.

Elona moved back to the gondola making sure she stayed in clear view but in a position where she could talk to Jaymis.

"You need to pretend you're still weak.

"I don't need to pretend."

"I mean, still not really awake. Still in a daze. So they'll let you stay there."

"That is not a problem."

"Good." She hesitated. "Jaymis?"

"I'm still here."

"Can I ask you something?"

"Yes, of course, I will marry you."

"What?"

"Wasn't that the question?"

"Of course not."

"Very well. What was the question?"

"Why did you follow me?"

"What do you mean? When?"

Elona sighed and made sure the men weren't coming their way.

"Why did you stay with me?"

"I didn't really have a choice. Things moved quickly."

"But when I said I wanted to try to kill Myrlask or stop him some-how. You could have said no. I mean—" she sighed, "—it's not a very good idea."

"I think it's an excellent idea."

"But it's not very likely to succeed."

He went silent for a few moments. "Are you fishing for a compliment?"

"What? No, of course not."

"Is that the truth? Because it really sounds as if you are."

"It's a serious question, you bastard. One girl against the might of the empire? Only a complete idiot would think that could work."

"So now I'm an idiot?"

"Yes."

There was a long silence as if she had really hurt his feelings, but she did not think that was true for a moment. He seemed impervious to any sort of taunt.

There was an outburst of laughter from the group of men round the fire. One of them, the one she hadn't named, stared in her direction for a long count of five. But she held his gaze even though it unsettled her.

Their battle of wills was disturbed by the patterner emerging from round the end of the gondola. He stopped a short distance away and stared at her cheek. Jaymis's voice emerged from inside the vehicle.

"You want to know why I follow you? Because the woman who single-handedly infiltrated Aris garrison, prevented the capture of its ley-circle, foiled the assassination of the Dragonblade heir, and thereby stopped the empire in its tracks, is a force to be reckoned with. Such a woman is a person to be followed, not abandoned. And besides, I love you."

The patterner stared at Elona and she returned his gaze though inside she felt as if she had collapsed in on herself, all her energy gone. The future had simply vanished.

"Are you still there?"

"I—I'm here, and so is the patterner."

There was a pause. "He heard me."

"He heard you."

Thankfully, Jaymis fell silent as the two contemplated one another. She did not know what to do. Perhaps she could conjure the void which might do her bidding and eat him along with his associates.

Or it might just consume her instead.

"What's your name?" she asked quietly.

"Metue."

"Greetings, Metue."

"You're the one."

"Am I?"

"No one ever said what happened at Aris, not officially. But there were rumours of a powerful patterner, or a Sister of Taymar. Or both, no one was sure."

Elona ran her hand across the bristles of her head. "I'm no patterner, Metue. I did not lie when you asked."

She watched as his eyes flicked towards the fire.

He turned and half-waved, she thought awkwardly, as if it was obvious, he was hiding something. "We're ready to go." He glanced up at the sky. "The wind has dropped enough and the *tekrak* is healed."

Elona dropped her chin to her chest and then turned a sideward glance at the captain walking towards them.

"I do not need your permission; I have given the orders. Let's get moving, the sooner we get back, the sooner we get paid."

"As you say, captain."

~

ELONA DID NOT SEE what the patterner did to bring down the wards but one moment they were there and the next they were gone.

She and Jaymis were tied into their seats once more—he maintained the pretence of weakness—this time it was not with their arms above their heads, though that was the least of Elona's concerns. She was hungry and they had been given no food.

The process of getting the *tekrak* attached to the gondola went smoothly and soon they lurched into the air. Elona's stomach wanted to eject the contents it did not have. The *tekrak* was hit by a forceful gust as they rose above the trees. The gondola swung and Elona found herself looking out and down at the greenery below.

And a perfect circle of brown and black. At twenty paces across it was clear the circle had no regard for grass, bush, or tree. Within the circle all was dead. The sharp boundary cut through the branches of a tree; the part within the circle dead, and what was outside, full of life.

It was outside of her experience although she could see it was not the void just that the very life of it had been drawn out.

Then the gondola swung back, the *tekrak*'s fire-tube erupted and they surged forwards.

CHAPTER 29

The next day passed slowly. The patterner managed to navigate them back to the river which they followed once more. The terrain remained much as it had, with high rolling hills covered in woodland bordering the drowned valley.

The almost stagnant lake continued for leagues. More than once she caught sight of drowned villages, some on the borders and others below the surface. For a while she wondered where the villagers had gone but she caught sight of smoke rising from the trees in a side valley.

They must be almost completely cut off now with the water filled with *dakasa* there would be no way to travel along the valley except on foot. It reminded her of Usala's village. The people who lived there did not seem to mind their lack of contact with the outside. It was almost as if they were alone in the world, which had been one of the things she had liked about it. But she had been told, there were markets in summer further downstream where people from different villages gathered and mingled.

It would be so much harder to do that here.

On the third day she felt the pull of a ley-circle, she was not sure how far away it was, nor its size. But it was distinct.

Jaymis could no longer pretend he was weak since he had filled out with the regular meals and rest. The captain had him sitting up during the day and tied to a post once more.

The patterner had not spoken to her again though every now and then he would catch him staring at her. It made her self-conscious, aware of the wound that marred her cheek.

It was almost impossible for her to have a conversation with Jaymis now, they kept him away from her. At night they were forced to sleep on the ground with the gondola between them.

When they descended that evening the patterner, who seemed to avoid contact with the captain and his men as much as possible, took the step of approaching the leader. Elona was sitting with her back to the body of the gondola and closed her eyes to feign sleep.

"There is a ley-circle nearby," said the patterner. "We must visit it."

In a movement that he seemed unaware of, the captain glanced at the sky where Lostimal hung, almost full.

"Why?"

"If you want me to maintain the wards, then I must."

"I am not willing to lose another day."

"We could lose more than that if we do not."

The captain's face looked like a gathering storm.

"It won't take an entire day."

The captain looked up again. "What if there's a feeding?"

"It's not likely."

"I can give you the morning."

"It will be enough."

Elona frowned. Was this something she did not know about *tekrasa*? How could a visit to a ley-circle have anything to do with the wards? But then how did he maintain them?

Then she caught herself. Why did it even matter? They were heading towards certain death; a random piece of knowledge had no value. She lay back, she just needed to rest. When the time came for action, she needed to be ready.

❧

ELONA WAS all set to have another day the same. Only able to see Jaymis and not speak to him. But they had just finished breaking their fast when a streak of golden light flashed across the sky moving astonishingly fast. She had been looking down but it was visible to her pattern-sense. Without thinking, she glanced up just as the golden line stopped extending. It was there and she could see it, just like the one back at the cave.

She stared at the line as it faded into the clouds. Then she saw the black dot, coming toward them fast. She managed to suppress her surprise and forced herself to look back at her food as the small bird swooped down. She heard the beating of its wings as it headed to the group of men gathered around their fire.

Trying not to look too interested she lifted her head slightly, just in time to see the brightly coloured—red and gold—creature circle the fire once and land next to the captain.

As if this happened every day, the captain reached down and picked up the bird. He fiddled with something tied to its leg and then tossed it away. The bird fluttered down, hopped about a few times then pecked at the ground.

Elona brought her gaze back to the plate in front of her, but she did not see it. Her mind was whirling with the significance of what she had just seen. A bird that carried messages, and could fly at a tremendous speed, there was no question in her mind that the golden trail was the bird. Not only that, it found them though even they really did not know where they were.

It was incredible and a powerful secret. The emperor must be able to send these messages to his forces wherever they might be, and what if they could go back?

The captain sent one of his men to fetch something from the gondola and called for the patterner. Elona tried very hard to pretend she was simply eating and paying no attention. The captain had small pieces of writing material in a wooden box. He inscribed a message and placed it in the small container. Bushy picked up the bird, who seemed quite unconcerned by the manhandling it was getting.

The container was re-attached and then Metue made a pattern on his slate and she felt the power flow as he energised it. The bird fluttered in the hands of Bushy who threw it into the air where it took flight and headed upwards.

Elona froze in indecision. She did not want the message to be delivered, it would tell the emperor that she was coming, and she knew she could bring down the bird—but if she did anything the patterner would know. What's more they were all watching the creature as it gained height and they would be expecting to see its golden trail.

She forced herself into inaction and did not watch. But she saw the golden trail come into being with her inner sense, heading east. Showing them the way they needed to go. She told herself that she had no choice but to let it go. She dare not reveal her power to any of these people.

THE CHANGE in the normal pattern of their current existence did yield one benefit. Their captors were in less of a hurry to move in the morning and, as she sat looking up at the overcast sky, Jaymis called her name. He had not seen any of the events since he had been on the other side of the gondola.

She stood, without looking in his direction, and walked to the end of it as if she was stretching her legs.

"Are you all right?" she asked into the empty air.

"I am much better; the wound hurts a little when I stretch."

"We're going to a ley-circle."

"I heard."

"I can feel it, it's a reasonable size."

"Can you use it?"

"To do what, Jaymis?" She was annoyed, it was almost as if he did not remember their previous conversations. But perhaps he didn't, he had been ill. "They are taking us where we want to go."

"Yes, all right, that wasn't what I wanted to talk about."

"What then?"

"Why did assassins try to kill us in Avakending?"

She started to say *because the emperor wants me dead*, then realised that made no sense at all. "Someone else must have sent them."

"Someone who doesn't want the emperor to have you."

"But doesn't like me enough to keep me alive."

"Someone who wants to put you completely beyond Myrlask's reach."

That made sense. Except it meant there was another player on the board, acting in opposition to her and Myrlask. Then she noticed the captain heading her way.

"I love you," she said making sure it was loud enough for the approaching man to hear.

"I love you."

"I told you not to talk to each other."

"Sorry." Elona dropped her eyes in a deferential fashion as the man strode up. She did not see the blow coming until it was too late.

He struck her high up on her damaged cheek, knocking her off-balance as the shock and pain pounded through her head. She staggered but did not fall, nor did she cry out. Instead she straightened and glared at him. All signs of deference gone.

"That apology didn't last long," he said with a laugh. "Get ready, we're moving."

THE PATTERNER NAVIGATED along the river a short distance and then turned the *tekrak* up a valley in the northern hills. Elona was certain now that the heights were getting higher—or the level of the river was going down in comparison. It amounted to the same thing.

He clearly was as able to tell the location of the ley-circle as she was. Did that mean all patterners had this ability? Another secret, but one she probably did not need to know. That Metue could do it was enough.

The *tekrak*'s fire-tube drove them along a wooded valley with steep sides, somehow the trees managed to cling even to some of the most angled slopes. A river, clean and fast moving, ran along its base with a flat area stretching out on both sides.

They came around a bend and the bed of the river widened with beaches on each side and grass rather than woods populated with a mix of *kelukisa* of different sizes and shades. The entire grassy plain was covered with tree stumps as if someone had intentionally removed the forest here.

Smoke rose from a collection of perhaps twenty buildings. Most were single storey and looked as if they might be for animals. The others had two floors with small windows, and it was from those the smoke rose.

"How far?" shouted the captain.

"The next bend in the river." The patterner pointed ahead perhaps half a league to where the woods started once more.

"Good. Let's stay clear of the locals."

If the people in the village were watching, it was from inside their houses. Elona saw no one during the quick glances she gave the settlement. For the most part she focused forward, looking at the ridge that stuck out into the valley like a castle buttress.

The forest in the valley floor was thick there although the area around the river remained open and grassy. She could feel the ley-circle clearly now, and its light burned her inner vision.

The wind buffeted the *tekrak* so the gondola swung sickeningly. She gripped the bench beneath her until her fingers turned white.

The fire-tube burned with a constant rumble, the vibrations fed through the whole structure and the ropes creaked against wood. She turned to Jaymis to find him smiling at her. It was probably meant to be reassuring, perhaps it was, a little.

As they approached the ridge, the view of the valley beyond opened up. The wide flat area continued, bordered on both sides by thick forest. Alive with who knows what? This close to an untended ley-circle who knew what abominations had crawled into the world during a feeding?

They were close now and the patterner was focused on his patterns, guiding the *tekrak* with a level of control that she had never seen with the Slissac. But their journeys had been simple, leave from here and fly to there. The most complex flying she had seen was when she had forced them to come down on the mountainside near Aris. It had been very windy and the patterner had struggled to keep the beast under control.

"There!" shouted the Kadralin from behind her. Habit made her turn to see where he was pointing, even though she already knew the direction. Somewhere to the left. She looked back at the rolling hill that climbed up beside them. Among the broken stones, landslides and smooth grassy slopes, a smooth cylindrical channel had been carved into the rock.

It dug into the side of the hill and, as she followed it down with her eye, it went further back into the slope with the rock face closed in around it until it was almost fully encircled. But her inner eye showed the ley-circle was not buried as some were. It lay there halfway up the slope, and there was a gash in the hill that gave on to the circle itself. It was bright but not as powerful as the circles at Avakending or the Wellspring at her home.

But if this had been in any place where people lived in greater numbers it would have had its own dedicated patterners. It was significant enough to be of use to the Taymalin.

The flying beast turned and headed towards it.

"To think this ley-circle is unclaimed," said Jaymis keeping his voice low in the hopes he would not be heard above the sound of the fire-tube and the wind.

"They would clear the ground below and make it into a military camp," she said. "A staging post for war that is both out of the way and easily defensible."

A ley-circle like this was a boon since any invading force would have nowhere to hide when they arrived. Surrounded on almost all sides by sheer cliffs, with one small entrance.

"Someone has cut stairs," said Jaymis.

She peered ahead and saw he was right. Zigzagging down the slope from the entrance, stairs at the top where it was steepest and becoming a path. Perhaps it was the villagers or people who came before them.

"Are there any buildings?" she asked, unwilling to look down.

"I think there might be, but the trees grow up the slope. The path goes into the forest."

There was movement behind them, and they went quiet as the captain pushed between them and went to stand behind the patterner.

Elona could hear them talking but was unable to make out what they were saying but the gesticulations and pointing was enough.

The captain stayed where he was as the patterner worked, she felt the energy flicking this way and that in the creature above them. The fire-tube would burn for a few moments, then stop, burn again as the great beast moved across to the slope, turned sideways and then descended slowly with the buffeting wind driving them away, and then terrifyingly towards the ground rising up to the side of them.

A sudden screech shattered the air as a huge, surprised, *sikechak* rose into the air beside them. Its leathery wings beat hard and it flew off beneath them. Then, as they came down more quickly, she saw the stairs and the path very close. Elona wondered briefly how the crea-ture controlled its height just as the gondola jerked and she heard branches cracking.

Like nails on a writing slate, the bottom of the vessel was scratched by the reaching fingers of the trees. It dragged from stem to stern and then disappeared. Trees rose around them and the gondola struck something solid. The wooded floor between Elona and Jaymis, cracked and split as a needle of stone pierced it and dragged back-wards before they came to a complete stop.

The captain spun round "Move! Get this thing untied before we're shredded."

The men moved and with the patterner's deft control of the *tekrak* they got it detached and planted in the ground in a short time.

Elona stared at the rock that had pierced the vessel's body. If it had been an arms-length to the left or right, it could have killed either her or Jaymis. Something the captain then commented on and laughed.

But they were on the ground again and Elona could feel the throbbing power of the ley-circle a short distance away. She studied the plants around her, everything looked normal and she sighed with relief. The ley-circle itself was above them, a good distance away and embedded in rock. Perhaps it was far enough that it did not distort the patterns of the creatures or plants that lived here.

She still could not fathom why the patterner had insisted on coming here.

Perhaps she would find out.

CHAPTER 30

By evening their captors had made a small clearing and had a good fire going. The patterner had set up his wards again, which in her mind's eye she could see as a thin blue barrier. He had not completely encircled them but left it open on the ley-circle side. He and the captain had climbed the path and stairs, disappearing for a while before returning.

The captain was still not happy about the delay.

Jaymis and Elona were separated again on either side of the gondola and they ate their food as night fell and shadows deepened beneath the trees. Lostimal lifted her full shining face into the night sky.

Elona shivered. The power in the ley-circle was chaotic, as if it bubbled and twisted. A feeding was coming, and the circle knew it. This was the worst place they could be, but she couldn't say anything without revealing her ability.

The patterner checked the wards and then, after saying a few words to the captain, he headed back up.

Can he not see it? He knew the circle was here, how can he not see what's coming?

But if he died, they would be stuck here, at best the soldiers would make them walk to Tirnia.

He must be able to see it.

Then something changed, the power above them was being manipulated. Metue was casting a pattern, and it was big. But no patterner ever tried to manipulate the World's Pattern when a feeding was happening.

Then there were voices.

Not their captors talking but others in the distance. Chanting. The people from the village—or abominations? If there was a feeding and they were Kadralin, they would be drawn to it for their rites.

The soldiers all stood and looked in the direction of the chanting.

Elona touched the frozen flesh on her cheek. Perhaps she could influence them without making it worse. There was so much power here just waiting to do her bidding. True power, not the void that distorted and corrupted.

She sighed. It did no good, even if she could make them investigate, she and Jaymis were still tied to the gondola.

Something struck her leg and she jumped, frantically brushing it away, not knowing what it was. But she saw nothing in the gloom, and she could feel no dangerous living thing close to her.

It happened again. This time she looked up and saw someone's hand disappearing behind the front of the gondola in the dim light. Jaymis? She stretched out her senses and perceived him on all fours in the darkness. He was no longer tied up.

That settled her decision.

She turned back to the four men who stood looking out into the darkness with the bright light of the fire behind them. This was not the same as stirring the lust in a man's loins. It was a thought that they were threatened and must all go to investigate. But here it could be like the wolves, all she had to do was influence the leader.

The sound of chanting was growing in the night which could only aid her.

She formed the thought that they were under attack and must

sneak into the woods to flank their enemy. She paused for a moment; she did not want to sacrifice innocents.

She changed the thought. The army attacking them was too great. Sacrifice the prisoners. Escape!

Then she focused on the leader she could perceive the patterns of his form, and those were easy to comprehend, but his thoughts? That was different. She had never done such a thing before. With her mind's eye she looked closer and saw the great swirling mass of thought, patterns so complex they defied comprehension, but she did not have to decipher them.

She took her own thought—she had conceived it and she could perceive it, just as complex as his. And, without understanding how she knew what she must do, she gave it to him. Like mixing more flour into dough she let it become absorbed. Yet she could still see it, distinct though it had entered the pattern cloud. Then one of his thoughts emerged distinct and separate. It touched the one she had made, as if this was a thought of his that matched hers.

She realised that was exactly what it was. The fear of a force greater than his, his traitorous self-preservation, his desire to live. So she fed it, strengthened it, pushed it.

He turned and looked at her. Then at the others.

"Come on," he said. "Let's get out of here, there are too many of them."

"What about her?"

"Leave her, we need to move before we're overrun. Move it! Now!"

It was the Kadralin who turned and stared at her long and hard. But even he obeyed, as if the thought of an overwhelming force had infected his fears as well.

They quickly gathered up their weapons, food and packs. Moments later they disappeared round the end of the wards heading along the edge of the forest.

Elona shivered. A cold sweat broke out across her body as she watched them disappear into the dark. She almost failed to notice Jaymis cutting her bonds.

She turned to look at him, his face in darkness against the fading blue of the sky. "How?"

"The patterner tossed me a knife as he checked the wards."

Elona looked up the slope. The lights of the ley-circle filled her mind. The turmoil in the face of the coming feeding, and the fixed patterning he was creating.

"He's making a path," she said.

"Let's go then."

She nodded dumbly. Her cheek was tingling and sweat ran down her back. He helped her stand. She stumbled at the unexpected freedom of her feet as he tried to pull her towards the path. She resisted.

"Our things."

"Leave them."

"No, I must have my knife."

Jaymis hesitated then relaxed. "Of course. Wait here."

"Do you know where they are?"

"Not exactly."

She turned and taking careful if hurried steps she made her way into the gondola. The light of her knife burned strongly in her mind. The box was underneath a pile of blankets. She opened it, extracted the knife on its chain and slipped it over her head.

Once outside she thrust the box into Jaymis's hands. "One more thing."

"But they're coming."

The sound of chanting was loud now. It was hard to tell how many voices there were.

"You start climbing, I'll be right behind you."

The huge bulk of the *tekrak* lay a short distance away. And she headed for it at a slow run. The plant was firmly rooted for the night, but she would not leave it staked down. Come the morning, it should have its freedom.

Her little knife might slice through the ropes easily, but they were thick, and it still took a couple of strokes for each one.

"So that milk-puke of a patterner set you free?"

Elona sliced through what she hoped was the final tie. Then stood slowly.

"I made him do it the same way I controlled you." Lying was easy. Perhaps the captain might go easy on the patterner, but only if he believed it.

There was amusement in his voice when he spoke again. "I wonder."

The chanting of the villagers filled the air. He turned his head towards the sound.

"He's making a path, up there, isn't he? That takes the balls of Taymar." He glanced up at Lostimal that hung full in the sky above them and Elona followed his gaze. The red disk of Colimar was separated from the white moon by only a sliver of black.

Elona shivered again. How could she be so cold?

"Let's do this the easy way. You sheath that little devil stick and I tie you up again. My boys will have your friend by now. You can't get away."

Elona frowned. There had been no sound of a fight. She couldn't see where Jaymis was from here, but she didn't think he'd been caught.

The blue light of the wards flickered and faded away.

The power of the ley-circle bubbled like thick soup and threatened to pour down on her. But there was nothing she could do. There was no magic she could bring to stop this man now.

Someone screamed. The scream turned into a gurgle and then cut off.

"Come here!"

His voice carried the hint of desperation and fear. And she saw the way he stood amid the darkness of the trees.

She turned away from the *tekrak* and strode toward the path.

"I said come here!"

The desperation was clearer.

"The feeding will consume you!"

"Let it," she said.

The ground rose then flattened; her pace increased. Looking back, she saw shadows moving in the shadows. The villagers, if that's what they were, came through the trees. Their movements erratic; shuffling and loping; arms too long for their bodies.

The captain lashed out with his sword. Something whimpered in pain as more shadows piled in on him and he vanished into darkness. His cry of fear and agony did not end abruptly as the other had. His haunting death cry echoed up the slope.

By Lostimal's brilliant white light, Elona broke into a slow run. Her legs were painful from the days of constraint and did not want to obey her.

The chanting from below continued unbroken and a glance down the slope revealed the monstrous forms of the abominations moving out into the open space and some climbing towards her. They were naked and their skin glistened sickeningly in the cold white light.

Then a smaller form twisted between them, dodging through their ranks.

Jaymis!

She cursed him under her breath for not doing as she had said. She would have choice words with him—if he survived.

It was almost as if she were watching a mummer's play. It was unreal under Lostimal's white eye.

Jaymis made the slope and scrambled up towards the path. Her heart missed a beat as a long arm reached up and caught him by the ankle, bringing him crashing down.

"No!" she reached out her arm and power flowed through her. The ground shuddered. Boulders shook loose and careened down the slope. The creature that gripped Jaymis's ankle looked up slowly as a rock bounced on the path and slammed into its face.

Jaymis scrambled up again, barely managing to dodge another rock.

The avalanche pelted the abominations, pushing them back, as Jaymis climbed.

Elona looked up. Colimar hung on the edge of Lostimal. She did not know how the patterner could maintain his path in the storm of power that surged around them.

She started up the slope again, hoping Jaymis would catch up.

The path zig-zagged once, twice, three times and she reached the stairs. Looking back, she saw Jaymis close behind. He had not taken the path but climbed directly up.

"Don't stop!" he shouted.

She reached the top and stared out across the ley-circle, only thirty paces from side to side. Encircled by smooth stone. The portal was a fiery arch with the silhouette of Metue at its entrance. He gestured at her to hurry and pointed up. Colimar was fully enclosed by the eye of Lostimal. When it reached the centre, the power of the feeding would be unleashed—any moment now.

She ran the final few steps.

"Get inside!" shouted Metue—yet it was difficult to know why. Though the power poured and tumbled around her, there was not the slightest sound from it.

Jaymis appeared at the entrance to the circle and ran.

She felt the gate flex as Metue stepped backwards and into it. The power beneath her froze as if it were suddenly ice. But above, the pressure of the feeding became real.

The first pulse was coming.

Jaymis would die.

She would die.

And it would all mean nothing.

She gathered herself, raised a hand to the sky.

"Stop!"

Blackness flowed from her. It rose to meet the descending energy of the Mother's milk.

The incandescent light of a thousand suns exploded around them.

Jaymis crashed into her, driving her back and into the portal.

CHAPTER 31

etween the scintillating lights of the World's Pattern, there was darkness.

She knew what the darkness was.

"Are you all right?"

"What?"

"I'm sorry I barged into you. Did I hurt you?"

Her chest ached where he had hit her, and her right arm felt numb, but nothing else.

"I'm all right."

She let him help her to her feet and then kissed him.

She had not meant it to mean anything, perhaps just a thank-you for saving their lives, but when her lips touched his it all changed. He was her anchor in the strangeness of the world. She wrapped her arms about him and clung to him as if he was the only thing preventing her from drowning. Her kiss was deep and passionate.

It must have surprised him, but he recovered quickly and returned it with the same fervent energy.

Metue made a noise.

Elona remembered where they were and pulled away, though she held on to Jaymis's hand. She looked back at the portal. There was

265

nothing to indicate that a feeding was tearing the natural patterns of the world to shreds and remaking them.

"What took you so long?" said Metue.

"Did you expect the captain and his men to just let us go?" said Jaymis.

"I left the knife so you could sneak away."

"Yes," said Elona. "Thank you for that. These things seldom work out the way they're planned."

"Why not?"

Jaymis seemed about to say something but Elona squeezed his hand.

"They just don't. I'm sure we should get on."

She turned and headed along the patterner's path still holding Jaymis's hand.

"I thought it was quite a good plan," said Metue. "I wanted to tell you, but we were interrupted."

"I know. Let's drop it."

"Where does this path go?" asked Jaymis.

"Glytheni."

"Never heard of it."

"My home."

Elona took a deep breath. "I would have preferred if we were going to the emperor's citadel."

"I don't know the pattern for that," he said. "Only those of the inner circle are taken there to learn how to recognise it. If we don't know it, we can't lead anyone there."

They walked on in silence for a while.

Elona took a deep breath, she knew that Metue had not helped them because he had any sympathy for their cause. All he was interested in was information.

"Ask your questions," she said.

"How can a healing go wrong?"

She gathered her thoughts as the twinkling lights of the World's Pattern moved around them, amid the dark void.

"We were in Avakending and I was attacked by Farahalek—"

"And you're not dead?"

"They only sent three."

Jaymis snorted and tried to turn it into a sneeze to hide his laugh.

"But I was very badly hurt and needed to get out." She hesitated; she did not really want to mention the void but if the patterner knew anything about such things it would be good if she had that information too. "Have you ever heard of the Mother's Kitchen?"

This time it was Metue who took a long time in answering, though the delay indicated the answer was obviously yes. He was probably being as circumspect as she was, wondering how little information he could reveal.

"It was a ley-circle at one time but is no longer."

"I don't think a journeyman patterner would have heard of a place that wasn't a ley-circle unless it had some special significance. You know what it is."

"In the old tongue, it is called a *kochulina*."

"Which is what?"

He ignored her question. "Tell me what happened to you?"

"There was nowhere else close by to draw power from, and it offered itself. It healed me, if you can call this healing. I stopped bleeding."

They walked on in silence for a while.

Elona tried the word out in her head. *Kochulina*. It was a strange one, even in the old language. Perhaps a scholar could have taken the word to pieces and made it understandable. She couldn't.

"What is it then?"

"You said it offered itself to you," he said. "As if it was alive?"

"I don't know. That's the best way I can describe it. I needed something and it was there."

"But you could control it?"

"Not really."

She remembered the *kikisa* in the Slissac ruin, tearing the men to pieces and dying as they were consumed by the power.

"If you can't control it, how did you make it do what you wanted?"

A grim smile appeared on Elona's face. She was glad it was too dark to see.

"You patterners are all the same, journeyman or Arch-mage, it's all about control and force. Look at the walls of this path, you see the World's Pattern and all you want to do is tame it and force it to your will."

"It's what my masters said, *fahain* have no discipline."

"And where has all your discipline got you? You're just shadows of the Slissac. You have nothing that was not stolen from them when we were slaves. You only have what was brought out of their lands when Taymar led our escape."

"We know more than they ever did!"

Elona slammed her mouth shut before she said something she would regret. Too late for that, she already regretted it all.

"Tell me what you think the *kochulina* is."

"Nobody truly knows—"

"You had nothing to bargain with except a meaningless word."

"Nobody truly knows, but—" He emphasised the word then paused to highlight her rudeness. "—but the prevailing theory is that it is corrupted *haileth*."

Elona hesitated. "I do not know what *haileth* is."

"I should not speak of it."

"But you are, we are bartering information."

"*Haileth* is what the common people know as Mother's Milk."

"You just have a different word for it, I suppose that makes it sound more mysterious."

"It's not just another word, it's the true word. We can't discuss the world being fed from the breast of the Mother in the sky."

"Yes, it's far too embarrassing."

Jaymis cleared his throat. "I have been silent."

"Yes, you have," said Elona.

"Do not start your games with me, Elona. I have been silent because I have been forced to listen to two adults bickering like children. Anyway, I'm hungry so would like to pause and eat. And perhaps you could refrain from souring my appetite any further by behaving like civilised people?"

Elona waited for Metue to say something. He stayed quiet but they stopped and shared out the little food they had. There was barely enough water for a mouthful each.

"I hope this path isn't too long," she said.

"I did not create it under ideal conditions!" said Metue.

"I know. I wasn't criticising." She tried to keep the edge out of her voice but there was something about Metue that raised her hackles. "I had no plan for escaping. I am grateful for what you did." *Even if it was self-interest.* "I can't make a path." Even as she said it her voice wavered in the middle of the lie.

"I was still an apprentice when the invasion of Taltia failed," said Metue. "But the story of Elona of Corlain is known to me."

"Come on," said Elona getting to her feet. "Let's get moving."

Her arm was still numb and in the dimness of the path, hidden from the men, she used the fingers of her other hand to feel her skin. Her heart sank, and she wished she could be shocked or surprised.

Jaymis hadn't seen the change in her face after the *kikisa* attack but nothing could hide the transformation she felt in her arm. The skin had become ridged and hard and she could imagine its charred and blackened look.

The power she wielded was corrupting her piece by piece.

THEY WALKED on in silence for a long time. They may as well have been standing still considering the lack of change in the path. It was always moving but always looked the same. She did not attempt to decipher it. She had become weary of power.

"So if *haileth* is the Mother's milk and the Mother's Kitchen is a *kochulina*, and I suppose that means there are more of them, what is the name for this other power?"

"*Kisheth.*"

She shook her head invisibly in the dark of the path. "Your words mean nothing. There is no knowledge in them."

"I don't know what you mean."

"I can take a stone in my hand and call it a stone, but the name reveals nothing of its pattern. To someone who does not know the word at all, I could call it grass and they would be none the wiser." She sighed. "You patterners cling to your words and symbols. You keep them secret as if knowing them gives you greater understanding. But you know nothing more than someone who draws a pattern from a scroll. If you replaced the words with the bellowing and bleating of a *kelukisa*, you would be neither wiser nor more ignorant. It would make no difference at all."

Metue said nothing for a long time. "You are right."

Elona did not feel vindicated.

"So how is it for a *fahain*, Lady Elona of Corlain? Is your knowledge deeper than mine?"

"It is not, Metue of Glytheni."

"So, there is no difference between us."

"There is one. I touch the patterns of the world directly. You work with symbols that are a poor imitation of the truth."

They went on in silence until finally, she could not be sure how long it was, she saw the arch of the exit ahead of them. She glanced at the dark shape of Metue walking beside them. She took Jaymis's hand in hers. Its solidity gave her strength.

Her greatest fear now was that Metue might decide to simply kill them, and she would not be able to stop him if he suddenly lunged for the portal and exited the path before them. It would collapse and they would be absorbed into the World's Pattern—or whatever it was that happened.

But there was no way she could communicate her concern to Jaymis without alerting Metue. She squeezed Jaymis's hand, he squeezed back. Probably just thought it was a game. She did it again. And again. Three quick squeezes in rapid succession. He gave a long slow one back, as if he had come to understand there was something important.

Or, he was just playing the game a different way.

The end of the path grew closer. She also had no idea what to expect at the other end. The circle might be below ground, or above it. They might fall. It was a chance she had to take.

They were only a few steps away from it and she thought she saw Metue move forward faster.

She threw herself at the way out yanking on Jaymis's hand. "Come on!"

She was dragging him forward for a moment before he got the idea and together, they flung themselves through the barrier.

Into dazzling daylight and sticky heat. Thick earthy smells of dirt and rotting vegetation.

And so much heat. The sun blazing even stronger than Avakending.

She squinted against the light and made out a phalanx of bowmen, who raised their weapons the moment they realised two people had appeared in the ley-circle.

Elona and Jaymis came to a sudden halt on the smooth damp stone. She could feel the power of the ley-circle boiling beneath her feet. They had left in evening darkness and arrived in late morning or early afternoon.

Some of the bowmen shifted their aim.

"You lied, Metue" said Elona. She did not turn towards him but glared at the armsmen. Of the ones looking at her, their eyes widened, and their crossbows wavered in their hands.

"Taymar's teeth! Elona, your arm!" Jaymis's voice crackled with horror. "Your *face.*"

"What's wrong?"

"What did you do, Elona of Corlain?" said Metue, only a little calmer than Jaymis.

She held her arms out in front of her. The one that she had flung up to protect herself and Jaymis from the power of the feeding. The one that had felt numb—still felt numb—was barely more than skeletal, with a thin covering of blackened skin. As if it had been burned.

With her untouched left hand, she felt her way up the arm to her neck and then her face on the right side. The scarring was gone, but that side of her face had been corrupted in the same way.

"It has a price," she said. "What's done is done." She lifted her head and looked about them. Thick forest of rich greens started a good distance from the ley-circle. There were even more armsmen further out manning siege weapons for hurling stones or arrows, all aimed at the circle itself. Several *tekrasa* floated above them and she could see more armsmen with bows at their windows.

"What is this place, Metue?"

Both the men were staring at her and the armsmen had not lowered their weapons.

"My master is waiting for you here."

"Not the person who is trying to kill us?"

"He would not appreciate your death."

"Not the emperor."

"No."

A sergeant of the armsmen moved forwards from the ranks and Metue went to talk to him.

"At least there may be an answer to this," said Elona and looked into Jaymis's face. The horror still hung in his eyes and she knew there was nothing she could do to prevent it.

"What did you do?" said Jaymis quietly so no one else would hear, and Elona realised he had asked this question before.

"You were too late when you ran for the path."

He stared at her. His eyes flicking to the right side of her face.

"Too late?"

"The feeding started, the first flashes anyway. It would have killed us both."

The meaning of her words sank in. "You *stopped* the feeding?"

She gave a short humourless laugh and shook her head. "I couldn't stop it. I just protected us. Like a ward."

"But with so much power why couldn't you use the Mother's Milk?"

"I didn't have time to think, Jaymis, and if there are patterns that can protect against the power of a feeding, I don't know what they are."

"But you're *fahain*."

She closed her eyes and sighed. It was not hard to understand him. He was trying to find excuses, reasons why it was not his fault for being late. Solutions that she could have thought of if only she had tried. Reasons why *he* was not the reason her body had been disfigured.

She placed her normal hand against his chest and could feel his heart pounding. If she had chosen, she could have seen it. "But it's not your fault, dear Jaymis. It's simply what happened." She shook her head once more. "Being *fahain* means nothing if I cannot see what I can do. I just react."

"Elona! Jaymis! This way."

"We can't trust him," said Jaymis.

"He wasn't bringing us to the emperor," said Elona. "And if Metue's master does not want us dead, it will be the emperor who does."

"Now!"

They turned and followed him, flanked on all sides by armsmen with weapons at the ready.

CHAPTER 32

The air was full of flying insects, some of which were interested in biting Jaymis. They did not, however, take much interest in Elona. The walk was not long and they came to some sort of staging post where the three of them climbed into the back of a covered cart pulled by four *kichesa*.

"Where are we going?" said Elona.

Metue did not answer for a while as the vehicle trundled along the smooth gravelled path. A small group of armsmen were still following them and the cart did not go fast. A passing thought had Elona grabbing the reins and them charging off, but that would be foolish, they were alone in a place very far from Tirnia, let alone Faerholme.

They were surrounded by the thick vegetation. So many trees, none of which she recognised, and nothing like the forests of Dirdin with a clear and open space between each. In this place all the plants intertwined, they climbed the trees and stretched between the branches.

The cart trundled round a bend and Metue pointed. Away on a hill, perhaps a league in the distance, stood massive defensive walls surrounding the towers of a huge castle. *Tekrasa* moved around its perimeter like buzzing flies. Elona frowned, feeling the hard skin on half a face pulling against the muscles. *What are they defending against?*

"What is this place?" said Jaymis. "I know of no country with a castle like this."

"We're a long way from home," said Elona.

It took most of the afternoon to approach the citadel, and they passed through many villages and wide fields filled with workers. Elona squinted at the sun as it descended in its great arc across the sky, there was something strange about the way it was moving.

They had not been tied up but the numbers of men escorting them was sufficient deterrent from doing anything unplanned.

"The sun is wrong," said Jaymis.

Metue laughed but did not offer any explanation.

"Who is your master, Metue?" said Elona.

He gazed at her for a long time, she could see his eyes drawn to the damaged side of her face.

"Why won't you tell us? What difference would it make?"

"I am wondering what will be better, seeing your reaction if I tell you, or when you are in his presence."

Elona glared. "Don't tell us, we don't want to know. Besides, how will your master feel if you tell us before he has the opportunity to spring a surprise."

The uncertainty now on Metue's face went some way to satisfying her desire for revenge. He opened his mouth to speak.

"Hush, journeyman," said Jaymis. "You've already said far more than you should. How would the guild feel if they knew how much you had told us of your secret words for magic?"

Metue's jaw tightened and he looked away, forward into the trees.

Elona pulled the sleeve of her shirt up her arm. Jaymis turned and looked at the skin just as she did.

"May I?" he said. She nodded and he touched his fingers against the blackened and ridged skin. "Does it hurt?"

"No, but it's stiff like wearing a leather jacket that's too small."

"It doesn't feel like skin."

She felt strangely detached from it, as if it was not part of her, exactly as if it really was starched cloth she could not remove.

Jaymis glanced at Metue but he was still pretending they were not there.

"Can you see its pattern?"

But she wasn't looking at her arm, she was looking into his face. When she didn't respond, he looked up and there he was, his nose barely a fingers-width from her own. She tilted her head to the side, leaned forward and kissed him. His free hand came up to hold her shoulder as their lips parted.

The trundling cart changed from mud and soil to cobbles and they were bounced apart.

The walls of the citadel loomed up before them. Narrow arrow-slits surrounded the entrance on both sides. They crossed a wide drawbridge spanning a chasm cut into the ground. If there was water at the bottom, they could neither see nor hear it. The walls rose directly from the chasm sides with no ledge to gain purchase even if an attacker could cross the gap.

Elona could feel wards permeating the stone. The lord here must have an army of patterners simply to maintain the defences of such a huge place. The cart ran for a short while in the dark. There was no doubt that there would be a dozen ways that death could be dropped from above.

But it all means nothing if you have tekrasa *to fly above the walls,* Elona thought. *The flying creatures might aid them in attacks on unprepared enemies, but the same would happen if the attackers became besieged themselves.*

Not that she could imagine a place this size, and so far from Faer-holme and the other realms of the Conclave, coming under attack. Who could possibly bring in a force strong enough to take it?

They went through a series of courtyards, linked by more tunnels always sloping upwards. There was no one in view and the ward-imbued walls of each courtyard were featureless save for more arrow-slits.

"This place is impregnable," said Jaymis.

Elona looked up and caught sight of a *tekrak* silhouetted black against the brilliant blue above. "Unless you can fly." Clearly the thought had not occurred to him but then she had had more experience, even if she disliked it.

"It reminds me of Canvor," she said. "And its attackers have much more of a climb."

"I wonder who the original builders were defending against," said Jaymis.

The only thing that Elona could think of was Slissac, but there had been no battle with them since Taymar had led them from the slaver's realm. At least nothing that Bejeren had taught her.

They came out into a proper courtyard, with people going about their business, there was a forge off to one side. The smell of horses and *kichesa* wafted through the air and everything seemed normal.

Normal save for the stares that she received from anyone close enough to notice her. It was a long time since she had felt self-conscious. It was a feeling she had lost amid the trials of her life. So, when it returned, it was a discomfort she barely recalled, but felt deeply.

They were led inside and Elona noticed the similarities between this place and the palace at Avakending. Now they were behind the barricades the windows were large and open. The passages wide and tall to allow the circulating of air. After the heat outside, it was almost cold inside, except where the sun broke through and burned the stone.

"You will be placed in a suite of rooms," said Metue, "until my master is ready to give you an audience. Please do not try to escape, the guards have orders to kill you."

"I thought he wanted to see us."

Metue shrugged. "My master is aware of your surprising ability to squeeze out of traps and certain death, Lady Elona. And that was before he knew you were *fahain*. He is keen that you should understand that while he wants to see you, he would not be concerned by your death."

He turned to leave but Elona spoke again.

"Why did you abandon your associates?"

Metue turned back, the expression on his face patronising, as if the answer were obvious. "Because they were not my associates."

Then he was gone, and they were hustled into a room through ornate double doors into their rooms.

JAYMIS CHECKED the windows while Elona went through every door and examined every cupboard. There was no other way out she could see.

"We could potentially escape through the windows," he said. "But we are quite a long way above the ground, and we would still be within the walls."

She made no comment about not being able to go out through the windows due to her fears. And neither did he.

"Do you think the captain and his men were working for the Emperor, while Metue wasn't."

Elona shook her head. "I don't know. If the Emperor is trying to kill me why didn't they just do it and take the body back?"

Jaymis sighed. "One thing is certain, I'm glad we know Metue is an enemy."

"Why?"

"Because if you thought he was on your side, you'd probably wake up with a knife through your heart."

Elona smiled. "So at least we know we can't trust him."

She got up and walked halfway to a window and looked out at the sun-drenched stones of the castle walls. "There is a bath, and water," she said. "And fresh clothes, though they aren't suitable for travel."

Jaymis nodded. "I suppose if we're going to meet this lord, we should make ourselves presentable." He hesitated. "You should go first. I'll wait."

Elona stared at him and finally shook her head. She held out her undamaged hand. "Come with me, Jaymis—" she paused for a moment. "—if my scars do not disgust you. I will understand if you prefer not to."

"Nothing about you disgusts me, Elona, but—" he hesitated once more. "—but are you sure?"

"Oh wait," she said letting her arm drop, "you didn't think I meant...*that*."

She watched as the horror of embarrassment crawled across his face. He opened his mouth to speak but not a single sound emerged.

Then she smiled, crossed to him, and placed her blackened hand against his cheek. He did not pull back. "You are a good man, Jaymis." She took his hand in hers and pulled him towards the room with the bath. "I can assure that, if you are willing, I really did mean *that*."

"You did?"

"I did."

CHAPTER 33

The sun's rays slanted across the stones and the heat of the day was relieved by a soft wind when they finally dragged themselves from the bed. Their first time had not been very successful, she had found his body to be quite strange—if exciting. At least Jaymis had some practical experience, unlike her, so it had not been awful. Everything she knew had been told to her by Savi.

Let her be with the Mother now, thought Elona offering it up as a prayer to soothe the pain she always felt with those memories.

In the bath, they had examined the new scarring to her body. It was not as bad as she thought. Her entire right arm was now scarred. Her right shoulder and shoulder blade, the right side of her face down her neck to her right breast but it stopped there.

She still had the hole in her left shoulder, of course.

The two of them dressed. Now that they had laid together, she had once more lost all embarrassment of her body and sorted through the choices of clothing without any attempt to hide herself.

She caught Jaymis watching her more than once, as he tried desperately to hide his body from her. She intentionally watched him. He was easy to embarrass and she took delight in it.

Eventually they were both dressed, and she wore a scarf so that she could raise it over her head and put her face in shadow. Jaymis wore a lose shirt and trousers that would not have been out of place on a summer's day in Faerholme. But he had to keep his worn and battered boots. There were plenty of sandals for Elona.

"Do you suppose the Emperor knows about this place?" said Elona.

"I doubt it, can you imagine him letting someone occupy a castle as strong as this?"

"But he must be a Tirnian lord."

"Probably, and close to the Emperor too," said Jaymis, "if he knows the Emperor wants you dead."

"But bold enough to send his own men to find us."

Jaymis came up behind her and embraced her. She allowed herself to enjoy it even though she knew it could not last—perhaps because of that. She wanted to be able to remember this, whatever happened.

Her stomach rumbled.

"Want some more fruit?"

"Only if we have to, I've had enough to last a lifetime."

Someone knocked on the door.

Elona pulled the material over her head and turned away.

"Come," said Jaymis loudly.

"My Lord Nemon begs your presence at the evening meal."

"We are at his lordship's disposal; we shall require a few moments to ready ourselves."

"As you wish, sire, your escort will wait for you."

The door closed and Elona turned back. "Nemon? Metue will be annoyed he didn't tell us after all."

"Seems we were right it was someone close to the throne."

Elona shook her head. "I was sure he was the one who summoned the Farahalek in Avakending."

"Perhaps he did, but then you escaped. He may have reconsidered."

"We had better go. Why worry over possibilities when we can get the answers from the man himself."

"If he tells us," said Jaymis.

"Why would he bring us here if he wasn't going to do that?" Elona's stomach rumbled again.

"Perhaps he just wants to feed us."

"If that's true, then Tirnians can't all be bad." Elona faced him and pulled the headscarf forward more. "Does this hide the damage?"

Jaymis hesitated. "Only if you are not really looking."

"That will have to do then."

"I could say you are indisposed."

"Kiss me and we'll go."

ELONA FELT this castle was unreasonably large. Now that she had rested, she gave it a more appraising eye as they walked its corridors. So large, in fact, there had been no attempt made to make much of it homely.

The floors and walls were bare, and no furniture adorned the passages. It was all simply bare stone—and much of that needed repair, there were even water stains and patches of mold in dark corners. If those could be clues to its age—and not merely the fact it had been abandoned for a long time—then she might guess it to be older than Canvor.

A stray thought crossed her mind. *What if not all people had been slaves to the Slissac?* Was that a heretical idea? She was sure the Slissac who lived in the central mountains had not been slavers. Why could there not have been humans—like the Taymalin, not Kadralin—who had never been slaves. Perhaps they had forged kingdoms here, wherever here was.

An even more heretical concept suggested itself. What if the people who built this had been Kadralin? Just because the ones she knew were farmers and traders, why should that mean they all were?

She shrugged. It didn't matter anymore since they were no longer here. Perhaps their world had died, or they had been driven out and become the scattered people they now were.

Their armed escort guided them somewhere. She had no sense of direction in this place. It seemed most likely they would end up near the main gate, simply because it would be more sensible to keep the people together in such a big place.

But who was to say what logic they chose to follow?

~

EVENTUALLY THEY CAME to a halt outside a large pair of double doors. She heard them being announced and the doors were opened.

The hall was large but not as big as she expected. Empty tables lined the walls—the most furniture she had seen in this place so far. The floor was intricately tiled in a complex pattern that looked to be for magic, but she sensed nothing.

A single table laid for dinner stood at the far end near a large fireplace. A small fire burned in it, dwarfed by the arch above. Only one person sat at the table. He rose as they approached. Halfway across the floor, their escort stopped, and she heard them moving to the sides of the room.

"Lord Nemon," said Elona as they approached. "I did not expect we would meet again so soon."

"Lady Elona, I am surprised we met at all." He moved around the table and gave her a short bow. She responded with an awkward curtsy; she was very out of practice. "And Lord Jaymis. Please be seated both of you. If I am not mistaken it will have been a while since you both ate well."

Jaymis held the chair for her and then waited until Lord Nemon took his place across from them before sitting himself. Rank has its privileges.

"You're very kind, sir," said Elona as the servants moved in swiftly to distribute the first course of sweetmeats. There was also wine.

They ate slowly, out of politeness.

"Thank you for your hospitality, Lord Nemon, though I will say that the Kadralin cook, among your mercenaries who kidnapped us, was very good. We did not starve even if the offerings were plain."

"They were not mercenaries, they were my armsmen and I trust they behaved themselves."

"I can't say they were very pleasant," she said. "Kidnapping is an unpleasant business."

"Better than death at the hands of assassins."

"Most things are."

Elona had expected a witty response but when it did not come, she looked up to see Lord Nemon staring at his plate and not eating.

Finally, he looked up. "Not all things."

"No, not all." *And I have suffered more than my fair share of those.*

The next two courses were equally light and eaten in a difficult silence. She had touched a nerve which she guessed had something to do with Nemon's betrayal of his Emperor.

"Why did you kidnap us?" said Jaymis finally.

"I have no interest in petty lordlings such as yourself, Lord Jaymis. My interest is only with Lady Elona."

She felt Jaymis stiffen and almost feel the heat of anger coming from him.

"Please do not insult my friend," she said quietly. "Not if you want my cooperation in your scheme to kill the Emperor."

In an equally calm voice, Nemon said. "The emperor is already gone."

Elona, and Jaymis looked up from their food and stared at him. They expected him to continue but he did not, he simply took another mouthful.

"Is he dead?"

Nemon looked to one side as if not wanting to face them, or perhaps looking for an answer to the question.

"He has been succeeded."

"I did not know he had any heirs."

"He appointed one."

Elona shook her head. This was like something from one of her insane dreams.

"But he is still alive?"

When Nemon finally looked up from his plate, his face was twisted with an emotion Elona did not recognise. It had the darkness of the void about it.

"He is the *Kisharuk!*"

Then he went back to eating.

Elona blinked once. Nemon must be completely insane. She knew from terrible experience how reality became twisted.

She glanced at Jaymis at her side but there was nothing they could say to one another that Nemon could not hear.

The silence dragged from awkward to embarrassing but there was nothing that she could think of to say.

She was grateful when Jaymis found his voice.

"You brought us here for a reason, Lord Nemon."

"I brought Lady Elona here for a reason."

"Yes, of course, I'm sorry."

Silence fell again.

"What reason?"

Nemon sat up straight and pointed his knife at Elona. "It was foretold, I have heard what prophecy was spoken. You must kill the *Kisharuk.*"

"The prophecy meant nothing," she said. "I was to bear a child to the Dragonblade who would grow up and fight a great battle."

Nemon slammed his hands down on the table and half stood. "That was *not* the prophecy. That was the interpretation of fools." He stood up straight and stared into the air over her head which was even more disconcerting than having his wild eyes on her.

"Shaven-headed warriors invade our land, defeating all who stand in their way: Lords, Princes and Kings all cut down. Then she, the child, walks onto the battlefield and picks up the Dragonblade. She fells the invaders like corn and drives them back. Across the deserted battlefield the king of the invaders appears. She battles him and kills him."

Elona shivered at his words, it brought back that moment, surrounded by the great and good of Faerholme, when the Revered Malea uttered the words that would destroy Elona's life. She glanced at Jaymis who was now staring at her. She realised that he had probably never heard what was spoken.

"It's already happened," said Elona. "It's history. It was Jaymis's mother, Metrid, she killed the Dragonblade and would have killed

Drahail but I saved him and then—" she looked down into Jaymis's eyes, "—I killed her."

"The *King* of the invaders, not some witch doing his work for him." Nemon spat the words at her. "It is the *Kisharuk*, he is here. Working to destroy us and now he moves in open battle."

"If that's true," said Jaymis, "then you were working for him too."

Nemon's crazy eyes turned on him. "And I have paid the price. That is why I am here now. That is why I captured her and brought her." He turned back to Elona. "I brought you here to warn you and arm you if I can."

He seemed to have calmed down or, at the least, become more introspective but an air of tragedy still hung about him.

"How do you know I was going to try to kill the emperor?"

"It could not be any other way," he said. "The prophecy dictates your actions."

"The prophecy destroyed my life."

"It was the *Kisharuk* that destroyed your life."

The Slissac-created monster was a tale told to children to keep them quiet. It was the creature that lurked in shadows beneath the bed, it was the thing that brought about all bad luck, and the name by which all curses were made. It was just an invention that made the flight of Taymar more dramatic.

Elona sighed. *My father, the Sisters of Taymar, and the Arch-mage destroyed my life.*

If Malea had not had her vision, I would have grown up as uneducated and vacuous as any daughter of a lord. I would have married Drahail and we would all have died at Apra.

Or, Metrid would have simply killed me.

But whatever it was that saved me from Metrid's magic would have saved me anyway, wouldn't it? And I would still have gone mad. Metrid would still have won.

She shook her head. There were too many possibilities and the one that had happened was the only one that mattered. Then a thought occurred to her and she looked at Nemon, still in his strange quiet bubble, she closed her mind and opened herself to the patterns around her, specifically to him.

When Metrid had been driving her mad, it had been her gifts and a thread of a connection between the two of them.

There was a singular lack of magic in this place, the patterns in the ancient stone and wood seemed flat and lifeless. Nemon's emotions bubbled within him though she could not interpret them, and she looked for a binding between him and something else.

But there was nothing. It seemed his madness was all his own.

"If the emperor is gone then I cannot kill him," she said.

Nemon's anger flared. "Have you not listened? The *Kisharuk* cannot die. It is that monster you must destroy."

"So where will I find him?"

The anger faltered. "In Myrlask's castle."

"And how will I know him?"

"You will make no mistake, *fahain*, you will know the *Kisharuk* when it stands before you."

Elona shook her head. There was no point in arguing with a madman, she knew that, there was nothing that could have been done to change the way she saw the world when her every sense was distorted.

She pitied him.

"And how will I destroy him?"

Nemon looked at her with his piercing eyes, the chair legs squealed on the tiled surface as he pushed it back. He stalked round the table and stood behind Elona. Jaymis stood up.

Nemon glared at him. "I mean no harm to the one that will bring us our salvation." With that he dragged the scarf from Elona's head revealing her scarred and blackened skin. "You command that which destroys patterns. Even the *Kisharuk* is a creature of patterns, you have the power."

It was strange, her discussions with the journeyman patterner had failed to provide any true knowledge of the void, yet that one comment from Nemon told her so much. Explained so much.

"How do you know what it is that is eating me?"

"The library of Myrlask is ancient and great, the *Kisharuk* has gathered the greatest texts and hidden them away so no others could gain this knowledge, least of all the patterners who might learn how to destroy him."

"But you read them." Elona pulled the scarf back over her head as Nemon returned to his seat.

"I sat at the Emperor's right-hand."

"And now you betray him."

"I will not serve the *Kisharuk*," he said. "You will leave tomorrow."

CHAPTER 34

It seemed Nemon did not care that Jaymis and Elona were unmarried. They were returned to the same room and locked in together. Elona went through to the bedroom and removed her clothing. The night was hot, and the clothes had stuck to her, at least where her skin was not scarred.

Jaymis seemed awkward and shocked that she did it with such a lack of self-consciousness. But he did the same though he tried to disguise and hide the state of his body.

Elona lay on top of the bed staring at the ornate ceiling. She felt Jaymis lie down. Her hand found his.

"He's hiding here," said Jaymis.

"What makes you say that?"

"Because he's scared, and this citadel is far too big for the staff he has."

"But all the armsmen and *tekrasa*?" said Elona.

"He could still be building an army."

She sighed. "I suppose so, but why would he be hiding?"

"Because he thinks the emperor is the *Kisharuk*."

"I expect he was the one that told the Emperor we were in Avakending."

It was Jaymis's turn to be unsure. "How do you go from working so closely with Myrlask, to this level of rebellion, in such a short time?"

"How does a new emperor take over the reins so easily? Surely there would be in-fighting among the lords of Tirnia. And what happened to Myrlask?"

"We didn't ask who the new emperor is," he said.

"Seems to be a sensitive subject." She rolled onto her side to face him. "What would you like to do now?"

He turned his head. "Sleep?"

"It's too hot to sleep."

"I think what you have in mind will make us even hotter."

She smiled. "You think you know my mind, lordling?"

"I hope I do."

"You really don't care about the scars?"

"I wish you didn't have them, my love," he said. "But only because you do not deserve them."

Elona rolled back and stared up. "Do I not? Perhaps this is retribution for my misdeeds."

"Retribution from who?"

"Oh, don't listen to my maunderings, just kiss me and make me forget."

THE BRILLIANT SUNSHINE reflecting from the tiled floor illuminated the room. Jaymis was already up and she realised she had been roused by him calling her.

"Breakfast, sleepy-head."

A gauzy blue robe lay at the end of the bed and she slipped it over her shoulders. It did nothing to hide her nudity, but it felt as if it did, not that she was much concerned with that.

She did however check there was no one else in the main room before slipping through the door.

Jaymis was dressed and when she appeared, he just stared.

"Well, you did leave it out for me."

"I did not realise I would be able to see through it."

"Enjoy it while you have the chance, the sooner we're away from here the better."

She sat down, breakfast consisted of the inevitable fruit, orange juice, preserved meats, fresh bread rolls but no butter.

Jaymis had torn a bread roll open and was busy stuffing meat into the space. She followed suit but used the knife to cut the bread first. It was dry but the juice washed it down easily.

"What's the plan?" he asked between mouthfuls.

She shook her head and finished off a roll before responding. "Nemon is crazy. I've been there and there's nothing we can say that will sway him. And we're at his mercy, we'll just have to play along."

"I suppose it might be worth investigating the new emperor," said Jaymis.

"Why?"

"We gather what information we can and carry it back to the Conclave, they'll be better informed for the decisions they make."

She put down the roll and reached out with her scarred hand to take hold of his wrist. "We have no reason to do that. It doesn't matter if Myrlask is dead, or just gone, what matters is if Tirnia continues its aggression, or not.

"If they stop then everything goes back to the way it should be, and if they continue to attack, nothing's changed. We don't need to warn anybody of anything. They'll find out soon enough."

"I thought it was what you wanted."

"It was but if Myrlask is gone, the attacks on me will stop."

"Why should they?"

She went silent. The new emperor might continue trying to have her killed and, even if that wasn't the plan, the Farahalek might not have been told to stop. Did the assassins have a rule about always killing their target no matter what it took? It was a thing that was said, but no one knew if it was true, after all they usually succeeded.

"But it was a foolish idea anyway," she said. "Nobody knows where we are now, if we get transported to Tirnia we can just disappear." *If you were not with me, perhaps I could return to Chara.*

"Who are you arguing with?" said Jaymis

She shook her head again. "I have no choice, do I? Very well, we'll go along with Nemon's plans to get us into Tirnia and close to the emperor. And then we'll find out whether this new one still wants me dead and if so, we'll deal with it."

"And if they don't want you dead?"

"We'll walk away."

"And have Nemon on our tail."

"He can't last long with this madness driving him, trust me on that. He will break."

ELONA WAS DRESSED in new travelling clothes that covered most of her scarred flesh, complete with gloves. They were too hot for the climate, but the next patterners path would take them into the north once more.

Rather than riding a slow cart back to the ley-circle, they boarded a *tekrak* that had been brought to rest in the courtyard. Elona found a place in the middle so that she could not see down in any direction and they were soon on their way.

There had been no message from Nemon, and he had not been there to see them off. Just armsmen and servants, who had supplied plenty of food.

It was not even midday when they disembarked at the ley-circle and were greeted by Metue.

"You're making the path?" asked Elona.

"Not today."

"And where are we going this time?"

His reply was given without even a hint of humour. "Glytheni."

"Really?"

"Yes."

She smiled. "How did your lord take the news that you had lost him four armsmen and a *tekrak?*"

Metue did not reply but led the way towards the ley-circle. There were other patterners working on the path and detachment of armsmen in Tirnian colours.

"You're not coming?" said Jaymis.

Metue shook his head.

"Then this is goodbye," said Elona. "I can't say I am sad."

If his glare could have cut her, she would have bled.

They walked on to the circle. Elona could see that the path was ready though she gave no sign of it. They waited for a few moments under the oppressive sun. Elona pulled the thick hood of the jacket over her head. It scraped on scars on one side of her scalp, and hair bristles on the other. She really should get them cut.

Finally, the first few armsmen headed onto the path led by one of the patterners.

"Did Lord Nemon tell you the plan?" asked Jaymis. "What are we supposed to do?"

"Kill the empress," said Metue.

And before Elona could ask why, they were hustled through the portal and left Metue behind.

THE WORLD PATTERN glowed the way it always did beyond the walls of the path, and beneath their feet. Elona wondered whether the shape of the path—from her experience they were always flat on the bottom with an arch—was created by the patterns used. Or it was that way because that's what the patterner wanted.

How did the power from the Mother's Kitchen work? How was it she could simply conjure it from nowhere at the other ley-circle? Why did it affect her the way it did?

"You command that which destroys patterns."

She shook her head in the dark. It made some sense, it made more sense than just claiming it was a corruption of Mother's Milk, but that wasn't the whole truth. If it destroyed patterns why hadn't it simply killed her when she tried to use it for healing? It had worked, but not the way that was expected.

It had shielded them from the feeding long enough for she and Jaymis to get into the path Metue created. It had driven the *kikisa* and then consumed them.

If she was unable to understand it, it would kill her eventually—because there would always be times when she needed power, and this would be the only thing available.

She put her withered arm through Jaymis's and lent on him as they walked. There was comfort in his touch, something she had never known. The only emotion she had ever seen in her father was when Elona had reminded him of her mother. And even then, only once.

The dark power allowed her to make a patterning, at least in the way she as a *fahain* could. But then it would stop working and, she searched for the right word, freeze.

That must be why the patterners thought it was a corruption. Had patterners of the past tried to use it? What would have happened if they did? They would draw a pattern and pull in the darkness to give it power.

"You command that which destroys patterns."

Did it destroy patterns? It was simple enough to test that, she turned her internal eye on her own skin, focusing on her arm. There were all the things she expected to see, the blood pumping through her veins, muscles, and bone, each one of them vibrant and shining with the complex patterns that made her body live.

She refocused on her other arm and it looked the same. She switched again and saw what was different. Her damaged arm had no skin. But of course, there was skin, she could see it with her eyes when she looked.

Concentrating harder she looked for the covering that held every-thing in. For a moment she thought she saw it, and realised it was the jacket. That pattern was complex but lacked the brightness and motion of living tissue.

What she was looking for lay somewhere between the two, but she could not see it.

"Where is it?" she muttered.

"What?" said Jaymis.

"I need to stop."

"Are you ill?"

"What's happening?" demanded one of the armsmen.

"The Lady needs to rest, who has water?" Jaymis's tone was that of a leader of armsmen, who expected to be obeyed without question.

He helped Elona sit down and she ran her gloved hands across the floor of the path. It felt both soft yet unyielding.

Water was procured and she took a mouthful of it. It hadn't been what she wanted but she was grateful for it, nonetheless.

"Are you ill?" asked Jaymis again.

"Not ill, but I need to rest for a short time."

It was clear that he was not happy with this answer, he had never known her behave this way before. But he did not question it and made it clear to the armsmen and patterner they would move on soon and had them move away to give her space.

Elona relaxed and removed her gloves. One hand was damaged and the other unharmed. *If I place the good hand against the bad, I can see where the skin stops, and I will know where to look.*

It proceeded as she planned. With the image of her good hand's patterns in her mind she traced it to the fingers that pressed against the hard, damaged skin of the other. She could even see where the pattern at the fingertip was distorted by the physical pressure.

She looked closer. And closer still. The detail of the living patterns grew in her mind and increased in complexity. She tried to block out the moving light of the living flesh so that she could focus on what she was touching.

There.

For a fleeting moment, she saw almost transparent frozen patterns obscuring and twisting the lights behind them—it was like looking through ice-covered glass. The patterns disappeared immediately, but she had seen it once and knew what to look for. The colours twisted and all the whites, reds, and yellows of the living patterns faded to blue, and dark red lines formed where, before, there had been nothing.

They were still patterns, these curious lines, yet they did not move. It was the difference between a rushing river, and damp mud.

As *fahain*, she manipulated patterns without even knowing them, without the painstaking studies that patterners must have done to find what could be used to create the desired effects.

This thing that her skin had become, it was a pattern and she could see it.

The true pattern for skin was here too, brightly coruscating lights that filled the sight of her inner eye when she looked at it. But she could see its pattern, and she knew now that the frozen pattern was the same thing.

The dark power did not destroy patterns - it took away everything that made them live.

Something slapped her face. She breathed in hard and suddenly.

"Elona!"

"What? Ow? That hurt." She coughed unexpectedly.

"You weren't breathing."

"Don't be ridiculous. I'm fine. Help me up."

He took her hand and she levered herself upright. Her head swam and she staggered into him.

"Can you walk?"

She knew there was something wrong because she didn't even think of anything cutting to say in response. Her legs felt as if they were going to give way at any moment.

"Can I have some more water?"

She drank some as she leaned on him.

"We need to move," said the armsmen.

"I'll be all right," she said. "Could you pick up my gloves, Jaymis?"

"You won't fall over?"

"I'll be okay."

She wavered when he let her go but he was back quickly and held her gently around the shoulders as she pulled on her gloves.

She took a deep breath and walked on slowly. The rest of their escort moved with them and at her speed.

"Did I really stop breathing?"

"I couldn't feel any air movement through your mouth or nose."

"Perhaps it was just very shallow." He said nothing but she could feel his muscles tensing. She sighed to herself. "I'm sorry I scared you."

"Can you tell me what happened?"

She pitched her voice as quiet as she could. "Not here."

CHAPTER 35

They emerged from the tunnel into grey drizzle, and a day very much colder than the one they had left.

Glytheni turned out to be a town of reasonable size with a very large armed force camped in the fields and valleys around the ley-circle. They were hurried off the circle by patterners and guards as Elona felt another portal taking shape behind them.

The place was busy. Despite the wet there was a constant movement of traders, *kichesa*, carts, and armsmen along the partially cobbled tracks leading in all directions.

Elona and Jaymis were stopped near a tent—all the constructions near the ley-circle seemed to be of canvas. It would make them easy to remove during a feeding but Elona didn't think they were very practical for continual use in such a busy place.

The leader of their escort went into the nearest tent and she could see him talking to a patterner.

"No *tekrasa*," said Jaymis quietly.

She glanced around. She couldn't help but be grateful.

"And no easy escape," she said.

"It would help to know precisely what Nemon had planned for us."

"How he expected us to get near this empress, for example."

The chief armsmen returned and promptly dismissed the rest of the men. They hesitated as if he had gone mad, but he glared, repeated his order, and they went.

Jaymis watched them go, but Elona stared at the man.

He took a deep breath. "My lord told me to give you this." He dropped a small but heavy bag into Jaymis's hand. "And according to them, there's a path to be opened to the place you want to go this evening. Troops and supplies mostly." With that he turned away.

"You're leaving us?" said Elona.

"I have my orders."

"Wait," she said, "please."

He stopped and faced them.

"Why did—" she glanced around to see if they could be overheard. There were many people moving around, some of them close. She continued more quietly "—why did your master choose this course? This rebellion?" She made the last word very quiet indeed.

He stared at her, his eye drawn to the scarred side of her face hidden in shadow, then looked down and shuffled where he stood. "Rumour says Myrlask killed his wife." She opened her mouth, but he held up his hand. "Don't ask me no more. You're on your own. Those are his orders."

PEOPLE WERE STARING, so Elona made sure her face was hidden, put her arm through Jaymis's once more and they wandered along the path in the direction of the town.

Once past the military encampment, she felt a little safer.

"What are we supposed to do now?" said Jaymis.

The stones were slippery in the damp and one or other of them would slip every few steps.

"Find somewhere where we can dry off and get something to eat."

It had been a long time from breakfast for them, and her introspection seemed to have worn her out.

After a while, they reached the stone and brick buildings of the town proper, and the street was lined with inns and hostels. They found one that looked neither expensive nor disreputable.

"Let's get a room," said Elona.

"But there's a path to the palace tonight."

"We need to talk, and we don't need to travel immediately. That's just what we were told to do."

"You think it's a trap?"

"I think Nemon is out of his mind and, given what we were told, desperate for us to revenge the death of his wife," she said. "And why do we need to do anything Nemon said if he's not forcing us to?"

They mounted the steps and went through into a pleasant interior lit by dozens of candles. They paid for a room three days in advance and arranged for food to be brought up.

The bed was not as comfortable as the ones at Nemon's fortress, but better than the hard ground. A washbasin stood near the window that looked out on to the street, with a potty under the bed. There was a small table with three chairs, and even a chest of drawers for clothes. They did not unpack their bags, just stripped off their damp outer clothes and hung them by the door. Rugs covered much of the floor.

Elona pulled back the eiderdown and top sheet. She sniffed.

"Not bad."

The meal arrived, Elona made sure she was covered before the servant was allowed in. They ate at the table looking out into the grey town beyond. There was a thick stew with plenty of meat and vegetables, accompanied by fresh bread. The drink turned out to be pear cider which Elona did not much like but drank anyway.

"Will you tell me now what happened to you on the path?" said Jaymis.

Elona put down her spoon and stared out, then she brought up her damaged hand and laid it on the table. She could not feel the surface, only the pressure of touching something. "I was looking at this."

"Your hand."

"Trying to understand what's happened to it. Everything is a pattern, but Metue called it a corruption and Nemon said I commanded a power that destroyed patterns."

"Did you have to do it then?" he said. "And why did you stop breathing?"

"I—" she broke off and reached out to take his hand in her damaged one. "I can't explain, I just had to look. I felt as if I was beginning to understand it, I couldn't stop looking."

"And the breathing?"

"I don't know, I was concentrating. Perhaps I just forgot."

"That's not a good thing to forget."

She said nothing but watched as she dragged her scarred fingers across the back of his hand. There was still no sensation even though she saw his skin wrinkle at the pressure.

"Did you learn anything?"

"Yes. Everything is a pattern."

"Even that?"

She nodded. "But it's frozen."

"Like ice."

"In a way," she said trying to think of a way of describing it. "Imagine a waterfall, all that movement and water splashing everywhere as it tumbles down. That's what a pattern is like."

"That's what you see?"

"It's hard to explain but I'll just say yes for now. What this power does whether it's corrupted Mother's Milk or not, I don't know, but it takes all the life out of a pattern. Imagine the waterfall moving so slowly there's no splashing."

"Like ice."

"No, it's not stopped, if that happened my skin would shatter, I suppose. It's more like it's old. Very old. Ancient. It still moves and bends but the pattern from which it's made has no life in it."

She stared at her skin again, it was as if it did not belong to her.

"Is it spreading?"

"I don't think so."

"Will it…" His voice trailed off.

She looked up at him expecting him to continue but all she could see was the pain in his face.

"Kill me?"

His expression did not change.

She shrugged and looked away. "I don't know. At present it seems only skin deep. I suppose if it went deeper it could."

"How can you be so matter of fact?" There was a sudden anger in his voice, and he stood up.

"How else can I be? I don't know how to mend it."

"There must be a way!"

"Why must there, Jaymis?" she said. "Things are not always simple. Stories are not always tied up in a pretty bow at the end. You know that as well as I do. We lived it."

"I don't care about me."

"But I do." She stood up and went to him. His body was rigid as she put her arms around him but within her embrace, the anger and tension fell away. He leaned forward until his head rested on her shoulder and she could feel his breath on her ear.

"I don't want to lose you."

"I don't want to lose me either," she said, "or you."

Elona looked out of the window. It was still light though the world was grey with rain. Somehow, she felt it should be dark by now.

"Let's go to bed," she said. It seemed as if the physical act of love was the only thing they had.

THE BED MAY NOT HAVE BEEN as comfortable as the one at Nemon's castle, but the weather was a great deal cooler and more in line with what they were both used to. As a result, they both slept better, even if there were periods of desperate lovemaking.

"We missed the path," said Jaymis. He lay face down but with his head turned towards the window.

"Good," she said and pressed her body closer to his. "What do you think we should do today?"

"We did not ask Metue if there was anything of interest to see in Glytheni," he said. "Somehow I doubt there will be much."

"I wasn't really thinking of that."

"Oh, you mean investigating this new empress?" he said disingenuously.

She slapped his bare behind, but the bed clothes meant she couldn't get a good strike.

"Use this money we've been given to buy clothes, food and equipment." He ignored her slap. "Discover if there's another way we can get to the capital."

"The first one of those will be easy, the second I am not so sure."

THE MORNING WAS BRIGHTER than the previous day, at least it wasn't raining, and the streets were busy. The main thoroughfares were cobbled so the rain was gone from them, though the side streets were little more than muddy tracks. The first part of their plan proceeded without difficulty, but their coins were severely diminished by the time they had bought better travelling clothes and new boots.

They could not hide the fact they were foreigners when they spoke, nor that they were of high class, and that attracted attention. Not violent, but just the curiosity of people who had never met travellers from foreign lands.

It was their visit to the cobbler that made Elona uncomfortable. Since they needed the footwear straight away, he had gone through his box of uncollected boots to find something that might fit, or at least be adjusted. And he liked to talk.

"We don't get many travellers here," he said after showing her a boot made of *kichek* hide that reflected in shades of dark green. She slipped off the one she was wearing. "Where are you from?"

"Faerholme," said Jaymis.

The cobbler held the boot and Elona poked her toes into it. The man had caught sight of her face beneath the hood and had glanced away. He said nothing about it but did not look at her face again. She was wearing her gloves so there was no other part of her disfigured body showing.

"Faerholme? That's a fair way."

Elona wasn't sure if he was being funny but he continued as if there had been no intention at humour.

"How does that feel, mistress? Stand up get a feel for it, is it loose?"

She did as instructed and put her weight on it.

"Walk to the door and back."

She did so. "It's a bit big," she said. "Length and the sides. It doesn't grip.

"I might have something that's a better fit. If you'll be taking it off."

He rummaged in his box as she removed it.

"Don't know as there's a regular path from Faerholme. What with the war."

"No," said Jaymis. "We came from Avakending?"

"Mirriasmia? Oh yes, now that's a very long way. Did you meet Lord Nemon?"

Elona glanced at Jaymis as the cobbler pulled another pair of boots, like the one she'd just tried, from the box. The man gestured for the one she'd removed, and she handed it over. He compared the sizes.

"This looks just right," he said.

"We didn't meet him there," said Jaymis.

"Myrlask is gone then?" said Elona changing the subject.

The man had just got down by her feet and now he did look at her. "The empress has taken his place." He went back and held the boot for her.

"I didn't know the emperor had been married."

"He wasn't."

"Then who is the empress?"

"Empress Hilaneena of the Empire of Tirnia, Warder of Esternes, Taltia and the Eastern lands, Protector of Umran." His words were almost a chant.

"Neither Esternes nor Taltia recognise Tirnia as their warden," said Jaymis. There was a hard tone to his voice as if he was barely suppressing an explosion of anger. "And I'm sure Umran does not feel very protected."

The cobbler slid the boot onto Elona's foot.

A *zatek* barked in the distance and the cobbler twisted round to look at the front door.

"Try the other one, lady."

With both boots on and buckled Elona stood. They hugged her feet. She walked to the door and looked out. The people were going about their business but the *zatek* hooted a little closer.

"This one is rubbing slightly on the side of the heel," she said pointing to the right.

"It will stretch." He glanced at the door again. "You need to go."

"How much?" said Jaymis getting to his feet and rummaging for the purse.

"A gift."

"Do not be foolish, you are craftsman, you should be paid."

"Please go, now." He opened the door. "I have a family; they cannot find you here."

"Who?" said Jaymis, but Elona gathered her things and grabbed him by the arm.

"Come on, Jay."

He let her pull him towards the door but tossed a few coins at the man as they exited into the cool air. Elona stretched out her senses but there were so many people it was hard to focus on anything specific.

The *zatek* sounded once more from the right, and there was another quieter one in the far distance.

"They're looking for us," she said and turned to the left.

"How can you say that?"

"How many people do you see here that come from beyond Tirnia?"

She had already noticed that not a single Kadralin walked the streets.

"How could I tell?"

"The clothes, they all have the similar cut here. We were the ones that stood out."

They hurried along the street though they were heading out of the town now. *At least we haven't left anything behind.*

"But if they want to capture us why didn't they do it when we arrived yesterday?" said Jaymis.

"Because we were supposed to be on the path to the Emperor's Fastness."

He stopped. "If you're right, we can't leave the town, there's nowhere to hide out there. If they're using *zatesa* and they have our scent it'll be harder for them to track us among more people."

"And we're away from the ley-circle," she said. "All right."

She turned abruptly left and went down a narrow alley. The shadow of the hills rose above the rooftops.

"Can you do anything about the *zatesa*?" he asked as they pushed along the dark and smelly passageway.

"I can't risk it."

"But you have a ley-circle nearby, surely you don't need to use the other."

She didn't reply. Her power scared her now. What part of her body would be taken if she chanced it once more?

The walls closed in and there was little sound. A baby cried somewhere while a voice tried to cajole it to silence. It was as if the town was holding its breath.

The hooting cry of a *zatek* echoed like a lonely spirit.

"How far away do you think they are?" said Elona.

"They aren't close, if they are on our track at all."

The hoot came again. Perhaps from a different direction, it was hard to tell.

"I may have been mistaken."

The alley they were following had been part of a network which spawned new paths at random without any suggestion of purpose. But now they came out on to a wider passage, though the buildings still overhung and blocked out the sky.

A deep gully in the middle of the street carried a stream of clean-looking water.

Elona turned immediately to follow it. Jaymis came on behind.

"They can't follow in water," she said and moved faster. Like any good town there was a river running through the middle of Glytheni. The path they followed ended in a plain narrow bridge, lacking any ornamentation, that spanned a river which while not wide was running deep and fast. It would not be easy to cross. Elona turned upstream. There were no boats, but a man was fishing on the far side. They were still close to the edge of the town and this part of the river had not been polluted by human waste.

The next sounding of the *zatesa* was much closer. The two of them found a place where they could duck back from the river's bank between two walls.

She sat on the damp ground, with Jaymis beside her, and placed a finger on his lips, staring meaningfully into his eyes. He nodded. She closed hers and sent out her inner eye, looking through the patterns of the world.

Their pursuers were close, almost at the bridge.

The *zatasa* were not wolves. They liked to live in groups but were individual creatures. She watched as the first one scented the two of them and pulled along the bank of the river. The man holding him followed, restraining him with a leash.

Elona felt the pressure building inside her. There was little time left, she wasn't sure what she could do. A fast-moving pattern in the river caught her attention, almost without thinking she focused on it and drew power from the ley-circle. The fish responded instantly; its simple mind was its undoing.

Just as the head of the first armsman was coming into view, the fish leapt from the water right beside the leading *zatek*. The sudden movement caught its eye and it shied. Then the flash of the skin, made the animal realise this was potential food and it lurched towards the water. It snapped at the fish—oblivious to the river. It reached the end of its leash and was brought up short. Its prey plunged back with a splash.

The *zatek* was not going to be stopped, it dug all four of its clawed feet into the ground and yanked hard. The armsman stumbled off-balance. The beast made it into the water and the armsman tumbled in after it.

The double splash sent waves across the river and she could hear the man spluttering as the strong current pulled them downriver.

Elona watched the patterns retreating.

She breathed out.

CHAPTER 36

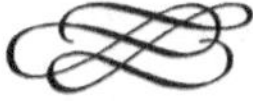

Once the kerfuffle had died down and the armsmen were out of range Elona and Jaymis stood.

"They won't give up looking for us," she said.

"I know."

She sighed. "What are we doing, Jaymis?"

"Trying to get to the empress."

"I cannot see how we can possibly succeed," she said. "The town is looking for us. We're obviously foreigners. We can't sneak onto the right path, even if we knew when it was going to be opened. It's hopeless."

Jaymis was silent for a short time. "Why do we have to wait for a path?"

The answer was so obvious she did not bother to answer.

He took hold of her arm and faced her. "Elona, why do we need them to make a path?"

"I can't do it!"

He just stared at her.

Then she realised what he was saying. "No, I can't control it."

"What difference does that make?" he said. "At least we'll be away from here."

"But we could end up anywhere. I might drop us in the middle of the sea."

He shook his head. "I don't think so."

"I appreciate your confidence, but I can't control it."

"What happened the first time? You ended up in Dirdin in a ley-circle. And the second time, you managed to take me, and we arrived in a cave, with a ley-circle."

"There are plenty of ley-circles in dangerous places."

"Exactly."

"You're not making any sense."

"There are plenty of places where you could have ended up and it would have been dangerous, but you didn't. You arrived in a safe place."

She hesitated; he did have a point, but it wasn't enough of one. "That was just twice."

"I know, but let me put it this way," he said. "What choice have we got?"

She couldn't deny his logic but there were still arguments she could make. "I'm not even sure how I make it happen."

"But I do."

"Oh, really?"

"You had no other choice."

SHE STARED at him for a long time. She shook her head. "You can't be serious."

He returned her gaze then leaned forward and kissed her on the lips. There was no force behind it, and she barely felt his skin against hers. But his breath brushed her cheek and she could feel his warmth.

"I love you," he said, "and I trust you."

But I don't trust me.

He gathered up their things.

"It's the last thing they'll expect," he said.

"I agree, suicide is not something people usually expect."

He looked around. The river ran beside them and the man was still fishing on the other side. Perhaps not everyone in the town was willing to inform on them.

"Which way is the ley-circle from here?"

She barely needed to think about it, the power was like a beacon if she chose to look for it. She pointed directly across the river.

"The sooner we move, the sooner we'll get there."

She didn't argue. She couldn't think of anything better. Instead she pulled her hood up and hid her scarred face from the world.

They went back along the river and crossed the bridge. The fisherman watched them. Once on the other side Elona took the path along the river on this side, away from the man.

"Wait!"

The sudden word from the fisherman jolted them both. They looked round in case armsmen were coming from the houses or across the river. But there was no one except the man and his line.

"I have fished these waters as a man and boy." He had pushed his hood back to reveal the shaved head and stained tattoos of a Brother of Taymar.

Elona took a step back.

"I have fished these waters and never have I seen a silverfin jump."

He made Elona nervous and she stepped back as the man got to his feet, still trailing his line in the water. Jaymis moved forward to protect her.

"What of it, old man?"

"A silverfin doesn't jump and you don't have the power, boy. It was her doing, the girl, let me see her face."

"It's none of your business, brother."

"The Emperor doesn't like the Brothers of Taymar, we have no homes here. I am no threat to you."

"We hear the emperor is dead."

"The emperor may have died but his will lives on in his successor. There is still no home for a brother in this place."

"Then why are you here?"

He smiled and shrugged. "I'm a spy."

Jaymis laughed. "Spies do not reveal themselves."

"Everyone knows I am a spy, I send reports back, such as they are. But these things are no secret. The real secrets lie in the Fastness of Tirnia and no one goes there without permission."

"What does it look like?" said Elona pushing round Jaymis. "The Fastness, have you seen it? Do you know what it looks like?"

"I have heard descriptions from those who have seen it."

"Tell me."

"Show me your face, girl."

"My *name* is Lady Elona of Corlain and you will treat me with the respect due my rank."

"Your rank means nothing in Tirnia."

"Very well, then we shall make a bargain. You will tell me what the Fastness looks like, and I will show you my face."

"I agree," he said. "But who shall go first since we do not trust one another?"

"You will tell me something of the Fastness. I will reveal my face and you will tell me the rest."

He shook his head. "It doesn't matter anymore. I know who you are."

Jaymis tensed. "Of course, you do, she told you her name."

"And I told *you* that the name means nothing. I know who she is. You, however, do not."

Elona looked at Jaymis, his face was expressing the confusion she was feeling. The man's mind must be full of holes.

"Well, if you know who I am you can tell me what the Fastness looks like."

He regarded her with pale blue eyes and his head slightly on one side.

"The Fastness is a great castle that sits on an empty plain. It is so huge that it takes a half day to walk around its walls. And those walls have defensive patterns within them that cannot be breached and there is no gate. It is impregnable from the outside."

"That's ridiculous," said Jaymis, "a castle must have a gate."

"I have not told you everything, boy. Do you want to hear the rest?"

"I do," said Elona.

"In the very centre of the Fastness, there is an ancient tower taller than any built by man, taller than any tower has a right to be, like a dark finger pointing at the sky. It has eight sides and is fashioned from black stone that has no seams. It was there before the Fastness, which was built around it."

"Where is the ley-circle?" said Elona. "How far out from the Fastness?"

The old Brother of Taymar laughed. "The ley-circle lies in the centre of the Fastness."

"He's lying!" said Jaymis. "A feeding would destroy the castle and this tower which is another invention."

"Hush, Jaymis."

"This is the reason why so few patterners are permitted to know the way to the Fastness. This is why so few are invited there. This is why the Fastness cannot be conquered. Its ley-circle can never be overcome, and they will always have a path to feed those within the walls. They will always have power for the wards. Even if an army could march across the plain to give siege - its weapons could not penetrate the walls and those within could never be starved out. The Fastness is impregnable."

"This cannot be true," said Jaymis again. "Nothing could survive the feeding."

"The ancient tower stands on the ley-circle."

Jaymis raised his hand in a gesture of surrender, as if the insanity of the old man's story had finally defeated him. "Come on, Elona. He's got nothing to say to us."

She laid her hand on his arm. "Wait." She looked at the old man. "Who am I?"

He shrugged. "The half-scarred woman."

She pulled back the hood and the man stared at her for a few moments before turning away. "Our bargain is complete."

"What is my destiny?"

He paused and looked back. "The same as anyone. To die."

~

Elona and Jaymis headed downriver with the rushing water on their left. Neither of them spoke about the man. The ground was muddy, and reeds grew up from the shallows along the river's edge. It reminded her of the first time Jaymis's mother had tried to kill her. The first time Elona's ability to heal herself had manifested so obviously. But it seemed that here in Glytheni, they did not harvest the reeds and they grew to their full height waving together as the river's current ran between their stalks.

"How far is it?" said Jaymis.

"We'll be there before sundown."

"Perhaps we should wait until it dark, we'll be able to get closer."

Elona looked at the overcast sky. It was difficult to judge the time of day when the sun was hidden. "I'm not sure it makes any difference."

The river bent this way and that as they followed it but eventually the angle of the ley-circle was sharply to their right and the water was no longer a guide. They headed into the town once more, passing dilapidated constructions which passed for houses. There were people all around them, she could feel them, but no one in sight.

"They're watching us from the buildings," said Jaymis.

"Stop a moment," she said. He moved on a few steps and stopped, keeping an eye on the muddy tracks and dark entrances.

Elona pulled back her hood once more.

"What are you doing?"

With her senses pushed out as far as she could, she was able to feel the change as people saw her. She turned slowly on the spot so they could see her face from all sides.

"Making legends."

"Why?"

"Because if they are impressed, perhaps they will be less likely to alert the armsmen," she said. "That Brother of Taymar was talking about prophecies. It seems I fulfil this one."

"I've never heard of any Scarred Woman."

"Neither have I but..." She sighed, covered her head and started walking again with Jaymis trailing after her. "I told you about Usala in the mountain village. When Chara brought me to her, Usala said she had been waiting for me. She had been born of noble blood, one thing she told me was that she knew of my mother and had met yours."

"My mother?"

"So she said, and I have no reason to doubt her words. But she was compelled to travel all that way from Faerholme or some nearby place, to the mountains south of Tirnia, just to wait for me."

"Who could have made her do that? How could they have even known where you would be?"

I have my suspicions as to who. "I don't believe they could know," she said. "I can't because if we are not in control of our own decisions, our own destiny, what point is there to anything we do?"

"But what this Usala said, and the Brother. How can that be possible?"

"Whose side are you on?"

"Yours, of course."

"Then do not question me on this. I do not know how these predictions can have been made without destiny being fixed, but if I believed it to be true, I would not be able to continue."

In reply, he put his arm around her shoulders, and they walked on in silence.

As they left the vicinity of the river the land rose, and the quality of buildings improved. But it also meant the streets were busier, with people going about their daily business. They stopped in a dark alley that smelled of something dead.

"How far now?" said Jaymis.

"Still too far," she said. "We can't get close without being seen."

"We'll have to wait for dark."

She nodded. "But we'll look suspicious if we hang around in this alley."

She heard the sound of wheels grinding on stones and looked back the way they had come to see a *kichek*-drawn covered cart heading their way, being led by a scruffy-looking man in rough clothes trimmed with fur. The *kichek* itself was smaller than usual but had the colouration of a fully grown animal.

They were trapped. Ahead was the street and there were buildings on either side.

Elona took a step to the side and leaned her back against the wall. "Kiss me."

Jaymis needed no encouragement. His body was against hers in a moment and his mouth drank her lips. She pulled away momentarily.

"This is just a disguise."

"I see it as an opportunity," he said and though she could not see his expression she knew from his voice he was smiling. "You are a fool, Jaymis Betlain."

"I love you," he said and silenced any reply with his lips.

She knew he was trying to shield her body both from sight and from attack. She had trouble understanding such affection, since the only other man in her life that she was supposed to care about had been her father, and he had not given her any regard at all.

But she would have done the same if it had been her with Chara. The Slissac woman had become family like no one else had ever been —except perhaps Jaymis.

Though they continued to press their lips together, both their attention were focused on the approaching cart. The grinding of the iron-shod wheels on stone. The steady slap of *kichek* pads in mud. The shorter, quicker step of the man. Coming closer.

Until it drew level with them. And stopped.

Jaymis pressed harder against her as if the problem might be a lack of space for the cart to get past, but it did not move. Elona felt Jaymis's hand moved to the knife at his belt. They breathed in unison. She felt the change in him just before he jumped to the side and pulled out the weapon.

Elona took in the stopped cart, the snuffling *kichek* and the man standing with his bare head bowed, gripping his hat in one hand, held at his side in a position of subservience. She immediately reached out and placed her hand on Jaymis's arm, to hold him back.

"Who sent help this time?" said Elona half to herself.

"You are the Scarred Woman." The man did not look up as he spoke, and his words were so accented they were barely recognisable.

Elona glanced up the alley and pulled back the hood a little, enough to show her face. "I am she."

"I take you where you want to go."

The cart was not large, but they would be able to hide beneath the coarse and stained cloth that covered the back of it.

"Can you take us to the edge of the town nearest to the ley-circle?"

The man tutted at the *kichek*, then went to the rear and pulled back the tarpaulin. Elona and Jaymis climbed on to a bed of hard vegetables that smelled of earth and the cloth was brought down over them.

"Now you know what it was like to escape with the traders in Dirdin," she said quietly.

The cart jerked and moved forward once more.

"Uncomfortable."

"This is nothing."

CHAPTER 37

The journey was not long but the whole time they were on edge, listening to the noises of the town around them. Waiting for some tell-tale that meant they were discovered.

But nothing came.

Shortly before the cart came to a halt, the town's noises faded, and the cart's wheels echoed. They were stopped for only a few moments before the tarpaulin was lifted behind them and they clambered out awkwardly. The hard, round vegetables turned and rolled beneath them.

They were in another alley but this one was covered with the building above.

"Thank you," said Elona. Jaymis followed suit.

"My gift to you, mother."

Elona guessed what he was expecting. She pulled the hood from her head completely, so the blackened and scarred half of her face was easy to see. "Blessings of the Mother be on you."

She was glad that Jaymis said nothing.

The man bowed deeply, then covered his cart and set off forward to the far end of the alley and disappeared. The hiss of heavy rain came from the nearer entrance.

"Making legends again?" said Jaymis.

"Come on'" She pulled up the hood once more. "Let's get this over with for better or worse."

"How do you want to do it?"

"Let's just head for the circle and when they realise who we are…" she let her voice trail off.

THE RAIN HAD CLEARED the streets of all but a hardy few. But everyone's head was bowed against the downpour, and the streets were already running with mud and effluent. The smell was unpleasant but that, with the rain, would make it much harder for any *zatesa* to catch their scent.

Elona turned in the direction of the ley-circle with Jaymis close beside her.

The prospect of what they were about to do terrified her and she reached out to hold Jaymis's hand. His firm grip settled her though she guessed he was as scared as she was.

"This is a long way from Avakending," he said.

"Certainly colder."

"And wetter."

"The food there was better," she said.

"The wine was very palatable."

"Stop," she said quickly.

"What's wrong?"

"I have to focus on the Fastness. I don't really know how this works. But if I'm thinking about how nice it was in Avakending, we might end up there instead."

"There was a nasty storm and you were attacked by assassins."

"I was nearly killed," she said.

"And you had to use that other power."

"I bear the scars of it."

"What did the Brother say about the Fastness?"

She tried to picture it in her head from his words. "Standing on a plain, great walls with no gate. A huge black tower at its heart, a pinnacle reaching for the sky, older than the works of man."

"Not just a Ziri Tower, you think?"

"It doesn't sound like it," she said.

"Can you picture it?"

"I can picture something, but whether it's a true image, I just don't know."

"Perhaps it doesn't have to be."

She knew he was talking to keep both their minds off what was to come, as well as hopefully making the magic work as intended—if it happened at all.

"What do you mean?"

"You said the patterns used by patterners are like a simple version of the real thing?"

"You think a simple image will be sufficient for the same reason?"

"It might."

"I don't think that really makes any sense."

The buildings that lined the street ended and the road turned slightly before heading off into the grey rain.

They did not pause, because that might have looked suspicious, but Elona trod this path reluctantly as she continued to imagine the Fastness. *How can there be no gate?*

The downpour slackened. Elona glanced up at the sky. It was still grey, but a lighter shade. The clouds were moving fast, and it looked as if the rain might cease completely. It made no difference to them— their cloaks provided some protection, but water had got in and she could feel cold damp patches.

"It would be nice to get dry," she said.

"Are we close?"

The power of the ley-circle was a burning light that filled her mind. "We'll be there very soon."

The energy was waiting for her to use it. Yet she had no idea how. Everything she did was accidental almost as if just a passing thought was enough to activate the Mother's Milk. The only thing she truly understood was the controlling of animals—even then it was the ancient ones, the ones like the Slissac themselves, that she had the least difficulty with.

As if that was its cue, in the distance a *zatek* hooted.

"Can you see anyone?" she said.

"Nobody on the road, nobody watching from the sides as far as I can tell."

"Doesn't that strike you as strange?"

"Yes."

"Slow down," she said. "Take my arm. I need to concentrate."

"Do you want to stop?"

"Keep moving."

He took her wrist and slipped his arm under hers. She leant against him as she closed her eyes. While her body continued to walk slowly, her mind went ahead. She found the *zatek* almost immediately and there were half a dozen others with it. Along with the men who looked after them.

She let herself drift down into the one that had sounded. She understood that he had caught their scent—one that he had been trained with earlier. It was his job to call and chase when he found the smell.

Elona suggested that the smell was that of a friend, a member of the pack. It was not like a wolf-pack where every member was really part of the whole, but even for *zatesa* the pack meant something. They worked together. The creature was quite happy to accept the idea. It liked having pack members.

She moved on to the next one, this one was not familiar with the smell, but it too was happy to associate that smell with the pack. Each time she went into the pattern of a *zatek* she found her task easier, whether it was experience, or that these creatures had something like the wolves binding pattern she did not know. Nor did she care. That it worked was all that concerned her.

Then she saw something she recognised.

A tiny sliver of power. Just like the one that hung about her own neck. A tiny knife that would cut through anything it touched like water. And the owner, a man whose patterns seemed hard, almost fixed.

Though he was the only one with a patterned knife, there were others with him possessing the same rigidness in their make-up. She knew what they were.

"Farahalek," she said, under her breath.

"Where? How many?"

"At the circle. Six. There are *zatesa* too, but they won't attack us."

"We can't stand against that many assassins."

"There's nowhere else to go, my love. And did we not come here because we have to be threatened with impossible odds?"

He said nothing but she could almost hear him saying *not six Farahalek*. It didn't matter, the danger needed to be real, and this was as real as it could get.

The rain was clearing, though moisture still hung in the air, and the buildings that surrounded the ley-circle were now visible, though she could see no one moving about. Still she did not want to make it too easy for the enemy to attack, after all if they simply walked into danger, there would be little reason for her to generate the power to take them elsewhere.

"Wait," she said and came to a stop, still holding Jaymis's arm. "They know we're coming. No need to pretend we're other than we are, but I have an idea."

Jaymis released her arm and got out his dagger. "I miss having a sword," he said, "and a bow."

Elona went to the side of the road and sat on the damp stones. She closed her eyes and let her mind stretch out once more. She was not sure how to do what she intended, but if it were true that the *fahain* had a natural understanding of patterns then she must trust it was so.

She wanted fog. In her experience fog was cold, so she wanted to make it cold here. She spread her sense out, this time focusing on what she could not see—the air around them, and all the way to and around the ley-circle.

There was so much motion that she could not grasp it. Then she realised she did not have to; this was like working with the wolves and the *zatesa* but less complex. These motions were not thoughts.

She tried to stop them, slow them down. It was like the strange power that had afflicted her, but less powerful. She simply leeched the power from the air. And it came to her so very easily, and she took it all in.

Something brushed her cheek and she opened her eyes to whiteness.

In the distance she heard shouts of astonishment and confusion. She looked down and made out the ground, covered with white. The air was filled with snow.

"Elona," hissed Jaymis. "Did you do this? Stop it." His voice wavered.

The freezing air bit into her exposed skin.

"I was going for fog," she said.

"Just as well there's no wind," he said. "It's hard enough to see as it is."

She stood up, though her damp clothes resisted as if they had become as stiff as her scarred body. "They can't see us."

"No, come on, let's cross to the other side of the road and then head for the circle. You can still see that?"

"I can see it." She closed her eyes and followed him through the whiteness. It was as if she had created the fog but then frozen it. Tiny droplets turning to ice. In the distance she could see the patterns of men, moving. The *zatesa* however were motionless. Guilt overcame her as she realised they would not be able to survive if this went on too long, like most ancient creatures they could not tolerate such levels of cold.

The other thing she became aware of as they crossed the road, was the intense silence that had fallen, as if she had even drained the sound out of the world. It reminded her of the silence in the mountains when she had been certain she was going to die in the snow.

There was little difference between then and now. The threat of death was just as clear.

The men she had identified as Farahalek were moving. Slowly, in twos, they had spread out from their previous position. One pair stayed on the road, each of the others went further out, but paralleling the others.

She found Jaymis's ear and told him.

He took her hand as they followed the line of the road in towards the ley-circle. Elona clung to him as they crept forwards, each step placed deliberately and as soundlessly as they could.

The cold ate through her clothes.

The Farahalek were close. She squeezed his hand twice in warning. Together they stopped and squatted on their haunches as the cold spread through her limbs.

Even though she could see their patterns, there was no sound as the assassins on the road moved past them, barely an arms-length away. They stopped, but did not speak. Perhaps they knew they should have found their targets by now.

The two pairs of flanking Farahalek soon came to a halt as well.

Elona jumped as one of the closer ones gave a short shrill whistle, and the others closed on the road—though still very slowly.

Jaymis pulled at her hand. She resisted and gave three sharp squeezes. Thankfully he got the message. She did not think they would be able to move without being heard.

It was at that moment the first of the *zatesa* started up a pained keening cry. She switched her attention and realised the poor beasts were suffering badly and probably would not last long.

It was joined by one and then another, hooting out their agonised blasts of sound. Jaymis squeezed her hand twice and gave a gentle pull. He was right, if there was a time to move, it was now. She squeezed back and pushed his hand.

Her legs had almost seized up with the cold, and sharp pains lanced through them as she rose and commenced the slow walk amid the crying of the animals.

She did not know what else she could do. The pain of the *zatesa* was tearing at her, all the more because it was her fault. There was only one course of action for her, and that was reverse what she had done to the air.

Taking the power had been easy but as they crept along the effort of putting energy back into the patterns was completely different, and much harder. If the ley-circle had not been available, it would have been impossible—she dare not imagine what using the draining power of the void might have done to the air if she had tried it.

Instead she focused on the ley-circle and created a conduit for the Mother's Milk to come to her. Then—not knowing how she did it— she imagined all the cold patterns in the air about her and fed the power into it.

The change was instantaneous.

Where there had been white, there was now fog. No, steam that hissed and burned her skin. She cut off the power instantly.

Jaymis must have been surprised at the change—there had been no way to warn him—but he reacted quickly. He yanked her forward and they broke into a run. He angled them up on to the road and they pelted forwards.

They had gone barely twenty paces before Jaymis came to a shuddering stop and pulled her round as she went past him.

She saw a rank of armsmen standing on the ley-circle. "How did they get there? They weren't there!"

Even as she said it another group marched forward out of nowhere. "Clever," said Jaymis to no one as the first rank raised their crossbows and fired. He ducked. Elona threw up her arm defensively and a translucent blue wall materialised between them and the armsmen.

The crossbow bolts glanced off it and fell harmlessly to the floor as the second rank fired.

"Behind!"

She spun round at Jaymis's warning; a sword was swinging towards his face. She gestured again and they were encircled in blue. The sword hung motionless, embedded in the warding she had created.

The Farahalek thundered up, and the armsmen ceased firing.

The tiny magic blade glinted as the lead Farahalek pulled it from its little sheath. With a practised swipe, the blade sliced through the patterns she had created. The blue light collapsed and the Farahalek lunged at her.

CHAPTER 38

The sun was setting in the west, highlighting the low hills of a vast plain. Cold air chilled her exposed skin, but the travelling clothes kept her own warmth in. They seemed to be at one end of a ridge, slightly down from the top which gave a view of the wide flat emptiness stretching out in every direction.

Something screeched into the night. Its voice carrying across the otherwise silent plain.

"The Great Waste," said Jaymis behind her. She already knew he was there because she had carried him with her.

"Probably."

"No Fastness."

"There's a big ley-circle nearby," she said, keeping her voice calm. "It's on the other side of this ridge."

"Do you suppose there's a flash of light or something like that when you do this trick?"

"Did the soldiers of Dirdin report a light?"

"No."

She turned and looked up the slope behind them. It was covered in short coarse grass. The same grass that stretched from her feet down to the plain and out to the horizon. The last rays of the sun shone

333

through the clouds from beneath the horizon in columns that stretched into the sky.

"That's nice," said Jaymis. "Shall we look before all the light is gone?"

They climbed, using their hands as well as feet. The slope was steep and the grass slippery.

As they approached the top, they slowed and got down on their bellies, squirming upwards. They saw the black tower first. Elona assumed they must be close because it was so big but as they crept higher and peered over the edge, her sense of distance adjusted.

They must be at least a league from the walls. The description had not been wrong. The outer defence looked as if they might be as high as her tower at Corlain, and at the lower levels they were featureless. Not even arrow slits marred the smooth surface. Higher up there were gaps from which arrows could be fired and perhaps unpleasant substances could be poured on to attacking troops. Though she could not imagine any force taking this place.

The ridge they were on did not afford them view of what was behind the walls, except for the black tower. Just as they had been told, it rose like a finger from the heart of the Fastness. Perhaps four or five times the height of the walls. A stupendous construction but looking at it she knew who had built it.

Jaymis breathed out as if he had been holding his breath. "Taymar's teeth."

"Slissac," she said in reply. "And it's sitting right on top of the ley-circle."

"That's impossible."

His response did not merit a reply. They were not imagining it. Here stood a tower that must be over a thousand years old—though it bore no sense of age in what they could see in the dying light—sitting in a place where the ley-circle feedings would have destroyed it the first time it was struck. Yet, who knew how many feedings later, it still pointed its finger into the sky.

It told a story that any patterner would understand in a moment: the Slissac had the knowledge to tame a feeding. And that was why patterners were kept away from here. Only the trusted few could walk the path, the only knowledge that had leaked out was a description.

Any army that attempted to lay siege to the place would have to cross who knew how many leagues of the Waste, even assuming they could find the location. Meanwhile the Fastness could be kept stocked with food, and bring in fresh troops, through its ley-circle.

"We must move quickly," said Jaymis.

"Why? They can't know that we're here."

"They know you, Elona. Someone will travel the path and tell how you disappeared from the Glytheni. We have to get inside."

"There's no gate," she said.

"There has to be one."

"Why?"

"We're here to see the empress, we need to get inside. We can't scale the walls. I suppose we could shout up for them to let down a rope."

Elona stared at the Fastness as the darkening night closed in. Lights from inside glimmered off the black surface of the tower.

She rolled onto her back and stared up at the thin grey blanket of cloud. The whiteness of Lostimal brightened one patch.

"There may be a way."

"You've seen something?"

The screech of a great flying beast—one of the *sikechasa*—filled the darkness again. Her skin crawled at the thought. She felt sick just contemplating it, but Jaymis was right, they had to get inside, and they needed to do it quickly. They must stay one step ahead of the empress.

Why had Lord Nemon shifted his position so quickly? He had sent them to Glytheni but could he have warned the empress so that, when they were not on the path, they were attacked.

"What are you thinking, Elona?"

Jaymis's words brought her back to reality as he leaned in towards her.

"I am thinking that I want you to make love with me now."

"Here?"

She reached up and pulled his face down to hers.

We may never get the chance again.

⁓

IT WAS HURRIED AND AWKWARD. Their clothes got in the way but neither of them laughed. And afterwards they clung to one another for a long time without speaking.

But it was getting colder.

"What's your plan?" he said after a long time.

"We have to fly."

"You can make us fly?"

She gave a short laugh. "No. I mean we must ride on the backs of *sikechasa.*"

"But what about your problem?"

She shook her head but realised he couldn't see her in the dark. "It won't be for long." Though she tried to keep her voice calm, terror grew inside her at just the thought of it. She forced it down.

"I'll bring two of them here and control them enough to get us up and over the walls. We'll find somewhere to land inside."

"And hope that bored armsmen on the walls don't try to bring down our mounts."

"Have you got a better idea?"

"I don't, but perhaps just one could carry both of us?"

"It would be easier to control just one, but I don't know if one could even get off the ground."

"The *zirichasa* can carry more than one," he said.

"How do you know?"

"What my friend said, about the woman on Esternes."

"These aren't *ziri.*" She shook her head. "We can't take a risk."

The screech went across the plain once more.

"They're hunting," said Elona.

"Should we wait until they've eaten?"

She shook her head. "Extra weight."

With that she sat up and stretched out her mind to the ley-circle. There did not seem to be anything unusual about it, despite the Slissac tower above. She drew its power and sent out her net to capture two great flying creatures.

∼

WANDERING in the snows of the cold mountains there had been very little sound, only the wind that froze her hair and skin, and the cries of the giant *sikechasa*. She had been sure she would die either from the cold or ripped to pieces by the talons of beak of one of those great ancient flying beasts.

The *sikechasa* came in many sizes and types but the huge ones that lived in the mountains, soaring on the winds, were almost as feared as the *nachasa*.

But when she had been dying in the mountains, she had barely any idea of what she was capable. Nor would she have had the strength or power to use it even if she had.

It was different now. She had the knowledge, and the ley-circle gave her all the power she needed. And yet, though she was able to find a pair of the creatures, hunting together and soaring across the dark landscape. They seemed oblivious to her attempts to control them. She found herself unable to insinuate herself into just one of them.

Time passed as she tried again and again to make some headway.

"Elona?"

Her eyes snapped open and she released the power of the circle.

"I...can't."

"What's wrong?"

She looked down inside herself and saw the terror that lay within.

"I'm scared."

His hand found hers and gave it a squeeze. "Me too."

She shook her head. "You don't understand. They are creatures that fly, I cannot be them. Just cannot."

"Time to find an alternative then." He was trying to sound cheerful, but she could tell he was disappointed.

She stood up and brushed herself down, adjusting her clothing that

337

was still a little askew after their ill-timed lovemaking. *We shouldn't have done that.*

"Yes," she said. "Another way in. We better hurry so we get to the walls before light."

They set off over the top of the ridge and down to the plain below.

It may have looked flat from a distance, but it was filled with humps and holes with no pattern. Most of the holes were filled with water and they tried to keep on the higher parts, but it slowed them down.

The Fastness grew slowly as they picked their way across the waste that lay before it. It had looked big from a distance, but as they drew closer the true enormity of it settled on them like a dark despair.

How can we possibly breach this monstrous place? Why do we even want to?

But the fact that she had been walking a path somehow predicted and known kept driving her. It did not matter. She was here now, and she must face this empress who wanted her dead.

"Perhaps we can climb the walls," said Jaymis, his voice at a whisper even though there was nothing to hear them.

"Perhaps."

But she barely thought about his words. She was considering what she had done back at the Glytheni ley-circle. Turning the air cold and then hot. But how could that help her breach a wall probably as thick as three horses nose to tail?

Whatever she did, they would need a distraction.

She stumbled on a clump of grass and fell forwards, catching herself as one hand went into the water and the other on grass. The ripples faded out and she saw the midnight black of her reflected silhouette against the greyer black of the cloud-filled sky.

And felt her tiny blade bump where it dangled between her breasts.

What magic can make a blade that cuts anything?

"Are you all right?"

"I'm fine. Hush."

She had never looked closely at the wicked little weapon.

She focused her inner eye and penetrated the pattern. And there it was, what she had realised must be there.

Though it was encased by a strong patterning, the core of the knife, embedded in the metal itself, was a tiny element of the void. She did not truly comprehend how such a thing could be made and the cunning that went into its construction but there it was.

The blade could cut through anything because it drained the power from the patterns it contacted. Yet it was made such that the pattern that contained it was not harmed.

She was sure that meant something in regard to her skin, but she did not know what it might be.

Climbing to her feet, she wiped her wet hand on her jacket and stared at the vast castle ahead of them.

"Come on."

She set off at the fastest pace she could towards the base of the nearest wall.

"What's your plan?"

She ignored his words, better that he didn't know.

Instead she reached out once more into the vast waste around them. Not just to the two hunting *sikechasa* she had contacted before, but to every single one she could reach. It was like the fish off the coast of Avakending, though they did not move together. There were hundreds of them, feeding off creatures that hid in the ground coming out only at night—she felt them as well.

This time she did not seek to control the *sikechasa* that had not worked with two, it would not work with more. But she knew how to tease their desires. They wanted food and she offered it to them. Within the smooth cliffs of the castle she promised them the chance to eat their fill.

A great cry from a large beast echoed across the plain and reverberated from the walls. That was not unusual. Then another one. She was sure the men inside could not distinguish one from another. Even in the short time she and Jaymis had been here they had heard more than one screaming in the dark.

Then another. And another.

The sound of wingbeats thudded through the air. The beasts flew in, first one or two, then there were dozens, then hundreds. They wheeled and turned above the ramparts.

Elona suggested that the men that stood looking up at them would be delicious treats to take back to their young.

She crashed against the wall of the Fastness as the constant cries of the *sikechasa* were mixed with the screams of men.

Jaymis had his back against the stones and stared up at the black shapes turning against the grey clouds.

Then he looked at Elona. He said nothing. He had seen her wrest the wolf pack from his mother and then turn it against her. He understood what this was.

Elona took her attention away from the *sikechasa*, though there was no change in the sounds from above.

She pressed the palms of her hands against the wall. And looked into it. The stone was as thick as she had imagined, and she could feel the wards that penetrated it, constantly powered, and fed from the ley-circle.

Walls that no army would ever be able to breach.

The wards did not shield the power of the circle from her. She reached out and felt it throbbing ready to yield to her, ready to form into whatever pattern she desired.

And she thrust it away. She wanted power but she would not take it from the circle.

Instead she studied the patterns of the wall, feeling them beneath her touch, even through the scarred skin of her right hand. And she accepted the power of the pattern into herself.

The stones beneath her hands cracked and splintered. Like dust it fell away.

She felt Jaymis move back. But she continued to focus on the patterns before her, spreading her attention in the shape of a hole, deep and wide enough for her to step through.

The stone crumbled before her. She pressed forwards and it gave way, turning to choking dust. Moments later her body was surrounded by stone.

Jaymis's voice floated past her. "Taymar's stinking teeth…"

Then she reached the ward. It glowed blue to her, powerful and strong. The ley-circle itself drove it, and she could not draw the power from it as it was constantly replenished.

But here, within the wall, was the pattern that made it. The patterners must have worked with the stonemasons, to place the patternings for the wards into the very stones. But if the patterns were in the stone—

The blue flickered and evaporated.

—when the stone was destroyed, the pattern went with them.

Elona continued forwards, step by slow step. And she knew Jaymis was behind her.

Her whole world shrunk to just the stone ahead and around her. Her body was tiring as the energy she absorbed grew. She did not know how much she could possibly consume and hold, or whether she would burn like kindling when it became too much.

She already felt as if her skin was on fire.

But she did not relent. This was the path she had chosen.

Step by step. She walked through the wall—

CHAPTER 39

Jaymis had been keeping his hand on her back. Partly for the comfort of knowing she was still there in the dust-filled hole she was making, but perhaps he hoped he reassured her that he was there. He had no idea what she was doing, and her power scared him.

It was simply too much.

Then she stumbled forwards and fell away. He followed quickly in case there might be enemies, but his feet became entangled with hers and his knees crashed painfully on the ground as he came down trying not to land on her, though he was not entirely sure where she was.

Light flashed nearby and went dark but further away, the entire room lit up. Despite the pain he got back on to his feet and drew his dagger in case there were enemies nearby.

He looked around trying to gain some idea of where they might be. All that he learnt was they were close to one end of a huge cellar, going off both to his right and left. Massive buttresses shored up the wall at regular intervals. The ground they were lying on was damp flagstones with pools of water collected at intervals.

He recognised the light was being generated by the moss that

Elona had shown him before. She said that the Slissac used it. She said the tower was Slissac.

Did that mean there were Slissac here too?

It didn't matter, this was the heart of the Tirnian empire. This was where they would find their answers and probably die.

Just as she had described in her story, she had overpowered the mosses nearby and they had died. The rest had lit up and they went off into the distance. Which might be a problem. He had no idea whether she could light the mosses through walls, but if she could it meant that every moss in a wide circle was now glowing and it would not be diffi-cult to find its centre.

He coughed as his lungs tried to clear way the dust. Looking back at the hole she had made he just shook his head. If she could do that to stone, she could probably do it to a person.

They could not stay here.

He knelt beside her and gently shook her shoulder.

No response. He panicked for a moment but could feel warm damp breath from her lips when he put his cheek close to hers.

Probably just exhausted. He gathered up as much moss as he could, shoving it inside his clothes and their bags.

He managed to get her into a standing position then hoisted her up on to his shoulders. She was not heavy, but he was glad he'd had time to recover his strength on the *tekrak*.

Though he had no real idea of the size of the place he knew that they had come through the wall about a third of the way along from the left corner. Which meant the main tower was forward and slightly to his right.

They probably did not want to go there until Elona was at least awake. But ideally, they should find somewhere to rest before trying to find the emperor—or empress.

There was no exit he could see but the buttresses hid portions of the chamber, so he headed left scanning the walls as he went.

The exit was just past the final buttress. It was so ordinary, it seemed out of place. If this had been an ordinary castle, he would have expected something defensible but if it were true the Fastness had no gates, then there was no need to make this door strong.

The builders, in their arrogance had believed their creation to be impregnable, perhaps it would have been against an army. But not against this one girl.

The door led to a corridor. The corridor led to more. The place was a warren and soon the moss lights faded. He pulled some from inside his shirt and held it as they moved on. His eyes adjusted to the dim light and they continued to make good progress.

He had no idea where they were going, he just wanted it to be away from the light Elona had created.

They reached a T-junction. The left turn headed into darkness but immediately to right was a spiral staircase going up and straight ahead was a door. This seemed a good place to stop. Elona was not too heavy but there were limits to what he could manage.

He stopped to listen and, just as it had been each previous time he checked, the place might as well be completely deserted. It was silent as a grave. He hid the moss he was holding and saw there was no light emerging from beneath the door, so he grabbed the handle and opened it. The dim light revealed several tables and chairs. Each table had a candlestick with varying amounts of candle. He shut the door and moved in.

Carefully he let Elona down and placed her in one of the chairs but leaning forward with her head resting on her arms, as if she had simply fallen asleep there. Then he extracted all the glowing moss and piled it up on another table. It lit the room enough for him to decide it had probably been a mess for off-duty armsmen. Or perhaps for castle servants.

Whatever it had been, the dust had been accumulating for years. Just as much as it had out in the passages. He was not fooling himself, once they managed to pick up his trail, it would be very easy to follow.

The door had a bolt, so he locked it. Then arranged his cloak at the bottom of the door. It would not hide the light completely, but it dealt with the worst of it. If he heard anyone coming, he could shove the moss inside his shirt as before.

Feeling marginally safer, he dug out the water bottle, bread—which had gone hard—and dried meat. He ate slowly and watched as Elona slept.

He could not imagine how exhausted she must be after what she had done.

He was tired too. He had been awake for an entire day. It had not been the first time but he was not as fit as he had been when he was a Dirdin armsmen, and they had not been required to carry a young woman for long periods of time.

He closed his eyes.

It was the sound that woke him. In his state of half-somnolence, he imagined what he heard to be a giant snake slithering across stone. But the sound remained at the same volume, as if it moved but never came any closer.

Then there was the light dancing on the other side of his eyelids. That was the thing that pulled him into reality. He kept perfectly still to prevent whatever it was from knowing he was awake. The light was not constant, it came and went but too fast to be a firelight, and too blue—not orange and yellow.

He separated his eyelids and peeked through the gap. There was something in the room with them, several somethings. He could barely make them out and they did not seem to have any specific form. He focused on just one, near him, though it was in constant motion. Part of that motion was the dust. It seemed to be made of dust, but the dust itself was moving, flowing around the shape of the thing, almost like a waterfall as it tumbled down the surface of the uncertain shape.

It was impossible to make it out. Then it went through a table—or some of it went across the top while the lower section passed beneath. Another one took its place, then a third came from the other direction and they passed through each other, giving off the blue flickering light as they did so—tiny bolts of lightning that crackled like dry sticks. While the strange susurration that filled the air was the dust.

It was about that moment he realised the strange dance of the dust creatures was centred on Elona whose head still rested on her arms.

He sat and his hand went for his knife.

"Shhh…"

He stared at Elona between the shifting dust clouds and saw her eyes were open. If the creatures had noticed him moving, they gave no sign but continued to circle her. There seemed to be five of them though it was difficult to tell. The mosses had almost gone out, and the only other light was the blue flashes.

Elona sat up slowly. If she was trying to avoid alarming them, she probably had not succeeded as they moved faster and in a more agitated way.

Jaymis wondered where the dust was coming from, since it was always pouring off them. He looked at the floor, but it was far too dark to see.

"What are they doing?" he said quietly.

"I think they want something."

"Do you know what they are?"

She gave a very short and quiet laugh. "Tahulin, I think."

"You don't believe in them."

"I was wrong, or they're something else."

"They don't look like the spirits of the dead."

Elona slowly got to her feet. She swayed and put her hand on the table to steady herself.

"Are you all right?"

"Dizzy."

Jaymis stood as well, but the dust creatures did not seem interested in him.

Only Elona.

It took him a moment to realise the mosses were getting brighter.

"What's happening? What are they doing?"

"Nothing," she said hoarsely. Her half-scarred face was like day on one side and midnight on the other. "Not them. Me."

But whether it was her and not them, the Tahulin, or whatever they were, were moving in increasingly complex patterns around Elona. It was almost like a dance, a fast and frenetic one; or the cogs of a windmill driven by a storm, even though there was barely any sound.

Then he heard a sound he dreaded from outside: Men shouting to one another, a triumphant noise.

"They've found us."

"I…can't…hold…it…in!"

The power in the room was so powerful Jaymis felt the hairs on his skin standing up. The mosses flashed white and went dark. But he could still see because the Tahulin glowed a constant blue now from the lightning within and lit the room with its eerie and silent glow.

Elona was standing rigidly, feet apart, and arms spread. Blue light flashed from her skin.

Someone thumped on the door. Something cracked.

The blue lights went white. Jaymis couldn't even look at Elona and the creatures that surrounded her as they flashed about in their complex pattern. It was like the Mother's Milk at a feeding. It spilt from Elona and shone out in all directions—even through him.

The door shook and the bolt cracked.

Everything went black and Jaymis saw spots. Then the door crashed open and three men stumbled in, one of them tripping on the cloak and falling with a cry.

The dim light of the lanterns cast black shadows.

Jaymis was on the first one before they had a chance to study the room. He jabbed upwards with his dagger through the stomach to the heart. This one went down without a cry. Jaymis yanked the blade free as he pushed the man away and was on the next in a moment. This time the knife went through the soft parts of the neck, slicing tendons. The second did little more than gurgle. It might not be a magic blade, but it was well-honed.

The man on the floor had got onto his hands and knees as, with both hands, Jaymis slammed the blade through his back. This would not kill him immediately but without a healer he would die soon.

But this victim cried out.

Something smashed across Jaymis's back driving him to the floor. Reactively he rolled away from the light just as another blow came down and the heavy club smashed into the stones. The man wielding it cried out in pain as the shock hit his hands and wrists. He dropped the weapon.

In a smooth move, Jaymis grabbed it up, swung it once to gain speed and smashed it into the knee of his fourth assailant. Something cracked, and the armsmen toppled crying out in pain.

The sound of two crossbow bolts being released was accompanied by thuds of bolt against flesh. For a moment, Jaymis thought he had been hit but it was the falling man who had taken a blow. Struck by his own side.

Jaymis swung the club again but this time at the edge of the door. The blow was not strong but sufficient to push the door closed.

"We need a warding, now!"

In the half-light from the door, he turned to Elona. She was no longer in that strange rigid position, but her half-scarred face was filled with surprise. Her hand came up and touched the second bolt that protruded from her breast.

Her other hand reached out to him. "Jaymis—"

CHAPTER 40

ime stopped.

Elona slumped to the floor.

He threw himself under the table to where she lay. The bolt had penetrated a good way, it had entered her lung but was not close to her heart. He resisted the temptation to rip it from her—though it was all he wanted to do. She was not bleeding badly on the outside, though her lung might be filling with blood.

It was best to leave it for now.

He wished he had her sight, wished he was a healer, but he was neither. All he knew was what wounds were quickly fatal and which could be survived long enough on the battlefield.

This one fell in the middle. It might not be bad, or she might die in a very short time.

But there were other concerns. He heard the unmistakable sound of crossbows being prepared. He had very little time.

He tore himself away from his beloved, scooted under the table once more, and launched himself through the door. At a time like this, attack was the only defence.

There were three more of them. Two with crossbows, and the squad leader with a sword. They stared in surprise at him, and that moment spelt death for the closest armsmen with his crossbow still not fully pulled back. Jaymis spun once, giving the club all the speed he could, and it smashed into the side of the armsman's face. Bones and teeth snapped.

The shock of the onslaught gave Jaymis the moment he needed to close on the second bowman and slash across his neck. It wasn't as clean as the one in the other room, but blood poured from the cut and the man lost interest in the fight.

Jaymis had steadied himself with dagger in one hand, the club in the other. He calmed his breathing. The sergeant positioned himself in a crouch, he too had a dagger while the sword in his other hand looked well-kept, and he held it as if he knew what to do with it.

Then Jaymis took a step back as something came through the wall. Moments later it had picked up dust and the susurration filled the air. It was larger than the Tahulin Jaymis had seen before.

The sergeant must have heard the sound and seen that Jaymis's eyes were no longer fixed on him. Perhaps he thought it was a trick at first, but the cloud of cascading dust moved up behind him. He spun round with a sweep of his blade, with the intention of taking down whatever had crept up behind him.

The sword blade slashed through the cloud without slowing and only succeeded in scattering dust where it exited. The lack of impact pushed him off balance and he stumbled forwards, into the Tahulin.

He coughed as he must have breathed in a lungful of the dust.

The quiet of the corridor filled with the man's pained and desperate breathing as he tried to suck air into his lungs. He fell to his knees and dropped the weapons as his hands flailed in a desperate attempt to get into clear air.

Jaymis had more important things to do than watch him die. Though he was grateful to the creature for saving him from a fight he would have most likely lost. Dropping the club, Jaymis sprinted past the dying man and back into the room.

Elona lay where he had left her. More of the Tahulin floated about the room—all of them larger than they had been, if they were even the same ones. Somehow Jaymis knew they were.

He dropped to his knees beside her and pressed his hand against her cheek. She was still breathing and did not seem to have coughed up blood in the time he had been gone. Which meant, hopefully, the bolt had not pierced a lung.

If only they had a healer.

He needed to trust the injury was not deep and remove the bolt. And for that he needed bandages but those were not among their supplies. The only option was to make do with clothing. He could use his own knife but that would take too long.

"I need to borrow your knife, my love."

He reached his hands to her neck and found the fine chain that held the scabbard of the wicked little thing. He acquired a cloak from one of the bodies and laid it out on the table then sliced through it creating regular strips with clean edges. Once he had enough, he knotted and rolled them up ready to wrap around her. He turned the remaining pieces of cloth into a pad for the wound itself.

They had no alcohol, so he had to trust that the wound was clean enough. The bolt had gone through several layers of clothing before penetrating her skin.

Carefully, since these were the only clothes she had, he cut up through the front so they could still be worn. But he had to remove the sleeves.

She lay there, pale in the dim light, her chest completely bare and the bolt protruding from it. Blood leaking from the wound, much of it had crusted but it had not stopped pumping which meant she still lived.

Causing her pain was the last thing he wanted to do, but this must be done. He placed one hand around the bolt and the other pressed down on her chest. Her skin was cold. He took a deep breath and pulled upwards, trying to keep the same angle.

Elona shuddered and groaned as the pain went through her. He had barely removed it more than a fingers breadth.

"Stop," she hissed.

"I must do this."

Her scarred and blackened right hand came down on his, stopping him from pulling again. She groaned as if moving her hand had caused the pain, as well it might.

"Wait, my love."

He hesitated.

"I must gather strength."

Even though it seemed as if she had once more passed from consciousness, he waited and counted his breaths. When he got to one hundred, he would start again.

But he had barely reached twenty before her hand moved away.

"Now. Go slow, my love."

Knowing she was awake made the act doubly difficult, but he took firm hold once more and pulled slowly. Another long and drawn out groan came from her lips and it was almost as if he was driving the bolt into his own heart as he inflicted the pain on her.

He could see the length of bolt he had withdrawn from her by the discolouration of its wooden shaft with her blood. He measured it by the number of finger joints. One...two... he felt its movement becoming freer, and Elona's pained cries became less ...three. He stared in horror as yet another length emerged. It was impossible that the weapon had not punctured something important. But the bolt came free of her wound and he threw it behind him. It clattered on the stones.

Quickly, as the blood oozed from the hole, he grabbed the pad and placed it over the wound. Then he pulled her up into a sitting position —she did not help him and must have lost consciousness. His makeshift bandage was enough to wind round her chest six times. He tied it off, made a pillow of his own cloak and laid her back. Carefully he adjusted her clothing and covered her with her own jacket.

He kissed her once on the forehead, stood slowly and sat back on one of the chairs. The strange dust Tahulin moved slowly about the place. At first it seemed to be at random, then he realised there was a pattern to it. Though he could neither follow it, nor divine its meaning.

Sleep overcame him before he remembered to hide the bodies.

~

HE FELT her lips pressing against his. Her scent as he breathed in. The softness of her cheek—and the roughness of the scarring.

"Thank you," she breathed in his ear.

He sat up and the memory hit him like a physical blow. He looked down to where he had left her, but she was no longer there.

"I'm here," she said and put her hand on his.

The chair clattered to the ground as he jumped up and gathered her in his arms. "I thought I was dreaming."

"No such luck."

Eventually his good sense overcame his desire to hold on to her forever. "I'm so sorry, Elona."

"What for? You saved my life."

"I let them shoot you." Then something else came to him. "How are you even standing?"

She shook her head. "You know I heal quickly. I used to do that even when I was young. But this time, at least at first, I was healing myself the way I did with Drahail." She pulled back the clothing he had sliced, there was barely a mark where the bolt had been. Elona shook her head. "But I did not do this."

Jaymis looked around. The Tahulin were still there, and still moving in that curious and complex pattern.

"What are they doing?"

"I don't really know, but they are making some sort of magic.

As he watched, her eyes unfocused.

"It's like a ward but covers the entire area and some distance outside. I suppose they are protecting us."

She came back to the world, smiled at him then went up on her toes and planted a kiss on his lips.

"You should eat," she said. "I've had mine. Everything left is yours. Sorry, I had quite a lot of it."

They sat down and he ate what was left of their food by the unsteady light of a candle.

"Did you carry me?" she said.

He nodded. "A long way, I think. Until I got here, and it seemed a good place to stop. You were exhausted after you breached the wall. How did you do that? I've never heard of a patterning like that."

She looked away and drew a circle in the dust on the table using her blackened hand which she then lifted and stared at. "I told you the void takes all the life from patterns. I took all the life from the stone.

"But it filled me up, I didn't know how to get rid of it. Like filling a waterskin with so much water it could drown everything around it, if ever it leaked." She looked up at him. "I did not dare to leak."

"When we were here with the Tahulin before, they were doing something and you—" he hesitated to say it. "—you were like a feeding."

"I leaked." She gave a small smile. "I had to let it out and they were desperate for it."

"They were?"

"Apparently so, they're bigger, aren't they?" she stared as one of them passed through the table beside them. "They were very hungry."

"Hungry."

She shrugged. "Best way I can describe it. I fed them."

"One of them suffocated an armsmen."

"Took your glory? You were doing so well."

"We would have been dead without its help."

She stared around once more. "And now they're protecting us somehow."

"You made some friends," he said. "Do you think they'll come with us?"

She looked up as if she could see the empress through the walls. Perhaps she could.

"I suppose we'll find out."

~

THEY WERE SILENT FOR A WHILE. Jaymis was happy just to hold her and she did not seem to mind.

"I wonder what the time is," she said.

"You want to go?"

"Want? No, what I want is to flee to the furthest lands and having nothing more to do with empires, patterners, and a destiny I neither chose nor want."

"But they will come after you," he said.

"Yes, they will come after me."

She moved as if she intended to stand and he unwrapped his arms. She brushed herself down and ran a hand across her head.

"Will you do me a favour?" she asked, looking down at him.

"Anything."

"Shave my head."

He ran his hands across his chin, the bristles were long and scratched him.

"I don't have a suitable blade."

She smiled. "I have the perfect one."

Reaching between her breasts she pulled out the Farahalek knife. She undid the chain and handed it to him.

"I don't want to cut you."

"I'm sure you'll be careful."

"What about the scarred side?"

She hesitated and rubbed the surface with her fingers. "If you can find any hairs."

Jaymis arranged the lights and lit three more candles to see what he was doing. The bristles on Elona's head were almost the length of his fingernail but, as he carefully dragged the blade across her scalp, it came away as if it had never been attached.

At first, he was cutting with some gap between the blade and Elona's skin, but as he gained in confidence, he simply let it rest against her head as he slid it across.

"When we ran from Usala's village," she said suddenly as he worked. "And we found the Slissac town, the matriarchs insisted I had my hair shorn. The human slaves had to cut their hair to mimic their masters."

"But you said you became Chara's sister?"

"Yes, there was a special ceremony. Although the matriarchs weren't keen, they had no choice."

"Does that make you a Slissac?"

Elona raised her hand to her scarred cheek and let it fall without replying.

When he had finished and stepped back, Elona ran her hand across her head once more.

"Thank you, that feels better." She turned to face him. "Do you want me to do you?"

"You think we should look our best for the empress?"

"I was only asking for you."

"Or do you dislike my bristles when we kiss?"

"That does not concern me."

"So you are truly asking for my own sake?"

"I am."

He placed the little knife back into its sheath.

"I am happy as I am."

"Very well then," she said. "Let us visit with the empress."

CHAPTER 41

$\mathcal{J}$aymis dragged the bodies from the outside into the room, although the blood trails could easily be followed. He took the sword from the lead armsman, it was a decent weapon though he hoped he wouldn't have to use it—they would simply be overwhelmed by numbers in this place.

He lit two of the lanterns and gave one to Elona, then extinguished the candles. They went out and shut the door behind them.

The Tahulin were still moving in their strange pattern, which included passing through walls. But as the two of them headed for the staircase the creatures did not follow them.

Jaymis placed his foot on the first step and looked back. "They're not coming."

Elona put her free hand in his. "They have been hiding us, I think, perhaps they are afraid."

"Afraid?"

"They were hungry, and I fed them, yet a powerful ley-circle is less than an arrow-shot away."

"So why didn't they eat the power from the ley-circle?"

She shook her head. "Not that, but why not from Mother's Milk as it comes down?"

"You think they're afraid of what's here?"

"Aren't you?"

He did not answer but gave her hand a squeeze and together they mounted the wide circular staircase.

The first level up looked as deserted as the place below, and the layout seemed the same as far as they could see. They climbed another floor.

The change was obvious. Whatever time of night they had finally penetrated the Fastness, it was now daylight. The stairs came out at what seemed to be the main level with corridors heading off in three of the four directions. Two of them had windows along one side letting in the daylight. From the orientation the lit corridors gave him, Jaymis surmised the third passage must be heading for the outer wall above where they had entered. There were lanterns at intervals along all the corridors, the ones in the third passage were lit.

Jaymis guided Elona to the darker corridor where they were a little less exposed.

"There's no point in hiding," she said.

"I'd rather not bump into any more armsmen who seem bent on our deaths."

"You need to trust me."

"I do," he said, and bit down on the *but* that wanted to follow.

"Come on."

She walked away from him along the right-hand corridor and stopped at the first window, looking out and then up.

He unsheathed the sword and followed her. The window looked out directly into a huge square composed of worn and uneven flagstones. Grasses grew up between them and, close to the surrounding walls, they were green with moss. He had known the Fastness was huge, but another three storeys towered upwards.

But even they were dwarfed by the black tower that sat like an obelisk in the very centre of the square. He estimated the base covered at least a third of the square, and its smooth sides tapered upwards. There was a great deal of grass gathered around its base.

The place went against everything he knew about ley-circles.

Anything within the area of a feeding would be destroyed. Any construction nearby would be twisted beyond use. While living things could be changed and turned into abominations.

If he did not know this tower stood above a ley-circle he would have sworn it could not be true.

"This is impossible."

She turned to look at him and the effect was strange as the blackened side of her face was turned to the light. But he could still see her there, it was almost as if the scarring was a mask.

The sound of leather on stone grabbed his attention and Elona's eyes moved to look past him. He spun round ready to take on the armsmen.

But there were none, just a woman standing at the junction as if she had wandered here though there had been no sign of her in any direction. Her clothes certainly marked her as the nobility, their colour and patterns were distinctive. The lines on her face said she was in her middle years but there was something in her eyes —agelessness.

The thing he found most concerning was her confidence. He lowered his sword because he knew that she would never let him reach her.

"Ah, there you are, children. I wondered where you had got to. Come along now."

She turned her back on them and headed along the other passageway with the windows on to the courtyard on her right.

Jaymis found himself walking and stopped immediately.

It was not magic, there was no coercion to keep moving. Yet it was as if she was drawing him along. He turned back to Elona, who had not moved from the window. She was however looking at him.

"Going somewhere without me?"

Words drifted from where the woman had gone. They were not shouted and yet they were still loud in their ears. "You are both invited."

"So that's the Tirnian Empress," said Elona. "Impressive."

"Her clothes," he said.

"What about them?"

"The designs and colours, same as Lord Nemon."

He saw the light of realisation in her face, and then she frowned. "Does that make any sense?"

"We won't learn anything standing here."

Elona glanced past him at the passage again. "Do you think you would be able kill her?"

He shook his head a little. "I think I would find it hard."

"I don't recommend trying."

"Why?"

"Because, for me, looking at her is like staring into a furnace. She is heat and light."

"She's a patterner?"

"I don't know what she is."

Elona placed her hand on his wrist and pulled him closer. They kissed. Just touching lips. He hoped this would not be the last time.

Then they turned the corner to follow the woman who was still ahead of them walking slowly. But Jaymis found the urge to follow her had become a desire to run away, taking Elona with him and escaping this place. While the dark tower in the centre of the castle was no longer a source of astonishment, it was a threat.

As they caught up with the woman, she walked faster. Jaymis fancied he could see the same thing that Elona had described. As if the power in this creature was so great even he could perceive it.

"I am so bored with this place," said the woman. "I've been here so long."

"Can't you leave?" said Elona.

"You will refer to me as Majesty."

"I was wondering about that, your majesty."

"Were you?"

"I believe you are the Lady Hilaneena of Nemon."

"What of it?"

"What happened to Myrlask, your majesty?"

"He became too old."

Their guide paused at a pair of double doors and flung them open.

As they swung back and crashed against the walls, she headed inside. It was a huge chamber with two ranks of galleries, and a domed ceiling of glass. The bright sky lit up the place.

Jaymis peered into the shadows beneath the galleries, there was something odd about them, almost as if they were a smudged painting. He tried to focus but it made no difference. That the power of a patterner was at work was clear enough.

If he had this much power at his command, he would place a small army where no one could see them. He had enough respect for the art of the patterners to realise that if one of them could conceive of a way of hiding something from plain sight, the pattern could be made to do it.

He reached out and took Elona's hand. He squeezed it and when she looked into his eyes, he pointedly looked at the side of the room. She nodded. Of course, she would already have seen—but she was now aware that he knew too.

They crossed the wide wooden floor, there was a layer of dust though the path they followed had been churned by many feet—now that he had noticed it he could see more footprints along the sides of the hall, confirming his suspicions.

At the far end was a large dais with steps going up to it, and a massive throne which looked to be carved from a white rock with lines of green running through it. Marble, perhaps.

There was a curious moment when even the empress seemed to blur and instead of walking in front of them, she was now sitting on the throne, her long dress draped around her crossed legs.

"You may approach, children," she said holding out her hand to them.

They continued until they were as short distance from the bottom step. Jaymis bowed though only enough to indicate a person who was deserving of respect. He did not go down on his knees.

Elona did not offer any obeisance at all. Instead she took another step forward.

"What are you?"

"Oh, so you're *fahain?*" said the empress. "That explains it. Always the rebellious ones, a troublesome lot. I was right to set the Farahalek on you. What's your name, girl?"

"I am Elona of Corlain in Faerholme. And this is Jaymis of Betlain."

The woman's eyes focused on him and it made him uneasy. "You're Jaymis? How lovely. I knew your mother."

"My mother was a traitor and a murderess."

"And I killed her," said Elona.

"Good. She failed me. If you had not done so, I would have."

"You?" said Jaymis. "I thought that would be your predecessor."

"Of course."

Elona looked around at the walls then back at the woman.

"What are you? Some sort of Tahulin?"

The woman laughed. "Little 'Lonie, you could not be more wrong."

Jaymis did not understand the name the woman had used but he could see Elona's whole body tighten.

"You're not her."

"I am everything that ever caused you pain, stupid girl," she said. "But no, I shouldn't take all the credit, after all my alter-ego did his best too. He laid the groundwork for me to turn your world into the nightmare it's become."

"I am not afraid of nightmares," said Elona. "I am no child."

"Perhaps not, Elona of Corlain, but it doesn't matter. Because you will be dead."

As the woman raised her hand, Jaymis threw himself towards Elona to protect her.

CHAPTER 42

$\mathcal{E}$lona had been expecting a burst of power as the woman energised some pattern or other. Instead, Jaymis thudded into her from the side knocking her to the ground.

Crossbow bolts whipped through the air, intersecting where they had been standing a heartbeat before. The armsmen hiding in the dark behind the curious wards had let loose at the signal.

From her prone position with Jaymis on top, Elona summoned the ley-circle and sent up a warding shield. The brilliant blue light of the dome flooded the chamber.

A scream of rage penetrated the shield, muffled but distinct. Jaymis rolled off Elona and they bounced to their feet. Volleys of crossbow bolts glanced off the ward as the men reloaded and fired with well-drilled precision.

Elona focused her attention on the blurring ward and felt its pattern—then disrupted it. The armsmen became visible. Suddenly able to see their compatriots on the other side of the hall they moved into more defensive positions though their ineffective onslaught continued.

"They can't touch us," she said to Jaymis and he relaxed. "And thank you."

"What now?"

The answer came in the form of blinding light that poured from the direction of the empress. Elona blinked against the flood of brilliance, she could see the raw power of it as it splashed against her warding. It was more like a feeding than a pattern, though it must be a pattern forming it. The empress was no *fahain*.

"The ward will hold, Jaymis," she said as calmly as she could. One touch from that power would turn them to cinders.

"But we can't fight," he said. "Can we run?"

She knew he was thinking of her instant patterner's path, but she could not summon it and even if she did. "She will come after us. Especially now."

The limitless power of the ley-circle was at her feet. The warding held against the empress and her men.

She closed her eyes and grasped the pattern she had created for the warding. And expanded it. Slowly at first, a hands-breadth and then another the circle that protected them grew larger. As she gained confidence, she extended it faster.

The stones that made the steps to the dais shattered and splintered as the ward intersected with them. The violence of it pleased Elona. She had always been the weak one, the one that everyone helped, the victim.

"Not this time!"

In a huge effort of will, she threw the ward out to the edges of the hall. The white light cut-off. The columns supporting the galleries around them, crashed away as the dome expanded.

Noise filled the air as the walls collapsed. She saw Jaymis flinch as the ceiling fell in, but it hit the warding and thundered down the sides of it. It took a long time but eventually the collapse ended.

Inside the blue walls the air was clear. Beyond they were surrounded by broken masonry piled against the blue light. And above them was open sky.

It was all broken masonry except for one flash of colour directly in front of her. The bloody corpse of the empress crushed and broken with not a hint of her power remaining.

"Oh dear. Look what you've done. You've broken it."

Elona froze. It was the voice of Jaymis but not his words. She turned.

He stood there, relaxed, with a condescending smile on his face. The bright light of power poured from him. The life went out of her. She turned away and wept.

"There, there, child. You should be pleased for him. He has achieved power far beyond you. Can you imagine what it was like for him to be in your shadow? I know everything he knew. How much he loved you and those tender moments you had together. And I know all your secrets, all the ones you made him promise to keep. Not that there is anything you knew that I did not. You could never win.

"You should be glad too because of all those who have stood against me, you have been the best."

Elona turned back and wiped the tears from her eyes.

She removed the ward.

The air filled once more with the roar of collapsing masonry while clouds of dust poured in on them. Elona conjured another protective ward but this time wrapped it tight around Jaymis.

"You bitch!" screamed the thing that had been her lover.

With only the slightest thought she shrank the ward forcing Jaymis to his knees—but she could go no further. She knew there was no choice but to kill him. But she could not do it. It was like trying to control the *sikechesa*, something inside stopped her.

"If you kill him, I'll just find someone else!" screamed the thing. "He is still here, if you kill this body, you'll be killing him too!"

Elona hesitated again.

Something struck her from behind with the force of a galloping horse. She was thrown across the ground and her skin tore on the stones and dirt. She screamed as pain seared through her calf. She rolled to the side as more crossbow bolts glanced off the ground. The protective ward went up—then dissolved again.

As she scrambled and limped painfully towards the nearest mound of collapsed building, she heard the clear laugh of Jaymis.

"I am not alone in this place, you foolish child."

Stop sounding like Jaymis!

She could feel the large number of magically charged devices that had entered the area. And the men. *Must be armsmen and patterners.*

The wooden shaft of a crossbow bolt protruded from her calf. The pain was excruciating and made it harder to focus.

"Stand up, girl," said Jaymis's voice. "No one is going to kill you except me."

She couldn't do a ward, at least one of the patterner's out there could nullify it in a moment. They could kill her easily enough anyway if they chose to.

Awkwardly, painfully, she got to her feet.

Jaymis stood there. Untouched and unharmed. If it had not been for that insufferable smile, she could have imagined it was him. If not for the tremendous power she could see.

"What are you?" she said again.

"I am nemesis."

"Who's nemesis?"

"Everyone's."

The words of Lord Nemon came back to her, the words she had dismissed as the ravings of a mad man.

The thing that had been Jaymis saw her face change.

"Yes, little girl, you have guessed my name. You cannot kill me, but I can kill you."

The power of the circle lay beneath her. And death in front of her.

Elona made a connection.

There was a murmur among the patterners. The creature looked towards the Slissac tower. Then back at Elona.

The ground seemed to vibrate beneath their feet.

"What have you done?"

Elona did not respond. The tremor in the castle increased. The broken walls shifted again, a scream sounded and then shut off. The walls around them that were still standing, cracked and more huge pieces crashed to the ground.

A shrill whistling grew from nothing until the air was filled with the shrieking of a wind that would not be denied.

The Jaymis creature took a step towards her, then jumped back. Staring up and out at the tower.

"She's opened a path!" shouted a patterner.

"What path, girl, a path to where?"

The screaming air subsided to be replaced by a liquid roar, like a thousand waterfalls. Stones cracked.

"To Canvor."

The creature's eyes went wide, like Jaymis when he was surprised. "But Canvor's ley circle..."

Its full attention went to the tower.

It felt like rain at first, pattering down on Elona's shaven head.

She turned and watched as a flood of water poured from the base of the tower, then shot out in great streams higher and higher until it finally erupted in a great geyser through the top.

Cracks formed and water gushed from them until, all at once, the ancient construction seemed to lose all strength and simply collapsed in a thunder of lake water and black stone.

Freed of all restriction the water shot skyward and then fell back in an increasing torrent.

"You have killed yourself, child."

"So be it. But I have destroyed everything you have built here."

"Unlike you, mortal, I have forever."

A flood of water erupted over the barricade of masonry and tumbled down towards them in an unstoppable torrent.

And Elona's last thought was not of her lost Jaymis, but her sister.

To be continued...

READ VEONA (PATTERNER'S PATH 0)

Discover the real beginning of this story...

Subscribe to my mailing list and download the prequel **VEONA** (Patterner's Path 0).

Go here: **taupress.com/vs-veona**

ABOUT THE AUTHOR

Steve Turnbull has been a geek and a nerd longer than those words have had their modern meaning.

Born in the heart of London to book-loving working class parents in 1958, he lived with his parents and two much older sisters in two rooms with gas lighting and no hot water (true!). In his fifth year, a change in his father's fortunes took them out to a detached house in the suburbs. That was the year Dr Who first aired on British TV and Steve watched it avidly from behind the sofa. It was the beginning of his love of science fiction.

Academically Steve always went for the science side but also had his imagination and that took him everywhere. He read through his local library's entire science fiction and fantasy selection, plus his father's 1950s *Astounding Science Fiction* magazines. As he got older he also ate his way through TV SF like *Star Trek*, *Dr Who* and *Blake's 7*.

However it was when he was 15 he discovered something new. Bored with a Maths lesson he noticed a book from the school library: *Cider with Rosie* by Laurie Lee. From the first page he was captivated by the beauty of the language. As a result he wrote a story longhand and then spent evenings at home on his father's electric typewriter pounding out a second draft, expanding it. Then he wrote a second book. Both were terrible but it was a start. After that he switched to poetry and turned out dozens, mostly not involving teenage angst.

After receiving excellent science and maths results he went on to study Computer Science. There he teamed up with another student and they wrote songs for their band - Steve writing the lyrics. Though they admit their best song was the other way around, with Steve writing the music.

After graduation Steve moved into contract programming but was snapped up a couple of years later by a computer magazine looking for someone with technical knowledge. It was in the magazine industry that Steve learned how to write to length, to deadline and to style. Within a couple of years he was editor and stayed there for many years.

During that time he married Pam (also a magazine editor) who he'd met at a student party.

Though he continued to write poetry all prose work stopped. He created his own magazine publishing company which at one point produced the glossy subscription magazine for the *Robot Wars* TV show. The company evolved into a design agency but after six years of working very hard and not seeing his family—now including a daughter and son—he gave it all up.

He spent a year working on miscellaneous projects including writing 300 pages for a website until he started back where he had begun, contract programming.

With security and success on the job front, the writing began again. This time it was scriptwriting: features scripts, TV scripts and radio scripts. During this time he met a director Chris Payne, who wanted to create steampunk stories and between them they created the Voidships universe, a place very similar to ours but with specific scientific changes.

But you can't keep a good writer restrained, so apart from the output of Steampunk stories Steve returned to his first love of Fantasy and Science Fiction.

Don't forget you can read VEONA by going to **taupress.com/vs-veona**